The

Christy Laughing

Beyond the Call of Duty

by

Christy Laughing

DEDICATED TO HIM
ALWAYS

ACKNOWLEDGMENTS

When my children were small I worked evenings at a restaurant. One night I was closing and a scared young woman tapped on the locked door. She was lost, and frantic for directions. All she did was turn the wrong way when she exited the highway, but she was so upset I couldn't convey that to her. So, I did exactly what Angela does in this story. I took her to her location.

Every writer out there knows when inspiration is striking them and this night it was overwhelming. It was windy, dark and rainy - just an altogether scary night, and there I was driving away from my home to the other side of town… It was the perfect scenario for a Suspense novel, so I took the experience, tweaked it a little, and created this story from it. I arrived home safe and sound that night – different from what happens to Angela and Susan.

Acknowledgement for the development of this idea, and thanks, go to that scared young girl, who will probably never know how much she affected me that night.

To Rich, Pete, Mike and Joe…..Love you guys!

To my audience: You really are the reason I do this. Thank you for your support. It's my true hope that you enjoy this!

A note from Christy:

While I based the geography of this book on real-life places in the Niagara Falls, NY area, any reference to the following is purely fictional:
The Niagara Falls Police Department;
Special Teams;
any officers or officials in the Niagara Region;
any specific crimes or criminals;
any stores, businesses, establishments, invented roads or neighborhoods – all fictional!

Kudos to the real Niagara Falls Police Department: Excellent work!

~ *Prologue* ~

Spring 2003:

From a distance, Angela Cahn could hear the sirens, not an uncommon occurrence on the boulevard where her store was located. She hardly noticed the sound as she checked the amount of topsoil bags she had counted against the number in her computer. It was inventory night; how she hated inventory.

Out of the depth of her concentration, however, the sirens suddenly seemed closer, louder and more violent. They were screaming, in fact, and as she looked up, a shot of fear raced through her chest. She was alone in her warehouse, and the door to the storage room suddenly burst open and a large man came running toward her. She screamed in shock and clutched her clipboard against her as if it could shield her somehow before she realized the intruder bearing down on her was really one of her employees, a seventeen-year-old young man named Michael Camden.

3

She stared at Michael in astonishment as he approached her, and in only a few seconds an entire drama unfolded itself. The frightened young man towered above her small frame, gripping her shoulders so her dark hair trailed down her neck as she looked up at him. He gazed frantically into her round brown eyes. "Angela, you've got to help me, *please!*"

"Michael, what's going on?"

"The cops are after me, Angela. I swear I didn't do anything. Please, let me stay here until they pass by! Okay?"

"Michael, what happened?" Her voice was stern and suspicious. The boy's eyes pleaded with her, his soul utterly panicked.

"Some guys I was hanging out with tonight stole a case of beer from a 7-Eleven. I didn't do anything," he rushed on, his voice imploring, "but I was there, and by the time I knew what was happening, they had already done it. The cops were chasing us all down Niagara Falls Boulevard and we scattered. Angela, if I get caught I'll have a record and they'll never let me into the police academy! Please let me stay here until they're gone."

Angela closed her eyes and sighed, feeling pressured. Michael was dead-set on the idea of becoming a detective. He'd confided the dream to her many times, and his ambitious blue eyes would light up when he talked about it.

While all the teens that landscaped for her during the summers were special, her very favorite was Michael Camden. He'd started working at *Lawn Care Products Unlimited* two years ago, the same spring an absurd, unexplained heart attack had claimed the life of her thirty-year-old husband, Jeff.

As she'd huddled within her cloud of pain that year, she remembered only a few people that could really reach her: her parents, her manager and good friend, Randy Tripp, and this teenage boy, who seemed stricken by the loss, and so very concerned for her pain. Indeed, he could reach through her haze of depression in a way the others never could, simply because he was there to do so. Many work nights would end late with Michael talking to Angela about everything from school, to girls, to religion, to careers. His friendship and company had gotten her through many lonely, agonized evenings.

She didn't want Michael's future to be jeopardized, or for him to experience monumental loss as she had. A police record *would* ruin everything for him... "Oh, for heaven's sake, Michael," she finally muttered. "What are you doing hanging around with kids like that?"

"I'll never do it again, I swear."

The discourse was suddenly interrupted and silenced by loud pounding on the door Michael had just burst through. Both he and Angela jolted and stared at it as if they expected it to open by itself and strike them to the ground. From outside, they heard a deep, threatening voice. "Police, open up!"

Angela drew in a quick breath, truly frightened by the thought of trouble with the police. She was an upstanding citizen. Never, *ever,* had she had a confrontation with the law and the prospect of doing so now wasn't at all appealing. "Oh, my God."

Michael ran toward the break room when he heard the sound of that officer's voice. "Just tell them I've been here working, okay?" he whispered loudly. "My father's a minister, he would *never* understand this."

"Well, *you* should have thought about *that* before you got *into* this!" Angela clipped in the same hushed tone. At twenty-seven years of age, this was the first time in her life that she had truly sounded like an adult, and she cringed at the thought even as she was galvanized into action for the sake of her young friend. "Now, get in there, and I swear if I get into any trouble I will *not* cover your hide!"

She was angry and she sounded deadly determined to carry through with this threat, but her protective instincts were churning. She knew she would go to great lengths to keep Michael from getting caught. "I'll tell them we're here doing inventory, and you've been with me all night. Now, go get an apron on!"

His quick smile was the picture of relief as he disappeared into the break room. Meanwhile, the officer outside was becoming impatient with this delay. Pounding harder this time, he began to shout again just as Angela opened the door and let him in, her face a bit white, but displaying only a reasonable amount of confusion.

"Officer. What can I do for you?"

Perhaps it was the beauty and gentleness in her voice and demeanor that settled him instantly, turning this raging officer into the very object of cultivated courtesy. Perhaps it was the quiet, settled atmosphere and the clipboard she was clutching that gave him the impression that nothing was amiss on these premises. Whatever it was, Angela was supremely glad for it, and smiled her sweetest smile to heighten the desired results. It worked like a charm.

"Miss, have you seen or heard anything unusual tonight, any young men in the area, any running or shouting perhaps?"

"No, I can't say that I have. My assistant and I have been doing inventory all night and it's been fairly quiet - except for the sirens."

"Well, do you mind if I look around?"

"Not at all."

Michael flushed the toilet loudly and came out of the break room as innocently as he could muster, clad in his *Lawn Care Products Unlimited* apron, and holding a clipboard similar to Angela's. When the officer saw him, his eyes narrowed and he looked back at Angela, who seemed intently occupied counting bags of fertilizer and marking the amounts on her clipboard.

"Who are you?" he asked Michael harshly.

"Huh? I'm - my name is Michael Camden. I work here."

"You know anything about the 7-Eleven down the street getting robbed tonight?"

"No, sir, I've been here doing inventory with my boss all night."

"Are you sure about that?"

The officer was looking suspiciously, discerningly, at both of them now, and Angela could feel burning heat rush into her face. Her heart began to beat wildly, and for a split second panic seized her and she almost blurted the whole truth out in great detail. Instead, she looked directly at Michael, and then at the officer in her stockroom, and declared with utterly affronted certainty, "Yes, I'm very sure. Michael is one of my best employees and we're doing our monthly inventory check. We've been here all night."

The officer looked skeptical, but turned to Michael and asked, "Well, did you see or hear anything unusual?"

"No – I didn't."

A long, nail-biting moment ensued as the officer looked them over with apparent knowledge of every misdeed they had ever committed. "All right, if either of you do see or hear anything, please let us know, and be careful because there are some thieves in the area; all right?"

"Yes, sir. We'll definitely keep an eye out."

"What time do you plan on closing up?"

Angela wondered briefly what business that was of his, but she answered sweetly, nonetheless. "Oh, it usually takes till about ten-thirty."

"All right, well, we'll be scouting the area for a while so we'll watch out for you until you're safely out of here."

"Thank you, we do appreciate that. Good night."

"Good night, miss... son," he tipped his hat to Michael.

"Good night, sir."

The door closed and they both looked at it again for endless minutes, feeling like an entire platoon of officers was standing outside and could still see and hear everything they said through the solid steel of the stockroom door. For several minutes more, they spoke in whispers, even though they were completely alone in the vastness of the room.

"Thank you, Angela, I can never repay you enough for that."

"No, you can't, but you owe me. *Big time*. Remember that." Then she smiled and her face lit up with beauty. Michael had always considered her pretty, but at this moment he noticed that she really was beautiful and he loved her sincerely, like a sister.

"Now, grab a pen and come into the office. You can start paying me now by really helping me with this inventory."

"You're on!"

*　　　*　　　*

They did finish the inventory that night, and when Michael opened his check the following week he was amazed to find that Angela had actually paid him for the time he'd worked over. None of the other kids he was with that night were caught for their crimes, so Michael had truly gotten away without repercussions. True to his word, and his own heart, he never hung out with that crowd again.

Michael worked at LCPU for two more years, and he and Angela remained close. Sadly, though, as much as they promised to communicate, after Michael left for college they began to lose touch. As the years passed each went their own way until, finally, they didn't see each other anymore.

Angela thought about that long ago night a few times over the years. Especially when she heard how good a cop Michael had actually become. Apparently, he was involved in some major drug busts throughout the city. One criminal in particular was one of the leading drug lords in the area!

She smiled to herself and guessed she had made the right decision that long ago night. She'd chided him then, saying that he owed her big, but it had only been a joke. She'd been glad to help such a dear friend, and a boy so worthy of a good future. She'd never expected repayment, had never expected that a young boy could really offer her anything in payment anyway...

Perhaps she was wrong.

~ *Part One* ~

~ *Chapter One* ~

<u>Spring 2013:</u>

Bullets riddled the thick inner-city air in stark, clipping cracks. For a brief, detached moment, it was that sound that kept this gang leader's finger leaning on the trigger of his pistol. It was the lust for blood, however, coursing relentlessly through his veins, that had brought him to this point in the first place. A rage... A threatening, choking rage that couldn't be contained and brought with it a powerful strength that must conquer. It controlled him, owned him, and he couldn't escape it.

His victim's body lurched backward as the first slug rammed into him. Then he jerked backward again, and again, and again, as the gun was emptied. A smile of vengeful satisfaction filled his attacker. Violence ruled. Power conquered all. And *he* was the ultimate, dominating force.

*　　　　*　　　　*

A young teenage girl sat distractedly in the crowded bleachers at her high school's last tournament basketball game. The team was well on its way to winning the entire season hands down; but that wasn't to be. Not today. Instead, today, in this pristine suburb of Niagara Falls, this usually innocent girl stood up, blending in completely with the screaming crowd. She looked around herself in an inebriated, lusting sort of haze, and lunged forward unexpectedly to dig a small knife into the neck of the girl in front of her.

No one really even saw it at first. Or perhaps they couldn't believe it, or didn't know what to do once the act finally registered on their shocked minds. So, she turned and plunged the knife again into the boy sitting beside her. Blood was in her eyes, and with a screaming, violent cry, she unleashed the rage within. The mob on the bleachers tried to scramble away, but there was nowhere to go. The girl simply stood there, dragging jagged edges ruthlessly through the bodies of her schoolmates.

A strange mixture of anger and glee shone in her eyes before she was finally stopped.

*   *   *

In a mall parking lot they waited. Cloaked by the darkness beneath a secluded parking ramp, the two grown men paced, punching their fists into their palms, kicking at the cement beams and guardrails. An impatient anger was brewing; was already present actually, with the need to expend it becoming overpowering.

A store employee finally emerged from the building, a young male, probably college age. Perfect. He was coming closer, closer, as they waited and watched in transfixed anticipation. Then, for some reason, the youth stopped. The men narrowed their seedy eyes as they watched, and became enraged when their victim seemed to sense their presence. He began to turn away! Slowly, trying to act casual, their chosen victim was turning away!

With one mind, they launched forward and grabbed him. One wrenched his hair back and the other came up quickly behind and leveled a pounding chop directly into the center of his face. The stunned young man crashed backwards and landed with a careening thud.

The rest of it went quickly. They might have wanted to watch him struggle; to gloat over his incapacity to fight against them, but they couldn't wait any longer. With punishing force, they came down on him. One encircled his neck with crushing hands, and the other held the flailing body completely down and watched the face with hungry intensity. Their victim's eyes bulged out, and his face reddened, then turned purplish, then blue. He was completely, and satisfyingly, dead.

It was then, after it was already over, that they beat him mercilessly, thrashing the unresponsive soul about in flinging, raging motions.

*   *   *

Blood was all over the city, and every cop in Niagara Falls was scrambling to clean it up. It was relentless and vile, and no one knew where it came from, or why this was happening...

~ *Chapter Two* ~

Sergeant Michael Camden looked at Niagara Falls Police Captain, Philip Jackson, with a level expression on his handsome face. Michael had strong, dark features and striking blue eyes that ordinarily sparkled with humor and intelligence. They weren't humorous today, however, and they weren't sparkling. Today they were dark and fierce with the crucial information he was disclosing.

Detective John Casey, Michael's partner, sat next to him, his soft brown eyes intense. His dirty blond hair stood out against the natural gold of his skin as he held his face against the side of his left hand and leaned the elbow on his desk. His expression was set, ominous and quiet, revealing how seriously he took this discussion.

"Captain, thanks for seeing us right away," Michael said gravely, "Casey and I were shocked when Marcus, here, came to us. We knew you needed to hear this." Michael nodded toward the fourth man inside the closed office, Detective Marcus Linden, who was scrunched into the chair next to Captain Jackson. Michael, like Casey, was a large, powerful man, but he wasn't nearly as huge as Detective Marcus Linden. Few men were.

"What's up?" Captain Jackson asked simply, with a degree of hardened nonchalance. He sat perfectly still, an artificial relaxation emanating from him, his dark, eagle-sharp eyes piercing and expectant. One heavy leg rested upon the other knee, and he tilted his white-gray head to the side.

"Well," Michael said, leaning forward intently, "we all know about these insane 'Blood Crimes' that have been paralyzing the city lately, right?"

"Right."

"And, Marcus is undercover downtown to eyeball everything that goes down in the Lex and Powell area..."

"Right."

"Well, lately, one name, Regis Black, keeps coming up in our busts. When we checked him out, of course, there's no record of the name, etc. etc., but apparently he's real and getting bigger, because Marcus has some news that'll blow you away." He stretched out his hand toward his Detective, giving him the opportunity to speak.

"What is it, Marcus?" Jack asked with curious worry.

"What it is, Captain, is a new drug being manufactured downtown, and this one's a bitch, let me tell you. They call it *'Racer'* and it's a variation on Spacebase."

"Spacebase!" Jack resounded in alarm.

"That's right."

"Spacebase has been dead for over fifteen years! And when it was out there we didn't see too much of it around here. I thought that stuff was too dangerous for even the crack addicts in L.A. to handle."

"It is, but they found a way to mix the crack and PCP without killing their users. I'm not sure if it has something to do with the heating process, or the amount they mix, or what the hell, but the results are a little safer, and they're calling it Racer."

"Hmm." Jack shuttered his eyes against the disgust he felt at this news, and against the inevitable dogfight that was about to ensue between this department and the dealers. Because that's what this

15

office did: fought against the nearly unleashable world of drug abuse.

They were a highly exclusive, secret team of investigators called the Special Teams, chosen and commissioned by the DEA. They systematically, and very quietly, dealt with drug related crimes that were bigger than the average police force was capable of handling.

They were the best, all of them, and Marcus Linden was no exception. At twenty-eight years of age, he was an amazing physical specimen, huge, and rather misshapen in his facial features. He was completely committed to his job. He worked specifically as an undercover investigator, living on the streets where it all happened.

There could be no family or friends in a situation like that. Even communication with the precinct was strictly limited. When an officer went into an area undercover in this manner, he was left completely alone, and, more often than not, he paid dearly for his effort. John Casey had actually originated this particular position, undercover patrol of the Lex and Powell Street district, only last year, and could no longer do it since his promotion into Special Teams administration. Casey only entered that realm now on the rare occasions when Marcus needed backup, and then only as his alter identity, street junkie, Jake Brown.

The whole picture was most important in every Special Team assignment. Each two-man team did their best to expedite their specific case, but facts must be compiled, witnesses found, trusted relationships must be established, and evidence had to be accumulated that was substantial enough to do damage to the criminal operations they investigated. It was never fast or easy, and was always taxing. Michael, the lead officer at only twenty-nine years of age, and Casey, a very close second-in-command at age thirty-three, felt the brunt of it all.

"When was the first incident?" Captain Jack asked Marcus.

"About two weeks ago - just about the same time the blood crimes started up - and it hasn't even had time to mushroom yet. When it does... look out. This stuff will be worse than crack ever was, with way more repercussions to deal with."

"Yeah, I could see it coming - just about two weeks ago, in fact," John Casey said, stepping into the conversation with crucial realizations. "There's been a stir going around downtown lately, but I couldn't get an accurate fix on what was up. Whatever it is, it isn't very popular around here yet, but it will be soon, and it's very hush, hush."

"Well, this is it," Marcus said. "*Racer*; and it's a mind-racer all right, let me tell you. Now, the real problem is two-fold. First, in some cases, the users trip out so bad they literally can't wake up for days. Who knows, maybe some of them won't ever wake up again... More important, it seems to cause a violent reaction in most everyone I've seen on it. Worse, I'm noticing that as it accumulates in the brain, the propensity for violence increases. So, the first time John Doe does the stuff he may not do anything particularly violent, but after the third or fourth time, he might start screaming and throwing things in a rage, then he may haul off and beat someone uncontrollably... hence the blood crimes. I'd stake my life on the theory that every one of them is connected to this drug.

"The word is power. It makes the users feel strong and powerful, and my guess is, they really are twice as strong, and definitely twice as dangerous, as when they're straight. I've been watching it happen, even to the mellowest guys, and they're loving it. It is *the* hottest thing to try, and the most addictive dope I've ever seen. Even worse than crack. I mean who knows, as it progresses, one of them, or a few of them, could decide to walk into the local burger joint one day and shoot the hell out of all the patrons. We're talking about a serious threat to society here."

"So, this is what's been going on in this city for the past two weeks," Jack mumbled.

"This is it. I'm almost sure of it, and it's beginning to leak in everywhere. Street gangs, to suburban malls, to high school auditoriums."

"Speaking of which," Michael said gravely, "we have evidence in that incident. The girl who stabbed all those kids at that basketball game was pumped full of a cocaine/PCP mixture. She's the first we can pinpoint, but she's also the only one of the 'blood criminals' who got caught. The other crimes seem to follow suit - irrational violence, signs of extreme rage - this makes sense."

"Damn. I knew there had to be a reason for all this insanity," Jack said on a disgusted rush of breath. "What's the street cost? I mean, who should we expect to be able to afford it?" he asked levelly.

"Anyone. The cost is fairly minimal, and you know, they can turn anything into a 'trade'. It's averaging a little higher than crack, and it lasts for two to four hours, which is a big improvement over crack's fifteen-minute-high. After the buzz wears off, all they can do is sleep. I mean, they literally can't do anything but sleep, which poses other problems, like theft and rape because these people are immobilized.

"What they're doing is using the crack houses. Everyone does the drug, trips on it for a while, does whatever else comes to mind, then they sleep - you know how that goes. Once they get a taste of it, though - I've already seen it - they'll fight, steal, kill, and everything else you can imagine to get a hold of the stuff."

Michael's angry, pensive glare found John Casey's and Captain Jack's. Their gazes matched his own. A slow rage burned there. The drug industry was, indeed, a depraved one. A whole level of underworld politics and psychological battles faced drug users and children raised in areas where drug dealings and usage were common. It didn't always mean a total lifestyle of addiction and destruction, but a drug like this new one, *Racer*, could affect their lives forever whether they intended it to happen or not. It could affect the lives of others, too, especially now, with this new, violent element included in the side effects.

Linden caught the tension in the air with wide, knowing eyes. "It gets worse," he said cautiously. "Or better, depending on how you look at it. According to my sources, the whole thing got started with a couple of junkie punks experimenting in their basement, but guess who's getting involved now?"

"Regis Black?" Jack asked with a rather wicked, hopeful smile.

"That's right," Linden said in a singsong way. "Word is, the inventors know they got a billion dollar product on their hands, and they need Black to finance them. If they succeed, their industry could skyrocket and become very lucrative, and very hard to discern... But!" Linden said with a gleam, "I got myself hooked right into it. I let the word out that I'd be interested in running for the operation if they ever wanted to make it big. They ate it up. Why shouldn't they? Not one of them suspects me to be a cop. They've seen me living with them, doing their lifestyle for almost a year now, and they think I'm some kind of psychotic killer."

A snorting chuckle escaped Linden at the irony of such a concept. Indeed the inhabitants of the inner city where Marcus had become quite a known and feared legend did think he was a violent, psychotic maniac. He played his role so well and had earned their implicit respect. He would reap the rewards of his endeavors now.

"Tomorrow night Black is supposed to come around to check it all out. You know... to see if this *Racer* crap is really worth his investment. If he likes what he sees, a deal will be made, and, when it goes down, I'll be right there, nipping the whole thing right in the ass." He sat back in ultimate satisfaction and glowed at the thought of such timely luck.

A certain fiendish gleam lit Captain Jack's eye and a small smile hovered over his face. "Well, all right!" It was more a statement of quiet amazement than anything else. Michael was much more readily enthused.

"Good work, Linden!" Michael slammed a strong, gleeful fist against his desk. "*Damn* good work!"

"Who are the inventors?" Casey asked, curious, as he was almost as well aware of the activities on Lex Street as Linden. "Do you actually know them?"

"Sure do, I've partied with them, too, and let me tell you - it ain't pretty. It's all in my report; their names are Marty Rhodes and Nick Kline. They live right on Powell. Hopefully, in a few days they'll be locked in a cell, along with Regis Black. Can't *wait* to meet him."

Michael actually laughed at Marcus's infectious enthusiasm. "I can't wait, either! Linden, you're *amazing*," Michael praised, with his own smiling gleam. The huge man glowed like a child.

"Thanks; it feels good to finally be in front of something, instead of behind it all, trying to clean it up, you know? I mean, we are actually in the position of preventing a major drug epidemic! They're planning to start producing it in huge quantities, and moving it everywhere. It's a billion dollar deal waiting to happen, and because of this department, it *won't* happen. Doesn't it feel good when the job actually accomplishes something?"

The three other men, all more experienced in this type of work, and familiar with the pitfalls that could inevitably accompany it, stopped and stared at Linden. They were a bit tongue-tied by this newer officer's idealistic awe. Most cases they dealt with were difficult to achieve and took long, dragged out durations of time to finalize. This one had fallen right into their laps, at a time when they could truly accomplish the most concerning it.

"Yeah, Linden, it does," Casey finally replied with his own smile and a nod of surprised agreement. "It feels *great!*"

~ *Chapter Three* ~

A lone man stood as straight and solid as a tower in the cool night air. His long black dress coat fit him in elegant, intimidating perfection as the breeze lifted it slightly and magnified his strength and size. A small gray Toyota rounded the bend of the quiet city street where he stood, its headlights just barely piercing the darkness. The man immediately began walking toward it. He knew who it was; knew she would be on time; that he could always rely on her.

He was opening the passenger door before the car had completely come to a stop, and quickly got inside. "Did you get the package?" he asked the thin blond as she continued driving again.

"Yes, it's in the trunk. Regis, what's going on? I don't like this anymore... that Max guy is really weird. I don't like doing this."

"Shhh, now don't start that, okay?" he crooned gently. "You know I need you to do this one thing for me. I wouldn't ask if it weren't absolutely necessary."

"Well, why can't you pick up these packages?"

"I've explained this before, Susan, your school pass gets you back and forth across the Canadian/American border without anybody getting suspicious. If I started going back and forth three times a week, Customs would wonder why."

The young woman looked into the face of the man she loved. A man almost ten years older than her, with way more experience about life and what went with it. "Oh, Regis... What are you doing, really? I'm not as stupid as you think. I know this has to be something illegal."

"It's nothing for you to worry about," he said, rolling his eyes with a gentle laugh as if he were placating a child. Reaching to cradle her cheek lovingly, he added, "Everything will be fine as long as you help me with this one small favor that I ask from you."

When he said it like that, any favors he might ask, legal or otherwise, seemed like hopelessly small requests. She was so very willing to do anything he needed her to do anyway. Protests, when he looked at her in just that way, only sounded unreasonable, and were usually left unspoken and forgotten. After all, she was indeed justified in crossing from Niagara Falls, Canada into Niagara Falls, New York everyday on an educational pass.

Susan was a straight A student in her first semester at Niagara County Community College. She had the distinctive look of frail innocence about her, she drove a standard, non assuming vehicle... she was the farthest thing from seeming like any type of threat or danger to society.

The inspectors who patrolled the Customs booths everyday at that particular intersection between the nations of Canada and the U.S. rarely even stopped her for more than a few brief questions anymore. When she approached, and her license plate number was scanned into their computers, they immediately saw that this innocent student had every right to cross back and forth for any number of reasons, and any number of times per day. What she had in her vehicle was never checked. She was absolutely perfect for Regis Black's plan.

She lowered her eyes, and felt the brush of his strong fingers against her cheek, smelled the intoxicating smell of him as he sat so close to her in the car. "That Max guy just gives me the creeps, that's all," she downplayed yieldingly.

Watching the effect he had upon this woman display across her face, a deep, knowing satisfaction filled Regis. Susan belonged to him. She would do whatever he asked of her. Tonight, she would become the necessary component to his truest use for her.

"Max is harmless," he replied, "and believe me he knows he's never to touch you. You're under my protection. I'd kill him if he ever tried anything." His eyes filled with a possessive rage, distorted yet genuine nonetheless, and of course, all this impressionable innocent saw was that he loved her.

She stared at him and latched onto his vow. He was beautiful to her. To most women, in fact, this man was an amazingly handsome, virile creation. To this lonely young teenager, however, he was everything. When he offered his protection, and reassured her with that calm strength, she forgot anything else in life was really important. Her eyes gleamed and searched his in awe. Very gently, he grasped her hand and gave it a short squeeze. All thoughts of danger and illegal activity, all nagging, underlying premonitions of what she was really helping him accomplish, vanished. She would do anything for this man.

"Now, what did Max say?" he asked her.

"Nothing really, he gave me the package, took the envelope, and I was on my way."

"Did you tell him to be ready next week with another package?"

"Yes."

"What about the note I sent, did he respond?"

"He said he could get his hands on some, but it'll cost."

"Yeah, well, it won't cost too much or he'll find himself out of business," Regis muttered bitingly, more to himself than to Susan.

She looked at him closely again as she drove, forcibly stifling her growing panic that there was a dark side to this man she loved. Instead, she insisted to herself that he had to be good, and loving and kind, because that's the only way he'd ever treated her. Anyone who could show that much attention and warm understanding to a scrawny, plain teenager, had to have good within. Right?

"So, where are we going tonight?" she asked.

"We have a stop to make, and I have a meeting with a very important prospective client who I want you to meet.

"Me?"

"Yes, you," he smiled again, his fingers squeezing hers in a gentle, circular pattern. "I want you more involved in what I do. I don't see you nearly enough, and I want you by my side." His eyes focused on hers with a passion as she stared back at him between quick, darting glances at the road. She was completely defenseless. "After we make the meeting tonight," he continued huskily, "it's just you and me."

Her eyes lit up softly, gently, as he touched her face again, promising the coveted reward of time alone with him. Then he began to talk to her, as he often did, and a black, rolling cloud hovered over the precious mood. A cloud that diminished his brilliance, that brought back the doubts, and struck fear within her.

"If I'm right in what I'm thinking about my new plan, we're going to be millionaires! Then, I'm going to quit this whole God forsaken hell-hole of a city and take you away to a tropical island where the two of us can live happily ever after. Would you like that?"

She would love that. He knew she would love that, and her heart soared at the thought. If only it didn't have to be done the way she suspected... She nodded her head anyway, her heart in her eyes, and smiled softly.

"Turn in here," he said abruptly.

For a moment, Susan had forgotten she was driving a car. The sudden command ripped her from her dreamy haze and she jumped, wrenching the wheel of the car to the right. A dark, formidable alley faced her. In spite of herself and the strong man beside her, the sight of that alley frightened her. It was too dark, too eerie, too... evil.

A tall, skinny man with bulging red eyes and a highly nervous edge about him, suddenly appeared before them out of the blackness. Already apprehensive, Susan was completely panicked by his sudden appearance and slammed to a screeching stop just before her car smashed into him. The man jumped backward and began to pace like a caged lion at the fright. As they jerked to a halt, Regis turned to her, "Relax, Susan," he said, "you're with me. Everything is all right."

A shaky breath escaped her. "Sorry."

Regis got out of the car.

"Hey what's-the-matter with you?" the wiry man scolded. He was actually walking back and forth erratically in a three-foot circle, unable to calm his drug-charged nerves. "You trying to hit me?"

"No, no," Regis answered with placating smoothness. "Marty, come on... we go back a long ways, don't we?" Marty looked skeptical. "Look, I got something for you; all right? Come on, Susan's just a little afraid of the dark, you scared her, that's all."

Marty looked at the thin, wide-eyed teen in the car. Her eyes were huge and obviously afraid. She stared back at him as if he were an alien that would snatch her up and carry her away if she weren't careful. A small smile curved Marty's lip and his paranoia fled. Actually, he wouldn't mind doing just that. At any rate, he believed this scrawny innocent wasn't trying to kill him. "All right..." he conceded sullenly. "Well... what you got for me?"

"How about a few pounds of coke, huh? To brighten your day?" A huge smile split Regis' face and Susan's breath caught as she watched him from the car. Marty, a sudden bout of camaraderie overtaking him, smiled back and laughed with glee.

"Hey," Regis said, "and you know what I got coming next week? A whole bus load of PCP so you can do your thing - that is - if what you've got is really all you're saying it is."

"Oh, man... it's better than what I'm saying. This stuff is un-be-lievable, you know what I mean, man?"

"Well, I'm hoping so, Marty, because I got big plans for it, and you're included in those plans. This can make us all very rich. Now, let's see it."

Susan listened with horror as Regis talked in an unrefined street slur, not even trying to hide the conversation from her as he usually did. A panic was beginning within her. A slow, crawling panic that made her struggle for air and almost jump from the car. She didn't want to be involved with Regis and walk by his side like *this*. She didn't want any part of what these men were saying. PCP? She wanted nothing to do with anything that involved PCP.

Regis opened the door for her unexpectedly, and the grinding squeak made her jump and shriek.

"Man, can't you quiet her down? With all the noise she's making, we'll get busted out here for sure," Marty said agitatedly, jumping and pacing again at the shrill sound of Susan's screech.

"She's fine, like I said, just a little jumpy in the dark." The retort was distinctly corrective, and directed at Marty. It was apparent that Regis wanted his girlfriend to be respected, even as he was respected, and would insist upon it violently if necessary. Marty backed off instantly, aware, even in his inebriated condition, that danger suddenly emanated from Regis Black. The thought of sustaining bad feelings from Black was frightening indeed. Not only could he kill without a second's warning, he stood completely above any law that would stop him from doing so. Marty fell silent at the thought.

Regis helped Susan out of the car with a reassuring gleam in his hard, dark eyes. "Susan... keep your cool, huh?" This remark was also distinctly corrective, and solely directed at her. A block of ice covered her soul. She began to back away from his hand, but he tightened his grip, and a moment of sheer terror filled her when she saw his eyes, intent upon her now. They were suddenly void of all the beauty and warmth he had always shown her. Instead there was chilling, deadly resolve in their depths. A hundred fragmented realizations came into perspective with that one heartless, determined look. If she tried to back away from him... she knew... her usefulness would no longer exist, and she would be eliminated.

She smiled nervously and slid her hand more firmly into his. "Are you sure he's okay?" she questioned, trying to distract him from seeing that she was rejecting *him.*

"He's fine; you're with me, remember." The warmth was back in his eyes, and the double meaning was clear. He would protect her, most assuredly, as long as she did exactly what he wanted her to do; was what he wanted her to be.

The three walked directly up to one of the huge brick warehouses they were parked between. Marty moved in continuous, erratic circles, as if the other two were walking way too slow. His arms would shake, then he'd take off his cap, turn it around on his head, causing his huge, bloodshot eyes to bulge out even more. Then he'd slap his leg and stomp his foot as if the anxiety was just too much for him. He'd look over his shoulder impatiently, nervously, then duck his head in sudden, dawning paranoia, as if something were flying over him, or a video camera was recording his every move from somewhere above his head. To some, it might have been comical to watch, but Susan saw it all in a span of under two minutes. To her, the sight was terrifying, and pitiful. The man was strung out.

They were right up against the abandoned building before Susan saw that there was a door, and Marty had already opened it before she actually discerned that they were going to enter through it. She clung to Regis now, ready to promise anything if he could protect her from the evil, threatening atmosphere that surrounded this place.

Yellow-gold light assaulted her in the form of one, solitary light bulb hanging from a ripped wire overhead. It was hopelessly dim, but compared to the darkness of the alley, the brightness hurt Susan's eyes and she saw spots for several minutes. When she could finally focus, they were in a hallway, climbing reverberating steps that loudly over-echoed each footfall. It was just a hallway with stairs, but it seemed ominous, and everything within Susan wanted to run far away from it.

The walls and floors were filthy with dirt and stank of body odor and stale liquor. Broken beer bottles were scattered to the sides of the steps in random piles, creating a tiny path where one might walk without stepping on them. Rats ran up and down the walls freely, until they heard the human footsteps. Susan cringed, grabbing Regis' hand in a pulling-back motion. She barely suppressed a scream as she saw them scurrying away. Regis looked at her stoically and glanced in the direction her eyes were darting. Then he tightened his grip on her hand and continued to walk onward, undaunted and unconcerned with the foulness around him.

Marty not only walked onward, but seemed to fit right in to the surroundings. Where he'd looked horribly out of place and freakish a few moments ago, even in the slime of the alley, he now seemed perfectly at home. He skirted past the obscenities spray painted on the wall, and bounded for an upstairs room.

It must have been the warehouse office at one time, Susan guessed as she entered the door Marty had unlocked with a key. It had a small reception area, empty right now, with a half wall of smudged glass that looked into another large room. It was an old conference room that was closed off by a solid steel door.

Regis and Marty congregated at the glass window as if they were perusing an art exhibit. Susan, too, looked into the larger room, but her mouth hung open in repugnance. Dilapidated couches and chairs were scattered about. Loud, obscene music reverberated against the paneled walls, the pounding rhythms seeming to jostle her bones. It could be clearly heard inside the reception room where Susan still clutched Regis' arm. He held her tightly against his side, as unwilling to let go of her, perhaps, as she was to be released. Other than that, he seemed completely relaxed and calm as he drank in the sight before him.

People were everywhere. Some were dancing, some were crying, some were staring off into space, but every one of them was high. In one corner of the room a poker game was being played. Five young men sat around the table drinking and playing, while barely dressed girls hovered over them. On the couches, couples were openly engaging in sexual acts, while others watched lewdly, and still others seemed to be standing in line, waiting for their turn.

In the center of the room sat one man behind a fold-up card table, ridiculously out of place with his wire rimmed glasses and ready cash box. He was obviously the keeper of this "store" and anyone who wanted to play, must come prepared to pay. A huge, formidable looking guard stood behind the man as he counted his change and kept supplies handy. This man also seemed out of place, but Susan couldn't figure out why. He blended in with the rest of the crowd perfectly, stood completely relaxed within the debauchery surrounding him, and yet, he was different. Susan didn't give him much thought. She saw what was going on around him more acutely, and she thought she was going to throw up.

"All right, is anyone in here on the stuff?" she heard Regis ask Marty from her stricken haze.

"Nope, I saved it just for you, but they all know I'm coming back with some tonight and they're waiting for it. I'm telling you the stuff's taking off like a rocket. *Racing rocket!*" he yelled enthusiastically with a guttural, frightening laugh.

Regis Black laughed back, slapping Marty's shoulder. "Well, let's see some action, man!"

Marty walked to the steel door separating the rooms, taking a brief second to note Susan's peculiar gray-white features with disdain. Then, with a swift movement, he ripped the door open. The music blasted into the air like a gunshot, then subsided again as the door slapped closed. Marty was gone for the moment, but Regis watched him closely through the glass. The music was suddenly completely silent and his wiry voice could be heard distantly, announcing that he was back with the good stuff. Everyone in the room surrounded him in a rush, reaching for the drug they had come out for tonight.

"Regis, let's get out of here, I don't like this," Susan said in a low hush.

"Well, you may not like it, but we aren't going anywhere yet, and you are now a part of it all, so you better cooperate." His eyes were dead again, and frighteningly void of the warmth she depended upon.

"I'm not a part of this. This is not anything I want to be a part of."

"Yes, you are. I can *prove* that you, little Susan Ventry, have been transporting illegal drugs across the Canadian/American border for almost two months now."

"What?" She was horrified. His words were treacherous and cold, but the tone with which he carried them was what tore at her heart.

"Yes, ma'am. Smuggling drugs, I do believe, means - Oh, a *long* time - in a federal prison. No more college degree, no more making a life for yourself. It's all gone, if you don't do exactly what I say."

"Regis? I... What...?" She stared at him with tears forming in her eyes. Betrayal lashed across her features in ultimate incredulous wonder. This wasn't the man she knew. It was the man she had always feared he truly was.

"Now, honey, there's nothing to worry about. All I need from you is exactly what you've always done. Nothing more. Just come back and forth across the border everyday, the way you've been doing. Bring a shipment here and the payment back to Max in the process. It's simple - and you're perfectly safe. No one would ever suspect you.

"My feelings haven't changed for you a bit. Now, if everything works out, which we're going to see in just a minute..." He indicated the crowd in front of them, jumping, kicking and scratching for their purchases, and his eyes lit up, distracted from her for a moment, satisfaction covering his face.

This was exactly what he'd been hoping for. The need was there. These people, who only moments ago were visiting amiably, were now ready to rip at each other's faces to get a hold of the drug Marty waved toward them. "Uh..." Regis seemed to remember Susan all of a sudden, "if everything works out, you and me are going to live happily ever after, I promise."

Except she didn't want to live happily ever after with him anymore. The more she saw the selfish fever in his eye as he watched the junkies snort the new drug, the less she wanted anything to do with him. If he had given her even the slightest bit of thought once the horrid festivities began, he might have noticed her utter rejection of him. It was to her benefit that he never glanced her way again. He would surely have killed her for the contempt and revulsion that filled her eyes.

The people in the room began to sway and laugh together in tremendous merriment. Some sat perfectly still and began to smile, others danced to rhythms only they could hear. A few sprawled motionless on their bellies and Susan truly feared they were dead. Still others held onto their heads as if some sort of terrific explosion had taken place inside. It was a site of human destruction. People sacrificing their minds, their dignity, their beings, so they might encounter this state of euphoria.

To Susan, it all looked disgusting, even devastating, but not to Regis Black. He saw only profit as the junkies took in their treats and began to sway in reaction to the drug. Everyone seemed so very happy and contented. Especially Regis, who was convinced that his designs for investment would provide incredible payoff.

Marty sprang back in the room with an overly bright wickedness laughing in his eyes. "See what I mean?"

"Yeah, it's looking good, Marty, I think we got a winner."

"Damn right we do!" The men laughed together, even hugged slightly in their joy. "Now, watch this... This is why we're going to be rich... I doubled the dose in those guys playing poker over there. Watch what happens to them."

"What?" Regis asked.

"It makes them *stronger!*" Marty rumbled deeply, in an overly exited, almost uncontrollable glee. "Just watch. You won't believe it."

After several minutes of watching, a stir began at the poker table, a disturbed agitation among the players. Then an argument started. Suddenly one of the young men jumped up, turned away from the others in seemingly impatient disgust, and slammed his fist against the back of his chair. When it hit the ground in a knocking crack, he became furious and flipped it up and around, then pounded it violently into the floor as if he couldn't stand the level of volcanic seething that boiled within him. He had to expend it somehow. Finally, he picked up the offending chair and crashed it uncontrollably into the wall.

Three of the other four men began to fight now while the fifth stood screaming at the lot of them in a black rage. Torrents of senseless, incoherent ranting spewed from his mouth as he raved on unseeingly. Susan was terrified and began to finally disconnect herself from Regis' hold and run for the door. He caught her before she'd even taken a step, and without saying a word, he pulled her back against him and forced her, physically, to watch the scene before her.

The men were starting to use their fists. A chaotic screech overtook the rest of the crowd as they saw the men fighting. Paths were cleared, paranoia causing some to shrink against the walls and cry like pitiful babies. Others still danced and laughed as if they couldn't hear a thing outside of the world they had drawn themselves into. Most, however, were thirsty for the bloody violence. Their eyes lit up with savagery, and they stared, transfixed by the beatings taking place in front of them.

One man of the three seemed determined to reign supreme, and as Susan looked on, she watched him beat the other two until they couldn't, or wouldn't, fight back any longer. Even then, he kept on, though, thrashing one of the other men with an unseeing violence, until blood swamped every pore on his face and his chest caved in like broken plywood.

It was then that the huge man who had been guarding the cashbox stepped forward. Violently grabbing the young man, he restrained the entire upper portion of his body with a twisting hold that began around the youth's chest and ended with the guard's other arm around the young man's ears. "Hey! Take it outside before the cops hear all this noise!"

A stunned hush overtook the rest of the crowd as that possibility struck them. The young man kicked and fought against the guard's hold, but at least he wasn't beating upon the other grossly still body that lay on the floor a few feet in front of him. When the guard released him, he sprang from the hold and howled like a mad dog, flexing his arms in a conquering victory bow. The crowd joined in, once again forgetting the threat of police overhearing them, and reveling in the staunch euphoria they depended upon.

Susan watched the huge guard carefully as he studied the lifeless body on the ground before him. He didn't touch it, or even go near it, he just watched it, almost willing it to move as the chaos resurfaced around him. She willed the body to move, too, but it didn't. In another several hours the young man who had savagely thrashed this other youth, would wake from a deep, deadened sleep, and discover that he had beaten his best friend to death.

Marty looked at Regis and slapped his hand in glee, a satisfied laugh transferring between them. "We definitely got ourselves a winner," Regis said with ultimate joy.

"Yes, sir, we do. That bear of a guard right there," he pointed to the man who had just stopped the fight, "he's our runner, ready to take this stuff to the ends of the earth if he's allowed to partake when the need arises."

"You've already got a runner set up?" Regis looked worried, and slightly angry that Marty was already setting up distribution procedures without his approval or direction.

"Yeah, listen, Black, this one's going to be easy as pie for you, and safe as hell. If you just get us the coke and the dust - especially the dust - and get the N.F.P.D. to look the other way, we got the rest of it under control."

That actually sounded rather nice. Almost no involvement meant less chance of getting caught. "I still get seventy-five percent."

"Seventy-five," Marty agreed without hesitation, "just like we said."

"All right, set up a meeting for two nights from now. I'll have Susan watch your runner for a day or two to see if I approve. After that, she's the connection. She'll give you the goods, she'll collect - everything. Don't contact me, don't talk about me, don't ever even look at me on the streets or I'll just put you in jail and stop all my troubles."

Marty's face went ghostly white, almost transparent if that were possible, and he stared at the man before him, believing every threat he issued. "Black, come on, you know I ain't no snitch. Jeez, you know I ain't ever going to say nothing about you and your cops. It's our own secret, no one else knows."

"Good..." Regis' face was unimpressed by this vow, and unafraid even if it wasn't kept. His threats were promises, and he had the ability to annihilate Marty, just as he said, and come out of it all completely unscathed. "If it stays that way, you and me are going to be *very* rich men."

Susan gulped hard as she listened without being paid any attention to, even though Regis still gripped her against his side. Her head was spinning, her emotions reeling. She felt like vomiting, or screaming, or crying pitifully in a ball, but still she was forced to hear more.

It couldn't be, it just couldn't be that she was to be used as a contact for his drug deals. It couldn't be that that's why he needed her. Had she heard him correctly as he asserted his unquestionable control? Were there really... *police* involved?

~ *Chapter Four* ~

At thirty-nine, Angela Cahn didn't look that much different than she had at twenty-nine, except for a few fine lines around her eyes and a drastically shorter hairstyle. She stood in the long, tunnel-like hallway that connected her store's showroom to its warehouse. Two steel doors were solidly closed before and behind her, effectively closing off the activity that occurred just beyond them. One entrance led to the cool, quiet atmosphere of her store, the other gave way to the occasionally insane hubbub of her warehouse. The hallway was neutral, and separated one aspect of business from the other as a time warp might separate different universes.

In stolen moments of quiet like these, she couldn't help but be awed by what her late husband had achieved. Jeff had begun their business as a teen, cutting neighbors' grass during summers. It should never have become as successful as it was today, but by the time he passed away, he'd built a modern store on one of Niagara Falls' busiest main roads.

Nearly everyone in the community knew of and used LCPU's services. If it wasn't to have their lawns and shrubbery designed and kept manicured throughout the summer, then they called for roofing or siding repairs. If it wasn't for any of that, then many households relied on LCPU's plowing services to combat the snow that so often paralyzed the area, or they came in and bought their own snowblowers, lawnmowers, rakes, etc. when the need arose. It was something to be proud of.

She remembered a long lifetime ago, when she seemed to be just a child, in love with an ambitious young teenager who planned on building an entire empire by simply mowing people's lawns. In her wildest nightmares she'd never imagined standing here without him, single and devoting her life to those dreams... and his memory. It seemed sad, and even empty at times, but it was a safe, tranquil way of life. Exactly what she wanted it to be.

Pushing herself onward, she entered the concrete enormity of the stockroom, her heels clicking sharply on the floor as she walked between the endless, perfectly aligned shelves. A few of them were running low on their stock, she noted absently as she glanced down at her infamous clipboard. It was inventory night again. It would never end. After all these years, Angela thought to herself, she really should have given this job to Randy, but she didn't have the heart to. He was such a wonderful manager and put so much time into making *Lawn Care Products Unlimited* a successful company. What few responsibilities he did not maintain, she could at least make an attempt to handle.

She did, however, pay one of her young employees to help on such occasions now. Long ago, she did it alone, until a particular night when someone had been forced to help her. She had realized how much faster and easier the job could be with two people working on it.

She smiled to herself as she remembered that night. The night her young friend had come crashing through her door to escape certain devastation. It was rewarding to believe that she had actually saved his future then, and to know, even if she hadn't seen him in years, that he had become such a vital and successful police officer. Had she not shielded him from getting caught that night, he might never have been able to accomplish that dream. That concept amazed her. She knew she was probably just a distant memory from his adolescence, but she would always consider Michael Camden, *Sergeant* Michael Camden, a dear friend.

She was still smiling when she turned to her young assistant, Lisa, and the girl smiled back as Angela closed the inventory book with finality. "Done!"

"Good."

"Yes, ma'am, let's go home. Do you need a ride?"

"No, that's okay, Mrs. Cahn, my mom let me use the car tonight."

"Well, okay then, you're free to go."

"Do you need any help cleaning up?"

"No thanks. It'll only take me a minute to set the alarm, then I'm out of here!"

"Okay, well goodnight then. I'll see you Saturday."

"Okay, Lisa, thanks again, and do good on that chemistry test Friday."

"I'll try."

When Lisa had pulled safely away in her mother's station wagon, Angela began the process of shutting down her store, turning off lights and computers, etc. It was an average night in her life, inventory had actually gone along much faster than usual, and that was always a welcomed relief. She had no way of knowing that on this typical, uneventful evening, her entire reality was about to change. Her very systematic and carefully unobstructed existence was about to sustain blows that would shatter it forever...

*   *   *

"A toast!" The seven family members relaxing happily at the dinner table lifted their glasses in unison and directed their attention to the graying, sparkling blue-eyed man making the toast. "To my son, Michael, and my beautiful daughter-in-law, Amy - may every year they spend together be better than this first."

"Here, here," the party resounded, and sipped at their drinks.

"The Good Lord knows," Reverend Frank Camden continued mischievously as he nudged his wife of nearly thirty years, "the man's going to need all the help he can get!"

Amy's father, retired police Lieutenant, Kevin Larsen, burst forth over the loud, sarcastic groans of banter, "Amen, Reverend!" and the table erupted in mirth.

Years of police work had graced Kevin with a dark strength that was almost tangible. His brown hair was spattered with gray now, and his perceptive brown eyes, which were even more alluring with the years of wisdom he'd gained, had a sober, savvy edge to them. A deep, flitting scar streaked up the side of his face from his back and neck, adding mystery to his rugged good looks. It seemed to symbolize all the pain he'd endured in his lifetime. Despite his past grief, however, an underlying humor lurked within him, and he often let it escape at the most unlikely moments.

He and the Reverend, both older, wiser men, touched their glasses together in a sort of shared confirmation. Apparently, they both knew how difficult the reality of marriage could be, even when the two partners shared an intense love.

The rest of the table continued to moan and Amy Camden, radiant with her silky light brown hair and soft green eyes, looked at her small, sturdy mother-in-law with a withering face. Their own sort of shared communication transpired within the humor. They were clearly outnumbered in the predominantly male Camden household, but it didn't matter. They held the life and breath of this family together within the warmth of their hearts, and every one of these big, strong men knew it.

"You're absolutely right dear," Jody Camden said with candy-coated sweetness, "you men rarely *can* keep up with us girls. You better pray for *strength,* too." With sarcastic expressions, and radiant smiles, the two women lifted their glasses high and tipped them gently together in a mock imitation of the two men. The table burst forth with more laughing oohs and ahhs.

"Dad's going to be on the couch tonight," Billy Camden, twenty-one and the second born son of Frank and Jody, said with huge, gleaming eyes.

"I think Michael will be, too," laughed the youngest of the clan, Sean Camden, a hugely muscled seventeen year old.

"Me? I haven't said anything!" Michael finally spoke up.

"No matter, son," Frank informed him with joking assurance, "you're male... and *we'd* appreciate a *little bit* of allegiance; you know what I'm saying?"

"Well, let's not forget who started it," Jody said, still grinning at the warm playfulness as she stood to begin clearing dishes.

With a sudden edge of sobriety, Frank spoke again. "Awh, honey, you know I'm kidding, we all know we'd be lost without you."

"Here, here," Kevin said again, and all the men lifted their glasses once more, serious now, to honor the ladies with a toast.

Amy stood to help Jody clear the plates. "I don't know, Mom, what do you think? Should we forgive them?"

"Well... I think if they can help us clear the table we could let this incident pass."

"I think so, too."

Michael was the first to jump up with his plate. "Good, because I have no intention of spending my first anniversary on the couch!"

"Yeah! Go, Michael!" Billy and Sean roared, high-fiving each other enthusiastically.

Amy's face flamed in embarrassment and Michael laughed and clutched her lovingly under one arm while the table began their playful banter once again. It was a wonderful thing to belong in this family. So much was different now that she and Kevin were a part of the Camdens. They had so much to be thankful for now.

"Hold on, hold on," she said to the group. "Before everyone gets crazy again, I have a toast to make, too." Everyone lifted their glasses and quieted to hear her words. Looking downwards, her voice shook with sincerity and she took a deep breath, trying hard not be too melodramatic. What she felt was so strong, though, what she'd been through was so deeply etched in her heart, and her gratefulness reached far into her soul. She couldn't help but show it, and Michael hugged her closely to his side reading her thoughts, before she even uttered a sound.

Michael hadn't even known Amy two years ago. Lieutenant Kevin Larsen, his father-in-law now, had been his partner then, and together they had worked the biggest of the Special Teams cases. Because of their excellent ability and a few surprise connections that would leave gaping, permanent scars in Kevin, they had brought down the most violent criminal in Western New York.

The experience, however, had left an imprint of devastation upon Kevin's soul that was irreparable. His wife was dead, his family dissolved, and he'd been betrayed more horribly than he could have ever imagined. It was at that time that he decided to retire, at forty-seven years of age, from the vital Detective Lieutenant's position he held in the Narcotics Division of the Niagara Falls Police Department. With commendations and honors from the DEA to the Mayor of Niagara Falls, Lieutenant Kevin Larsen had graciously retired from duty.

Michael, however, had been promoted, due to his excellent service in that same case. Today he was a Sergeant in charge of Supervision of the Special Teams, and there were many more facets to their investigations than he'd ever imagined being a part of. Beyond all of that, he had found Amy in it, and he had the privilege of calling Kevin a friend - and family. Those were the two things that mattered most to him.

He looked at his wife now as she spoke what was in her heart, knowing she couldn't possibly express it all, and knowing, too, that she wouldn't really have to.

"To my father. Less than two years ago, we all thought he was dead. I'm just so glad he's alive, and that we can be a part of this family."

The table fell silent for several seconds, but Kevin's eyes were brilliant as he looked meaningfully into his daughter's face. It was true. Nearly two years ago he'd been presumed dead, and his and Amy's lives had sustained blows they never thought they'd recover from. Then, Amy had been distant, almost lost to him, the true secrets of her life kept carefully hidden within Kevin's mind and heart. Now she was truly his daughter, and he knew he could never love anyone quite the way he loved her. He, too, was glad to have recovered from so long and agonizing a trial.

"Amen to that." Frank broke the silence with a quiet, sincere tone, no joke held within the comment this time.

"Here, here," the table resounded again in subdued reverence. They sipped their drinks once again as Kevin rose from the table and hugged his daughter.

"I love you, honey."

"I love you, too, Dad."

*   *   *

While Kevin Larsen and the Camdens laughed, joked, and shared a family warmth that secured their hearts, Michael forced himself away from the festivities. It seemed unfair that on his first anniversary he must leave his beautiful wife in the company of others; but he must. It was his job, and tonight, especially, he must be available as Marcus would be meeting with the *Racer* contacts. His teams must be securely in place and ready on a moment's notice.

He told himself how important this was as he kissed his wife goodbye and her soft eyes glazed with disappointment at his departure. An entire drug scheme would be stifled tonight and never be allowed to begin. That was important, right?

Yes, it was, he decided as he closed the door to his parents' home behind him and turned his cell phone on. It was critically important.

But it wasn't worth it.

*   *   *

As Michael drove back to work to begin the setup of surveillance for Marcus, a young woman was racing down the highway in terror. She must get to her destination on time. She must warn her contact of the things she had learned. If she didn't, it would all be too late.

She gripped her cell phone tightly until her knuckles turned white, her face twisting in panicked fear. "Hello?" her voice shook. "Is this the cop?"

"Cop?" the voice queried in obvious shock and confusion.

"I know you're a cop, so don't try to screw with me, I don't have the time!"

"Who are you looking for?"

"I'm looking for the cop that hangs around Lex Street. I'm your contact, and I'm supposed to watch you. I know you're a cop, I saw you go into the police station yesterday."

Marcus's face fell and his heart began to hammer painfully. He couldn't have been spotted so easily. It couldn't be possible after all the effort he'd expended on remaining completely indiscernible as a police officer, that at this most crucial time he'd been observed. It just couldn't be. "Who is this?"

"I told you, I'm your contact. We're supposed to meet in the dead-end warehouse on Powell Street tonight with the other two dealers. I'm supposed to set up a distribution plan with you for my boss."

It was a female. Marcus hadn't expected the contact to be female, although he was pretty sure who this was. It would be almost as good to bust her as Regis Black, from what Linden had heard about her. Almost - but not quite - and her boss was sending her, rather than come himself. That was a huge disappointment. "What do you want?"

"I - I want help."

"What?"

"I want help. I don't want to be involved in this, I swear I don't, and I can tell you everything you want to know. I know whose involved, I know what they want, what they're doing, everything. I don't want to be involved in this, I swear I don't!" she repeated desperately.

"Wait a minute, wait a minute. What's your name?"

"First tell me yours. Are you a cop? Tell me! I have to know!" It was the sheer anguish in the plea that struck a chord within Marcus Linden. It was primal and terrified; and it was real.

He hesitated for only a moment, a monumental split decision facing him. Someone had seen him go into the police station yesterday when he'd been forced to let Michael know that a deal was definitely to be made tonight. This could be a con-job, an innocent-girl ploy, designed to make him confess. If he fell prey to a trap like that, the entire *Racer* bust would be immediately blown and lost forever. Or, this terrified girl could be telling him the truth - that she was mixed in over her head and wanted to assist him in busting the case.

Silence hung in the air as the two frantic souls held their phone lines. Then it was broken, the decision made, the risk taken.

"Yes, I am a cop." Even his voice was different as the confession was made. A deep strength emanated from him now as he spoke, and an authority that hadn't existed only a moment before, overtook him. Yes, he *was* a cop.

Susan began to cry. Wrenching, gulping tears that she couldn't control and sprang as much from relief as fright for her situation. "My name is Susan," she said. Just as Marcus had thought; he'd heard all about Susan Ventry on the streets. She was Black's girl, where all the good stuff came from. He could never have guessed her next words. "I have proof of everything you want to know on a tape. I'll give it to you if you just keep me out of it and keep them away from me. They're going to be watching us tonight so I have to meet with you before then."

"Where are you?"

"I'm in Ontario, on my way back to The Falls. I tried to run away, but I'm so afraid they'll catch me. I don't have anywhere to go, and I don't know of any other way to stop this except to tell you what I know... and hope to God you're one of the good guys..."

*   *   *

It was Marcus Linden's turn to grip his phone in desperation. There was so little time left. Someone was watching, and people surrounded the pay phone he was using. People who might be listening as they drank and partied their time away. People he'd seen a hundred times before, who suddenly seemed like nameless, faceless masses. Why couldn't Susan have called earlier?

The relatively short ringing into Michael's private office line seemed like endlessly long, dragged out moments. The line finally clicked, and whatever hope Marcus had of reaching his sergeant to tell him of this radical change of plan, ended. This was a line used only by authorized agents. It would be checked immediately when Michael returned to the office, but that wasn't soon enough. Marcus needed to speak with him right *now!* Where was he? He was supposed to be setting up the surveillance!

"You have reached the office of the Niagara Falls Drug Enforcement Administration. Please leave a detailed message and your call will be returned. If there is an emergency please press star zero, and an operator will assist you."

Marcus rolled his eyes, then closed them in a silent prayer. The entire project was on the line this very minute. Marcus stood completely alone in his ability to direct it into a positive outcome or a negative one. He would have to leave a message, he decided, then call Michael's cell. There was almost always some way to reach him.

"Michael, this is Marcus!" he lowered his voice and tried to speak slowly and clearly into the receiver, but the noise around him muddled the words. "There's been a serious change in plans. My contact called me, she knows I'm a cop, and she's willing to supply important information. Her name in Susan Ventry, I've heard of her... she's Black's girl. She must have decided to blow him in... Anyway, I'll be meeting her at - "

Marcus never got a chance to try Michael's cell. The message was cut off with a sharp grunt, and the sounds of the loud voices from the background were clear for a split second. Then the line went completely dead.

~ *Chapter Five* ~

While she was collecting a mass of papers that had accumulated in the inventory process, Angela saw a single pair of headlights turn into the parking lot. All was dark and quiet, a peaceful humming of the exhaust fan filling the air as the rest of LCPU settled. The sign on the door stated clearly that *Lawn Care Products Unlimited* was closed, but the light from inside the office must have alerted whoever this was that someone was inside.

It was a young woman. Angela watched her walk up to the storefront and peer inside, cupping her hands to either side of her face so she could see through the dark glass.

"Sorry," Angela called, "we're closed."

"Please, I just need directions, do you know where Cane Street is?"

Angela looked a bit leery, aware of the many horrible things that could happen to a woman alone in a dark building at night. Then she looked at the slight figure ensconced in darkness outside of her storefront and the desperate eyes that looked genuinely beseeching, even in the darkness. Shrugging, she went to open the door. The young woman rushed in frantically, and Angela was instantly on edge. An electric tension seemed to fill the air as this frightened youth entered into it and began to speak with a shaking quality that she was trying hard to control.

"Hi, thanks for letting me in, I was on the highway and I got off at Niagara Falls Boulevard, but I can't find Cane Street."

"Oh, well Cane Street is down the other way," Angela said soothingly, trying to calm the upset radiating from the young woman. "When you got off the highway, you must have turned left. If you'd have turned right, you'd have seen Cane about one mile down."

The poor thing looked like she was going to cry. She had straight blond hair and was so thin as to appear unhealthy. She looked like something straight out of a back-to-school ad, with impossibly skinny jeans, platform shoes and dyed-pink jean jacket. Angela thought the look was hideous and not complimentary to any body type. She must be getting *really* old.

"My friend said to turn left when I got off the highway... I'm going to visit her... I'm from out of town..." Her voice faded. "I don't know where I'm going."

"Oh, isn't that the worst feeling? When you don't know where you are to begin with and then you get lost?" Angela smiled reassuringly and the young woman seemed to visibly relax a bit.

"Yeah."

"Well, just go straight back down Niagara Falls Boulevard until you get to the highway again, and then keep going. You'll see Cane Street about a mile down."

"So, I turn right out of the parking lot and just go straight?"

"No, you need to turn left out of this parking lot and go back into the direction you came. See, you made a right turn into - " Angela could see the girl getting more confused and frantic by the minute, even though the directions were fairly simple and clear. Niagara

Falls Boulevard was a busy, fast paced semi-highway, though, with stores and businesses cramming in everywhere. It was understandable that this young woman's fear and unfamiliarity with the situation were distracting her. This particular young woman's fears, however, seemed enormous. Angela's tender heart only wanted to calm her down because she truly looked frightened. "Oh - why don't I just take you there."

"I have to get to my friend's house." It was a quiet, hopeless statement that seemed inappropriate as a response. It made Angela look deeply into her face. Instantly, the first connection was made; a connection of the heart, a connection that made Angela's entire being rear up with a primal, protective instinct. This child was frightened. More than frightened, she seemed... frail... unable to shield herself from a world that could do her serious harm for it. Angela, however, wouldn't harm her. She would help her, and she would see to it that nothing else harmed this innocent, either. At least not tonight.

"It's okay," Angela said soothingly, speaking right into Susan's troubled soul and seeing a visible relaxation in her. "I'm on my way out anyway, I'll take you there; there's nothing to worry about. I'll just drive out that way and you can follow me in your own car. Do you know where you're going once you get to Cane Street?"

"I think so, my friend lives above a pizza place. Arnie's? Arnold's?"

"Armondo's?"

"Yes, I think that may be it."

"All right then, I'll drive right into Armondo's parking lot and you can follow me. Everything will be fine, I promise... What's your name, dear?"

"Uh - it's... Susan."

"Well, okay, Susan, give me a minute to lock up and we can go. I'll drive slowly and you follow close behind, all right? And don't let any of these nut cases who drive on the boulevard scare you. If you want to drive nice and safe and slow, you just do it and never mind if they like it or not. I swear, everyone is in the biggest hurry these days..."

Angela babbled on easily as the two left LCPU and got into their cars. Susan, still leery about her situation, began to smile as Angela carried on about crazy drivers. Once inside her sharp, red Lexus, with its gold lettering and symbols flashing starkly against the flawless gloss of color, Angela situated herself and looked in her rearview mirror to make sure Susan was following behind her. Driving slowly, she pulled onto the boulevard and turned left.

It was a relatively simple jaunt, about ten minutes out of Angela's way, and Susan seemed glued to her rear fender as they drove. If she had to make any sudden stops, Angela thought nervously, Susan was going to ram right into her. Luckily, no such incidents occurred, and shortly into the ride, she led Susan down Cane Street, and turned into the parking lot of Armondo's Pizzeria.

Pulling to an exaggerated stop, Angela turned to smile at Susan and announce their obvious safe arrival. The young woman would naturally be gushing with gratitude for this act of genuine hospitality. Instead, Angela was assaulted by an incredulous, anticlimactic sense of bewilderment. Before she could even muster her thoughts of this good deed together, and extend further comfort and reassurance, Susan had parked her older model Toyota with a decisive jolt and had run into the building. Not a word of thanks or acknowledgment followed.

Angela stared after the girl's hurrying form as she disappeared inside Armondo's and the door closed with a slap. That was it. She was gone.

Unable to believe how rudely she'd been treated after Angela had literally gone out of her way to help, she sat and stared at the solid door. She truly expected it to open and Susan come rushing out with great torrents of appreciation. She was mistaken. Silence seemed to encompass her rather suddenly; a feeling of complete foolishness followed as she found herself staring expectantly at the back door of an old, shut-down pizzeria.

Sitting upright in thorough affront, she eventually began to pull out of Armondo's parking lot. She looked back only one more time to be absolutely certain Susan wasn't trying to reach her. For a long time to come she would wonder if she should have simply accepted what had happened for what it was worth and been gone forever; but she didn't. She looked back; and when she did, she *did* see Susan. She was running, but not toward her, not to say thank you for the directions and the kindness. She was running *away* from someone else.

A large, hulking man dressed in dark, meshing colors was chasing Susan out the door of Armondo's and through the parking lot. Some sort of weapon was raised toward her, a club or a hammer perhaps, as if he was itching to smash it into the girl's skull if he could just get close enough to do it. From Angela's assessment in her rearview mirror, he seemed only seconds away from achieving that goal.

Angela sat there, frozen. It wasn't that she didn't want to help, it was just that it was all happening so quickly, and it simply didn't occur to her to render aid, at first. She just sat and stared, a gripping, sickening fear engulfing her as she witnessed a violence that was undiluted in its raw hatred.

Until the man actually did strike.

With a jolt, Angela heard the crash as Susan neared her car in a frenzied attempt at escape. The weapon came down, and Susan wrenched herself sideways just as the hammer crashed into the window of her Toyota. She screeched and twisted, beginning a frantic sprint away from her attacker as he pulled his bloodied hand up and out of the broken glass. Staring at it dumbly for a moment, he looked up with renewed rage and lunged after Susan again, refusing to be dissuaded.

It was then that Angela began to move. Not with any real plan in mind at first, not even fully aware that she *was* moving. An abrupt, instantly-arrived-at decision simply laid hold of her, and before she could process the consequences of involvement, she was racing her car backwards into the parking lot. Fierce protectiveness guided her, and red rage propelled her toward Susan's assailant.

Susan and her attacker both saw the car speeding toward them as soon as it began to move, and stopped in shock to watch it come toward them. Turning around quickly, Angela sped forward directly at the hulking man. Amazingly, instead of running as Susan did, to get away from the car aimed at him, he redirected his attention at Susan in a determined attempt at completing his task of violence toward her.

Angela was incensed. Apparently, this maniac didn't deem her a threat. Stepping on the gas a little harder, Angela tried to intimidate him, and at the very last second, he seemed to realize his danger. It was too late. He looked up in the mere fraction of time that he had and Angela saw the whites of his eyes just as he realized she was truly bent on killing him if he didn't leave the girl alone.

He jumped to his side, but the movement confused Angela, and, out of reflex, she tried to swerve away from him just as she was about to make contact. In one thumping crash, she ran right into him.

The man's face and body smashed sickeningly against Angela's windshield in a grotesquely misshapen mass before it rolled off to the side and fell to the ground. Screeching to a horrified halt, Angela looked at her steering wheel unseeingly for several seconds, wondering what had just happened, and unable to believe that she had just hit another human being, almost deliberately. Was he dead? Oh, God, had she killed him? She turned suddenly, in a panic, to see if she had actually just taken another human life. Before she could focus on the scene, however, that same man was up, very much alive, and right in the window of her Lexus.

He pulled the door open with a vengeful rage that was directed solely at Angela now. His face was the picture of ugliness. It wasn't so much the shape of his features or color of his hair that made him so hideous, it was the hatred that filled his eyes. It was evil, determined anger that seemed rooted to his very soul. Angela was petrified and stunned by the impact of that repulsiveness. A mere split second later, it registered upon her that this picture of violence intended to do her serious harm.

Reaching into her car he grabbed her harshly by the neck and yanked at her awkwardly in a dazed, injured attempt at wrenching her from the car. Obscenities Angela was rarely accustomed to hearing spewed from his mouth as he grabbed again, hurting her in his insistence to get her out so he could accomplish his violence.

With every ounce of strength she possessed, Angela held her seat and tried to push him away. She was too close to the edge of the parking lot and the large bushes beyond it to step on the gas, and even if she could have made the simple movement, she didn't really think of it as she was being physically assaulted. All she could think of was getting this brute off of her.

"No!" she screeched. "No! Somebody help me!" Her words were muffled and then cut completely off as his large, grubby hands grabbed at her face, clawing a handful of the sensitive skin as he tried to silence her and pull her out of the car yet again. If she hadn't been fastened securely in her seat belt, he probably would have succeeded at that last attempt.

Dizziness was engulfing her due to the blows she was sustaining to her head, and the overpowering feel of his huge hands yanking at her mouth and face. She was reaching for the gearshift now, finally realizing she was in a car, for God's sake, she should pull out of here and leave this madman dragging in the pavement. It was useless, however, for although she was attached to her seat by the restraining belt, he was pulling her enough to keep her from being able to actually reach and maneuver the gearshift.

Then, all at once, his hand slackened, and he collapsed almost as if in slow motion. As he fell onto, and almost into, her car, Angela saw the slim form of Susan standing behind him with deadly eyes and an unwavering, remorseless look on her face. The hammer that this man had chased her through the parking lot with only moments ago was dangling from her hand as if it weighed several hundred pounds: Heavy, unbearable, but stuck, nonetheless, in her grip.

It took Angela a second to figure out that Susan had just bashed this man in the head with it. For a few minutes nothing was said or done. A stunned silence filled the air along with a peculiar dumbness, as if both women were watching it all from a distance that didn't really touch them. It touched them very deeply, however, and after a moment Angela realized that with force.

Pushing at the bulk of this stranger's weight, which was slumped constrictively into the door of her car, imprisoning her feet and movements, she finally succeeded in a violent shove to free herself. When she finally got out of the car, Susan was watching her. "Oh, my God, what have we done?" Angela spoke out to her in a loud whisper.

"Nothing worse than what he was going to do to us," she said lifelessly.

Angela took only a second to peer into the young woman's dead face. Bending low, she reached to press her fingers to the throat of this creature. Amazingly, there was a pulse. She jumped up as if his flesh had scorched her, and hissed sharply, "Oh, my God, he's alive!"

"What?"

"He's alive, Susan, we've got to get out of here, right now, before he wakes up. We won't get into any trouble for simply defending ourselves; he tried to attack us! Come on, let's just get away, and we'll call an ambulance to come get him. No one will ever know."

"No one except *him!*" Susan screeched, pointing her finger at the man on the ground.

It was the desperate tone in Susan's voice that made Angela comprehend this man's degree of danger to her. He had, after all, been trying to kill her only moments ago, so he obviously knew her and hated her enough to go to great lengths trying to achieve that goal. Beyond that, Angela realized, if this man found out she had been the one to come rushing to Susan's aid tonight, he could come after *her* as well! Somehow, the possibility that he might do just that seemed all too likely to occur. "Oh, my God, Susan, who is he?"

"He's no one... Go... please... just go, I'll take care of everything from here, don't get yourself involved in this." Time was beginning to pass, and although they were in a quiet, shrub-enclosed parking lot that was abandoned and private, it was possible that someone might see or hear them.

"I'm not leaving you here."

"You have to, please, there is danger here that you know nothing about. I'm so grateful to you... you saved my life. Now, please, I'm going to leave in my car and you leave in yours, and I'll never tell anyone about this night. As far as he goes - just leave him there, it's only my own lousy luck that would keep him from dying."

"Susan - " Angela began, but was cut off as the huge, monstrous man began to moan and roll to his side. It was like an alarm bell to Angela and Susan.

"Oh, no; run! Go, now!" Susan screeched in a whispered rush. "He's moving."

"Come on, Susan, we have to get out of here! Come on!" Angela was pulling at the younger woman's sleeve, trying to make her move.

Susan seemed momentarily paralyzed as she watched the huge hulking man lift his head off the pavement and focus his gaze upon them. That was all the convincing she needed. She began to tear through the parking lot after Angela. In only a moment, both women were streaking down Cane Street in Angela's bright red Lexus. As they shot out of the parking lot, they could just make out a distinctive set of flashing lights at the far end of the street.

Police.

"Oh, thank God," Angela sighed, "we can stop and tell the police everything."

"No! No, oh, my God, we have to get away from them!"

Angela was stunned. Susan seemed very near an actual fit of hysteria. She had plastered her back against the seat she was in, and held one of her arms out in front of her, gripping the dashboard in a rigid posture. The other hand held onto the door handle so hard her knuckles were turning white, and Angela knew she would jump out of the car to avoid a confrontation with the police.

"Turn down this street! Quickly! Do as I say; we can't let the cops see us!"

Without thinking past the urgency in Susan's tone and the utter certainty her desperate features displayed, Angela swung the car to the right and pressed the gas pedal hard. They sailed down the street. "I don't think they saw us," Angela said airlessly.

"Just to be sure, turn down here," Susan replied as she nervously twisted almost completely around in her seat to look behind them. Angela turned again. Everything was quiet and undisturbed, but now they were tucked away in this maze of city streets, and the only way out was to backtrack through Cane Street. Apparently, that wasn't an immediate option.

"All right," Susan said gently, resignedly, when it was quiet behind them for several more minutes, "pull over and let's just try to blend in for a while, maybe they won't see us."

Angela pulled over near a field and parked. Empty vehicles lined the street the same way, so they blended in with the rest, although most of the other cars weren't so nice, or so red. With the motor off, the two women sat in sudden stillness. Shaken, and frustrated by confusion, Angela turned to the young woman beside her and asked, "Susan, what on earth is going on? You obviously weren't meeting your girlfriend."

"No. That was just a story. Please don't ask me about the truth. You can't know. I swear, if they catch us, I'll tell them you don't know anything." It was a sincere promise.

"About what?" Angela insisted.

"I can't tell you."

"Well, why was that man trying to kill you? Are you involved in something illegal?" Angela's eyes widened in horror at this just-realized possibility. Susan was obviously involved in something quite illegal.

"Actually I was trying to make it all right, but I guess that isn't to be," Susan said dejectedly as she looked out the window and tears pooled at the corners of her eyes.

Angela looked at her closely. A distinct air of hopelessness and confusion was radiating from her, and Angela's heart bled. She had no idea what was happening, but she believed that whatever it was, Susan was caught in the middle of it. She also believed that Susan did, indeed, want to make everything all right. "What have you done?" The question was gentle and knowing.

Susan turned her head and looked at Angela with a sarcastic air of self-disgust. "What *haven't* I done is the better question. Look, I have to get out of here..." She opened the passenger's door and began to exit abruptly.

"Susan... wait!" Angela was preparing to get out of her own door when Susan stopped her with her voice, once again both desperate and demanding.

"Listen, you can't help me, now do what I say or you will end up in this...trouble, that never ends. I have to get out of here. Just wait about an hour or so and then, if everything is still quiet, slip away. I don't think anyone saw us, but if they did, just tell them some girl held you at gunpoint and made you take me around town tonight. Just, please... don't ever tell anyone my name. Tell them it was just some crazy lunatic that threatened you."

"I'm not going to say that."

"You've *got* to! Now listen to me; this is not a game, and don't try to protect me! This is some very big, bad business, and if you don't tell it the way I'm telling you to tell it, you will wind up dead! There isn't anything you can do to help me – not a thing... except to say nothing about tonight! No one can know where I went tonight, or that I even exist. Please, please let it be. Promise me that you'll let it be!" She was becoming frantic again and rather hysterical as she pleaded.

"All right! All right. I promise. I won't say anything about what happened, or about you... I promise." Her eyes bore the promise into Susan's as she ended her vow in quiet sincerity. For all of Susan's rough edges and peculiar behavior, Angela knew she was trying to protect her, and Angela could sense in the very air around her that she may just need that protection.

Instead of answering with any number of appropriate responses, Susan looked deeply into Angela's face, tears filling her eyes and that look of desperation and fear still lurking behind her features. "You're a good person. I haven't met many like you in my life. Thank you... If you see anything... If anything weird starts to happen to you... I mean if you feel like someone's watching you, or following you... be very careful... and..."

Susan looked again at this woman who had shown her a wealth of needed humanness in one simple act of kindness. She was, apparently, debating whether or not to say something else to Angela. Something critically important and secretive. Something that could save her life. With an acute decisiveness, Susan's shoulders squared for just a moment of courage and she shot the words out that she obviously would have preferred not to say.

"And... Don't call the police! Ever! *For your own good.* Trust me on that."

It seemed a simple enough statement. Most young adults seemed to believe the police held some sort of enemy status. It was the way she said it, though, that made Angela stare into her eyes to try to catch a glimpse of the depth which the statement carried. A deep meaningful depth that wasn't simple adolescent rebellion, but stark, knowledgeable fear. A warning.

Before she could discern anything more, however, Susan slammed the door to Angela's car and ran. She was ensconced in thick trees and lost to Angela's sight before anything could be done to stop it.

~ *Chapter Six* ~

Kevin opened the door to his home and a wave of silence assaulted him. It was too damned quiet compared to the fun and laughter at the Camden's house. Usually it didn't bother him, but sometimes it was the most depressing sound in the world. Because there was no escaping it. This was his life. Alone. Without family. Silent.

He threw his keys down on the end table in his living room and immediately switched the TV on. The noise of a popular sitcom filled the air, and the glow of TV light threw everything else in the room into shadow. The sound was grating, almost invasive, because it wasn't what he was seeking. He wanted life. The television only added... noise. Oh, well, it was better than the silence, he told himself. At least this lack of pulsing vitality also lacked the pain and disasters that came with a life filled with love and excitement.

Peace. He'd sought it so long, and now he was glad to have achieved it. Whatever pitfalls came with it, he would gladly bear. Gladly. Silence and all.

~ *Chapter Seven* ~

Utterly dumbfounded, Angela stared at the dense foliage just ahead of her, and was deluged by sudden darkness and ominous silence. She looked around her quickly, feeling conspicuous and endangered. Everything was quiet. The organized rows of Cape Cod houses that occupied the street started about twenty yards away from her. The road wound into a circular curve beyond the houses and gave way to a small playground and thickly treed park.

As Angela peered into the darkness, expecting any number of terrors to abruptly overtake her, she could just make out groups of benches scattered throughout the trees. This was obviously a lovely little spot to relax or picnic. Funny, Angela had been down the busy hubbub of Cane Street so many times, and had never noticed this quaint little residential section that extended just beyond it.

She would have to enjoy the scenery another time, she thought nervously as she slammed her entire vehicle into a locked state with the automatic controls at her fingertips. Slinking down, she looked at her watch and hunched into her seat. Susan had said to wait about an hour. It was almost eleven-thirty. If things stayed quiet, she would not wait an entire hour. Her nerves were raw, and as she thought through everything that had occurred tonight, she was absolutely stunned.

It had been a normal, uneventful evening in her life. A young woman had come in and asked for directions, an occurrence that happened almost everyday at LCPU. People rarely knew where they were going on the boulevard where the store was located, and the road extended for countless miles that began in the city of Buffalo and ended in the city of Niagara Falls. Tourists of all persuasions were forever getting lost and wanting to know where they were, and how to get where they wanted to be. So, another person asking directions was hardly an unusual incident.

The events that had followed that request, however, were mind-boggling. Some deranged lunatic had tried to kill both her and the young woman she was trying to help; that same, seemingly helpless, vulnerable innocent had more raw street smarts than she ever let on to possess, and was involved in something deeply illegal. On top of that, she, Angela Cahn, had almost been involved in a murder tonight. It was incredible.

Yet, through all of it, Angela's thoughts were most upon the frail young Susan who seemed to be running for her life even now. Susan's face filled her mind, with that look of dejected desperation that had covered her features when she told Angela how she wanted to make everything all right for herself. It was heart-wrenching.

Some sort of deep bond had been forged between the two women amid the events of this night. Something vital had transpired emotionally, a quality of soul, as essential to Angela's life as it was to Susan's. That child needed help, and Angela needed to help her. It was as simple as that.

Shaken by the impact of her terror, and the interchange between herself and Susan, Angela sat up abruptly and decided it was time to leave. She couldn't sit here any longer in this dark quiet, wondering about Susan's and her own safety. She wanted to go home where she would immediately forget this whole issue and wrap herself back up into the secure life she lived.

That, however, wasn't to be.

Across the density of the black foliage facing her, Angela saw a sudden movement. Apparently, this park was connected to more than this one quiet, picturesque street. Thinking the movement was Susan, that she may have reconsidered her offer to help, Angela sat still for just a little while longer. For just another horrible few moments, she trained her eyes on the scene before her, which was coming closer and clearer with every second. It wasn't Susan.

It was a group of three men, and they trudged through the semi-forest of the park with ill concealed haste. They looked, to Angela, like they were trying to get further and deeper into the density of the trees, but they obviously didn't realize that in doing so, they were getting closer and closer to its opening on the other side where Angela sat watching with a horrified catch in her heart.

Two of the men dragged the other along as he kicked and fought against them. He was gagged with some sort of wide tape strapped across his mouth. His hands were bound with the distinct, metallic shackling of handcuffs, and the other two men forced him forward as they held him between them.

All three of them were in dark silhouette to Angela's limited vision. She couldn't see their faces even a little; they were just black masses in the night. Their movements and actions, however, were distinct. The starkness of the moonlight, combined with the streetlights surrounding the street where she sat, somehow made the shadows vividly clear and frustratingly obscure at the same time. A deep, sickening upset was forming in the pit of her stomach as she strained her eyes to absorb the scene. A dreading knowledge of something she didn't technically know yet clutched her heart till her breath was constricted. She began to sweat. A foreboding she wanted to turn away from, yet found herself mesmerized by, chilled her to the bone as she continued to stare, unable to turn away.

The man being forced through the woods was the man who had attacked Susan. There was no mistaking his size and sheer bulk, and Angela shivered at the sight of him, and the thought of how much a man like that could have hurt a woman of Susan's tiny stature. Where Angela might have understood a man like him being involved in something illegal, she could not understand the two men who were beside him, obviously trying to find a safe place to conduct their business. For they were, unmistakably, with their hats, uniforms, and bulking revolvers holstered at their sides, police officers.

Susan had warned her about the police, and now a slow, inching dawning was showing Angela why. Obviously, whatever Susan was involved in, there were police officers involved in it, too. Now, even though Angela wanted to believe in Susan's total innocence, she couldn't help but wonder if she was connected to these men, and a party to their violence.

The group stopped abruptly and the two policemen looked around. They faced the man at a distance, and one scurried behind him and tried to shackle his feet together with another pair of handcuffs. The other assailant held on for dear life. It might have been comical at any other time, in any other situation, to see these men fall over each other in their attempt to further bind this huge, powerful creature. The last thing Angela saw in this scene, however, was humor.

They finally secured his feet, then left him writhing violently on the ground where he had landed in the scuffle. The officer who had actually had the trying task of clipping the cuffs around the monster's ankles got up angrily from the ground where he had fallen. Both men readjusted themselves for a fraction of a moment before they towered over the other, and faced him down levelly. A swift, agitated kick to the bound man's ribs reinforced their unquestionable control before the officers settled into their mission.

They began to talk. Of course, Angela couldn't hear them, but she could tell they were, very quietly, talking to the man. The hulking mass on the ground, still gagged with the heavy tape, shook his head vehemently and the officer kicked him. The man doubled forward and settled once again.

Hunching down, the police officers pushed only inches away from their victim's face, and, holding his lapels in a customarily threatening hold, began speaking again. The man shook his head again, and this time convulsed his body into a writhing mass of movement. His hands and feet were bound, his mouth gagged, and still he presented a frightening and formidable picture.

The officers must have thought so, too, because they jumped backwards, then one of them lifted up his billy club and heaved it down upon the monster's head. It didn't help. The man was still writhing and kicking with his legs fastened together. He squirmed violently, and the other officer cracked him against the head as well. Then again. Then again, with a suddenly uncontrolled violence and insistence, they both began to beat him. The huge man's body went suddenly stiff and slightly convulsive. Then it was still. Permanently and horribly still. He was dead. Angela's hands covered her face in absolute, rejecting horror. The man was dead.

The two officers took only a moment to check his pulse and discover the reality that they had killed this man. They removed the handcuffs and tape from his body, and put them carefully away before they rolled the man over and began rifling through his pockets. They were searching for something, desperately searching, and when they came up empty after rummaging disrespectfully through the dead man's person, one officer pounded his hand against the ground in ultimate frustration. Whatever they wanted they hadn't found it. Worse, they would never find it now.

They spoke quietly for a few more seconds, apparently trying to recover, to regain what had escaped them. They seemed suddenly fearful as they looked around themselves into the darkness, and Angela froze, thinking she might be visible to them. Apparently, she wasn't because after another several moments of quiet discussion, they ruthlessly kicked the lifeless form one last time, turned around, and left.

*　　　　*　　　　*

Above Armondo's, a silent stranger stared out of the tiny slit of draperies he pinched to the side of the window. He'd seen everything, and wished vehemently that he hadn't. For if he saw, he must accept, and if he accepted, he must be responsible for it. He tried to close his eyes, to block it out, but he couldn't.

A bright red Lexus had pulled into the parking lot, and the small gray Toyota had followed. He knew who drove that Toyota, just as he knew who the huge man waiting downstairs was. He wished again that he didn't know anything at all. All he wanted was to protect what was his, to make sure harm didn't come to any of his own. Beyond that, he didn't want to know anything at all, and most certainly didn't want to be a witness to it.

Nevertheless, he'd heard the madman scream with rage, then watched him chase after Susan, and attack her. He'd watched the beautiful woman in the unique red Lexus come to Susan's aid. He knew her, too. On several occasions he had utilized the services her store on Niagara Falls Boulevard provided. She was an innocent bystander, he was certain.

He didn't want to see, but he had. Now a decision collided into his conscience, and ripped at his mind and soul.

Should he protect the innocent? Or protect his own?

~ *Chapter Eight* ~

Michael's blood iced in his veins as he entered his office and casually pressed the retrieval button on his answering machine. Nothing could have prepared him for what he heard. Nothing. Marcus Linden's voice was strained and desperate as he tried to convey a monumental disruption in the night's plans. Then his voice was cut ruthlessly off.

He and Jack listened to the message over and over again after sending the four Special Teams designated to assist tonight, out to scout the area. Casey had left quite a while ago, to properly place himself on the streets as Jake Brown. He was immediately informed of the trouble. If anyone could find out what happened tonight, Casey could. Michael and Jack took a tremendous reassurance in that fact.

They could, however, only discern a few things in the message Linden had given, and that made them tense with distress. To look at them, they almost seemed casual, staring at the machine as if it were forming words they might read into. It was essential to be able to act and react with calm, professional decisions. Inside themselves, though, almost in another part of themselves, the dread and fear lay deep.

The name of the contact, Susan Ventry, and the fact that she supposedly wanted to confess everything to Marcus, was the only clear part of the message. Then again, it was the only thing on the message, but it was obvious that Marcus was going to try to convey much more before he was cut off. That left Jack and Michael straining to figure out anything they might otherwise glean from his few chopped words.

It was useless. Marcus had obviously been in a bar, at a pay phone, which was usually where he made any calls because his street persona didn't have his own phone. He'd been rushed and worried, and he was obviously going to meet somewhere with this contact before the originally scheduled meeting in the Powell Street warehouse took place. He never had a chance to say where, though, or at what time. As of right now, according to Casey and the Special Teams that were quietly surveying Powell Street, Marcus was nowhere to be found...

*   *   *

"Hello?" Regis' voice was groggy from sleep as he grabbed for the phone to stop the annoying ring.

"Yeah, Regis, it's Goldie, we got trouble." Officer Dwight Golden was panting for breath and glancing around himself nervously as he spoke into his cell phone. His partner drove just a bit too fast down the boulevard in his attempt to put distance between himself and the scene behind him.

"What?" Regis questioned deeply, instantly more alert, his blood beginning to pound through his veins.

"We just killed a cop!"

"*What!*"

"We killed a cop! Detective Marcus Linden! He's a Narcotics Investigator, Regis, and he knew everything! *Everything!* God, what the hell is going on?" Panic and desperation emanated from the officer. He was shaken and amazed by what had just transpired.

"Slow down, Dwight, just slow down. What happened?"

Officer Dwight Golden, a twenty-six-year-old, second-year patrolman, took a deep, shuddering breath. His features fit his name perfectly, and his cousin, Regis Black, had nicknamed Goldie when they were just children. He had golden blond hair, small green eyes and a full face that always looked a bit too red. So far, his record was exemplary. No one would have ever guessed...

"All right, we patrolled the warehouse area tonight, just like we planned... and the two junkie inventors showed up alone. There were supposed to be three of them, right? The inventors and their runner?"

"Yeah."

A note of tightly restrained hysteria laced Golden's voice and made his words breathy and unsteady. "Well, there were only two, which we thought was fishy, and then Susan never showed up."

"What do you mean she never showed up? She had a hundred grand worth of PCP with her that she was supposed to deliver to Marty and Nick!"

"I know that, so we went looking around a little. I mean who knew what might have happened to her, right? Then we thought about the lab and got worried, so we drove past there, just to make sure everything was kosher. When we get there, we're listening to the scanner to see if Susan might have gotten busted or something, and we see her car in the parking lot. We checked the building; everything was locked up tight, so now we're really starting to worry. Where the hell was she, and why was she even there to begin with?

"We pulled out and started looking around Cane, and all of a sudden we see Marcus Linden running down the street like a freak. You should have seen him; he scared the hell out of us. Blood was dripping down his face; his hand was all cut up... and he was high as a kite - *Racer* high - I couldn't believe it."

"This cop was high on *Racer*? Are you sure?"

"I'm dead sure. I know that kind of high, it's the reason we're all going to be millionaires. There's no doubt in my mind that Linden was a user, and what's more, I think he was supposed to be the junkie's runner, and instead he was meeting with Susan."

"That's impossible!" Regis said abrasively, affronted by the notion.

"Yeah, well when we tried to act innocent and help Linden into the car, he turned on us like a demon. He was strong as a bear and foaming at the mouth; he almost killed Hewitt and me, I swear. He knew everything; names, places, even high he knew it all. The crazy bastard tried to arrest us. Then, he said Susan gave him some envelope that'll prove everything."

"An envelope? What kind of envelope? Where is it?"

"How should I know, I'm assuming she gave it to him tonight. If that's true, we've got to find it."

"Why would Susan give a cop an envelope? What was in it?"

"I told you, I don't know! All I know is Linden was running down Cane Street, and says Susan gave him an envelope that'll bust us!"

"He must have tricked her into meeting him there. She probably didn't know he was a cop."

"Or, little Miss Susan ain't playing on our side anymore."

"That can't be," Regis said again, with the same note of incredulous affront, "Susan would never turn on me."

A short sniff escaped Golden, and an air of derisive impudence laid hold of him that he rarely showed to this particular man in charge - cousin or not. Regis Black was dangerous, and Goldie, of all people, knew that. He obviously disagreed with him at the moment, however. "Well, there she was Regis, you explain it. Why were both of them together, five miles away from where they were supposed to be? And why did the two junkies show up alone, where they *were* supposed to be, without their runner, who just happened to be built like a damn monster? All of this is just coincidence? I don't think so. How else would Linden have gotten that *Racer* he was stoned on? No one has access to *Racer* yet - except someone who might be in real tight with its makers."

A peculiar blanket of gray hovered over Regis as he shifted in his bed, staring unseeingly into the darkness. All of a sudden, everything that was supposed to finally be perfect was turning against him. His plan, that would have made him rich enough to live in the lap of luxury, far away on some remote island, was crumbling beneath his fingertips.

His young cousin's words and utter anxiety reached into him. The runner Marty had known so well was a cop? A cop Susan had been assigned to watch for the last two days? He recalled the colorless white her face had drained to when she'd met Goldie and his partner, Bob Hewitt, dressed in full, intimidating uniform. She couldn't believe her eyes. Police were involved in the business she was being forced to work in. Regis had seen the mistrust within her, and that was exactly what he'd wanted to see. If she didn't trust cops, she would never go to them.

"We're all in this together," Goldie had said to her slyly, purposely implying to her sickened soul that the entire police force was made up of drug dealers who wanted to profit by this deal.

"Of course, Susan, what do you think?" Regis had added, seeing that she needed a bit of education in this matter, "that city folks, with all their riches and prestige run these types of things? Not quite. It's always the big-timers, the ones you would never suspect, the ones with the money, who really run these kinds of shows."

It was so true. Regis Black knew that better than anyone. After years of struggling in this depraved little section of the world, he'd finally woken up, and began to use what he truly possessed.

Last year, out of the blue, the biggest drug dealer in the city had gotten busted, and the entire area was in shock over who and what this guy really was. Regis, too, had been stunned by it. He'd known Tim Rush casually on the streets; had even worked for him in reality, like every other user and dealer in the city had. Also like everyone else in the Lex and Powell area, he'd feared and respected Rush. Any sane person would have. He'd owned the entire area, and if one was ever found to have crossed him, that unfortunate soul would never see the light of the next day.

Shortly after the citywide sensation of Tim Rush's arrest, Regis' mind had begun to turn over, and he had contacted Goldie, his cop cousin. In Regis' opinion, Goldie never did fit the role. Apparently, he had always been right, too, because when Regis made his suggestions, Goldie jumped at the opportunities presented. Incredible amounts of money could be made due to this unprecedented collapse in the drug industry. Almost overnight Regis promoted himself from small time drug dealer to prince of the international connection; with *Racer* the most prized jewel in his crown.

He had everything he needed to accomplish it, too: a few police officers, the entire inner city, and last, but not least, his ultimate defense - The Judge - who he held securely, right in the palm of his hand. Racer would cause Regis' ventures to progress into millions of dollars. At least it was supposed to progress that way. Racer was the only part of the world he ruled that belonged to him; it was his idea, had his signature upon it. For him ever to be considered successful, and cultivate the respect of the industry, it must, absolutely *must* progress!

They'd never counted on an undercover cop, however, and Regis, most certainly, had never counted on betrayal from *Susan.* Goldie was right. She knew everything, and... she must have turned against him. *His* Susan! Panic raced through him. It didn't fit his

72

strong, capable temperament at all, and for several moments he couldn't cope with it. Totally unexpected betrayal, even hurt, assaulted him. Susan knew everything because he had entrusted her with everything! As a reward for that trust, she could slam them all right into a cell at Attica.

They must find her, and she must be silenced!

"Dwight? If you ever speak to me like that again, I'll kill you." It was said with calm, almost polite assurance, but Goldie blanched, and knew his cousin meant the threat. "Now," Regis continued with a business as usual tone, "the cop is dead." It was a flat statement that carried the enormous degree of selfish power this man had become accustomed to.

Gone was the black panic, deeply hidden was the incredulous sense of betrayal he felt over Susan's defection. Cold, hard strength emanated from him now. "That gives us time to find the PCP and whatever proof Susan gave this cop before she decides to squeal again. I'm certain she won't go to the police station; she'll be afraid we'll see her. She might try to make inadvertent contacts if she's desperate, though. In that case, she'll be needing someone to help her..."

"What if Linden was investigating this, Regis? What if he's got a partner whose going to want to avenge his murder?" All traces of the previous impudence were gone from the young officer now. Shriveling panic had replaced it.

"Dwight, shut up, and calm down! You're of no use to me like this! The damn cop was a user, do you really think he had a partner who knew about that? Now, if you can't play the game, you'll have to be cut from the team, you know what I'm saying?"

Dwight Golden knew exactly what his cousin was saying. "Yeah, all right, I'm all right..." Dwight took several seconds to calm himself as his partner, Bob Hewitt, watched and listened to the conversation in horrified silence. "What next?"

"That's better. Now, where is Susan?"

"We don't know."

"You know, Dwight..." a short, humorless laugh escaped Regis. "I don't want to hear another thing that you don't know about tonight! She must have been somewhere! Is her car still there?"

"I... didn't check."

"Well, do so, if you don't mind," Regis said with acid sarcasm. "And find out where the hell she went!"

*   *   *

They would surely find out, too, and their plan to terrorize would work. Except for two things that they hadn't counted on: One was the instantaneous bonding and loyalty that had developed between Angela and Susan. The other was, ironically, the other side of the law.

Two patrolmen found an abandoned gray Toyota on the side of a downtown road. The window had clearly been smashed deliberately, and distinct streams of blood smeared down the jagged, broken glass.

"Whoa, we better call this in," one officer said to the other.

"Yeah, looks like someone had some trouble."

But it was nothing compared to the trouble that would follow.

~ *Chapter Nine* ~

Michael's face was twisted in a deep, formidable scowl. Anger emanated from him in great, biting currents. He had lost a man. Marcus Linden was found this morning in a bloody heap, beaten to death.

The scene of the crime had been the most gruesome, heart-wrenching sight Michael had ever beheld. He'd seen death before, had seen beatings before, but never had he been forced to witness the mutilation of a friend, ripped open and lying in his own blood, the way Linden had been. He had never lost a man he'd assigned to a job. There could be no description for the way he felt. It was raw, hard pain; and under it, he was forced to proceed on.

To intensify matters, his department was in an impossible situation. A murder had been committed, which meant homicide investigations must take place, but the information pertaining to this case was extremely confidential and explosive. It could not be handled through regular channels, and keeping the lid on it, with the body being found in a public place, and reporters already cramming in for the details, was going to be nearly unachievable. It must be done, nevertheless.

On that note, John Casey was scrambling to piece it all together, working fast as the primary homicide investigator for the Special Teams. With his other undercover duties, now even more crucial with Marcus's unexpected absence, the pace was grueling. It was necessary, however, to get all of the ends properly covered. He stood like a rock as he read off a computer sheet in front of him, rattling off the information in hard, unimpressed tones. It was unspeakable that someone would have the gall to kill a police officer in this way. It ripped at the peace of mind, and showed a disrespect for authority, and a collapse in society that must be fought against.

"All right, Michael, here's what we got..." Casey said with quiet rage. "We checked out the name Susan Ventry; easy as pie, the name came up. She's a straight A student at Community; she comes in from Canada everyday to attend her classes - how convenient - she lives alone at 101 Ontario Street in a hell-hole of an apartment; waitresses three nights a week at a Pizza Shop on the strip; she's got an educational pass; and drives a gray Toyota, license plate number B5J-201.

"Last night this same vehicle was found on 10th Street, supposedly heading toward Canada. The window was smashed, and blood was found on the broken glass. Blood type matches Linden's, but DNA match-ups will take a couple of days. Susan Ventry has since disappeared, did not show up at her apartment last night, nor did she attend classes this morning." He threw the printout down on the desk in angry disgust. "I think we've got ourselves a murderer."

"We sure got enough for an official suspect," Michael said.

"Here's a picture of her. It's a copy of her student ID card."

Michael picked up the tiny card and peered into the face of the most average college student one would ever hope to encounter.

The picture of frail innocence faced him, but in his mind, it was the picture of a murderer.

"What about Marty Rhodes and Nick Kline, from Linden's report? They were supposed to have been meeting with Linden last night in the downtown warehouse, what happened to them?"

"I'm afraid they disappeared." Casey said a bit shamefacedly. "When we got the call that there was trouble with Linden, everyone sort of panicked, and when we got back to watching the warehouse, those two stiffs were gone."

Michael looked steadily at Casey, both of them knowing full well that professionalism wouldn't have allowed such a thing to occur. No one was thinking particularly professional last night. Besides, the safety of an officer always took top priority. That was basic police procedure.

Picking up his phone almost casually, Michael began to quietly punch a few numbers as Casey watched. "Yeah, Jack, it's Michael. We got a picture of Ventry... No, she's disappeared, along with Marty Rhodes and Nick Kline - how cozy - she hasn't shown up at home or school since yesterday... Right."

Casey stared at Michael as he put the phone back into its cradle. There was a deceptively quiet, gentle surety to the act. "Jack wants that photo enlarged, and he's going to broadcast it all over the city today at noon. If this little piss-pot is hiding, she won't be for long. Did you check out Customs?"

"Yes. She hasn't gone back into Canada since yesterday."

"Good, then she's stuck here. We need to find her. Our main goal is still containing *Racer*, so whatever comes up, we need to be able to handle quickly. I just hope we don't blow the whole damn thing."

Casey's eyes looked strangely dead, and alive with fire at the same time. "Me too, Michael; me too."

~ *Chapter Ten* ~

Angela dressed and went to work trying to act like this was any other ordinary day. She couldn't help feeling, though, as if the ordeal of the night before had permanently altered her universe. She'd thought of little else throughout the night, and as she applied makeup to her bruised face, the events renewed themselves over again in her head.

Thankfully, the swelling from that monster's attack had gone down, and it hurt worse than it actually looked. She felt as if a large slab of burning, hardened beef was attached to her lips and cheeks, but when she actually looked at it, it wasn't that puffed at all. A heavy coat of foundation would alleviate the slight discoloration, and so she would enter her day as if the troubles of the night before had never occurred.

It was the only way, she told herself; the only way she could possibly cope with what she had seen was to forget about it, to act like it never happened. She did not see two police officers beat a man to death. She did *not!* she insisted to her rebellious conscience. She must not say anything about last night! Who would she tell anyway? Other police? No way! Susan was right, she must stay quiet... and she would never trust the police again.

She'd inspected her car twice already to see if the monster had left his mark when he was hit. Thankfully, the brunt of his impact had been on the windshield and there was no discernable damage to the vehicle. She checked one more time as she managed to get out and enter the office of LCPU as if everything were normal. She would be glad to throw herself into her work and not think about anything else throughout the day.

The office of LCPU was situated behind the checkout counter. It was typically functional, with two matching desks, which faced each other in the very middle of the room. Angela's desk faced the door, and she could see with a simple glance if anyone came up to the counter to cash out his or her purchases. Randy's desk faced hers, and to the side was a large wall of window where they both could see the parking lot and whatever tumultuous action was occurring on Niagara Falls Boulevard.

A computer printer, copier and several filing cabinets were placed efficiently toward the other wall, creating a cool, relaxing atmosphere inside the office. What little space was left was decorated with a soft pastel wallpaper, and the gentle hum of the exhaust fan in the warehouse made all other sounds blend peacefully. Randy was already there and greeted her with a smile and a wave from inside the showroom as she walked behind the counter and into the office.

Turning on her computer and preparing herself in general for the day ahead, she reached over to get a cup of coffee, glancing down, half interested, at the newspaper on her desk. She didn't see anything. She could barely focus, and a sip of the hot coffee brought on an agony of pain in her injured lip. The memories that refused to leave her mind for long, came rushing forward once again.

She wondered, first of all, about Susan. Was she safe? Where had she gone last night after they bolted out of Armondo's? Did she have anything to do with that man's death? Angela wanted to believe Susan was completely innocent of the despicable deed she'd witnessed, but she wasn't at all sure that was the case.

Susan had just about confessed her involvement in something illegal. In fact, she had risked her own neck to make sure Angela wasn't connected to it. What an ironic twist. Last night when that scared young woman had come into LCPU, Angela had been assaulted by a protective instinct toward her. Now that same young woman, who had seemed so vulnerable, was protecting her with the same instinct. For God's sake, they didn't even know each other! Still, Angela worried about her, fretted over whether she was safe, and wondered what in the world such a shaky, vulnerable teenager had gotten into that was as corrupt and dangerous as what she'd seen last night.

"I have to stop thinking about this!" she told herself as an acute sense of panic began to rise within her. She was overwhelmed with the sensation that she had done something wrong last night, however unintentionally. It made her want to confess something, or at least to explain to someone in authority that she and Susan had been innocent. Again, she wasn't sure Susan *was* innocent. Besides, there was no one to tell. She would simply have to wait this out to make sure she hadn't been spotted last night, then live with what she'd seen until her dying day.

"And that's all there is to it!" she said out loud in a determined, resolute tone, just as Randy walked into the office.

Randy Tripp was thirty-seven years old, with white-blue eyes and sandy brown hair that he wore very short and off of his face. He was handsome and capable, dressed in a shirt and tie, with pleated dress slacks. Randy and Jeff Cahn had been childhood buddies, and they'd worked together from almost the inception of LCPU.

In truth, the business was better run in his capable hands rather than Angela's, simply because he had physically experienced every facet of it. He had a lovely wife, Joanne, and two strikingly beautiful teenage daughters. He often swore that raising teenage girls in this millennium was a job designed to bring about heart attacks, and that the worry alone would probably be the death of him. "That's why there's an increase in heart-attacks," he would say with the utmost conviction, "they probably all have teenage daughters." He was comical in his dissertations, but serious within himself. He was an excellent husband and father.

"It has to be what way?" he asked Angela as he entered the room, referring to the comment she had just spoken into thin air. Embarrassed at having been caught talking to herself again by Randy, she replied with a blush and a short chuckle, "Oh - nothing."

"Talking to yourself again?" he asked with a sly smile.

Angela shot him a sarcastic, guilty look as he sat down across from her, preparing to go over the accounts for the day. Thankfully, he jumped right into business. "If you call Mill Supply today, you better order some more bags of beige stone. The Connor's job used up every bag we had in stock, and it's still not done. I think those are going to be big this year so tell them to send whatever they can."

"Okay." Angela made a note, then looked up expectantly, waiting for him to say more.

He did. Shifting slightly into the conversation, Randy took a deep breath and plunged into an altogether different topic and mood. "Well, boss," he said proudly, leaning back heavily in his desk chair, "the season has officially begun, and *I* sold *three* of those new power mowers to prove it!" Randy looked confident and proud as he waited for Angela to lavish her praise upon him, but his face fell as she spoke. Her mind must be in the clouds today because she didn't seem to be comprehending.

"Three! Just today?"

"Well - no - not *today*, but in the last week."

"Oh, I was going to say..." When she saw the comically offended expression on Randy's face, she laughed and backtracked. "Not that three in one week isn't good, it's excellent, Randy, really, it's just the way you said it sounded like you meant... Forget it."

He replied with immediate confounded humor, feigning over-sensitivity. "Yep, that-a-way to make the personnel feel good about themselves, Angela. Just take a shot right into the heart whenever you feel the need to do so, you know, I'm here for you."

Both looked across their desks and laughed, no real offense being taken. Randy was an excellent manager and salesman, and both parties knew it. It would have been quite a feat to sell three power mowers before ten a.m. on a Tuesday morning; especially when summer and deep-down grass cutting season wasn't in full swing by any stretch of the imagination.

With a sarcastic wag of his head, Randy was about to drop the subject and stick to relevant business. Considering Angela's preoccupied state, it would probably be best. Then he really looked at her. This lack of sharp wit was uncharacteristic, and she seemed... rather lost. "Anything wrong, Angela?"

"No... No, nothing. I've just been thinking about some things. So, what's on the agenda for today?"

Randy looked into Angela's face for a moment. He almost pursued it, then stopped. Whatever was bothering her was her own business. He would watch out for her, though, most assuredly. He'd been doing so since Jeff's death, and genuine love and affection kept him carefully protective. She often tried to act happy and content, but Randy knew better. He knew too much, and he didn't like the forlorn look of depression that would settle over her at times.

It wasn't healthy that such a beautiful woman had remained so unattached for all these years. She needed to get out and live, to be alive, and although Randy had loved Jeff, and would honor his memory forever, just as Angela did, he felt she needed to let him go. Instead of addressing that issue right now, though, Randy answered her with the business of the day. Something about beige stone... Afterward, Angela couldn't recall.

She did manage to complete a few of her daily tasks, keeping sufficiently busy, but severely shaken and disoriented. She purposely avoided Randy to keep him from noticing, but every once in awhile she would catch him watching her with a concerned expression. By noon she had lulled herself into her work and was just beginning to feel a bit more normal. Nothing terrible had happened so far. No police officers had come crashing through her door to take her away. No huge, hulking ghosts had appeared to her, warning of certain curses to come. Maybe everything really would be okay.

She sat at her desk again and turned on the noon newscast as she unwrapped the sandwich Randy had brought her from the local sub shop. She took exactly two bites before she dropped it back onto the waxed paper and stared at the small television in horror. The Newscaster was relaying a headline story that had just come in. The image of a huge, hideous looking man was suddenly pictured on the screen and an attractive anchorwoman began speaking, declaring this late breaking issue with a grave, monotone quality. Angela's heart raced with the words.

"A local Narcotics Investigator was beaten to death last night in Woodland Park off Cane Street in Niagara Falls. Twenty-eight year old Detective, Marcus Linden, was found this morning near a clearing in the woods by a local jogger and his dog. The Detective died of a cracked skull after having been beaten repeatedly with a heavy instrument. Police would not comment on the Detective's duties, investigations, or if this was a drug related attack, but say a full scale investigation is underway."

An interview with the jogger followed as he detailed where he'd been running and how his barking, insistent dog had come upon the body and led the man to it. Angela phased out at that point and began to stare unseeingly at the television. The picture of the...*detective*... that had been on the screen was clearly the image of Susan's and her own attacker from last night.

"Oh, my God!" she whispered in ragged gasps. Her hand was held up against her mouth in horror and her round eyes were huge. She sat in a frozen posture of crossed legs with her forgotten napkin in her lap. "He was a *detective!* No... this can't be. It just can't be!"

But it was, and as Angela's mind began to simultaneously shut down and race, she was even more convinced that the police were "very big and very bad," as Susan had said. That... beast... had certainly not acted like a police officer. The way he'd chased her and Susan hadn't seemed at all policeman-like. In fact, Angela couldn't believe he actually *was* a policeman. He was so far from anything that looked capable of upholding the law and protecting citizens that she shivered with the thought. He had been violent, dangerous and evil last night. That must be common nowadays, she thought bitterly as visions of the other two officers' brutality filled her mind.

Her heart skipped. This would mean the persons responsible for that Detective's death were other police officers. The news made no indication of that whatsoever, and as Angela heard the noise of the TV distantly from her tangled, frightened thoughts, her heartbeat doubled. It was the anchorwoman again, and as she spoke, Angela cringed, because the fresh, young image of Susan's college ID card was suddenly displayed across the screen and accompanied her solemn words.

"The police do have one suspect in their case, and they are asking for the community's assistance. If anyone has seen, or knows the whereabouts of this young woman, please call the Police

Department immediately. Please do not try to apprehend her. Simply call your local police station, or dial 911."

It took a long time before Angela could move, and it was only because she didn't want anyone to guess her true distress that she finally did so. She clicked the TV off and wondered what she should do now. Susan was, somehow, known to the police and was a suspect in the murder. How on earth had that come about?

How did that involve Angela? Would she be connected to it as well? If she was, she knew the true story, and if she had to she would simply tell it to whoever would listen. That line of thought made her wonder if she should at least try to tell someone that Susan hadn't killed that man. Angela knew the truth; should she try to absolve Susan from the blame being attached to her? She truly didn't know what to do, and stark fear made her decide, once again, that she must remain quiet. Quelling the over-boiling emotions within her, starting with fear and progressing steadily to condemning guilt, she insisted to herself, made herself believe, silence was the right thing.

It was an effort to move through the rest of the day at a somewhat believable pace, but she forced herself to act normal, to involve herself in her tasks, to avoid any type of deep thought. She was in the warehouse counting bags of white stone to see if they could fill an order that had just been called in. The season was indeed beginning, she observed, looking around her stockroom, and worrying that they weren't going to be prepared for it.

In the past few years, landscaping had taken on a whole new dimension. Virtually every household was slowly but surely replacing the traditional masses of clumped bushes and flowers that had always been popular. The new, more spacious designs of sculpted shrubbery and uniquely shaped bushes were the rage. The biggest feature of these designs was the use of small mountains of stone to set the creations upon, and Angela agreed with Randy, there wasn't going to be enough.

It was after she'd been in the warehouse for several minutes that she got the acute feeling she was being watched. Looking around suspiciously, she went very still. It seemed her easy movements of casual counting were suddenly loud and conspicuous. She turned slightly and looked to her left. Nothing was there, but a prickly fear was, nonetheless, upon her, and she turned to walk toward the door, which would open into the showroom where she would find Randy and other folks to be around.

Just before she reached the door, a flurry of shuffling motion was suddenly loud in her ears, and she looked toward the sound with wide, expectant eyes. Before she could properly discern what it was or where it was coming from, a voice called out, and a hand grabbed her arm. "Wait; please?"

Already on razor edge from the feeling of imminent danger by an unknown observer, Angela shrieked and turned. A desperate face assaulted her senses as she focused on it. The young woman, seeing her fear, let go of her arm as if it were a snake, and jumped backwards. "Oh, my God..." It was Susan.

"Susan!" Angela grabbed her into her arms and hugged her tightly. "Oh, you scared me." She released the embrace and peered into Susan's eyes. "Are you all right? Did you... get away safely last night?"

"Yes, I was all right, what about you?"

"Well, I'm here and functioning, let's just leave it at that. I'm not ashamed to admit, though, that I am scared to death! What did... what happened to you after you left me?"

Susan looked at Angela for a second, then said discerningly, "I see you've already heard the news." There was a distinctly hurt catch in her voice.

Angela gaped at her. She'd scarcely recovered from the relief of finding that the intruder in her warehouse was relatively harmless. Everything else was moving too fast. "Yes... Susan... yes, I did."

"Angela... I came to ask you, *please*, not to tell anyone you saw me last night. It's very important that no one know about me." Sheer terror, and hopeful desperation filled Susan's face. Her movements were even more jittery than the night before, and she wore the very same clothes, the same hair, the same expressions.

"Susan, I know you didn't kill that detective. I was there, I saw the whole thing."

"You did?"

"Yes; two police officers killed him."

"I know; I saw it, too."

Angela took a deep, cleansing breath. The strange bond that lay between them was confirmed as they looked into each other's faces. "Do you want me to tell someone you're innocent?"

"No! Just don't say anything. The best thing that can happen is for me to get out of town and never be seen here again."

"Why are *you* being accused?"

Susan looked at Angela with complete torment, physically fighting whether or not to tell the older woman what she knew. With a rush of breath and a fierce shaking of her head she blurted out, "I can't tell you anything. I have to get out of here. I just want you to be careful and know that I'm innocent. I didn't have anything to do with Linden's death."

"So... you're not *involved* with these police officers; right?" Angela's words were slow, her expression speaking of how much she wanted to believe that.

"Police officers, yeah right," Susan spat disrespectfully. "They're not police officers, and neither was Linden... at least not the good kind... and no, I swear to you I wasn't involved in his death, but the cops want to pin this on me. They want me to be guilty and they want to trap me because..." She stopped herself in renewed torment. "Just please don't tell them about me. I can slip out of town and no one will ever know."

"But, who are you? Why do the police want to accuse you of this detective's murder if you truly didn't do it?"

"Because they're dirty cops, that's why. Their whole station is loaded with them. I'm... just someone who got in their way. They know I didn't kill Linden, they know I had nothing to do with any of it, but they've got my face plastered all over town trying to blame me because it'll get them off the hook. If I get caught, they'll have me right where they want me. That's why they've got the whole damn city looking for me! I have to get out of here! You won't tell on me, will you?"

Angela was getting more enlightened and more confused by the second. She didn't know what Susan was involved in, but she knew that she had somehow gotten in these officers' way and was now being bullied and blamed for murder to keep her quiet about what she knew. If this young woman had ever sounded like a desperate child, it was now. Looking at her with her heart surging with compassion, wanting to protect her from the injustices that were claiming her life, Angela answered, "No, I won't tell on you."

"Thank you." It was simple and heartfelt.

"Where will you go? Do you have a home?" Somehow, Angela knew this youth did not have the security of a home she could run to.

"No, but it's okay, I'll get by... I always have."

Angela nodded as if she understood, but both of them knew she didn't. Their ways of life were worlds apart. What seemed to be common, expected behavior to Angela, like the love of solid parents, was completely foreign to Susan. Likewise, what was everyday instinct to Susan, like the ability to survive alone, seemed heartbreakingly unfair to Angela. Nevertheless, these two women

88

accepted each other just as they were, and as they embraced like the mother and daughter neither one of them had, they clung desperately, and truly prayed that the other would be all right.

Unwillingly, Angela released Susan, and as she ran for her life, out the back door of Angela's warehouse, tears fell from their eyes. The door shut automatically behind Susan with a loud smack that made Angela jump. Rows of neatly stocked shelving faced her, and the incessant humming of the fan made everything seem huge and quietly frightening. She felt so completely alone, so totally unsure of what was to become of her and Susan from here. She turned suddenly and ran toward the showroom door to try to surround herself with other people, and escape the fear that engulfed her.

She wouldn't escape, though. It would follow her everywhere she went, along with a burning insistence that the young Susan be helped. The problem was, she would never be able to get away from one feeling, without sacrificing the other.

~ *Chapter Eleven* ~

By the time Angela flicked on the lights in her upscale condominium, which overlooked a gorgeous stretch of the Niagara River, she was ready for tears. The end of the day brought no relief to her senses, and her nerves were raw from worry.

"Just wait it out," she told herself out loud, "time always has a way of making things better; and when you see that nothing bad is going to happen, you'll begin to feel all right again." A logical and much relied upon pattern of thought, which she had used frequently and with much success over the years. It was, however, quite naïve in this case, and deep down she knew it.

Slipping off her shoes with a sinking exhaustion, she thumped down unceremoniously upon her cool, clean, cream-colored sofa. Her home, like her, had a refined class about it and a light, easy atmosphere. Quiet peacefulness hung in the air and the softness of gentle whites and pastels colored her world with comfort and welcoming relaxation.

She rested her head back upon the sofa and thought again about Susan. She absolutely could not get that young woman out of her mind. Was she safe right now? Was she desperate with fear as she'd been last night and this afternoon? Was she cold and alone?

What had she done that had gotten her into this much trouble? Who, for God's sake, was she in trouble with? Police or criminals? There were obviously no answers.

Tossing her head in frustration and perhaps an attempt at clearing it from these nagging thoughts, she noticed she had a few messages on her answering machine. Desperately needing some distraction, she reached her hand toward the country-white end table that stood gracefully next to the couch, and pressed the retrieval button on her machine.

The first two calls were hang ups, which usually drove her crazy with wondering who had called and not left a message. Tonight she cast it off. She just didn't care to worry about such non-essentials. The third call was from her mother, and she smiled at the voice as it floated gracefully through the machine.

"Angela? It's Mom, honey. I didn't really think you would be home yet, but I thought I'd give it a try anyway. I've been thinking of you all day and just wondered how you're doing. Call me when you get some time, okay? Love you."

A moment of true relief encompassed Angela. Fourteen years ago, her parents had moved to Florida to spend their senior years in blissful warmth and paradise. At that time, Mr. and Mrs. Jonathan and Rita Kholer had seen their daughter grow into a beautiful young woman who was happily married to an ambitious, successful man who loved her deeply. Mr. Kholer, a faithful employee for Niagara Mohawk Power Company for thirty-three years, retired early with the full benefits an employee of that duration could expect. A lifetime of wise investments, too, had paid off well.

Seeing that their only child was stable and on her own, they had made the move to Florida with a degree of sadness, but few worries. Little had they known then that their daughter would experience the devastation of widowhood only two short years afterward.

They'd actually considered coming back to Niagara Falls permanently after that, to be with Angela. They did come back for a time, until Angela was able to stand on her own two feet again, and truly, they had gotten her through that dark time. Life really does go on, however, and both parties had come through it. The Kholers eventually went back to Florida, and Angela, to her store.

She stopped the machine and replayed the message, listening to the sound of her mother's voice with a wistful grin. It was just like her mother to be thinking about her when she was troubled. How did mothers always know? A lighter mood was just beginning to claim her when Angela heard a muffled beep, and another message began. This one, however, didn't leave her feeling warm and blissfully forgetful of her circumstances. It confirmed them instead.

Sitting bolt upright, Angela stared at the machine in fresh terror as a dark, ugly voice began to sound from it. "Angela Cahn?" the voice slithered. "Hello, Mrs. Cahn, how was your day today? I've been watching you and I must say I *do wish* this was a social call, but unfortunately, it isn't. This is business. Are you scared? You should be because you're in deep, *deep* trouble. You see, we saw you helping Susan last night. We saw everything. Did you know there's a room above Armondo's that overlooks the parking lot? Probably not. And did you know someone was up there watching? I'm sure you didn't.

"Now, I know you didn't mean for any of this to happen," the voice continued in deceptive understanding, "why, you were just being a nice person, a good person, who went above and beyond the call of duty to help a scared little lady. But, you see, *now* you have information we need, and you're very lucky, Angela, because you get to tell us what you know instead of us killing you because of it. I want to know where the envelope is, and *exactly* where Susan Ventry is. If you tell me, this whole nightmare will end for you, and you'll never hear from us again. If you don't, I promise, you will wish you were dead." Click.

The call ended and Angela found herself backed up against the wall of her living room, staring at the machine as if it were responsible somehow for the call that was on it. She knew nothing about an envelope. Had Susan been carrying an envelope? She didn't recall... Someone had been watching her. Someone not only knew Susan existed, but they knew what happened at Armondo's, and that Angela had helped her. They wanted to know where Susan was now. They said they would leave Angela alone if she just told them...

Feeling suddenly conspicuous to the entire world, and afraid of what anyone might see as she stood in her own living room, five stories above ground level, she inched along the wall and closed her window blinds in a swift, awkward movement. She was shaking all over and trying very hard not to panic.

Before she had the time to ponder the issue, though, the phone rang. It seemed glaringly loud and Angela jumped at its sound, rushing at it in an unthinking attempt at silencing it. "Hello!" It was a frightened, apprehensive bark.

The caller actually chuckled. It seemed obvious that he had indeed made Angela fear him. "Hello, Angela. I see you got my earlier message. Now, let's make this short and sweet, shall we? Then you can get back to relaxing in that pretty, white condo. Very sharp, I must say."

The voice was intentionally over polite and terrifying. He spoke to her with a familiarity Angela had not granted him. How did he know her condo was decorated in shades of white? How did he know if he liked it or not? Had he actually been in her home? "Who are you?" she asked the caller.

"Well, now, I couldn't tell you that; and in the future, just leave the questions to me because, you see, you're in no position to be *asking me* anything, got it?" The dominant air of exactly who controlled this situation was established with that statement. She didn't answer it, but her silence indicated her complete obedience to anything this caller would demand.

"Now, where is Susan?"

"I don't know where she is."

"Don't lie to me! Where is she?"

"I swear to you, I don't know where she went."

A pause followed, the man seeming to hear the truth behind the terror in Angela's voice. "All right then, where is the envelope?"

Angela opened her mouth to speak, then stopped. She didn't know anything about an envelope. She tried to think, to remember anything that might give her a clue as to what he was talking about, and how she should respond to it, but she truly didn't know.

"Angela? Where is the envelope? Now, don't play games with me, I mean it. Tell me or suffer for your silence."

She opened her mouth again. She may have promised to help Susan, but this was going too far! Her own life was in danger now, and for what? For some girl who had obviously embroiled herself in some sort of criminal act? How did that obligate her, a person who simply tried to help a stranger? It didn't obligate her, she thought with resolution and anger. She must make this lunacy stop! She must make this man understand that she knew nothing!

"I don't know! I never saw an envelope!"

The caller was quiet for several seconds after that, seeming to believe her once again. "Where is she?" was all he said after that, but it was said with a quiet, demon rage that terrified Angela, both for herself, and Susan.

"I don't know," she enunciated desperately.

"Do you know if she left The States? Went back to Canada?"

"I..." Angela wasn't sure if she should tell him. She knew Susan was still in The U.S. because she'd been in her warehouse this morning. Why did he want to know? Would he hurt her even more because she'd made further contact with Angela? "I..."

"Yes? Come on... You don't have to protect her, Angela, you don't even know her. You don't owe her anything, and no one will bother you again if you just answer my few questions." The voice actually sounded like a helpful, encouraging comrade now, coaching her into a difficult, but ultimately correct decision.

Strangely enough, with all the slithering evil crawling through this man's voice, Angela believed the only thing he wanted from her was information. She further believed that if she gave him that information he would leave her alone. She could sense that he didn't want anything to do with her. He wanted Susan. All she had to do was answer him and this nightmare would end.

"Angela?" The voice jolted her back to reality. She could not betray Susan. As much danger as that might mean to her own self, she would continue to protect her. She certainly couldn't betray her to a man like this, and she wouldn't tell him anything that could cause him to find her.

"I will not tell you! And don't ever tell me that I can or cannot ask a question or say anything I please!" Click.

In ten seconds, the phone rang again. Her Caller I.D. identified the number as "Private". Of course... he didn't want to be traced. Unfortunately, she'd never taken the steps necessary to un-list her home phone number. It was published, for all to see, in the local phone book. Thank God, they apparently did not have her cell phone number. She picked up the ringing receiver angrily, and slammed it back down, her determination radiating right through the line. Instantly, she took the phone off the hook. She may be crazy, but she would *not* betray Susan to a man like that.

"Okay, Susan," she said into the air, "wherever you are, we're in this together now, I hope you appreciate that."

She was answered by terrifying, all encompassing, silence.

~ *Chapter Twelve* ~

She was two hours early for work the next day. She'd been up, literally, all night long, and although she was freshly showered and made-up with a deceptively bright red pantsuit on, Angela looked deeply strained. Her eyes were a glassy, puffed red, and worry lines creased and shadowed her face.

In spite of her early arrival at work, Angela did nothing business related whatsoever throughout the day. She deferred all responsibilities to Randy, and kept a careful, apprehensive eye on everything around her. Her nerves were tense and raw. Every car that pulled into the parking lot of LCPU might be a potential madman come to make her pay for her defiance last night. Every customer was a possible killer in disguise. The delivery man, who was finally bringing those precious white and beige stones, could be a maniac, come to wreak havoc in her life and deliver the promised threat of misery so bad she would wish to be dead.

Her total lack of sleep over the last two nights, of course, made everything bigger and far worse than it really was, but then again, how bad was it, really? She'd met a young woman who, for some inexplicable reason, touched the very roots of her soul. She worried about this youth almost every minute, certain that danger was waiting to swallow her. She, herself, had been viciously attacked by a police officer that acted like anything *but* a law enforcer, then had witnessed that man's murder by other police. Now, she felt sure that someone, who apparently had access to her security-locked home, was ogling her every movement. How much worse could it get?

When the harassed Randy finally came into the office a full hour after he usually left for home, looking worn and worried about his boss, Angela cast him off dismissively. He tried to insist that she come home with him and have dinner with the family, feeling that this newest depression was the worst he'd ever seen her go through. It seemed to have come on her frighteningly fast, too, leaving her fearful and silent. She must need some company, it would do her good.

Angela flatly refused his invitation to dine with his family, becoming uncharacteristically cross when he persisted. Randy had no idea what was happening with her right now, and he thought he did. She couldn't share her feelings with anyone; including Randy. That, and the fear, made her abrasively tense. Only one possibility crossed her mind in the hours of pondering she'd endured over this issue. Just one hopeful possibility.

"All right, Angela," Randy said in an offended, shocked tone at his boss's curtness.

"I don't mean to be rude, Randy, it's just that... I have a lot on my mind."

"Well, why don't you tell me what's happening? You're really worrying me."

"I know, I... I'm sorry. It's nothing."

"Are you thinking about Jeff?" Randy broached the subject sensitively.

Angela was shocked to discover that, no, for the first time in twelve years she was not thinking about Jeff. She didn't tell Randy that, however. "Yes, that's it, I'm just... thinking about Jeff again."

"You know, Angela, I'm not going to preach at you, because it's probably the last thing you want to hear, but you have got to get on with your life. It's been twelve years, don't you think you can let it go now?"

Angela looked downward as Randy implored her. The topic was so completely irrelevant she might have laughed in another circumstance. He was grave and looked at her sincerely. Obviously, he had wanted to discuss this with her for quite some time. His words, however, were not completely without substance to her troubled mind. If she'd really been able to concentrate on them, she might have agreed for once. She'd loved Jeff with all of her heart, but yes, it was time to let go. Her emotional disruption of the last two days with Susan had made her realize that.

"You're right, Randy. That's kind of what's been bothering me. I feel like in a way I *have* released it, and I feel guilty about it."

"Well, you shouldn't. We both know Jeff would want you happy."

"Yes. I do know that."

"All right," Randy conceded gently, feeling he had accurately deduced the true problem, and that the profound depth of his words had finally spurred Angela on toward change. "If you reconsider my invitation, let me know. I know Joanne would love to have you."

"Okay, thank you, and tell Joanne and the girls I said hi."

"I will."

Randy donned his coat and said good night for the evening. Angela would lock up from here in another hour or so. Randy opened the store every morning and worked the warehouse and sales details from seven a.m. until four, and Angela came in at around ten and closed up at six everyday, except Saturdays when they both stayed on until nine to cover the rush of customers who did their lawns over the weekend. They closed the store completely on Sundays and Mondays, except during late spring and summer, when they stayed open from ten a.m. till five p.m. on Sundays. It was an easy, accommodating schedule, and they found that even when business was at its peak they handled it well.

Angela looked around herself. Everything was ominously quiet now that Randy had left. There was one young man left in the warehouse in case an order came in that Angela couldn't handle alone, but everything else seemed so very quiet. That young boy's presence was hardly a comfort to her.

She looked out into the traffic that lined the boulevard at this time of day. Perhaps she would close up early tonight, she decided. It would be better to lose a sale or two than sit here by herself, feeling shaken and ultimately unsafe. She was a sitting target, alone as she was in the quiet of the store. Funny, she had never been afraid before. Why did it seem now as though she should have been taking precautions all along?

Her young employee was, of course, thrilled to close up early. He gathered his things quickly and LCPU was locked up for the night. The never-ending line of traffic Angela had to endure was unexpected, but her mind fazed out anyway. She had other things to concentrate on. Like trying to form some sort of plan for the next few days of her life. What if she went home and found more threats on her answering machine? What if the police somehow connected her to Susan Ventry?

Actually, considering the fact that police officers had been the actual murderers of Detective Linden, and the news had said the police were now in pursuit of Susan Ventry, and someone had seen her with Susan, it was very probable that the police already did know about her. Oh, God, if that were true, she might be accused of murder. What if they tried to make her talk by accusing her of murder or of being an accomplice in Linden's murder? What if a complete nightmare laid hold of her life? She must have a plan!

There was, however, no real way to prepare for such things, and she was making herself sick with worry over them. There was only one hopeful possibility. The one option she had thought of again and again throughout the hours of agonizing she had gone through over this issue...

She finally turned off Niagara Falls Boulevard after ten minutes of bumper to bumper honking and congestion. It was a welcomed relief. She usually missed the rush hour because she was still working when it occurred. She didn't mind the delays, she had nowhere special to go, and home would probably not bring the relief that it usually did, but the traffic and noise only added to her tension.

A dark blue sedan turned off the boulevard, too. She saw it in her rearview mirror and her heart immediately began to race again. It wasn't an unusual looking vehicle; actually, it was rather average. It wasn't following too closely behind her, and quite possibly wasn't following her at all. Yet, for some reason, she was afraid of it.

She moved along steadily as she covered the distance to her home. The car was still behind her. Her mind raced, her heart pounded, but she kept on driving as if everything were normal. No one could harm her by simply following her, could they? They already knew where she lived, where she worked, and what she'd done two nights ago in her spare time. What possible benefit could it serve them to follow her? Except to terrorize her, and they were succeeding in doing just that.

With that thought, she suddenly jerked the wheel of the car to the left with an angry, decisive snap. Purposely not signaling the turn, she was abruptly careening down a quiet side street. The car followed. She did it again, this time turning to the right, the car followed again. She began to panic. She was definitely being followed. Someone was watching her and following her, and had promised life worse than death if they caught her.

She began to cry as she practically hydroplaned down the road and exited back onto another busy street. She'd had it with the fear and paralysis she was feeling lately. She couldn't take the pressure of what was happening to her. Her carefully ordered life was being turned upside down, and a terror and helplessness was pervading it with absolutely no escape and no one at all to turn to. She couldn't take it!

The blue sedan kept up closely, purposely tailing her now and obviously aware that she knew it. She had only one option. She would use it now. There was one police officer that probably could help her. One who she knew she could confide in, who would keep her secrets, and who knew, without a doubt, the ins and outs of an investigation.

Sudden, dawning relief swept over her, and, as if it should have been completely obvious before this, she instantly knew what she must do. A small smile lit her face in remembrance of a playful vow made so many years before that was never, *ever*, meant to be taken seriously. She needed his help now, though, and she would take him up on his promise to repay.

Picking up her cell phone, she turned her car once again, this time into the direction of the Niagara Falls Police Station. She would drive right up into the parking lot, she decided with a note of angry determination. See how they liked *that!* "Hello, may I speak to Sergeant Michael Camden? It's an emergency!"

"Who's calling please?" the solid female voice on the other end inquired.

"I'm - uh - an old friend, my name is... my name is Angela Cahn."

"Please hold."

Angela held the line as she continued driving. The car following her kept its distance but remained with her. "Wait until you see where we're going," she taunted uselessly from the safety of her own car. "You won't be trying to scare me then."

She was ready for a complete meltdown by the time a sharp click sounded and a slightly familiar voice said, "Hello?"

"Michael? Is this Michael Camden?" Her voice was suddenly weepy and desperate with her relief.

"Yes. Angela?"

"Yes, Michael it's Angela. I know this is probably very strange, but something terrible has happened, and I'm in big trouble. I'm afraid I need your help."

*   *   *

The occupants of the blue sedan did not follow Angela into the parking lot of the police station, but neither did they worry when she entered it. They had friends there, plenty of them who would be only too glad to help them with their cause. The fact that Mrs. Cahn was willingly going to the police seemed only to show how little she really knew, and that was good for them. They'd been wondering how much Susan Ventry had told her. Apparently not much. They could get the information that the defiant Mrs. Cahn had easily now. She was about to spill it right out for them.

~ *Chapter Thirteen* ~

Detective Sergeant John Casey ran a strong hand through his wavy blond hair, and sighed deeply. Marcus Linden was dead. How could something that had started out so full of hope, full of ease, have turned out so devastatingly wrong? He remembered the words the young giant had spoken so enthusiastically just three days ago. "Doesn't it feel great to finally be in front of something, instead of behind it, cleaning it up all the time?" It was the comment of hope, of passion to see change in his society. It died mercilessly with his beaten, bloodied form.

Casey punched in a few codes on his computer with an un-anticipating lifelessness. It was unlikely that anything new would show up so early in the *Racer* case, especially with Marcus's very basic report their only guide. The dealers were probably in hiding, what with all the hype surrounding Linden's death, and would put the project on hold now until they saw if any other cops were lurking about with information that could incriminate them. Unfortunately there weren't.

The mundane scanning of pertinent files would now be required every single day to begin to find links. The main goal of this operation was still the same. They must contain *Racer* before it really hit the streets.

Since Linden's death, the bizarre acts of violence that had been flooding the city had ceased conspicuously. That was good, to be sure, but it wasn't permanent, and Casey could feel that it was all just beginning to brew. It would explode in uncontainable fury very soon, and without Linden, they had no way of regrouping quickly enough to keep *Racer* from starting its flow.

It might have been possible if they'd had more warning, or more men on the case, but Linden had only discovered the drug two weeks ago, and no one had been expecting it. The dealers were onto the fact that a cop had been in their vicinity now, so they would take care to keep all newcomers distant. They would relocate their bases, and sink deep into the underworld of the city.

The photo of Susan Ventry had brought nothing to them that they didn't already know. Canadian/American Customs, of course, was extremely willing to help, but they hadn't seen Susan since the time she'd crossed over into the U.S. three days ago. No one else had come forward at all. She'd simply disappeared into a city large enough to swallow her whole, and small enough to keep her tightly contained. It was all too likely that she had hiding places with the city's drug dealers that police didn't even know about. Her face being publicized would at least keep her where she was without much ability for her to move about. That point was in the Special Team's favor.

The shrill ring of the phone offered a welcomed interruption. Both he and Michael lunged at it, each one eager to be relieved of the monotonous perusing of the files. Michael reached it first, and picked it up quickly, glaring triumphantly at Casey's lack of speed. "Camden here. Yeah, Greg? What...? Are you sure?"

An incredulous, distraught silence thickened the air, and Casey looked up at his partner. Michael's face had gone white and he seemed unable to respond to his caller for several seconds. Then, obviously struggling to regain himself, he choked out a response.

"Has anyone else seen this report? Good. That was good thinking, man. All right, Greg, it's very important that no one else, even your staff members, see this; all right? You know DEA procedure from here: total confidentiality, okay? I appreciate it; thanks, buddy."

Casey looked up expectantly. Something had gone down, and he wanted to know what. "What was that all about?"

If Michael's face could have possibly gone any paler, or more stricken than it had been a moment ago, incredibly, it did. "That was the medical examiner's office... guess who had crack and PCP in his bloodstream at the time of death?"

Casey paused, rejecting the thought. "Linden?"

"Yeah. He had four times the normal dosing hit in his blood."

"That's impossible."

"I know, but it's confirmed; and the blood on Ventry's car was definitely his."

"What the hell is going on?"

"I wish I knew. Is anything coming up on your files?"

"Not a thing. No incidents of overdose or PCP related drug use are being reported at all. In fact, if anything, the usual drug arrests have been down, and when they've occurred, they've been very ordinary. As far as the police and hospital files of this city are concerned, there isn't even a *threat* of a new drug."

"Yeah, but Regis Black knows about one, doesn't he? He knows this drug is the real reason kids all over are flipping out and killing each other. He got our man killed for his knowledge of it, too. I wish we could find *him*."

"Well, unfortunately, we both know he doesn't really exist. That's just an overly dramatic street name for a common low-life."

"A common low-life with a lot of cash, and a lot of connections."

Michael and his partner exchanged the same penetrating look of confusion. Surely, they were losing ground on this case before they even got started. Neither of them spoke for several moments, and when they did, they were truly afraid to voice what both of them thought. Michael forced himself to begin, gentling the way he might broach this subject.

"Casey...? You've worked the streets... sometimes in a situation like Linden was in... well... Do you think he might have become a user without us knowing?"

"No. No way. God, Michael, I hope not."

The sound of the phone interrupted their musings, making them jump.

"DEA," Casey said with strained professionalism. "Yeah, Liz, he's right here." Casey covered the phone against his shoulder. "Michael, an Angela Cahn called the switchboard asking for you, says it's urgent that she speak with you."

"Angela Cahn? As in Angela Cahn from *Lawn Care Products Unlimited*?"

"I don't know, Liz didn't say. Do you want me to have her ask?"

"No, that's all right, I'll take the call."

"Put her through, Liz," Casey said easily, and pressed the hold button on his line.

A puzzled look shaded Michael's features as he punched a button on his phone so he might connect with the line Angela was holding on.

"Whose Angela Cahn?" Casey asked, noticing Michael's sudden expression.

"She's... an old friend."

~ *Chapter Fourteen* ~

Michael waited anxiously at the door of the Police Station, craning his neck to see the individual cars that were entering and leaving the parking lot. He saw Angela the minute she pulled in, and watched in growing alarm as she jerked her car to a stop and flew up the steps of the building, looking over her shoulder in fear with each movement she made. When he rushed out to meet her, she jumped in frightened shock, then literally fell into his arms without greeting or preamble. She was obviously terrified, and she looked as if she hadn't slept in days. Whatever she had found herself involved in must be very serious.

It took several minutes to calm her down and assure her that everything would be all right. She shook in his arms as he guided her protectively into the building, up through the elevator, and into the quiet corridor of the third floor of the precinct. A large glass wall greeted them menacingly until Michael slipped a card into the magnetic strip on the door, then punched in a series of numbers. The door swung open quietly without further delay.

Directing Angela along with his hand at the small of her back, he studied her apprehensively as she moved along in jumbled silence. Amazement and relief kept her thoughts occupied and almost unable to speak. Michael didn't push her, he wanted to be sure they were securely ensconced within the private office of the DEA before they began the discussion.

John Casey was standing at the file cabinet with papers laid out in unorganized sections. He'd gotten engrossed in something while he was standing there, and it had progressed into a mild disaster. He was still deeply disturbed over the notion that Detective Linden might have been involved in the *Racer* issue outside of the interests of the law.

It seemed to be a more and more believable theory, though. When an officer lived among a crowd like that, bombarded everyday with their lifestyle and system, it became easier to play the role, even lower your defenses and shed some of your standards. Sometimes you must do that, or get caught. Linden was so very good at this game, too; better than Casey had ever been at it. He was more natural, more enthusiastic and violent in his role. He'd been full of the drug at the time of death. It was all too possible that Linden had gotten involved over his head. If that were true, though, surely he'd only been a casual user. He couldn't possibly have been willingly involved in distribution.

Could he?

Hearing the door open, Casey turned and began speaking, "Hey, Michael, everything all right?" His partner had just bolted out the door after the phone call had come in from his friend. Casey stared at him in shock now, and Michael looked slightly guilty. "Oh... Hello."

"Hello," Angela replied, still shaky from her trauma and overwhelmed by the realization of protection and safety.

"Michael? Whose your guest?" Casey asked with eyes flashing a warning. There was no such thing as a 'guest' in the office of the Special Teams. This was a serious breach of rules, and Casey wondered at his partner's sanity for bringing someone up here.

Michael, of course, saw the expression on Casey's face and pleaded in his own way for a little leeway. Casey would give it to him, of course. Nothing needed to be said to anyone else about this infraction, but he better have an exceptionally good reason for committing it.

"Casey, this is Angela Cahn. Angela, this is my partner, Detective John Casey. We will ask that anything you see in this office be kept completely confidential. Can you agree to that?"

"Y-Yes," Angela answered the authority questioning her. Undoubtedly, this boy had grown up.

Since Michael had every confidence in the character of this woman, he needed no other assurances of her complete silence, so this simple answer satisfied him. Casey, however, seemed comically astounded by his easy acceptance as he watched Michael seat Angela into a comfortable chair, and begin the conversation without further warnings or ado. Intrigued, Casey sat down himself and listened with rapt interest as it all began.

"Are you all right, Angela?"

"Yes, I... I... guess so. You look so different, Michael... all grown up." A short smile transferred between them, and their eyes both held the respect and admiration they felt for each other. Michael's eyes held an added note of compassion. This woman was as decent as people were allowed by nature to be, and she was obviously very frightened by her present circumstances.

"No one can get in here, right? I mean, you're the only one that can hear this," she said with a sobbing catch in her voice that she was trying pitifully to hide.

Casey's gaze connected with Michael's. This woman seemed completely out of place in a police office, and it seemed wrong that she should be in a position of feeling threatened or frightened. Casey questioned Michael with his eyes as they looked at one another, wanting to know why. Seeing Casey's reaction to Angela,

Michael relaxed slightly and answered his gaze with a shrug, turning to continue speaking to Angela.

"No, as long as you're under the sanction of this office no one will be able to get to you."

That seemed to relax her in a great rush of relief, and she dabbed at her eyes. They seemed unable to stop flowing with tears.

"Angela, what is this all about?"

"Oh, Michael, something terrible has happened. I swear I wasn't involved in any of it," she replied desperately, "and I'm so afraid because... the police *are* involved in *all* of it."

Michael and Casey connected again, this time with shock. What was she talking about? And how did it seem way too similar to a situation they had been wondering about only moments ago?

"All of what?"

"That detective's death."

"What?"

"I know who killed that detective who was found in the park yesterday."

Michael and Casey sat bolt upright and looked at each other again, intensity in their eyes now. Michael suddenly held up a hand to stop Angela from saying anymore. Looking at Casey, he said gravely, "We better get Captain Jack in here."

"Right." Casey was punching in the number to the Captain's office before the statement was completely out of Michael's mouth. Angela watched them with wide eyes, suddenly realizing how critical this situation was.

When she caught her first glimpse of Captain Philip Jackson, a renewed sense of awe filled her. He swept into the office and, in typical fashion, seemed to completely dominate the room. "All right, what in hell is so important that you had to get me - " Jack looked at Angela, who sat staring with huge, round eyes at the white-haired force that had just entered the room. Looking back to

Michael with a gleam that promised certain anger, Jack said, "Who is this?"

"Captain Jackson, this is Angela Cahn," Michael said, standing to his feet rather disruptively, before his captain showed his temper. Only authorized personnel were allowed in this office, and it was obvious by Jack's expression that he didn't consider this woman authorized. "Angela owns *Lawn Care Products Unlimited*, over on The Boulevard." Jack exaggerated one single nod in acknowledgment, still unimpressed. "She's a friend of mine; she says she knows who killed Detective Linden."

Jack's expression changed instantly. "Is that so? Well then, hello, Ms. Cahn, I hope for Michael's sake that your story is good." A small smirk hung in the corners of his mouth as he spoke and held out his beefy hand. Angela took it, but she wasn't at all sure if he was serious or not. Neither were Michael or Casey as they exchanged glances, but Jack sat on the corner of the desk and waited for the story to begin.

"Okay, Angela, go on," Michael encouraged her gently.

She took a deep, cleansing breath before she began. "Well, it was all so simple. I was doing inventory two nights ago, and this car pulled into the parking lot of the store. A young woman got out of the car - "

"What kind of car?"

"I don't really know. It was one of those tiny little things. I think it was a Toyota, something or other, and it was gray."

"All right, go on," Michael said as he scribbled the information down.

Feeling that her words were suddenly important and enlightening, and needing desperately to get it all off of her chest to authorities that could actually help her and Susan, Angela continued with a renewed sense of confidence and vigor. "She got out and asked directions to Cane Street. She said she was from out of town

111

and visiting her friend who had just had a baby. She seemed... scared, and desperate. My heart just went out to her. She was so upset that when I tried to explain the directions she got all confused."

"Did she mention her name?"

"Well, yes, she... said her name was Susan."

"Susan Ventry?"

"Yes, but she didn't say her last name at that point. She just wanted to get to Cane Street, and she was so frightened and confused that I drove her there. I went in my car, and she followed me in hers. She said her friend lived above Armondo's Pizzeria, but when we got there the place was closed, and she just ran into the building. She never said thanks or spoke again. I was shocked, so I just sat there for a minute. When I finally started to pull out, I saw her come rushing out the back door, and this huge man was chasing her through the parking lot with a hammer."

Angela hesitated slightly, checking their gazes before she went on. "It was the detective they showed on the news yesterday, and he was going to kill her, he most definitely was. In fact, when she tried to get into her car he swung at her and smashed the side window. I didn't know what to do, so I thought I would just threaten him a little and try to get Susan out of there, but when I came at him, he didn't move... and... I swerved, and hit him with my car."

"You hit him with your car?" Michael repeated, sharp concern in his tone.

"Yes, but he wasn't hurt. In fact, he got up and attacked me. Michael, this man did not act like any police officer I've ever encountered. I never would have guessed he *was* a police officer if I hadn't seen the news yesterday. He was vicious and angry and he was out for blood. He didn't care whose blood it was, he was just going to kill anybody that got in his way. It was terrifying."

She looked desperately between the three men, from Michael, to Jack, to Casey, feeling guilty about her methods. With a sudden, panicked sense, she prayed they would believe her.

"You're telling me," Jack broke in skeptically, "that the detective who was murdered yesterday attacked you and your friend in this manner?" He obviously didn't believe it, but Michael and Casey knew Linden's blood had been pumped full of *Racer* at the time. This extremely uncharacteristic behavior, which at first seemed unbelievable, was actually quite likely to have occurred. It also confirmed Angela's credibility. They didn't want to explain these things to Jack in front of her, though, so when Jack caught their eyes, and they lowered their gazes intentionally, he stopped himself from further criticizing Angela's words.

"Yes, he did act exactly that way," Angela responded to the cynicism defensively.

"So, what did you do?" Jack asked levelly.

"Well, I really couldn't do anything. I was strapped into my seat belt, but he was hitting me and scratching my face, and I felt like I was suffocating. Then... he just collapsed... and I saw Susan, standing there with the hammer. She'd hit him on the head and he'd passed out. We thought he was dead, but I swear to you he wasn't!" she added quickly. "In fact, after a few minutes he started to move, and that's when we got out of there. To get away from him. When I looked back, he was getting up and he was very much alive, far from being 'beaten repeatedly', and far from dead.

"We drove around the streets for a while and then Susan got out of the car and left me there. She was scared to death and she said that if I got caught, to tell the police that some crazy-woman threatened to kill me if I didn't take her around town, so I wouldn't get into trouble for being with her. She said that what was going on was very big and very dangerous and that I shouldn't be involved in it. Then she said not to tell the cops anything because they couldn't be trusted."

"She said the *cops* couldn't be trusted?" Michael seemed confused by that, and slightly offended.

"Yes, and with all my heart, I agree with her."

"Why?"

"Because... cops killed him."

"*What?*" Jack actually stood to his feet and stared down at Angela, donning an intimidating expression of utter, rejecting shock.

She started to weep again, and Casey put his hand on her shoulder, as much in an urgency for her information as in a comforting gesture.

"When we drove around, we ended up stopping by this park. I didn't even know where we were really, but that's when Susan got out and ran away. She told me to stay there for about an hour and if everything was quiet then I should leave. So, I sat there, only for about twenty minutes, and I saw some movement in the trees. I thought it might be Susan so I stayed and watched, but it wasn't her. It was three men. I could tell by the size and shape that the one man was our attacker... Detective Linden... and the other two were dragging him along against his will... They were uniformed policemen. At least they were dressed like police."

A long silence filled the air as the three men stared at Angela. "Is there any way you might have been mistaken in what you saw?" Jack asked acidly.

"I know what I saw. I could show you the exact spot. They weren't very far away. I could only see the outlines of their bodies, but those outlines were clear. I could even see the shine of the handcuffs they used to bind him. That's why I didn't come to the police right away. I was so terrified of what I'd seen, I didn't know what to believe, or who to trust."

Jack seemed to phase into a world of incredulous, violent silence at this point.

"Have you spoken to Susan since that night?" Michael asked, momentarily distracted by the expression on his Captain's face.

"Yes, she came to see me yesterday. She wanted to ask me, actually she begged me, not to tell anyone she existed, or that she was in the area that night. She said this station is full of dirty cops, and that they wanted some type of information from her, that's why they were framing her. Apparently she was right."

Michael glanced at Casey, and they stole quick, uneasy glances at Jack, but neither of them said anything. The Captain felt as though he'd been slapped, and he was seething. Angela didn't notice, she was continuing on in a haunted voice.

"Last night I got phone calls from someone who knew all about Susan and me." She began to tear up. "He said... he's been watching me, and he knew what my house looked like, on the *inside*. He wanted to know where Susan was, and where some *envelope* was." Angela's face twisted in sarcastic confusion. "I didn't know what he was talking about, but that's all he wanted... that, and to know if Susan had left the country or not. He said he'd leave me alone if I told him... and if I didn't, he'd make me wish I was dead."

"Did you tell him?"

Angela seemed lost in thought. Michael's question jolted her out of it. "Huh? No, no I didn't tell him. I couldn't betray that innocent young woman to a man like that, I just couldn't! But tonight when I left work, someone was following me! That's when I called you."

It seemed obvious that the three officers looking into her face were wondering just how innocent this young woman really was, but they didn't reveal any of their thoughts. Based on Angela's account of the night in question, Michael believed Susan was innocent of the murder, but probably not innocent of other crimes that weren't mentioned yet.

For one thing, Michael knew Marcus Linden; a female of any size would have an extremely difficult time harnessing a man of his incredible mass, let alone to actually achieve the monumental task of crushing his skull. In fact, Angela had said that Ventry had actually struck him once with a hammer, and the action had only caused him to pass out momentarily. There was no way she could have kept him still long enough to beat him until his skull cracked.

As he thought about it, it made more sense that there were two grown men involved, and, even then, Michael believed they would have needed handcuffs to accomplish the task, especially with *Racer* being in Linden's system at the time. It didn't matter, though. Susan Ventry was the key to a lot of questions, and her guilt, quite possibly, went beyond murder. She must be found.

Casey handed Angela a cup of hot tea, and when her hands could barely hold it he reassured her, "Hey, hey... relax now. If you remain quiet about what you know, and rely on us, everything will be fine; I promise."

His warm smile did wonders by way of relieving her, but Michael wasn't at all sure that Casey's assurances were likely. This office could do very little right now to protect Angela, with the *Racer* case so hot and in such a precarious position. Certainly, Susan Ventry, even with Angela's testimony of innocence, was still a criminal at large. He knew with one look at Jack's face that this was true, and as the Captain stood slowly and walked toward him, Michael was deluged by awareness of the countless complications involved in what had just been revealed.

"Casey? Can you take Mrs. Cahn into the other room for a moment, please?" Jack asked.

A deeply strained look pulled at Casey's features. "Yeah, sure. Mrs. Cahn?" he stretched his arm out politely, as if to show her the way out, and she followed his lead into another office. When the door closed, Jack turned again toward Michael.

"Well, what do you think?"

"I believe every word of it, and it lines up with Linden's file. The small gray Toyota, its broken window, the blood, how Susan Ventry was involved... all of it. You've got to admit, it would have been pretty hard for a little teenager to beat a man like Linden to death."

Jack took a deep breath and turned away from Michael, letting it out in a rush of thoughtful torment. "Do you think there are officers in this precinct involved in distributing drugs? I can't believe any of my men would do that." Agony and denial covered Jack's countenance. This news, above anything else Angela had revealed, obviously concerned him the most.

"Well, we can't be certain of that yet, but it sounds that way. Neither the way Linden acted, or the way his murderers did, sounds like any police procedure I've ever been taught; and I doubt the officers involved wanted information from Susan Ventry for any type of legitimate investigation."

Michael stopped and looked downward, seeing Jack's pain and betrayal. "Sir, we didn't have a chance to tell you this yet, but we warned Greg at the Medical Examiner's office to let us know of any type of crack-PCP mixtures in any of their autopsies - Linden had huge doses of each in his bloodstream at the time of death."

"...What? Not Linden."

"That's how we felt about it, too, but there it was. To be honest we were beginning to wonder if - well - maybe he was involved in it on a not-so-professional level, but I think Angela just shed some light on that.

"He was attacked early in the night, according to the message left on my machine. Then he's seen by Angela, keeping his appointment with Susan Ventry on Cane Street - that's what he was trying to tell us in his message, where he was meeting her, and maybe about this mysterious envelope Black and his men want to find. When he makes the meeting, though, he's pumped full of *Racer* and reacts the way a *Racer* user has been reported to act: Violent and out of control. The question is, who did this to him?"

Michael looked downward considerately. "I think she answered that question, too. These big distributors we're looking for... may be officers right out of this precinct."

Jack closed his eyes, then leveled his gaze on the floor, puckering his mouth thoughtfully. "Well, what's your plan in finding out for sure?"

Michael answered very quietly. "The first thing is to get on this Armondo's thing right away, check it out, see if there's anything there. Second, I'm going to get some more details about that autopsy, make sure Angela's story really checks out. I mean, I believe her, but who knows, maybe the people who did this were... I don't know... coast guard officials or something, with similar uniforms. In the dark who would be able to tell?

"If they were real uniformed police officers, they would have used a billy club. That should be easy enough to check out - if the wounds came from that specific type of club. How many times was he actually hit, and how hard? Could a woman have accomplished it, or is it likely that there were two grown men involved? What about the angle of the wounds? Was he being hit from two sides at once? The report should tell us all of this, especially if we ask specific questions. As far as the handcuffs - that should be easy, too. If Linden was fighting against his attackers with regulation cuffs on his wrists and ankles, there will definitely be abrasions on his skin. Those things scrape like hell."

Jack looked at Michael with quiet respect in his eyes. He was an outstanding detective, and, as usual, his mind was already working fast. "Good. Start there, and let me know what you find out immediately. What about Mrs. Cahn?"

"I don't know, I was going to ask you about that. Someone's following her, and they know who she is and that she's involved with Susan. She needs police protection."

"Hmm... There's a problem." Jack said dispassionately, all signs of listening admiration and painful denial gone as the dominance of his position reasserted itself. "If we start protecting her, it'll be obvious to this whole station that she's involved in something, and it's also going to alert whoever is watching her that we're onto them."

"Yes, but we can't just leave her for a target. If nothing else, she's a witness to a murder."

"True, but they don't know she witnessed that murder or they would have threatened her about it when they called her. All they said was that they wanted information about Ventry. Now, I'm not suggesting we leave her completely alone, I'm just saying we need to be cautious about the way we handle this. We can't forget that busting *Racer* is still our primary interest."

"Angela's a part of the *Racer* case now."

"Yes, she is, and she can lead us to Ventry, and probably to whoever else is involved in this fiasco, but not if she's got an armed guard around her. We need to be discreet."

Michael didn't like the sound of that. Jack didn't seem to be taking Angela's danger very seriously. "How discreet?"

"Well, we can get a few men to watch her building and a few to watch her store in case anything goes down, but I don't want it to be obvious. If we time this properly, we can bust the whole case through that little lady."

"Captain! I don't want to use Angela as bait!"

"Why not?"

"Because she's an innocent citizen, and it's dangerous!"

"We've used innocent citizens before." The implication was overwhelming. A direct challenge laced Jack's eyes as he looked at

Michael, demanding that his personal feelings be put aside. It was his duty to use whatever tools were safely at his disposal to close a case.

"Besides, I don't think she's in as much trouble as you think. They want her information, and if she just plays the game a little bit, they'll keep her alive for it. In the meantime, if they do make any moves, we *will* be there. Again, I'm not suggesting we abandon her. All I'm saying is that we act wisely."

"Well, I don't like it."

"Listen, we'll inform her of what's going on. She'll feel better and she'll be safer with a few guards around her. Really, she will be."

"And who are we going to use as guards? Cops? We don't even know who we can trust. I say we get her out of town and into Witness Protection until this can be solved."

"Michael... That's not a good idea."

"It is to me."

"But it isn't best for this case!" Jack said coldly, suddenly impatient with Michael's resistance. "Now, get your head on straight and open your eyes. You are a DEA Sergeant, and you are sworn to this case. I don't care if the witness involved is a good friend, an enemy, or your great Auntie Bev!

"This is a nasty business, Michael. People you know, and like, are used all the time when it serves a greater goal, and if that's what we have to do, then we do it! Jack paused, then added for effect, "Let's not forget, we're already overlooking the fact that Mrs. Cahn broke a few laws in withholding the evidence she did."

What did that mean? That because she'd been terrorized into silence, she now owed them a favor? A long pause followed in which Michael looked steadfastly down at his desk. Feeling protective of a friend was one thing, acting unprofessionally was another. At this moment, he couldn't separate the two, and he was stunned by the concept that he had to.

Was he acting unprofessionally? Or was Jack simply hitting below the belt to make him concede? Michael wasn't really sure, but as Jack looked at him steadily, Michael realized how important this case had suddenly become to his Captain. He was willing to make sacrifices to achieve the goal of solving it that Michael, perhaps, wasn't willing to make. "I understand," he said quietly, pride leveling his voice so the sting didn't show.

"Good..." He softened a bit. "Hey, if you want to know worry, and anguish, try wondering if the men you invest in, trust, and believe in with your entire life, are dirty drug dealers. Now *there's* something to worry about."

~ *Chapter Fifteen* ~

As Michael drove home that night, the weight of the Racer case surrounded him. His career was, sometimes, way more demanding than he wanted it to be, and tonight that demand was crushing him.

He'd gone against the rules before, that was for sure; he'd been blasted by Captain Jack before, that was also sure. His levels of responsibility and accountability were so high now, though, that everything changed form. The simplest stretching of the rules, which he'd regularly pushed to the limits as a detective, became glaringly relevant and critical as a DEA Sergeant.

The one benefit of his job was that only a few crimes were investigated at a time, therefore the workload wasn't profuse. The intensity each one presented, however, was indeed overwhelming, and the threats each of these cases posed to the innocent people of the city were always dramatic. Any slip up could result in total loss and failure.

At this moment, with someone he cared so very much about involved in the whole of it, he really didn't think he could stand the pressure. Because he *could not* do anything more to help her than provide an obscure surveillance team. What good would that really do her in a one on one attack? No good at all, and he was appalled by the fact that police business should so readily risk a life so dear to him.

The *Racer* case, though, could *not* be lost, he insisted to himself, and neither did he want it to be. There was a much greater goal involved in all of this, and that was the truth of it. Still... what about Angela?

He turned his dark green Dodge Ram down the remote road that would take him home. Everything would be better when he got home. Amy was home, and every tension eased in his beautiful wife's presence. He parked the truck inside the garage of his new country house. Once the edges of city limits passed, Niagara Falls was made up of beautiful country and productive farmland. While Michael and Amy didn't actually live on a farm, they had a beautiful view of cultivated farmland within their private, treed lot. A few minutes one way, and Michael's parents' house could be reached, and a few minutes the other way would bring them to Kevin's new home. They were family oriented, all of them, and their past trials had increased that bond.

"Hey, Babe."

Amy's face lit up. She had a very natural beauty, with straight, silky brown hair, and warm green eyes that overflowed with genuine kindness and honesty. She moved instantly toward that voice; the deep, resonate timbre she loved to hear, especially when he spoke in just that way. "Hi."

A deep kiss complimented the greeting, and Michael held his wife in his arms for a few moments of peace while she reveled in the feeling. "How was your day?"

"Okay. Student teaching is a blast! Those kindergartners are so cute, I can't believe how smart they are. We had a lesson on Dinosaurs today, and almost half of them knew all the different names of the dinosaurs! The hard names, too, like Triceratops! I couldn't believe it! I don't remember being that smart when I was five, do you?"

"Ohhhh, speak for yourself, *I* was brilliant when I was five... That's why I decided to be a *cop* when I grew up."

The statement started off in a light, humoring attempt at arrogance, but Michael finished it with a bitter tinge as he broke the embrace and started for his living room sofa. Crashing upon it heavily, he closed his eyes and extended one hand forward without even looking, as an invitation, a need, for his wife to follow. As he knew she would, she accepted the offer and sat beside him, a curious look on her face.

Michael had a very stressful job, and Amy was aware of almost every detail of it. The only way for an officer to win the 'battle for the family' that they always fought, was to be able to share their world with their spouse; and have a spouse that understood and accepted it. Michael was very good about leaving work behind him when he came home. He was usually able to do it, too, because of the few cases that were concentrated on at any one time. While he often discussed the specifics of the cases he was working on with Amy, he was rarely weighed down by them during his time with her. Something was different tonight.

"What's the matter, Michael?" she asked sensitively, her hand moving across his forehead in a soothing, worried movement.

"Everything."

"Like what?"

"Like work, and work obligations. Sometimes this job is just too much, you know? They want us to be inhuman. Unfeeling."

"What happened?"

Michael took a deep breath before he launched into the tale. "Did I ever tell you about Angela Cahn? My boss when I was a kid?"

"I think you did. Was she the one who kept you from getting caught by the police when you were seventeen?"

"Yes, that's her. I haven't seen her in... God, I don't know how long, at least eight years. She's one of those people you never forget and you always care about, you know? I don't think I've ever met someone as good at heart as she is. She's still like a sister to me."

Amy smiled softly as her husband spoke. "So, how has she made your job unbearable?""

"Well, remember when I told you about Linden's new project, Racer?"

"Yes."

"It seems that Angela met the contact sent by the ringleaders of the drug, and then witnessed the murder of Detective Linden."

"What? Oh, my God! Is she into that type of thing?"

"No! That's the problem; she was an innocent bystander, a victim even. Two nights ago Angela was working late, and this young lady came into her store asking for directions. It was Susan Ventry, our suspect in Linden's murder. Angela had no idea who the girl was, or what her involvement was with drugs. I'd bet my life that even after everything that's gone down, if we asked Angela what *Racer* is, she wouldn't have a clue.

"Anyway, to make a long story short, Ventry was scared, and Angela, being the decent human being that she is, took her where she wanted to go. After she dropped her off, she saw this man chasing Ventry with a hammer. It was Linden. We think someone shot him up with *Racer*. Angela tried to help, but Ventry's assailant started attacking *her*, so Ventry hit him on the head with the hammer, and knocked him out. Angela swears he was alive, and she and Susan took off because he was waking up and they were afraid of him. Then she's sitting in her car waiting for everything to quiet down, and she sees two cops drag Linden into the woods and beat him to death."

Amy sat perfectly still while Michael spoke, her eyes huge and transfixed with the story. Now she took a deep, sharp breath. "Oh, my God! *Police* killed him?"

"That's what Angela says, and I gotta tell you, it's looking more and more like she's right. Now she's witnessed a murder, Susan Ventry seems to have taken an interest in her kindness and is likely to call her, and someone at the top of this whole mess knows about her. Last night she got a few phone calls from someone asking about an envelope she knows nothing about, and threatening that if she didn't tell them where she took Ventry, they were going to kill her, or worse. Today they were following her. Now, I don't know who is involved in this, or how deep it goes, but she is going to be in serious trouble if these guys come after her for that information."

"Well, just don't let that happen."

"It's not that simple."

"Why not?"

He looked away and waved his eyes at the ceiling sarcastically. "Because she is... umm... *instrumental...* in this case. She'll be watched, but at a distance, so that if anything happens we'll be there, but we don't actually want to *stop* it from happening."

A horrified, confused look covered Amy's face, not only at Michael's words, but at the bitter note of absolute conviction with which he spoke them. "Why not?"

"Because she's our best chance of catching the individuals involved."

Amy looked incredulous. A touch of horrified rebellion laced her eyes. "Michael, that's insane. I don't care what anybody says, you cannot just leave that woman alone if you know someone is going to come after her! You all talk, talk, talk about your cases, but your job is to protect the innocent. Angela needs protection!"

"You don't understand."

"I understand that if that woman winds up dead, you'll never forgive yourself!"

Michael took a deep, scowling breath. He was suddenly agitated with this conversation. "We're not exactly going to leave her wide open for attack. She'll be watched very carefully, and I'll do my best to get on this case so she *doesn't* end up hurt. I have to catch the leaders involved in *Racer*. When I do, she'll be safe."

"You hope! It could take months to solve that case."

"Not anymore, we don't have months. Whatever is going to happen is going to happen in the next few weeks."

"Regardless, just because you need to solve the case doesn't mean you will, and it doesn't mean Angela will be safe in the meantime! She really needs some protection!" Amy was incensed, and it showed in her eyes. She sat before Michael with her head tilted sideways in absolute astonishment that this conversation should even be taking place. She couldn't believe Michael would use another person to achieve his goals; even a goal this worthwhile.

Michael sat up abruptly, his eyes blazing with anger. He wanted to silence his wife's words because they hit too close to his heart. He knew she was right and yet knew how powerless he was to really be of help to Angela right now. His voice was raging steel as he shouted, "Amy *stop!* Just stop! I can't help her anymore! Do you think I feel good about that? It's killing me, but all I can do is stand back and wait. This wasn't my idea, I wanted to get her out of town, but..."

He stopped short, clenching and unclenching his fists while he took deep breaths and hung his head in a gesture meant to recompose himself. He was in charge of this case, he wouldn't begin laying blame, even if he wanted to make Amy understand. When he spoke again, he was much quieter, but no less strained in his demeanor. "I'm not a rookie anymore; I've got responsibilities now that I don't even think I can handle sometimes. I can't afford to think with my emotions, I've got to think with my head."

"Who said *that*? Captain Jack?"

Michael's eyes shot to hers. How did she know Jack had said that? "I say it."

"Well, *Sergeant*," she mocked, "the day you stop using your heart is the day you better turn in your badge."

Michael gave her a withering look, but then he smiled at her. His wife. "You know, you're such a female."

"Is that supposed to be an insult?"

"No," he leaned into her closely and imprisoned her against the sofa with the strength of his arms on either side of her. "It's meant to be a compliment." Then he kissed her.

"I'm still right," she said, trying to fight the effects of his kiss.

"I know you are, there just isn't anything I can do about it."

"This was Captain Jack's decision, then?"

"Yes."

"Good... It was really upsetting me to think you were such a cold jerk."

Silence filled the air, and a thick tension came along with it. Michael looked at Amy for a long moment, thinking about that. Was he so cold? Was he willing to use someone to solve the *Racer* case? What if the witness was a stranger? Would that make him feel differently? Probably, he decided, but it wasn't cold. He wanted *Racer* off the streets because it was a menace to the city, not because he wanted some sort of personal gain from it. Amy was right, too, though, and Angela's present danger was grinding at his soul and causing him not to see clearly because of it. How could he manage both? How could he ensure her safety and not blow the case?

There was no way.

Was there?

~ *Part Two* ~

~ *Chapter Sixteen* ~

Kevin Larsen was outside at seven a.m., waxing his new boat with meticulous care. It sat securely inside of its trailer, off to the side of his driveway, bright red and dark, contrasting black. It was a gorgeous piece of machinery and was steadily becoming Kevin's new love. Retirement was good. At least it was when there was something to do, and this morning he was content as he rose early. He was still unable to sleep late after all the years he had trained himself to get up at the crack of dawn. In little more than one month, he could be cruising this boat along the scenic waters of Lake Erie during his long days at home. He couldn't wait for that!

As he continued his task with great attention and enjoyed the warmth of the spring sun as the entire western part of the state seemed to thaw from the frigid temperatures of winter, he saw his son-in-law's truck pull up to his house. With a pausing curiosity, he watched the young man approach.

Michael walked up to Kevin with a smile as the older man looked at him with that comical expression. For as close as they lived to each other these days, they didn't get much time to actually spend together, and certainly never did so in the early morning. Now Michael needed help, and his long night of deliberation had brought him to only one conclusion. He was right in wanting Angela's close protection, and so was Jack in wanting the case to take top priority. Hopefully both opinions would be satisfied, right now, with the possibility Michael had come up with.

"Michael! What are you doing here at seven a.m.? Aren't you supposed to be working or something?"

"Yeah, well, I thought I'd drop by to see my old-geezer father-in-law, you know."

"Hey, you better watch it with that old-geezer stuff, little man, cause I'll show you just how much I still got, and it'll put you to shame."

A hearty laugh escaped Michael, and his eyes shone with affection. He had no doubt whatsoever that in a one-on-one tussle Kevin could, indeed, put Michael to shame, even in his youthful, excellent physical condition. At forty-nine, Kevin was still strong and capable, with a muscular, fit body. He was the type of man who bettered with age, and the rest and relaxation he'd experienced this past year had increased his physical appeal as well as his disposition. A handshake followed the mild teasing, and Kevin looked directly into his son-in-law's face.

"So, what's up?"

Michael looked around a bit. "The boat looks good."

"Yeah." Kevin's eyes gleamed for a brief second as he regarded his beautiful craft. "So, what's up?" he repeated knowingly.

Michael took a deep breath, unable to figure out exactly how to broach the subjects on his mind. "Amy and I had a disagreement last night."

Kevin smirked and began the process of little circles again with his wax. "Really? Well, son, I'm afraid it won't be your last, but I'm a bit surprised after a year that it was your first!" His light, jesting attitude ceased when Michael spoke again.

"Yeah... it was just... can we talk?"

Kevin glanced at his son-in-law more acutely, and answered with a quiet, concerned sincerity. "Sure, come on in, I think I got some coffee left."

Michael followed Kevin into his house, a beautiful new ranch that was set in a lot similar to his own home. The house itself was rather small, suitable for a widower living alone, as Kevin was, but the lot surrounding it was spacious and treed, with a gorgeous stretch of woods behind it. The inside was decorated with modern, clean fixtures. Michael entered the kitchen with familiar casualness and immediately went to get a coffee cup.

"What's the matter, Kevin, you don't know how to wash a dish?" he chastised humorously as he saw the mountain forming in the sink.

"I do them, sometimes, it's just that the cleaning service will be coming in... what... two days? I'll let them earn their money."

Michael shook his head and laughed at the lame response, sitting down at the table in the otherwise fairly clean kitchen. He pushed his cup of coffee out before him, resting his forearms almost full length on the table. "I know it's hard to put them in the dishwasher, I mean it's a whole foot and a half away. Uh... this is a clean cup, isn't it?"

"Yeah, yeah, yeah, it's clean, now what's up?"

Seriousness eclipsed Michael's smile. "I have to ask you a favor."

"All right, ask. Does this have anything to do with the disagreement last night?"

"Well, sort of, I mean, well, just listen to this..."

Michael went on to detail everything that had transpired within the last three days. As he unloaded the truth to his friend and respected former partner, he felt a tremendous weight being lifted from him. It was good to talk to Kevin, and Michael knew that anything he shared with this friend would be kept completely confidential, so he allowed himself the luxury of telling him everything. Kevin's insight was always valuable, and he could handle the ugliness of anything police work could shell out. After all, he'd been the best for a long, long time, and had dealt with the very worst in his day.

Information regarding a new drug and details about Linden's death were fascinating news items to Kevin. In spite of his vow of abstinence from the police force, his blood was beginning to pump with the ideas and instincts of an investigator. The secrecy of Michael's Special Teams work certainly wasn't news to Kevin. He'd maintained his own secrets inside that division less than two years ago.

"I'm really sorry about Linden."

Michael sighed and looked away. "You can't imagine how it feels to lose a man."

"I think I can... So, you honestly believe cops are involved in it all?"

"It's a possibility."

"Damn... That's something." Kevin looked distant as he pondered it.

"Yeah, the problem is, we have to move immediately, and we're not really sure where we're going. I mean we got some great leads, but we still don't have an accurate fix on the whole situation. Now Jack is afraid that if we look too interested in Angela, they're going to retreat, then the whole case is blown."

"Not necessarily. Maybe you'll just throw them into a tailspin that'll make them screw up. An operation like what you're describing can't be dropped in a day. The dealers can't just shut it all down the way you're thinking because they see the DEA involved. If they brought the stuff in, the game's in motion already, and they'll have to get it out there because someone else probably wants to get paid for their efforts. It's that kind of game. There's always someone bigger behind these guys, waiting to reap the rewards of their labors. Not even dirty cops are immune to that. Mark my words, they'll still be trying to distribute their goods, but they'll be crapping their pants and falling all over each other knowing that you know something. That's when you gotta get in there and nail them."

Michael looked at his former partner levelly, a sense of amazement halting him for a moment. Kevin had a way of bringing a whole new light of reality to a situation, and had pegged this one accurately within minutes. His experience on the streets made him wise to a whole other side of the tracks, which was crucial in times like this.

"I suggest you get started immediately, though," he continued, "because time may be a problem for you. If they do succeed in getting the stuff out there, you'll never be able to stop it. The streets take over, and the demand for the stuff will get it to them all by itself. If you give them too much time, they'll cover their tracks, and you'll never be able to prove who was involved, and to what capacity. Right now, though, you may be in a key position, and you need to make it work for you. Get Casey out on the streets to keep an eye on things there, and get yourself busy investigating that pizza place and getting wind of what's happening inside the precinct, etc. etc."

Amazement gave way to awe as Michael listened to Kevin's wisdom. Everything seemed suddenly clear and attainable. Angela's appearance at the police station, and her involvement with Michael and the DEA, may be causing the *Racer* industry to launch into a sudden and unexpected collapse. If that were occurring, Michael needed his department to be ready.

"That's all true, Kevin, but I'm still worried about Angela. Jack wants to use her as bait!"

"And he blasted you because you *don't*, huh?"

Michael looked away, the sting of the incident still too fresh. "I wouldn't say he blasted me, but he made me wonder if I was acting unprofessional. What does professional mean, anyway? That you can't feel anything at all? Or aren't we allowed to care?"

Kevin looked at Michael steadily for a moment. There was no sorrow in his eyes for this younger man's turmoil, but there was an understanding. Michael held a place in Kevin's heart that no other person held. He was a son, a brother, a friend. There was no one closer to him in his life, and at the most crucial of times Michael had shown himself true. Now he was struggling, and Kevin wanted to shield him from all of it, but there was no way he could, and no way that he should. Michael must grow into this new role, growing pains and all. Kevin, however, would help where he could.

"You can care, but it's at your own risk, and on your own time. Beyond that, your whole life belongs to the case you're working on. Believe me, I know... So, were you acting unprofessionally?"

"No! I was right. Angela needs protection... And so was Jack... right now Angela is very useful to this case, and we don't have much time. That's why I'm here."

Kevin's brow furrowed deeply. "How can I help you with that?"

"Well, it's Angela. I can't help her anymore, and to be honest, I don't really want to. I'm too close to this case and my focus has to be on *Racer*. I can't see straight with her at risk, though. These people have been in her house, they're calling her on the phone, watching her. I don't know where they'll show up next or what they'll do to her when they get to her... And I can't waste time worrying about her. She gave us a huge edge with her confession, enough of an edge to really get somewhere fast."

"So? What? Do you want me to do some surveillance for you or something?" A deep recess within Kevin was hoping Michael would say yes, that he wanted Kevin's help investigating, but he didn't.

"No, I wondered... if you could keep an eye on Angela for me...?"

"What?" It was a distinctly negative response. Kevin's entire being was rejecting this request. "How do you want me to do that?"

"I don't know - just go over to the store and see if she's all right. Jack's going to get some men out to her place today to watch her, but I don't know how close they're going to be... and if we can even trust them."

"You want me to watch her all day long? She's going to need twenty-four hour protection!"

"I know..." A long, enduring look pleaded with Kevin.

"Awh, Michael, come on! You don't really expect me to play *bodyguard* do you?"

"Kevin, you're the only one I trust, and the only one I can possibly ask. Since you're not on the force there's no conflicting interest, and I would feel a lot better, I'd be able to actually work, if I knew you were with her."

"But... how long will this take? I don't even know this woman; what if she doesn't want me hanging around?"

"She'll want you there if she starts getting threats, and she's already so scared she'll probably be grateful that you're there."

"Michael? You *can't* be serious. You are actually asking me to stay with this woman for however long it takes you to solve this case? I don't want to do that! I do have a life, you know."

"No, you don't; all you have to do lately is wax your boat."

"That's a low blow. I've earned the right to do nothing but wax my boat!"

"Yes, you have; and I'm not knocking you. It's just that I don't know what else to do!"

The desperation in that comment affected Kevin more than the actual words. With a capitulating shrug, he shook his head.

Seeing that Kevin was wearing down, Michael drove home for a positive response. "Look, will you just go over to her store and meet her today? If the two of you absolutely can't work together or you can't come to some agreement on this, then you're free to leave. Would you at least do that? Just go talk to *her* about it?"

A long, begrudging moment ensued. "Oh, all right! *That* I'll agree to. I'll go talk to her, and see how much trouble she thinks she's really in."

"She probably doesn't know how much trouble she's really in. *You* do."

"All right! I said I'd talk to her!"

"Today?"

"I'll go over to her store right now, I promise."

A deep sigh of relief cut through Michael. "Thanks, Kev, I appreciate this."

"Yeah, yeah, never mind the thanks; I guess I could use a little excitement for the next couple of weeks. I'm warning you, though, once the lake is opened for sailing, I'm gone."

"It's a deal," Michael agreed with a smile; a deep, inner smile. For he knew that once Kevin met Angela, he would do whatever he could to help her. He had agreed to meet her. Fine, that was all he would need. Michael could almost guarantee that once he did, neither hell, high water, nor the call of the sailing seas would keep him from helping her.

He was right, too.

~ *Chapter Seventeen* ~

"Hello, Angela."

A muffled screech escaped Angela's throat before a leather-gloved hand reinforced its position over her mouth.

"You know you really should have cooperated because now things have to be done the hard way, and I must tell you we're very annoyed by your obstinate attitude."

Tension compressed every joint in Angela's body. Rigid fear paralyzed her as her eyes widened in dreading shock over the gloved hand that held her. She had made it home after last night's trauma at the police station with the help of Detective Casey. He'd come right into her condo to make sure she was safe and that no one had been in there during her absence. All had been well. She had actually allowed herself to believe that everything was all right now that she had told the proper authorities about the problem. She hadn't received any more phone calls last night. She'd thought it was over!

Apparently it wasn't, because here she was, being accosted in the private, underground garage of her building. Where were the guards Michael had promised?

"Now, we're going to go for a little ride. If you cooperate, you'll be fine. If you don't, we'll have to get *very* rough."

The dark shadows and spaciousness of the garage both echoed what went on inside of it, and muffled those same sounds. The noise didn't matter right now anyway because at 9:45 a.m. on a weekday morning, everyone else in her building had already either left for work or was deeply ensconced within their homes. No one was around to hear her struggle. The dark, masked figure that had slithered up behind her could do whatever he wanted, and it would go quietly unnoticed.

He started directing her body toward the small entry door that would take them outside. The two large doors that would give access to the residents' cars were closed, but the small side door was opened, and he tried to push her through it.

Parked about twenty feet away, a waiting car, large and black with shaded windows, sat perfectly still with its engine running. Angela's eyes rested on it as if it were the only sight before her. It seemed to represent the terror consuming her. It was waiting to abduct her; she could *not* let them get her in it. She simply *could not!*

She began to fight. It was useless at first; this man was big and strong and his simple hold had secured her entire body. As she saw herself getting closer to that car, though, sitting menacingly in the distance, ready for its getaway, she began to riot hysterically. There was no way she was going to get in that car!

With a growling screech that came from somewhere deep inside of her, she kicked and twisted. The man stopped, but he didn't let go. Feeling trapped and frantic, she fought harder, and, with a flailing effort, finally wrenched herself sideways very suddenly in sheer, primal desperation. Her attacker's hold slackened just slightly in his surprise. Then, remembering the one and only Martial Arts move she had ever learned, in a moment that was lightening fast but seemed to her like concentrated slow motion, she resisted the urge to stand and fight, and, instead, slid her body *down* quickly, through the circle of his arms. Scrambling forward then, in an awkward attempt to gain distance from him, she ran for the elevator door. If she could only get inside, he would not be able to access the rest of the building without security clearance.

He was right behind her, in his own desperate rage, snatching the air at her back in powerful, swift sweeps of his arm. She barely went three steps, and was just inches away from being caught again, when she heard a sudden shuffling in front of her. The elevator door opened, and she came face to face with another man, apparently there to aid the attacker.

She screamed and backed against the sidewall of the garage in horrified defeat. One man blocked her path toward the door to her home, and the other man blocked her path out through the garage. She regarded them both with blazing eyes as she compressed herself against the sidewall. There was nowhere else to go. Bunching her hands into tiny fists, she hunched down into a ball and prepared herself to fight. There was no way she would win, but she wouldn't just allow herself to be taken, either.

To Angela's complete amazement, she watched as the man in the elevator doorway, after assessing the unexpected assault taking place for a split second, began to enter the garage. He wasn't looking at Angela, he was looking, violently, at her attacker. Coming at him with a predatory rage, Angela saw the masked man back up and stop in distinct shock and fear.

The man in the elevator began to speak, seeing the startled fright his presence caused this intruder. Swaggering forward with a slow, knowing, ultimately intimidating smile, an eerie dominance settled. "You know who I am, don't you?" he asked ominously. "Yes, you do... and you know what? You *should* be afraid. Because we already know what you *don't* know, and we're going to nail you for it. Whatever you want with this lady, you can bet you'll *never* get it."

Such a strange set of words, spoken with quiet, threatening precision as the man stalked toward Angela's attacker. Strange words, but they seemed to set the attacker's soul afire. Bending low into a football run, he suddenly slammed full force into the dark man who was talking to him, and bolted for the door. He was inside the passenger's seat of the black car, and it was speeding away, before a minute had passed.

Recovering himself instantly, the man ran to the door and jerked to a stop as the car sped off with an ungodly screech of grinding tires. Grimacing and smacking his hand against the doorframe in frustration, he turned to Angela, who was still hunched down, with her eyes wide with wonder at this stranger in her garage.

He stooped down and reached a steady, non-threatening hand toward her quaking form. She jerked away from him and stared into his face.

"It's all right, I'm not going to hurt you. Just calm down, everything is all right. Michael sent me; my name is Kevin Larsen. I'm a retired police lieutenant, and Michael is my son-in-law. Just relax... that's it, everything is going to be fine."

Somehow, looking into the strong, sure eyes before her, Angela believed those words - that she would be all right. She began to relax and shake all over at the same time. She didn't know that she was crying until she hung her head forward in a surrendering gesture and saw the tears drip to the ground. Then she began to truly wail. Desperately, Angela flung herself forward into the safety this man presented to her, and Kevin received her into his arms as she clung to him.

In the line of duty, it had happened often. Women, children, and sometimes even men who found themselves suddenly safe often dissolved into tears in the arms of a protecting officer. Why was this different? Why did Kevin see and feel more in one glimpse of this woman's face, than he sometimes saw in people he knew for many years? Why was he enraged by the thought of her being bullied and brutalized? Why did he feel such a fierce, protective instinct jump to life by the sound of her weeping, terrified soul?

He enveloped her in his arms, and allowed her to reassure herself there for several minutes as he cooed to her gently. When she settled into a quiet mass of intermittent sniffs, he finally turned and directed her toward the elevator door that would take them to her condo.

With her own key he admitted them into her home, and sat her down in a soft, fabric covered chair at her kitchen table. Then he positioned himself directly across from her, gazing uncertainly as he asked, "Are you all right?"

"Yes, I'm fine."

The response was way too quick, and she didn't look like she was fine at all. He smiled slightly at her attempt at bravery. "Well, you don't have to worry about a thing. I'm here to see that you're protected."

"W-what did you say your name was?"

"Kevin Larsen."

"And you're - Michael's father-in-law?"

"Yes."

"I didn't even know he'd gotten married." She smiled a bit at her own lack of knowledge, then her face fell, and she reared back suddenly. "How do I know Michael sent you? He never told me he was married..."

"Shhh, shhh," Kevin reassured, smiling again at the smart suspicion that suddenly radiated from her eyes. She was pretty tough in her own way, and intelligent. "Listen to me, Michael *is* married, and I *am* his father-in-law. We used to be partners, but I retired a little over a year ago. Now, he can't help you anymore because of his involvement on a particular case he's working on, but he asked me to look after you because he knew you might be in trouble.

"Well, how did you get in the building?" she asked desperately, afraid that if he could get in, anyone else might be able to as well.

"Your maintenance man let me in. He - uh - knew me. I told him I needed to reach you, and he let me in. Said you had just left for work, that I might be able to catch you if I took the elevator down to the parking ramp. I guess he was right." He smiled reassuringly, and she nodded back.

Kevin could see her relaxing as he explained, but she still seemed slightly unconvinced. Reaching into his back pocket, he pulled out his wallet. When he made the move, Angela gasped, catching a clear view of his shoulder holster and the menacing gun sheathed inside of it. "It's okay, I just want to show you something." He pulled a picture out of his wallet. "Look."

It was a photograph of an enchanting young couple alive with love on their wedding day. Angela smiled and took the picture into her own hand. It was Michael and Amy.

"This is your daughter?"

"Yes. Her name is Amy."

"She's lovely."

"Yes, she is." Kevin's eyes shone with pride.

Angela smiled slightly, noting the gleam. Then, looking into the smiling young woman's image, she commented, "She doesn't look like you, does she take after her mother?"

Kevin's eyes dropped, and he hesitated for a brief second. "Yes, she takes after her mother."

Angela hadn't meant the comment to be offensive. It was just simple small talk, but she sensed that she had unknowingly said something untactful. Trying to recover it, she said, "I'm sorry, I didn't mean anything by that, it just - "

Very gently, Kevin interrupted her. "It's okay. She looks and acts a lot like her mother. It's just that – my wife passed away a few years ago, and I still feel it sometimes."

Boy, did Angela understand *that*. She studied this man as he placed the picture carefully inside of his wallet, and put it back into his pocket. She thought it was possible that he was lying about all of this, that he could be one of the bad guys, just coming in disguise, but she doubted it. There was something fine and honest about him and his love for his family that she could see in the depths of his handsome face and comforting brown eyes. Something like that couldn't be imitated, and he didn't give the impression that he was trying to. It was real and natural. She believed him.

He looked up at her again, and her eyes jerked downward. Had she just been staring at him? And had he just caught her? How utterly humiliating. She hadn't had an experience like that since high school.

"Are you sure you're all right?"

Much calmer now, and much more steady, Angela answered, "Yes."

"Good. I'm afraid everything around you is somewhat wrong, though, so prepare yourself for some rough times. Someone wants to know where you took that Ventry girl the other night, and they don't seem to want to give up."

Surprised by his knowledge of the situation, Angela asked, "Who are they?"

"Mrs. Cahn, I'm afraid you've gotten yourself into something very ugly. Whatever you see and hear from here on must remain completely confidential, because you are now in the very middle of a police investigation."

"What?"

"Yes. You're also very lucky because you know Michael. If you wouldn't have went to him, I don't know what might have happened to you."

"So, the police *are* involved, aren't they?"

"We think so. The problem is, we don't know which ones, or how many."

"But... involved in *what?*"

"An illegal drug operation. It's a new drug I'm sure you've never heard of - a street drug, called *Racer*. It's highly addictive, and is expected to become very popular once it hits the streets. It causes extreme, violent behavior in its users, which has more than likely been the cause of the 'Blood Crimes" the news has been telling everyone about. We think there are some officers out of the N.F.P.D involved in trying to distribute it."

"Oh, my God!" Angela's hand went to her throat in horror. *"I'm* involved in something like *that?"*

"I'm afraid so."

"But, how?"

"Susan Ventry was the drug leader's contact person."

"Oh, my God... then... Susan was..." She stopped and looked at him intently for a moment. "What...? Exactly how is Susan involved in this?"

"She apparently contacted Detective Linden, claiming she wanted to give him information about the case. Detective Linden was an undercover investigator."

"Well, he didn't act like one."

"We believe he was found out and exposed, possibly by Susan Ventry, and was injected with *Racer*, causing the violent reaction you saw. He was posing as a runner for the drug."

"Runner? What's a runner?"

"A runner is a person who delivers or distributes a drug. They work for the dealers, getting the drugs where their bosses want it to go, wherever it will be most lucrative. Sometimes it's around town, sometimes to other cities so distribution can be set up in those areas. I understand you developed quite an attachment to Ventry. Can you tell me something about her?"

Angela was horrified that Susan had been a part of something so sordid. She looked at Kevin with her mouth hanging open in utter, rejecting astonishment. Her face was pasty white as she tried to respond. "No, I really can't. She was just a desperate, frightened young woman, and I wanted to help her. I had no idea she was involved in anything illegal. I just thought she was lost in a strange city and that's why she was so scared. I can't believe she's involved in something like this. She - didn't seem the type... I believe she wanted to confess to that police officer, though, because she said that to me; that she'd been trying to make everything all right."

It was Kevin's turn to stare at Angela. He was astounded and strangely touched by the compassion that lay within this woman. It was genuine and unusual in its essence. She'd met a frightened young woman, and in a matter of minutes had seen into her emotional trauma, and had become embroiled in her circumstances. Instead of scaring off when a huge, violent man threatened the girl, she'd rushed to her assistance. She'd kept Ventry's secrets when they could have incriminated her own life, and, even now, she fought for that youth's innocence and worried over her predicament. This was a very special woman. She was extremely beautiful, too.

"I know all of this seems strange," Angela said when she caught the look on Kevin's face. "It's just that - well I don't know - she just seemed so helpless and distraught. Then all of a sudden I was there, involved in what was happening. It was so quick that I didn't have time to think about what I was doing. If you're thinking that I'm some sort of heroine for not telling on her, I'm not. I'm a coward and I was afraid of the police because of what I saw."

An absorbed, staring intensity still hovered over Kevin's face, and Angela found herself very nervous by its depth. Without really thinking about his words, they simply fell from his mouth in a murmur that silenced all other thought and tingled her spine. "Oh, I think you knew exactly what you were doing. You knew you wanted to help that girl, and you risked your life to save her. I don't think there's a cowardly bone in your body..."

Silence fell suddenly. They were strangers, but a world of knowledge passed between them, lasting only a split second, but seeming to stop and redirect whole lifetimes. Angela's mouth hung open, then closed, then opened again as she tried to respond to the potency of this man's words. In a whisper that sounded strangled and ridiculously lame to her own ears, she finally spoke. "Thank you."

Kevin was jolted back to reality. "You're welcome." He cleared his throat nervously and plunged forward. "Listen; are you sure you're all right? Do you need some tea or something?"

"No, really, I'm just a bit shaky, that's all. I feel much better knowing you're - that someone - is here to look out for me. So... now what?"

"Well, originally Michael asked me to meet you, and see what kind of danger you thought you were really in. Now I can see you need twenty-four-hour protection. These guys mean business, and have ways of getting what they want."

"Yeah, like getting into my building." She looked spooked and nervous by the thought.

"Exactly; and I'm afraid they would have gotten pretty nasty to get that information."

"Why? What do they want with Susan? She's just an innocent kid."

"She's not so innocent, I can probably tell you that for sure, even if she was trying to come clean. There's some envelope out there

147

with information in it. She may have betrayed her boss, and knows where, say, his hideout is. She could have knowledge of the *Racer* industry's central location. She could be in sole possession of thousands of dollars in illegal drugs. Maybe she stole money from him. There are a million possibilities, and he wants her and this supposed envelope back, so he can be sure of it all."

Angela stared at him in shock and horror. She absolutely could not believe that something so simple had turned out to be so intricate and involved. That she was, somehow, connected to it all and had vital information concerning it was incomprehensible. "Well, if that's true," she replied with wide, serious eyes, "shouldn't the authorities be checking Armondo's, to see if they can find this information out?"

"Yes," Kevin said with a short chuckle at the naive astonishment emanating from her. As if she were the first to think of this obvious plan. "Michael is already doing that. I have to tell you again that you did the right thing in going to him. It's really a freak coincidence, the way everything happened: That you knew him, and were afraid to talk to anyone else... it's amazing.

"I'm afraid your life has changed, Angela - drastically. Even though you were just an innocent bystander in all of this, you have knowledge that some very nasty people want to get from you, and they don't care if they have to tear you limb from limb to get it. I scared them off a little, but they'll be back. We may have to get you out of town for a while, until everything is cleared up."

"Out of town? I can't leave town, I have a store to run, and... and... I just can't up and leave town!"

"Well, you might have to; you just got attacked in your own home. Do you really think they won't come back?"

"Yes! They shouldn't keep coming back now that I've told the police what I know! That man was afraid of you, maybe he'll leave me alone."

"He won't leave you alone. If anything it's all going to intensify, and you've got to prepare yourself for it whether you like it or not."

The phone suddenly sounded in a subdued buzz that might have been an explosion by the way Angela jumped. Her eyes swung to it with rejecting fear. This whole thing was too much for her. She hadn't done anything wrong! She'd simply helped a scared individual, that's all. Now her entire life was being turned upside down because of one single incident.

Kevin looked at her with violent dislike for the anguish on her face. She obviously thought her attackers were calling to make further threats, and she looked at him desperately for a fraction of a second, asking him with her eyes what she should do. He walked right up to the phone with her, his arm comfortingly across the small of her back as if to reassure her of his strength and presence. "It's okay. Answer it."

She picked the receiver up slowly, halting twice before she finally managed to say, "Hello."

"Angela? This is Michael. I called the store, and Randy said you weren't in yet. Is everything okay?"

A rush of relief washed over her. "Michael – Oh, thank God, it's you."

"Why? Something is wrong, isn't it?"

"Well... sort of. Actually not anymore. Are you married?"

"What? Yes, I got married last year. Why?"

"Did you send your father-in-law over here to help me?"

"Yes; actually I thought he was going to your store. Is he there?"

"He's here, and thank God he is. Someone tried to kidnap me this morning."

"Oh, no..." Michael droned.

"I thought you said I was going to have protection."

"Yes, starting this morning. They are waiting outside your store wondering where you are. We're sorry, Angela, we didn't think they'd move that fast."

"Well, it turned out okay because - umm - Officer Larsen came just in the nick of time. Michael, I was so scared!"

Kevin was listening to the whole conversation as closely as possible without actually having the receiver at his ear. Now he leaned forward and said, "Here, let me talk to him - and you can call me Kevin, I passed the rank of Officer years ago."

A quick smile in her direction preceded the deep intensity that filled his eyes when he spoke to his son-in-law. "Michael? Yeah... Well, I went to the store, and she wasn't there. Her manager said she didn't get in till ten. There I was at eight thirty, just standing around uselessly, so I thought I'd come to her house."

"How did you know where she lived?" Michael asked from the other end of the line.

"I pilfered a voided check from her desk, and it's a good thing I did. Where the hell were your men?"

"We didn't think they'd move on her this fast. I really thought once they knew the DEA was involved, they'd back off."

"Well, that wasn't too smart. I told you they'd be tripping over themselves. She can't be left alone; now, are your men in position?"

"Yeah, they're at her store."

"A lot of good that does her here."

"Kevin, give me a break; all right? I'm just now getting a chance to call the shots here. Jack's been elbowing in up until the last few minutes because he's all concerned about this internal thing. Now, did you get a look at these guys at all?"

"Not really, they were masked, but they were driving a black Buick-type car. Real nondescript, real neutral. One was about six-two, built strong, and he knew me, let me tell you."

"Why do you say that?"

"You should have seen the look in his eyes when I showed up. He couldn't even function for a few seconds. If they didn't know your department was onto them before this, they know it now, and it could very well have been a cop because he seemed confused that *I* would be involved. Like maybe he knew I was retired, and wondered what the hell I was doing here. Again, I could be wrong... but..."

"Hmm... chances are you're exactly right. Damn..." Michael seemed to stop and regroup, then said, "All right, what's your plan?"

"Well, if I get her to her store, will she be all right with these guards?"

"I don't know... What do you think?"

Kevin pursed his lips sarcastically, a gesture Michael couldn't see, but could sense. He'd set Kevin up just by asking that he meet Angela - and Kevin now knew it. Without answering the question, he simply said, "I'll talk to you later, Michael."

He hung up the phone, and stared at it distractedly for a few moments. Angela had been watching him and listening to the entire conversation. It was awing to watch the authority and decisiveness that emanated from him, just as it was awing to think of Michael in such an important position.

"You're not going to leave me, are you?" It was a desperate plea, rather than a question. Angela had taken comfort in the strength and knowledge of this ex-police officer. She felt safe with him where she didn't trust anyone else. She didn't want to be cast off on some other police officer; she wanted him to stay with her.

That realization made Kevin's chest swell with a certain resolved pride. He would indeed protect this woman with his very life. No one would harm one hair on her head while he was around.

A long subdued pumping of blood began to course through his veins. Instinct, too long denied and too long suppressed, surged to life. He *would* protect this woman. Hadn't that been his motive years ago, when he'd accepted the call into police duty? To protect the innocent? Yes, that's exactly what he'd wanted then, and as he looked at Angela Cahn, it was what he wanted now. His reply to her question was quiet and simple, but the force behind it was intense and dramatic as he looked into her eyes. "No... Of course I won't leave you."

~ *Chapter Eighteen* ~

Susan watched the man escorting Angela to his car with intense curiosity. He was rather frightening, in a revering sort of way. Straightforward, unadulterated authority emanated from him as he scanned the area around him with one sweeping, all encompassing glance of his hard eyes. It was certainly obvious that he would cause Angela no harm. He had a protective arm around her back, and an acute awareness of his surroundings. He had come in the very nick of time and saved her life as if he'd been commissioned by God to do so. Who was he? Police? Not like any she'd ever met. He'd seemed real, genuine; and Regis had been afraid of him.

Susan had known it was Regis under that mask as she'd watched him in Angela's garage. She would know Regis anywhere, dressed in anything, and this was the first time she'd ever seen him afraid. Susan was glad the stranger had shown up, because even with all the hell that had taken over her life because of Regis, and the betrayal and deception he'd caused her, something deep within her was connected to him in an almost tangible way. He'd been so kind to her once... She didn't want to have to kill him.

But she would have, to save the life of Angela Cahn.

She'd run almost three full blocks, in terror, when it was all over and Regis came charging out of the garage toward her hiding place. Thankfully, he hadn't been coming for her as she'd feared. He'd gotten into the big black car that had waited for him, and had fled. When she finally inched her way back to hide again, and capture the vital few possessions that she kept here for her survival, everyone was gone. Angela, her strange friend, Regis and his big car, apparently had all escaped. Good.

It was the very smallest of movements that drew her attention away from the handsome stranger, across the street now. He seated Angela in his own car and looked at her closely before he started around to the driver's side of the vehicle. Only a tiny movement, more like a breeze. She crouched low in her hiding place, where she'd been staying close to Angela for nearly three days now. It was an old maintenance shed, barely used, and perfect for overlooking the parking area surrounding Angela's building. Whether she stayed there to ensure Angela's protection or her own was beyond her ability to assess at this point. All she knew was that she wanted to be where this woman was.

She must be very careful to stay completely out of sight. Her face had been exposed to the entire city as a wanted murderer. A murderer who would, if caught, stand before the court to make her plea. A court controlled by Regis. If he ever found her outside of the court... she would be worse than dead for her betrayal.

Her car was of no use to her. It had been impounded for evidence. She might have been able to drive across the border if she'd done so immediately after Linden's murder, but she'd been so stupidly afraid. It made her furious now. If she'd just left right away she would be back in Canada right now, and possibly long gone into British Columbia, or some equally far away province. Instead, she'd panicked immediately and had abandoned her car for fear of detection, and with it, had abandoned her chances of getting back into her country before the authorities were notified.

Actually, she hadn't been afraid of the authorities then. She'd been afraid of Regis and his men, who, ironically, *were* the authority in this God forsaken city. After that, she'd been amazed at how fast her name and face had appeared in the news. The whole city must be completely corrupt and under obligation to the few that followed Regis. Then again, Goldie had said that, hadn't he? That cops were all involved in this drug deal, and wanting to profit by it. Apparently that was just so, because look what had happened with Linden. After all the trust and promises of goodness and protection he'd given her over the phone, he'd turned out to be one of them; high as a kite and trying to kill her for her betrayal.

Maybe she should just let them do what they wanted. Why should she care if the city had access to this new drug? If people wanted to take this stuff, why should she risk her life to stop them? If the police and judges didn't care, why should she? Perhaps she should just give Regis his dope and his money, and try to get him to let her go. She'd have a much better chance of surviving that way than this.

Something within her knew, however, why she cared, especially when she thought of Angela, and watched her strange friend lead her to his car with attentive concern. In truth, had she known what was to become of her simple contact with Linden, a police officer who was already involved, she never would have called upon him for help. She had made the contact, though, and everything had exploded around her. Now she *did* care very much that she not be a part of such ugliness. If there was such a thing as a "good guy", she wanted to be one of them. For now, however, until she could figure out who the good guys were, and who could truly protect her from the corruption within their system, she must stay completely obscure. Unless she could escape.

It wasn't a breeze, it was a rush of ice cold wind, and when Susan turned to see it, she took a sharp, painful breath. Through a tiny, unnecessary window placed high upon the wall of the shed, she could see Regis Black, standing just outside of her shelter, watching the couple across the street with blood in his masked eyes. She ducked inward, even though he obviously hadn't seen her. She should probably just surrender, she thought again, then maybe Regis would leave Angela alone. She was frozen into the corner of the tiny shed, though, unable to move. She knew that if Regis Black got a hold of her, he would make her tell him where the PCP was, then he would kill her.

Susan watched him carefully, unwilling to take her eyes off his movements, and expecting any second for him to turn and see her there. He would look into her soul as he'd always been able to do, and she would be caught in his grip. It was an agonizing moment. She wanted to scream, or run, anything to get away from his nearness, but she didn't dare. He stood perfectly still for several seconds, just watching Angela and the stranger. Then, when the man had settled Angela in the passenger seat of his car, and his body was exposed as he stood straight and began to walk around to the driver's side, Regis lifted an easy, gliding arm upwards. The barrel of a gun came into view, and he cocked it distinctively.

"No! Angela! Look out!"

It was a scream, and Kevin heard it before Angela ever knew it had been directed at them. He flew over the car and pulled her from it in a jerking glide. They were on the ground, shielded by the vehicle when they saw Susan run full force for the security of the garage. The masked man who had attacked Angela less than an hour ago stepped into the parking lot, his gun raised at Susan as he began to chase her. He only took two steps before he stopped hesitantly, looked into Kevin's direction in a seeming debate as to which target was more useful to him, and pointed the trigger decisively at Susan.

Kevin was up in an instant, and as the shot from Regis' gun struck the air, the shot from Kevin's gun exploded. Somehow, the two interrupted each other, and both missed their targets, but the masked man was now running again, and Kevin was now going to chase him down.

In his attempt to keep Angela shielded, Kevin literally threw her back into the open door of the car, more out of reflex than wisdom, and ran full force toward the masked man in her parking lot. From there, it was chaos, and no one really knew what was happening. Everyone had a different concern in mind, and went after different targets while they avoided their pursuers at the same time.

Kevin was after the masked man, red rage in his eyes. The masked man, Regis, was still chasing Susan, his ultimate goal to get a hold of her so he might regain the incredible amount of goods and money that were rightfully his. Susan ran from all of them, heading first for Angela's garage, then turning toward the street when she realized there would be nowhere to go once she got in there. She was truly terrified at the thought of Regis catching her.

Angela's only concern was Susan. She watched in horror as the hulking black figure behind her caught up easily with her scurrying steps. She shifted, but there was nowhere for her to go. The street seemed far away, and what would she do when she got to it? Run in and keep going forever? The man would surely catch her.

Kevin was there, however, and with swift, powerful steps, he was set upon catching this criminal. "Police! Freeze!"

Regis Black turned, if only for a second, to see how close Kevin Larsen was. How the hell had Larsen gotten involved in this? He was supposed to be retired!

Abandoning Susan suddenly, out of necessity, Regis turned into the garage of Angela's building. Before Kevin could adjust to this unexpected change, one of the large garage doors was opening, and the black car that had been waiting to kidnap Angela a short while ago came crashing out. It was aimed directly at Kevin at first, intimidating him to a halt, then was purposely turned away from him when Kevin reared back to avoid being hit. The car was aimed directly at Susan then, who was almost to the street now, racing away, thinking Regis was still behind her on foot.

One of the back doors of the Buick was opened slightly, and from Angela's vantage point she could see that with one sweep the man inside would have Susan securely ensconced within that car.

"Susan! Behind you! Run, run toward me!" Angela bolted from the car with that scream, once again not having a plan, but intent on Susan's safety. Susan reached for that voice. Terror guided her, and all she could hear was the security present within that voice. Angela's face came into view as she stumbled into the street.

Susan never even knew the car was behind her. With a sickening, merciless shriek, Regis' car swung in front of Susan, and ground to a stop, trapping her as she skidded before it. Primal desperation overshadowed her.

Regis jumped out and moved toward Susan in lion-like, predatory rage while Susan backed up cautiously as if any sudden move would cause him to accurately lay hold of her. All the while, she watched his eyes in knowing horror, but, oddly, his eyes didn't hold the malice she expected. Instead, there was a gentle sort of pain, an agony of the soul, and it gave her pause, if only for a second.

Angela didn't see it. She stopped short in gut-wrenching horror. She couldn't move for several seconds as it registered upon her battered senses that Susan had been caught. The Buick loomed in front of her as if it were the only thing present on earth. It looked huge, monstrous and heartless.

Kevin, too, reared from uselessly chasing the car, trying, if nothing else, to get a license plate number and accurately assess the model and make of the car. He watched helplessly from his distance as he saw Susan's retreat, only able to glimpse the side of her face from his angle, but seeing her panic and fear nonetheless. He could see the masked man's reaction perfectly, however, and he stared curiously. It was Angela's screaming that finally penetrated the haze that had momentarily doused him. Her scream, and the sight of her, running in outrage toward the masked man.

With exasperated alarm, and a guttural howl of his own, he ran straight toward the scene, purposely trying to divert attention away from Angela. It worked for everyone. The entire party seemed to stop to watch Kevin run toward them, protective ferocity emanating from each pounding step he took. His gun was waving out in front of him more like a sword, but no less aimed at the man in his ridiculous mask. Regis jumped back into the car in jolted shock, and in seconds the car screeched off down the street with grinding tires and unquestionable speed.

"Get in the car!" Kevin howled, not missing a step. Angela rushed to obey, suddenly wondering if she might have done something wrong by the way he was growling.

"Where's the girl?" Kevin barked as he started the car.

Angela looked around. "She's gone!" It was a desperate observation.

Kevin didn't even blink. He was racing down the street after that Buick. If he could only get his hands on the men inside of it, he knew he'd have the whole *Racer* industry with them. As he sailed onward, though, his surroundings were ominously quiet, and when he connected with the traffic of the main road, which Angela's quiet, upscale street veered off of, there was no black Buick, no criminals to be seen, and no Susan Ventry.

~ *Chapter Nineteen* ~

Kevin wished everything could have gone differently. He wished fervently that he could have held onto the drama that had just erupted before him, but he couldn't have. He'd only come here this morning to *meet* Angela, and here he was, caught in a battle for her life. What would have happened if he hadn't been here?

He looked over at her now, with her huge, round eyes, and a forced quiet that did little to hide the shock and terror of what she'd found herself in. Could she, Angela Cahn, possibly be racing down the street in a car-chase, pursuing a huge Niagara Falls drug dealer? No, this couldn't be - but it was.

"They didn't get Susan," she said in distinct relief. Kevin had stopped the car in the parking lot of a donut shop, and his eyes were upon her.

"No, and we didn't get them, either."

"Oh... I'm sorry."

"No, you're not. You're just glad Ventry got away."

"Can we go back and try to find her? Maybe those guys are waiting somewhere to get her."

"I doubt that. *Those guys* are long gone into that traffic." Kevin pointed toward the growing line of mid morning traffic that seemed to fill the air with tense heat.

"Well, maybe we could find her."

"You're really worried about that kid, aren't you?"

"Yes, I am."

"Are you sure you only met her the other day? You two seem to have quite a connection going."

Angela looked at him sharply, thinking he doubted her story. "Yes, I only met her the other day. Still, I am very concerned for her. Don't start thinking..."

"Whoa, whoa, whoa," Kevin interrupted with an amused smile. "I'm not accusing you of anything. Actually, I'm well aware that during a crisis situation people who don't even know each other often become instantly and remarkably bonded for life. You're just very special in your particular loyalty."

There was that look again. "Oh... I'm sorry... I just want her to be all right so badly, and she almost got herself caught trying to help *me*. What was she even doing out there?"

"Actually, Angela, we can't rule out the possibility that she was there with your attacker by choice."

Angela looked at him sharply again, this time with savage denial and shock in her eyes. She had such beautifully expressive eyes...

"That's *not* what was happening! I will not believe that Susan was a party to having me abducted!"

"Why not?" It was a goading question.

"Because... she *wouldn't!* It's something you just don't understand. I believe her, and I trust her, and she trusts me."

"Yet, you went to the police when she begged you not to; made you promise not to."

Angela was outraged and hurt by this seeming accusation. *"That - was - different!"* She enunciated each word as if they were being carved out of rock. "I did that to protect her, and me, because there was nothing else I could do. And I didn't just *call the police*, I called *one detective*, who I knew I could *trust!*"

"Maybe she thinks the same thing." It was a gentle, revealing statement that shed light on his point, and silenced Angela. She looked directly at him, a tormented expression on her face as she waited for him to expound on his theory.

"Maybe she thinks that if she listens to her bosses, or if she connects you with the right people, that they won't harm you. I'm not saying she isn't genuine, I'm just saying that she might be playing by a completely different set of rules than you. It seems obvious that she doesn't want you hurt, otherwise she wouldn't have put her own life in danger by calling out to you when that bastard was going to shoot you. Like it or not, though, she was the main contact person for the first *Racer* deal, commissioned by Regis Black himself. She's not an innocent.

"I know it seems like all drug dealers should be obviously ugly, evil, black souls, but they aren't. Sometimes they're just kids, mixed up with the wrong people and the wrong ideas. Not that that makes them any less guilty.

"Think about it... She was in that shed with your attacker, then when he's about to shoot you, she calls out your name and runs toward the garage. It's not like there was anywhere to hide in there. Unbeknownst to us, however, the car your assailant was using was parked in there. It stands to reason that she was trying to reach it to get away from the man she had just betrayed by calling out to you."

Angela closed her eyes, enlightened and confused at the same time. What Kevin said made sense. Why else would Susan have been with that man in her parking lot after not being seen for over three days? "Do you think, then, that she is still involved with those people? If she is, then that would mean she betrayed Detective

Linden on purpose, and drew them to him. In that case, she might not have killed him, but she may as well have because she caused it. Do you think that's what happened?"

"Everything right now is speculation, but it's very possible."

"But she told me she had nothing to do with the murder..." Angela said desperately, confusedly.

Kevin just looked at her: One long, knowing look that made her feel as if she were being incredibly gullible. "Do you really think she would have confessed?" he asked. It was a gentle, genuine question.

"I don't know. At the time I felt she could have told me anything... I thought she was being completely honest."

"What exactly did she say?"

"She just told me she was innocent, and I told her I knew that because I'd seen the murder. Then I asked her if she had anything to do with those officers, and she said... She said *no.*" Angela's voice grew in strength until her eyes shone with hard confidence. "She said they weren't good cops, and that she wasn't involved! I believe her!" Absolute conviction radiated from Angela's face now, along with a slightly rebellious challenge for him to try to prove her wrong.

"I don't know all of what she was involved in, but I believe she was trying to get free of it, and that she had nothing to do with Detective Linden's murder. If you'll remember, *he* was trying to kill *her,* not the other way around. If anyone was guilty that night, it was Linden!"

"Linden was shot full of *Racer,* Angela, and not by choice as far as we can see. Someone drugged him, probably trying to kill him. What if that was Susan Ventry?"

"That's impossible, she was in shock over his actions. If she'd have drugged him, she wouldn't have been surprised by it."

"Unless the amount pumped into him was intended to kill him. Maybe she was shocked because he was still alive."

"She did *not* kill Linden!"

On a deep, cleansing sort of breath, Kevin asked her quietly, "How can you be one-hundred-percent sure she's innocent?"

Angela stopped and thought about that for a second. "Are you one-hundred-percent sure she's guilty?"

"...No."

Angela stared out the window as the line of traffic thinned out dramatically with the simple changing of the traffic light. "I guess I can't be completely sure, but there was something about her, Kevin; something innocent and vulnerable that can't be faked, you know? She was terrified the night she came to me, and so hopeful, too. I could see it then, without even knowing anything about her.

"It's almost like my perception is tainted *now,* when I know some of the facts, and when I knew nothing, my intuition was right. When she walked into my store, she belonged to me. I can't explain it. It was almost like I was commissioned by some higher authority to make sure this one soul was kept safe. As if she were the daughter I never had."

It suddenly struck Kevin that he knew very little about Angela Cahn. Why had a woman like her not had a chance to have children? Michael had told him she was a widow, but why had she remained unattached? At the same time, her quiet, sincere words melted his resolve because he understood exactly what she meant.

He'd relied on fact more often than not in his line of work, but it had always, *always* been the gut feeling within that was most accurate. Sometimes it took the facts to realize that he'd known them all along, but when facts came in direct conflict with instinct, and instinct still held its beliefs, it was something to be heeded. In a way, he was feeling some of the same things right now about Angela that she had felt about Susan: An instant connection, a commissioning to guard and protect, and a knowledge of this woman's soul that transcended the knowledge of the mind.

Suddenly, it was very quiet in the car as they looked around themselves. "I understand what you mean," Kevin said, bringing Angela back into the conversation with an easy tone.

"I have to know if she's innocent, Kevin. Please, can't we just try to find out if she's truly involved before we tell the police she was with my attacker today? It all sounds so convincing: He was there, she was there, I was being attacked. Everybody is already questioning her validity. Can't we please try? I promise if she's guilty, I'll work just as hard to try to bring her in, but if she's innocent..."

"Angela..." he was obviously struggling with her plea, "that's illegal."

"It is?"

"Yes. I have to submit pertinent evidence to the proper authorities."

"Why? You're not a policeman anymore."

He looked shocked. "It's still illegal, they call it Obstruction of Justice. Besides that, my own son-in-law is heading up this case. To withhold information would be an extreme insult to him."

"Oh. I didn't think of that."

Silence filled the air.

"On the other hand, he did ask me to help, outside of police business."

She looked up hopefully. "Oh, Kevin, couldn't we just go look for her? She can't have gone far, and if we find her, we can question her and decide what's best. It can't be obstructing justice to simply *talk* to a murder suspect."

"No, it's not. In fact, I was going to go after her anyway, but not with the intention of seeing if she's *innocent...*" His voice was wry, but his expression was capitulating. "What if we find her?"

"Like I said, we can decide what to do then."

"It's still wrong," he said, but he was already starting the car and pointedly redirecting it back toward Angela's condo. When he turned out of the donut shop parking lot, Angela smiled and reached to touch his arm very gently, relief and gratitude in her eyes. "Thank you," she said sincerely. Then she faced forward, and set herself firmly toward the next part of the journey.

~ *Chapter Twenty* ~

Angela's heart was pounding, her knees shaking, and her eyes were shining with certain elation. Perhaps it was wrong, she thought, to be reacting to this situation with such thrill, but creeping stealthily around behind her building, watching quietly as if they weren't really there, was making her feel as though she'd stepped into some sort of James Bond movie. It was far from the predictability of her daily routine, and the man she was with was so very good at it. His eyes were everywhere at once, and his ears could pick up the slightest sound. She felt positively sneaky, and she found herself thoroughly alive with sly excitement.

She stood behind Kevin, straining to peer around his large frame to see what he was seeing. It was useless. "What's happening?" she asked, a bit of exasperation escaping her as she choked back her exhilaration.

"Nothing, all I see right now is your parking lot. But hold tight there, Special Agent Cahn," he teased, sensing her exaggerated excitement with a smile, "there's nowhere for her to have gone around here except down the street in the direction that Buick went, or jump in the river and take a ride over The Falls. My guess is she won't want to do either. If she's been hanging around here on her own, she'll come back sooner or later."

"What if she doesn't?"

"Then we lost our lead, and we start over again."

"Oh, that can't happen, we'll never find her then," Angela cried in a genuinely despairing singsong voice.

Kevin looked back at her for a second, intrigued once again. "We'll find her," he said quietly, his own resolve coming through. He was beginning to want to believe in Susan Ventry's innocence almost as much as Angela did. He was determined to find her, and give her a fair chance, if for no other reason, because Angela wanted him to so very badly.

She held back any more wailing, and looked into Kevin's face. If he said they would find her, they *would* find her. Angela was sure of it. He turned again to peruse the parking lot.

"Bingo!" he said as his eyes scanned the area a short while later.

"What?"

"No offense, but your friend isn't too bright. She should have at least waited until it was dark out."

"Is she there?"

"Yep, running straight for that shed."

Angela bullied her way around him now, determined to see what he was seeing. Sure enough, there was Susan, nervously glancing around herself and making a quick, trotting walk toward the shed in Angela's parking lot.

"What should we do?"

"I'm not really sure. We can't just jump her or she may scream bloody murder and get us all caught. I'll have to sneak up behind her and try to convince her we're the good guys before she makes a scene. Let's sit back for a minute and see what she does. If she comes close to us, it'll make it easy."

"If she sees me, I think she'll be all right. Why don't I just go up to her and try to talk to her? It won't look so bad for a woman to approach a woman, and I don't think she'll scream or make a fuss with me."

Kevin thought about that. "All right, but listen carefully, Detective Cahn. You have to follow the plan as closely as possible for it to work. You approach her, get her talking to you, and get her out of sight, preferably inside that shed so she can't bolt away from you. I'll go get the car and pull up to the building. Your job is to convince her to get in quietly, like nothing is wrong, okay?"

"Yes. I can do that. I know she won't run from me."

"Okay. Good luck. If anything goes wrong, keep yourself safe until I get there."

"Okay."

Kevin crept back toward the far end of the building with the most amazing stealth Angela had ever seen. He stopped and looked at her just before he turned and disappeared around the corner, on his way toward the street. His car was hidden in the parking lot of another apartment building a few hundred feet down the road.

Angela turned back toward the corner of the building, watching Susan trot nervously through the parking lot. There was that feeling again. Her stomach felt as if she were tipping over the edge of a roller coaster. She couldn't move for a minute, completely overwhelmed with this spine-tingling experience and the important task ahead.

Susan had entered the shed. Now was the time. Angela ran through the parking lot, trying to make her tiny frame move as quietly as Kevin's huge one had just a moment ago. It was insultingly impossible to achieve. Nevertheless, she made it to the door of the shed while Susan was still inside and occupied within. She jerked her head around violently when she heard Angela approach, and for a moment Angela truly thought the young woman was going to pull out a weapon and kill her by the harsh look in her eyes.

Angela entered the shed quickly. "Susan, it's Angela."

"Angela?" Relief washed over Susan in a great, weakening rush. "I thought you went after - that man."

"We did, but we didn't find him. I came back to see if you're all right."

A distinctive quiver started in Susan's lip, and her face seemed to crumble in waving sections, as if she felt herself falling apart, then tried hard to regain control, but ended up falling apart again anyway. "I - I don't think I am." She bent low and clutched a dark green gym bag to her chest as if it were the only sure thing in her life. "Are you okay?"

Angela's lip began to quiver the exact same way Susan's had, except she didn't fight it, and it came from a heart of compassion rather than confusion and fear. "Yes, I have a friend who is helping me. He wants to help you, too."

To Angela's complete bafflement, Susan backed against the wall of the shed as if Angela were pointing a gun at her. "No, I don't want his help, I have to get out of here."

"Susan, stop running, can't you see there's nowhere for you to go? We can help you."

"He's a cop, isn't he?"

"No! He's not a cop!" she replied, as if being a police officer was an ultimately distasteful offense. "I mean - he was, but he's not anymore, and he's one of the good guys. Susan, you've got to believe me."

"If he's a good guy, then he can't help me." It was the most desperate, heartbreaking statement Angela had ever heard, because it came from absolute conviction and utter rejection of herself. Angela wanted to physically silence her from speaking that way.

"Susan! You stop that! I mean it! He can help you, and I don't care what anybody says, you are *not* one of them."

The last shred of strength Susan held onto cracked with that statement. Angela had been so kind to her, and believed in her so much. Oddly, that very kindness was breaking her. If Angela had only rejected her, yelled at her, looked at her with the disdain she felt she deserved, then she could have gone on being strong. This love, however, this belief in her innocence when she truly hadn't wanted to be guilty, was her undoing. Great, gulping tears wracked her body, and her entire frame seemed to surrender. Just for a moment.

Behind Angela, the sight of Kevin's car suddenly appeared in looming shadow, and Susan stiffened. Without any warning at all, she made a desperate screeching sort of cry, and bolted toward the door, running right into Angela, and nearly knocking her down to get past her. She was running through the parking lot, and away from Kevin before Angela knew what had happened.

Luckily, Kevin had seen this coming and was prepared. With one flying leap, he got out of the car, grabbed a hold of Susan's streaking form, and the two went sprawling to the ground. Taking huge, deep breaths, Kevin jumped up as quickly as he could regain himself, looking down at Susan with intense concern. "Are you all right?" His hand was stretching forward, unsure whether he should help her up, or insist that she lie still.

Susan looked completely stunned, but in a matter of seconds she, too, jumped up. Her elbow and shoulder were badly scraped and bruised, but she was unaware of the pain. She took one look into Kevin's knowing eyes as he settled his hands on her shoulders in a calming gesture, and turned around to dive away from him. She hadn't taken two steps before he caught her and restrained her entire body with one firm grip around her waist.

"Hold on there, you. You're not going anywhere."

"Susan, please let us help you." It was Angela again, and Susan stopped flailing to look at her, confusion and desperation in her eyes. Then, with a sob, she dropped her head, and finally relaxed in complete surrender.

Kevin seemed to be the only one aware that they were in a parking lot where gunshots and commotion had undoubtedly been heard and reported less than two hours ago. Anyone might be observing this drama. With that risk in mind, he pushed everyone quickly toward his car and pulled away from the scene as soon as he sensed Susan's willingness to come along. Angela sat in back with Susan, shielding her in a motherly hold while they allowed Kevin to take them away from everything.

"I'm so glad you're all right. I was so worried about you," Angela said sincerely, shaky tears in her eyes.

"Me too... Oh, Angela, I'll never be able to get out of all this trouble." Susan finally collapsed with this wail, and Kevin looked at her desperate form in his rearview mirror as she burrowed herself into Angela.

"Yes, you will, yes, you will. We'll help you get out of this, but you have to tell us what's going on. Everything, so Kevin can stop this for you."

"I tried, I really tried to do what was right, and it all fell apart on me."

"I know, I know it seems that way, but you've got to listen to me. Kevin is a friend, he's a retired police officer, and I have another friend who is a narcotics investigator. He wants to know the truth, and he wants to help you. I promise, they can keep you safe."

Susan looked up toward the mirror, where she could feel Kevin's gaze upon her. It was a candid look, a searching one. "I'm not innocent," she said, weeping with confession to both of them, but directly speaking to Kevin, "but I swear to you, I didn't know what I was doing. I'm so sorry."

Unbidden, a protective compassion filled Kevin. He saw the stark torment in this young woman's eyes. It was desperate, pleading and real.

He believed, beyond a doubt, that she was innocent. He knew, too, his duty in this matter; and that to save this young woman, and ensure Angela's safety, he would go far above, and beyond, the call of duty.

~ *Chapter Twenty-one* ~

By the time Kevin pulled into his driveway, he realized that a tremendous conflict was now set before him. Susan Ventry was wanted for questioning. He was an ex-police officer. He knew what he was supposed to do. He was supposed to turn her over, and allow Michael and the DEA to do their job. She would be questioned, and her information would be used to stifle *Racer*. That was good, that was what was supposed to happen. Michael could be trusted implicitly to carry through on that fairly.

So, why did it *not* seem like an immediate option? Why did Kevin's entire being rear up against the idea of giving Susan over to anyone until he could prove her case? Whatever that actually was.

His garage door opened at the press of a button, and in seconds they were sheathed within the room's darkness. It was only when the door closed with finality that Kevin began to breathe normally. He hadn't been followed, he'd watched closely to make sure of that, but it wouldn't really matter if he had been. Whoever was underneath that mask had known him. His home could be easily pinpointed, especially if these criminals had access to the precinct computer system, which Kevin strongly suspected they did. They would soon discover that he had Susan Ventry, and his home would not be safe for very long.

What a treacherous position he was leaving himself in. He'd threatened a band of drug dealers, and was now about to alienate himself from Michael and the police who would side with him against those dealers. There was no protection in this no-man's-land he'd created. To think, this morning he had nothing to do but wax his boat.

"Ladies... I hope you enjoyed the ride."

"Where are we?" Susan asked suspiciously.

Kevin smiled. What did this child hope to accomplish with her smart distrust? "We're at my home, young lady."

Susan and Angela both looked around themselves. It was a typically dark, functional garage, complete with tools, shovels and lawn equipment pushed neatly to the sides of the walls, and a bicycle hanging from a hook in the middle of the far wall.

"Would you two like to get out or shall we sit in here all day?" Kevin smirked. His humor was genuine, and Angela caught it, smiling herself as she began to move, guiding Susan along with her.

Kevin opened a small door inside the garage and allowed them to pass ahead of him, into the living room of his home. "Make yourselves comfortable, ladies, is there anything I can get for you? A cool drink or anything?"

"No, thank you," they both replied, almost in harmony, and sat down wearily on the couch. Susan was following Angela's every lead, and it was obvious as she looked around at this typically middle class home that she was awed by it. Indeed, to her this small house seemed magnificent, even extravagant, and was everything she had ever dreamed of living in. Kevin watched her, and found himself looking around too, at the nice but ultimately unimpressive things he saw everyday of his life. Somehow, through this little lady's eyes, they seemed awing. Again, a touch of compassion laid hold of him.

Angela, too, looked around with distinct interest as she entered Kevin's home. It was woodsy and comfortable. Windows were everywhere, and stunning visions of the woodlands surrounding the house made her feel as if she were camping outdoors, rather than in the middle of a semi-residential part of town. The living room, where they were now, had an amazing wall of sheer glass at the far end to heighten that impression. It gave way to a deck, and the whole room seemed to be placed in the middle of the woods. It was gorgeous.

"You have a beautiful home," Angela said shakily as Susan drew to her side in a slightly clinging posture. She clearly didn't know what to expect.

"Thanks. I just moved in last year. It's the kind of place I always wanted, but could never really afford until... I retired," he said, disregarding a certain mystery about the comment. He looked steadily at the women, observing Susan's wide-eyed awe and distrust, and Angela's motherly reassurance. They continued to stare at him, expecting something, but unsure exactly what.

Pursing his lips, he walked purposefully into his dining room and came back with a chair, setting it down directly in front of Susan. She and Angela tracked his every move as if he were performing an act in a play for them. He turned the chair backwards and straddled it. It had an imprisoning effect on Susan. With a direct look that carefully displayed none of the compassion grinding at his soul, Kevin said, "So, young lady, what do you have to say for yourself?"

Susan gaped at him in frightened reverence. She didn't know what to say, or more accurately, what he wanted her to say. She felt like an errant child being scolded by her father. A father she'd longed for, with tough brown eyes, and an understanding that he was trying to hide. With an almost dreamy, curious smile, she asked, "About what?" It was an actual question, not a smart-mouthed reply. She genuinely needed him to define which of the many things he wanted her to explain.

Kevin leaned back slightly, readjusting his position, and wondering about her strange expression. "Let's start with today, and then go backward, okay? What was going on at Angela's building today?"

"I only know what I saw. Regis was - "

"Regis?" Kevin interrupted, purposely drawing specifics from her.

Susan nodded. "Yes, Regis Black is what he calls himself, I don't know if it's his real name."

"Okay, go on."

"I've been hiding in that maintenance shed by Angela's apartment building since - the other night. I just wanted to make sure nothing bad happened to her." She looked at Angela, whose eyes were filled with understanding and pity for Susan's situation. "Anyway, today I saw him go into the garage and start harassing her, then I saw you come and help her. Who are you?"

"My name is Kevin Larsen."

"He's a retired policeman, Susan," Angela explained yet again.

"I figured you had to be something like that. Anyway, that's all I know about today."

"If you were hiding in the shed and saw Black go in, didn't you also know he came back and hid the car in the garage?"

"No. When you chased him out of the garage the first time, this morning when he tried to kidnap Angela, I ran away for a while because I thought he might have seen me. When I came back, you were taking Angela to your car."

"And you had no idea Black was still there, or that he hid his car in Angela's garage?"

"No, I swear I didn't know."

Kevin considered that for a moment with a hard, furrowed brow, attempting to remain impartial. "All right... what about the other night? What happened to Detective Linden?"

Susan's lip began to quiver. "He was supposed to help me."

"With what?"

She hesitated openly, then her words came out in a choked, painful whisper. "Get away from Regis."

"Why *didn't* he help you?"

"Because he was strung out, that's why!" she spat belligerently, obviously confused and hurt by Linden's betrayal. "We were supposed to meet together, and I was - supposed to tell him what I knew."

"You were supposed to meet at Armondo's?"

"Yes."

"What happened?"

"When I got there, he was leaning against the wall, sort of laying his head on it, you know? I knew right away he was stoned. When I said who I was, he jumped up and ran toward me... really weird... like he was looking right at me, but he couldn't see me - like I shocked him. He kept shaking like he was real confused - definitely strung out. I didn't know what to think, I was going to turn around and leave because I figured for sure he was one of Regis' men after all, but he stopped and asked me for the information I had, like he remembered all of a sudden. I gave him an envelope that I put together purposely to give to him - "

"An envelope?" Kevin interrupted intensely.

"Yes."

"What was in it?"

"Information about Regis and his men. There's a tape of them talking about business. They're all laughing and acting like they're going to be millionaires and stuff. I taped it the day before the meeting was supposed to take place. Marty, Nick, Goldie, and Regis are on it, and they're talking about how much PCP is to be delivered, how long it will take to manufacture the *Racer*, how Goldie was to watch the lab and make sure they were never caught... stuff like that. I also put the formula for *Racer* in there."

"A formula?"

"Yes, when Regis agreed to fund *Racer*, he made Nick write down the formula and give it to me. I was supposed to give it to Regis, but I never did, and he must have forgotten to ask for it. I put it in the envelope."

"Oh, God... that's why they wanted it back so bad. We need that envelope, Susan. Where is it?"

"I gave it to Linden... He grabbed it, and then... I don't know what happened to him - he just went crazy. He started pacing like a caged lion, and then he threw it across the room and started coming after me. That's when I really knew he must be working for Regis, and I had just been caught. So, I ran, and that's when Angela saw me in the parking lot with him. I never saw the envelope again after that."

Kevin closed his eyes in denial, knowing this piece had been lost. Regis didn't have the envelope, though, because he had specifically harassed Angela for it. Could it still be at Armondo's? Only a profound miracle could have kept it there this long. If it was, Michael could find it. That would be a tremendous break. On the other hand, if Regis and his men knew about it, and hadn't found it, it probably wasn't there. In that case, where was it?

"What about before that night?" he asked Susan sensitively, knowingly. "What exactly is it that you know? Why did you need to get away from Regis?"

Susan's gaze shot to Kevin worriedly. Retired or not this man was undoubtedly still a police officer, and however good and kind he might have been up until this point, he was still a danger to her in harsh reality. "I was... well... I was a runner for him..." Susan's eyes fell away in shame.

Angela's face dropped, and her eyes filled with a masked disdain. Her hopes that all of Kevin's theories about Susan were just unfortunate mistakes plummeted to the ground. The love and concern she had labored with for this young woman diminished into fragments with this admission.

Until Susan saw it, and began to speak. She couldn't bear to lose Angela. Not her love, concern, and respect. She must make her understand why she'd done it all. She must make her see that she wasn't as evil and ugly as it sounded. She was so, so sorry. "I swear to you I didn't know. I didn't know until he told me that's what I'd been doing."

"How could you *not* know something like that?"

Susan sighed deeply. "I don't know, I guess... I probably knew something was wrong, but I never guessed it was as bad as it really was. You see, I... he... we... were lovers." Angela looked away in embarrassment, more so because of Susan's reaction than because of her actual admission. She seemed profoundly ashamed, and afraid of the way they might view her because of this revelation.

Kevin, too, looked away, certainly not shocked, but sensing the feminine discomfort, and thinking how young she seemed to be engaging in a relationship at that level. "How old are you, Susan?" he asked.

"I turned eighteen in September."

Well, technically she was old enough. "How old is Regis Black?"

"Twenty-seven."

Kevin looked at Angela. A distinct glare laced her eyes as she connected with him. A twenty-seven year old man with an eighteen-year-old college freshman? Heaven only knew what kind of manipulation had taken place.

"Where are your parents while all of this is going on?"

"I used to live with my grandmother. She's in a nursing home now. My mother is an alcoholic, I haven't seen her in years, and I never knew my father."

"How did you meet Regis?"

"He used to hang around the college - Niagara Community - and I met him there."

"You attend Niagara Community?"

"Yes, this is my first semester. I have an educational pass that allows me to go there. That's why Regis was so nice to me: Because I could get back and forth into Canada everyday without Customs getting suspicious. I was so blind. I really thought he loved me.

"He used to give me large gold envelopes, and I was to deliver them to a man named Max. We met in an alley off Ontario Street. He was really weird - I was afraid of him, but Regis used to say I was under his protection and that Max would never hurt me because of that." She scoffed at the notion with a sniff now. "He was right, I was under his protection, and Max never touched me, but I used to think that was such a wonderful, heroic thing to say. Like I was his lady, and he was my knight. What a blind fool I was. He knew exactly what to say, and how to say it, to make me do whatever he wanted.

"Anyway, I'd give my envelope to Max, and he'd give his envelope, or several envelopes, to me. Then I'd cross the border with them and deliver them to Regis. I never knew what was inside, and I never asked, even though, to be honest, I knew it had to be something illegal."

Kevin looked downward thoughtfully. "How did you finally find out for sure?"

Susan took a shaky breath. "Regis made me go to... I don't know what it was... an old warehouse in the city, a drug house I guess. He made me watch these people all strung out on drugs. In fact, that's where I first saw Detective Linden. He was a kind of bouncer at this place. He looked the same as everyone else, but different, you know? Something about him was different.

"Anyway, we could see everything inside the room because there was a glass window looking into it. I don't think the people inside could see us, though. It was kind of like an old conference room, where you walked into the reception room first, then you could look into this other room from there. Regis and I stayed in the office part, and this other guy, Marty, was talking about this new drug that he had. I guess Regis was going to start giving him money and drugs to produce it, but he wanted to see how everyone reacted to it first.

"You wouldn't believe what was going on in this room... it was disgusting. Marty walked right in, and started waving this drug around, and everyone got crazy almost knocking him down to try to get some of it. Then he came back in the reception room and said to watch these guys in the corner who were playing cards. He said he'd given them more than everyone else because he wanted Regis to see that it made them stronger.

"It made them go *crazy*. They started fighting with each other, and smashing things. I wanted to get out of there, but Regis made me stay and watch. Then this one guy started beating another guy up really bad. I mean, he wouldn't stop, he just kept beating him and beating him while everyone cheered. It made me sick. I really thought I was going to throw up. How can people be so... *mean*? She shook her head, a bit preoccupied and saddened.

Kevin and Angela sat frozen with interest, their wide, riveted eyes giving Susan a sense of purpose as she continued. "Then the bouncer, Linden, finally came and told the guy to quit fighting or take it outside because he was afraid the cops would hear all the noise. The guy stopped, but his friend wasn't moving. I think he killed him, and I think Linden thought so, too, because he just kept watching him, waiting for him to move, and the kid just laid there.

"I don't know what ended up happening to him because we finally left, but when I told Regis that night that I didn't want to be a part of this, he told me that I already was a part. He said I'd been transporting drugs across the border for four months, and he could prove it. He wanted me as his contact person for this new drug - *Racer*, they called it. They were going to begin shipping large amounts of PCP in from Max to make it. Linden was the runner, Marty and his sidekick, Nick, manufactured it, and I was to make payments and deliveries to each party.

"I noticed Linden the night that kid was beat up, and I checked him out. Actually, Regis wanted me to check on him for a few days, and I saw him go into the police station the day before our meeting. I knew if he was going in and out of the police station he had to be a cop, and then I was *really* scared. So, I took off. I just drove straight down the highway toward Toronto.

"Then I started thinking how easy it would be for Regis to catch me with all his connections. I mean, where would I hide? Regis had cops, criminals - everyone - on his side. I had nothing. I knew he would kill me for betraying him... I was so scared and confused, I finally turned around and decided the only way out was to call Linden. We arranged to meet, and the rest is history."

"And after he was killed you stayed in Angela's shed?"

"Yes, for the most part. I didn't want to cross the border that late at night in case word had already gotten out about Linden's murder: I thought for sure they would have called it in and reported me. Customs would have picked me up in minutes."

"You thought *they* would have reported you? Whose they?"

"The cops that run with Regis, and The Judge, who gives them all their ways in and out of whatever they need."

"A judge?"

"Yes, I don't know his name, but he's connected somehow. I've heard Regis and Goldie laughing about it. I think Regis gets money from him."

"You know for sure that officers, *and a judge*, are involved in this?"

"Yes, I met the cops, and I saw them kill Linden. If you don't believe me ask Angela, she saw it too."

Kevin looked at Angela, and she nodded as if this might be startling new information for Kevin. "I believe you, Susan, what I want to know is, are you sure that real police officers are involved, and that these same officers killed Linden the other night?"

"Yes. They were the same ones. They work for Regis. After he tricked me into this, Regis did everything he could to make me know *exactly* what went on. The one cop's name is Goldie, I think he's Regis' relative or something, and Goldie's partner is in on it, too. He said the whole department was loaded with cops who wanted to profit by the *Racer* deal."

"Well, that isn't true at all," Kevin interjected defensively. "Although I'm sure some officers are in on it, the precinct isn't loaded with drug pushers. I know one investigator for sure whose department is not dirty. Were you supposed to drop drugs to Linden the night he was killed?"

Susan looked surprised for a moment that he would be aware of things on that level. "No, I had a shipment of PCP that I was supposed to drop to Marty so he could start making *Racer*, and a payment Marty gave me the other day that I was supposed to drop to Max after the meeting. See, Nick keeps all the accounts, and they sort of figure out all the ratios and agree on a price before anything is delivered, so Marty can't cheat. Like, say Max sends two thousand dollars worth of PCP; then he expects - I don't know - something like five thousand dollars in return, no matter what. If Marty can double and triple the prices and make fifteen thousand out of it, that's his business, but eventually Regis knows what's going on, and then expects more, so it all evens out, even though everyone knows Marty is a scam artist.

"They would make payments to me three times a week. I've been doing this for months without knowing it - back and forth - except now Regis makes sure he tells me *everything,* even things I don't want to know about. *Especially* things I don't want to know about. I'm the one who's supposed to deal directly with Marty to oversee it all.

"So, Marty gave me the first direct payment day before yesterday. I was to divide the money in half and give one half to Regis, and the other half to Max. The night of the meeting, I was to collect anything more that Marty had, and meet with Linden so we could set up a distribution time. It would have taken Marty about a week to prepare everything."

"What about the crack needed to make *Racer*? Where does that come from?" Kevin asked, intently interested in this detailed description of the operation.

"I guess Regis has access to cocaine from this side," she said, meaning the American side of the border. "Then Marty makes the crack. I think the PCP was a problem to get a hold of, because I heard Marty tell Regis once that if he can just keep getting him 'the dust', everything would be fine."

"Apparently Max has access to 'dust'?" It was part question, part statement, as Kevin's mind absorbed everything. Susan nodded affirmatively. The whole operation was both complicated and overly simple, and Kevin had to concentrate to get his facts straight. Angela just sat staring, slack-jawed, and unable to believe, or possibly comprehend, what was being said. If the facts being disclosed weren't so utterly important, Kevin would have had to laugh at her expression. As it stood, there was absolutely nothing to laugh about.

"All right," he said, shifting into an even more straightforward position before Susan. His forearms rested on the edge of the chairback so that his entire torso leaned intimidatingly forward, and his eyes were searching and absorbed. "Let me get this straight. Max supplies Regis with the PCP; right?"

"Right," Susan answered evenly.

"Regis supplies Marty with the cocaine *and* PCP; right?"

"Right."

"Marty then creates *Racer* out of it; right?"

Susan's lips twitched slightly, wanting to smile at his deliberate, organized repetition. "Right."

"Regis and Max, then, split the profits in half; right?"

Her lips twitched further. "Right."

"So, they obviously have the money to secure the stuff in the first place," he smiled at her stiff, observing form as she tried not to laugh at him; "right?"

She smiled back full force, then sobered. "Right. They fund everything, and therefore, feel that they own everything. At least I know Regis feels that way, I've never talked much to Max."

Kevin sighed with a sense of knowing, and sat up straight again. His eyes narrowed, and in a disgusted, sarcastic tone, he said finally, "And you're the little go-between that makes it all happen... right?"

She looked down, twisting her hands in her lap in nervous shame, and answered quietly, "Right."

Kevin looked at her sensitively, his eyes sparking with realization. "But you never made the drop that night, did you?"

"No."

"So, what did you do with all that PCP?"

"I hid it."

He smiled proudly, as if she were his child, and had just performed an incredible feat. "Where?"

"In the basement of my apartment building."

He took a deep, quiet breath and held it for dear life, hoping against hope that she hid her package well. Everything was on such a time chase with this case, and Susan's apartment would be easy for Black to access. "Is it safe there?"

"Yes, I think so. There's a loose board in the ceiling. I put it inside, you can't even tell it's there."

Kevin let out his breath. "Okay, what about the money?"

Susan hesitated for a moment, then reached down at her feet to present the green gym bag she'd risked everything to go back to the maintenance shed for. She'd known it was dangerous to go back, although she'd been afraid of Regis showing up again, not Angela. She'd been clutching the thing since she'd gotten in Kevin's car. He knew before he ever opened it what was inside. When he saw the stacks of money crammed within, he smiled genuinely at Susan with an approval she cherished.

Then he looked at Angela and spoke. "We need to let Michael know about this."

"What's going to happen to her?"

He seemed to reflect on that disturbingly. "I'm not sure, but if the evidence is intact, and her story checks out, we may be able to keep her out of jail."

"Jail!" Susan stood completely up, and shrieked at Kevin. "I can't go to jail, I didn't mean to do anything wrong!"

"Hold on there now," Kevin rose and towered over her, placing his hands on her shoulders in a calming gesture. "Don't panic. What you've said will carry a lot of weight, and if it's all true, you'll have helped bring in one of the city's most dangerous drugs, along with the real suppliers who fund it, and an international connection if we can find this Max character. That's big stuff and it won't go unnoticed, or unrewarded."

"Then why would they send her to jail?" Angela demanded, standing too.

"Because she violated international customs, she transported illegal drugs across the border, and she knew, like it or not, that she was involved in an illegal activity."

"But I didn't know." It was a pleading, grappling whisper.

"Yes, you did." Kevin looked dead into her eyes, and Susan hung her head, then slumped to the couch in utter dejection. Kevin and Angela watched her closely for several seconds as reality dawned on all of them. Slowly, Angela sank down as well, touching Susan's arm in the gentlest of gestures.

"Did you know, Susan? Did you know what you were doing?"

She was quiet, staring into her hands for a long time. Her reply was a mere whisper, a choking admission. "In a way. I didn't ask too many questions, but after a few trips back and forth, and especially after I met Max... I knew."

"Yet, you did it anyway?" Kevin asked, not as a criticism, but more as a need for the facts.

"Yes. Because I loved him, and I didn't want to lose him. I would have done anything..." She dropped her head and cut her words off.

"Not anything," Angela said soothingly. "You wouldn't allow *Racer* to be brought to the city of Niagara Falls." Susan looked up at Angela, shocked that she had, in fact, done something right after all. "Most women find themselves willing to go to great lengths for the man they love," Angela continued. "A young woman only feels that all the more, especially when she's dealing with an older, more experienced man who can tell her, maybe even *give* her, everything she's always needed."

"He was going to take me away to a tropical island where we could live happily ever after..." she stated pitifully. "How I would have loved to go... far away... from all of it."

"Trouble is, men like that never have any intention of carrying through on those dreams." Kevin's deep voice crashed in with the reality he conveyed.

"I realized that. I also realized that I didn't want to go with him anymore. Not after I'd seen what we were really doing."

Kevin reached down and touched the top of Susan's head with a gentle, fatherly caress. "Good girl."

She responded with awed adoration and slow, running tears.

"Listen, how would you like a hot bath, some clean clothes, and a good meal?" Kevin suggested suddenly, warmth and security shining through him.

Susan smiled and nodded, still staring at him worshipfully.

"All right, I'm going to let Angela help you; the bathroom is right down the hall. We'll clean you up and get you all set for the adventure ahead of you."

"Adventure?"

"That's right. I have a feeling we're all in for *quite* an adventure."

~ *Chapter Twenty-two* ~

When Susan was safely tucked away in her bath, and her clothes were washing, Kevin and Angela finally looked at one another with the inevitable, knowing dread they shared. Adventure indeed. They both knew that what lay ahead of them would be anything but an exciting adventure. It would be more like a roller coaster ride through hell.

They entered the kitchen, and Kevin groaned inwardly. Not that he'd been trying to impress Angela, but an absurd rush of pride had filled him when he saw how she admired his home. He was mortified now, however, when he looked across the kitchen and the mountain of dishes Michael had teased him about just this morning loomed before him conspicuously. Angela saw his expression and laughed.

"Sorry about the mess."

"That's okay, it restores my faith in bachelors."

"Just - uh - have a seat."

Angela took the chair he indicated, and smiled again over Kevin's embarrassment.

"Do you need anything? A cool drink or a cup of coffee? Anything?"

"No, thank you; right now I'm still too shaken up. Thanks for taking care of Susan that way, though, it's sweet of you to be so nice to her. I think she's in love with you."

Kevin shot her a wry, withering look. "That's not love. Not romantic love, anyway. That's a young lady who needs a father."

Angela was shocked. This man was certainly proving to be more than he appeared to be. She would never have guessed he possessed the degree of sensitivity and emotional perception it would require to observe such a point. "You're right. She needs a lot of things. So, what are we going to do?"

Kevin stared downward at his kitchen counter, both arms stretched out, bracing himself against it as he pondered that same question. When he looked up, he was decisive, but somewhat regretful as well. "I have to call Michael."

To his surprise, Angela nodded; he had really expected a fight from her. "I figured as much. Do you believe her?"

"Yes."

Distinct relief covered her face for a second. "So, what's really going to happen to her?"

He answered on a resigned gush of breath, looking first toward the ceiling then straight at Angela. "Just what I said before, but she's going to go through quite a hell before it's all said and done. Even then, it's going to be up to a jury to decide if she's innocent."

"But with all the evidence she can provide... surely she won't be charged for being young and stupid enough to fall in love with a man like that."

"She won't be on trial for that. I wish she would be, most jurors can understand it when it's put that simply, but it's not. She still committed a crime. She transported drugs across the border. That's major. Just like any other crime that's committed because people think they're in love, this will have to be prosecuted."

"But she didn't know!"

"Try to convince a jury of that. It's just like when women steal, or walk the street, or kill their kids because the man they love tells them to. They might think they're justified, but no one else does."

"That's different."

"No, it's the same; exactly the same. She knew what she was doing. The only help she's going to get is possibly from her young age, and because she's willing to confess now."

Angela looked away, feeling slightly angry by the truth of his words, and the stark certainty with which he spoke them. She also felt lost that what seemed like innocence to her, really wasn't, and was unlikely to be interpreted as such by anyone else.

"On the other hand," Kevin said, watching her closely and seeing her anguish, "she is willing to give names, places, and huge, pertinent facts about a criminal industry that will make crack look as harmless as candy cigarettes. Did she actually say there was a judge involved in this?"

"Yes, she did."

Kevin shook his head. "Well, if she can provide that kind of information, she deserves to have her few transgressions overlooked."

Angela's face sprang to life. Kevin noticed it, was even taken aback by the beauty of it for several seconds, but he was already picking up the phone and beginning to dial. Before the last number was punched, though, he stopped and looked into her eyes. "Just so you know... I'll do everything I can."

Angela wasn't sure how much, realistically, that was, or the degree of depth he actually felt about all of this. She knew he meant his words, though, and she took immeasurable comfort in his strength and sincerity.

He stabbed his finger at the last button, which would connect his call to Michael's office. "All right. Here we go."

"DEA."

"Michael? I'm talking to you way more than I want to lately."

"Kevin! Where are you?" There was a distinct note of alarm in Michael's voice and it registered on Kevin only slightly at first.

"I'm at home. Did you hear what happened?"

"I heard there was shooting around Angela's building. Is she with you?"

"Yes, she's fine, we're both fine."

"Well, why didn't you call? I got Special Team officers searching the whole damn city for you." He seemed acutely irate.

"I couldn't call right away, I had a little business to take care of."

"Like what?" A knowing quality entered Michael's voice, and his irritation seemed to vanish with it.

"Like, Susan Ventry was out there when that jack-ass attacked Angela."

"She was there? *With* the attacker?"

"I thought so, but she wasn't actually with him. By the way, his name is Regis Black, big shock, but Ventry says she's sure it was Regis Black under the mask, and she would know."

"Why?"

"Because she's his *Racer* contact, just like you thought, and she's also his lover."

"Hmm. Surprise, surprise."

"Yeah, well, none of this is what we thought, Michael."

"How do you know?"

"Because I talked to her."

"You did! Where is she?"

"She's... safe."

"Safe? That's all?" A long, thick silence ensued, Michael sensing what was to come. "You're not planning on withholding evidence, are you, Kev?"

"I'm going to tell you everything I know, then I'm going to hang up this phone. Now, listen carefully, that kid is innocent... well, at least somewhat innocent. She met Black at her college campus, apparently he hangs out there. He used the romantic knight-in-shining-armor crap to seduce her and pull her into the game because she lives across the border. She could get in and out of The States on a regular basis without seeming suspicious. She didn't know what she was transporting until he told her last week."

"Oh, come on, Kevin, you believe that?"

"Yes, I do. She was in love with this jerk, and did whatever he told her to do. Now, listen to her story, and *you* tell *me* if this doesn't check out.

"Last week he brought her to a drug house downtown, an old warehouse. While she was there, Regis Black and a man named Marty brought *Racer* out and they intentionally overdosed a few kids. She says one of the kids beat the other one to death. I don't know names or faces, but she claims it was done. She said there was a guard there, a bouncer type, and that he broke up the fight, but not in time to save the kid. It was Linden. Then she says she followed him for a couple days, according to Regis' instructions, and saw him go into the police station. That's how she figured him for a cop.

"She called him and they set up a time to meet at Armondo's. When she got there she gave him *an envelope* with all her information. Problem was, he was already strung out on *Racer*, and threw the envelope across the room and attacked her. That's when she ran, etc."

"So, the famous envelope," Michael mused, interested.

"Yeah, and you've got to find it. Among other things, there's a written formula for creating *Racer* in there."

"Awh, no. No, no, no..."

"Yes, yes, yes. Black wanted the formula written down, and given to Susan. She put that, and a tape of all these guys doing business, inside this envelope as proof against Black. There are at least two cops that work for Regis, possibly more, but she's only seen and heard of two. One of them is called Goldie, and the other is his partner. Susan thinks this Goldie is some kind of relative of Black's. He claims there's a ton of dirty cops in the precinct, I think that's bull, but that's how he scared her into doing what they wanted. She also said there's a judge involved."

"A judge?"

"That's what she says; doesn't have any names, and never saw him, but she's heard Regis and Goldie, specifically, talking about him. I don't know how any of them found out about Angela, or who drugged Linden in the first place, but if you can find Black, possibly through this Goldie person, you got your case.

"One other thing. Susan Ventry was supposed to drop the PCP to Marty Rhodes that night. She never even brought the stuff over. She had no intention of delivering it, or even meeting with him. All she wanted was to get to Linden so he could help her. She's confused, and now, without a doubt, thinks all badges are the enemy."

"Kevin," Michael interjected worriedly, "why are *you* telling me all of this? Why don't you let *her* tell me?"

Kevin ignored the question. "The drugs are in the basement of her apartment house. There's a loose board in the ceiling. She put them there."

"Kevin?"

"Michael, I've got to do what I've got to do. Check this stuff out, get that envelope from Armondo's, if it's still there. Ventry put a whole load of information in it that will incriminate Black. Verify what I just told you, and see if she's not telling the truth."

"Kevin!" Michael nearly shouted in alarm, seeming to disregard all the import of what his father-in-law had revealed. "You have to bring her in! Kevin...?"

With the most calm, quiet movement, that was almost imperceptible to Michael as his mind screamed against what his father-in-law was obviously electing to do, Kevin hung up the phone.

~ *Chapter Twenty-three* ~

"Kevin!" Michael yelled frantically into the receiver one last time. It was useless. Kevin had said everything he intended to say, and had hung up the phone. What did this mean? What, in the name of God, was he planning to do, harbor a suspect wanted in a drug and murder case? He couldn't possibly do that; and if he *was* going to do it, why?

"Michael, you okay?"

Casey stood in the doorway to Michael's office as if he wasn't sure if it was all right to enter. His partner was standing at his desk, looking at the phone as if it were a sword that had unexpectedly cut through his heart. Strangely, in a way, that's exactly how Michael felt.

"Yes," he blurted out, way too quick and sharp.

"Are you sure?"

"Yes, what have you got?"

"Well, Armondo's is just a dilapidated old pizzeria. The city inspectors would have a field day writing up ordinances on it, but all we saw was an empty building. There's an apartment upstairs, broken down to hell, but someone's been in it recently."

"How do you know?"

"There are some fresh dust trails throughout the place, a few obscure footprints, some papers... There's no electricity, though, no heat, no water; everything's been shut down since..." Casey thumbed through a few pages of a small spiral notepad, in search of the exact information. "...September 5th of 2010. So whoever was up there wasn't there for long."

"Maybe it was Linden."

"Could be, there was no forced entry, though, so he must have had access to the place. The owner is Eugene Fonta; he had a stroke in 2010 and the place shut down the next day - no relatives or next of kin. He's in a nursing home now, trying to sell it off, but so far, no dice. The city's tried taking him to court a few times for maintenance, but what can they do? I guess he's cognizant enough to deal with the situation, but he's sick enough not to be able to do much about it. It's a sticky situation. At any rate the place *is* up for sale, and Mr. Fonta *is* trying to sell... I think the city finally just gave up."

Michael ceased all movement for the briefest of moments. "It's been taken to court, huh?" His mind was beginning to reel. He was still thinking about Kevin, and wondering franticly what his father-in-law was doing. Kevin knew that if he were hiding something, or protecting Susan Ventry, his actions would put Michael in an incredibly difficult position. Technically, Kevin would be under arrest for such actions. That's why he hadn't said anything about what he was really doing. He'd only relayed the information that Susan Ventry had obviously given him.

How did she come to tell him these things? He must have been talking to her for quite some time to obtain that much information, and that much conviction of her innocence. Did he let her go? Or was he hiding her?

The information itself, though, that had been eye opening. The whole mystery had been spelled out to him in detail, including what to look for, and where to look. That sudden knowledge was causing the itching feeling of instinct to jump to life as he listened to Casey's additional discoveries. Armondo's owner had been taken to court... Interesting.

"Casey, can you check who the judge in charge of the Armondo's case was?"

Casey stopped as if Michael had switched conversations without notifying him. "Sure, but what does that have to do with anything?"

"I'm not sure." Michael looked at his partner, his friend, with uncertainty crossing his features in obvious waves. He was debating whether to tell Casey that Kevin had just called him. To do so, however, would be to allow another officer to know of an indiscretion. In turn, that would be both exposing Kevin, whom Michael would protect with his life if he had to, and putting Casey in the difficult position of having to conceal critical information.

"Michael, what's up?" Casey asked, his eyes knowing and full of the trust he would always offer.

Michael hesitated, then walked behind Casey and closed the door to his office. He looked slightly bewildered for a moment, wondering how to begin, and caught between excitement over the facts he'd just learned, and concern for the way he learned them. "Kevin just called me. He went out to watch Angela this morning."

"He did? Good. Did Jack okay that?"

"No. Kevin is a citizen. Any citizen has the right to visit another citizen without the police telling them it's okay."

"Hmm. Right. I'm glad you called him."

"Anyway, to make a long story short, Regis Black tried to kidnap Angela, and somehow Kevin got Angela away. In the process, he also got a hold of Susan Ventry."

"*What?* That's perfect!"

"No, it's not. He's not bringing her in."

Confusion covered Casey's face. "Why not?"

"Would you believe, he thinks she's innocent?"

"So? What does that have to do with anything? She still has to be questioned, he knows that."

"I don't know what the hell he's thinking," Michael responded, shaking his head with an edge of disgust. "Apparently he wants us to be able to prove her innocence before he gives her over to us."

"*What?* What is it about this kid that makes everyone want to believe she's innocent? And how are we supposed to *prove* she's innocent without talking to her and hearing her story?"

Michael hesitated again, looking painfully serious. "Casey... I don't want anyone else to know what I'm about to tell you, and no one can know that he's been in contact with her, okay?"

Casey's interest was piqued, and he could sense the vitality of this information. "You bet, Michael, I won't say a word, but... how much contact has he actually had?"

"I'm not sure. I suspect he has her with him, although he didn't say that he did. He only said he'd talked to her - and wait until you hear the information she gave him."

It was almost an hour later when Casey, transfixed by the story and the details Michael revealed, finally commented on all he was hearing. "So, the officer involved in all of this is named Goldie?"

"That's what she told Kevin, have you ever heard of a Goldie around here?"

"No, but I can check that out easily enough."

"All right, let's get on that right away. You didn't happen to find an envelope laying around at Armondo's, did you?"

"No. The place was bare, but I could check again."

"All right, let's do that; we'll go together. I want to see this place. Then we've got to get that PCP, today, right now, immediately. We need possession of it. After that we should see if we can find Max, not that he'd tell us anything about Regis, but at the very least, he needs to be put off the streets. As for Marty Rhodes and Nick Kline, we'll have to have you go under as Jake for a few days to try to see what happened to them. While you're at it, we need to check out the death of that kid. See if there have been any reports of missing persons or deaths in that area in the past two weeks, etc. etc. What's got me suspicious about it is: Linden would have reported a murder. *Should* have anyway."

"Maybe he didn't know he was dead. You specifically said Ventry seemed unsure herself. Maybe he just got the crap kicked out him. Doesn't mean he died."

"Maybe. We'll need to confirm it in any case.

"Got it."

Michael paused and looked steadily downward for a few moments. "You and I will go for the PCP right away, but by tonight I want you on the streets as Jake. Trouble is, I need you out there and in here at the same time."

Casey shrugged, somewhat honored.

"I'll just have to get one of the other teams to work on the rest of it. You stick to the downtown area and find out what you can, but I want to have contact with you. I'm not leaving you there alone, not after what happened with Linden. I want you checking in every two hours, no exceptions, and I'll try to have a team standing by in case you need assistance."

"Fine, but make sure they stay the hell away unless I call on them. If investigators start barging in where they don't belong, it could be more dangerous to me than being stuck in the middle of a gun fight."

Michael sighed resignedly. "I know; but I need to have contact with you." It was an almost desolate statement, showing just glimpses of Michael's grief in having lost an officer in the line of duty, and his utter unwillingness to lose Casey. Worry lines dug into his brow and began to strain the corners of his eyes. He was too young to look so hard, so seasoned, so familiar with the ugly truth of life.

"All right. Every two hours." Casey smiled considerately at his friend, moved by the concern in Michael's face. It didn't come from simply putting one of his men in another dangerous position, it came from having to put him, specifically, in a dangerous position. "We'll bust this in no time."

"I hope so, Casey. Because if anything is going to happen here, it's got to happen right *now.*"

~ *Chapter Twenty-four* ~

Goldie sat quietly in the shadows just as twilight finally turned into darkness. Huddled behind a cluster of trees in the lot across from Kevin's house, he picked up his cell phone and punched in the number to the infamous payphone at *Lucy's* Bar. The call was answered almost immediately. "Yeah, Regis? They're not here."

"Well, where in hell are they?"

How was Goldie supposed to know that? "I don't know, I've been watching the place for about an hour, though, and there's no sign of life."

"Have you gone in?"

"No, I haven't gone in!" Goldie responded with sarcastic incredulity. "Why risk breaking and entering? They're not going to be sitting in the dark. No one is in there."

"Well, he took her there today," Regis said as if Goldie was somehow responsible for making Kevin, Angela and Susan disappear.

"Well, they're not there now."

Regis took a deep breath, and held the phone away from his mouth for a minute, trying to think with all the noise going on around him. The bar was full of people tonight, smiling at him, giving him certain, meaningful looks of approval. Even looks that wanted his approval. Word was definitely out that he was funding *Racer*. Great, that was all he needed.

Since Linden's death, Marty and Nick had vanished, along with Susan, all the money, and her hundred grand worth of PCP. Even if he could get his hands on it, what in hell was he supposed to do with it? Give it back to Max and try to explain that he didn't have the money to pay for it? Hardly. Everyone was expecting payment very soon, and Regis couldn't give any of them anything. On top of that, some sort of evidence against him, which Susan had provided, was supposedly floating around town somewhere, and he didn't know where it could be or what it was.

Regis Black was brand new at this game, and he shook with apprehension at the problems he was facing. Cops were onto his business. There was no doubt about it now, and they had all the evidence they would ever need in the form of a witness. Susan. *His* Susan! Had she really given Linden evidence against him? Would she really betray him that far? Did what they share truly mean nothing to her? How could that be?

Susan had turned against him. He wouldn't believe that. He couldn't let go of her anymore than he could let go of the *Racer* project! They were both his, and they were both meant for him alone. If he didn't get control over what was happening, his whole existence would be futile. Worth nothing. He must recover the PCP and relocate himself, Nick and Marty. He must get *Racer* manufactured, and start distribution and payments right away. Most of all, he must get a hold of Susan.

Damn Kevin Larsen. This was all his fault. What was he even doing in all of this? He'd always been a nuisance, and now, after he'd crashed the entire industry already only a year ago, he was back, making himself a pain in the ass again on *Regis'* turf. He'd have had Angela Cahn *and* Susan *and* whatever evidence there was against him early this morning if it wasn't for Larsen.

"Did you look to see if Larsen's car is gone?" he asked, finally returning himself to the conversation with Goldie.

"No, I can't go sneaking around his house, Regis. It's suicide. The guy's a bull-dog, and if I get caught, we're all dead."

Regis thought about that for a moment. It was true. As much as Goldie's personal existence meant very little to Regis, if he sacrificed him, and got him caught, he might blow the whole operation. "All right. See if you can track them somehow."

"How do you expect me to do that?"

"I don't know, you're the cop!"

"And what do you expect me to do? Put out an APB on him?"

"The cops got their methods, Goldie. There must be some way to find his car and track them."

Silence.

"Goldie?"

Goldie's body was stiff and unyielding as he looked downward toward his right side. He could see the shadow, but it was the feeling of cold steel against the side of his head that immobilized him. The phone still stood frozen against his ear, and, obedient to the command that had just been issued to him, he didn't move a muscle. From the other side of the line, Regis' heart sank and his blood curled as he clearly heard what was happening.

"Hello there, Goldie. We've been looking for you. Now, don't move a muscle or I might be forced to shoot you. Who knows, you could get badly hurt from a shot fired at such close range." Michael stood straight and tall, his eyes blazing anger and contempt. "Is this what you always wanted to do when you grew up, little man?" he continued, purposely goading, his voice slithering out in a deceptively congenial tone. "Be a dirty pig?"

Goldie stiffened.

"Face down, Golden. We're going to take a little trip down to the station so you can answer some questions for me."

Michael took the phone away from Goldie's ear as he sprawled face first on the ground in front of him. His gun pointing directly at him, Michael took only a second to look up and across the street. Kevin's house was quiet, deadly still. A pang of anxiety coursed through Michael. He knew Kevin was alive, was so far unharmed, but where was he? Did he know how close Regis Black was getting to him? Did he know that Black knew where he lived, and was looking for him and the women he was protecting? Would Kevin be able to shield them all by himself?

*   *   *

Regis disconnected the line with an instant jab at the payphone in the *Lucy's* bar. Goldie had just gotten busted. A whole hell was breaking loose. What was he going to do? How could he regain everything?

The door to the bar opened, and a ragged man walked in. No great stir followed his appearance. Jake was a semi-familiar face around here these days. He was a harmless junkie, who used to have very big connections. He sat down at the bar and a beer was set before him. He drank quietly, saying his few hellos and talking the inevitable small talk of the bar. As usual, everyone around him was stoned. Except one man in the corner, who was staring at his table with pasty white features.

Bingo!

A certain throbbing started in Casey's chest. He narrowed his eyes in an attempt at covering any anxiety, and rose from his stool. It seemed like an endlessly long walk across the bar, and when it was done he stood before Regis Black. Finally. Marcus Linden had known the name Regis Black for quite awhile, but Regis had kept himself out of the limelight enough to keep Linden from ever knowing the face. Black was letting himself be seen among the crowds now, and Casey was glad his job was being made easy.

Regis looked up from staring at the phone. A mangy looking character stood before him. Jake Brown. The man with the many connections.

"You Regis Black?"

"I don't know."

Jake snorted, unamused and unimpressed by this game. "I have a message for you."

"Oh?"

"Yeah, the message is: the stuff's at your girlfriend's place."

Regis stood straight up. "What?"

"The stuff's at your girlfriend's place," Jake repeated condescendingly, as if his words had been unmistakably clear, and shouldn't need restating."

"What are you talking about?"

A snapping ferocity exploded in Jake's countenance, and he leapt forward to whisper in hoarse, intimidating anger, "Listen, I don't play your little games, okay? I work for power so big, you can't even stand in its shadow. The message is: 'The stuff's at your girlfriend's place.' Consider it a favor that someone *wants* you to know."

Dawning covered Regis' face. Someone high up, probably cops, had found out where the PCP was, probably through the trouble with Susan, and someone even higher up than that wanted Regis to know about it. Thank God for him. His connection. His protection. As weak and victimized as The Judge had always been, he was always there, and always looking out for Regis.

Casey watched Black's expression carefully, applying his lead to the conversation in noncommittal jumps until he was sure he was saying the right things in the right way. It was tricky, but Jake's hard edge, and narrow, dangerous eyes made up for any inconsistencies.

Indeed, he set the tone, rather than followed it. "I'm just his ears and his eyes," he said cryptically, as if the comment meant something insidiously deep, on a level only they were aware of. "See you around."

"Wait! Does he know one of my men just got busted?"

Casey knew of no such thing since he hadn't spoken to Michael since this afternoon. He wondered if the mysterious judge Black knew was powerful enough that he could be aware of a Special Team bust that quickly. He almost lost his carefully fixed gaze as he struggled to think fast. "He knows now."

"What will he do about it?"

"I'm sure he'll do what he can."

"He *has* to. It's Goldie, and he could *destroy* us!"

Something within Casey clicked with admiration at the news that, somehow, Michael had caught Goldie. A frantic note, however, had crawled into Regis' voice. Jake stared at him, wanting to know the information he was willing to tell, but unable to continue the conversation on a level that required specific knowledge of people he didn't really know. He shook his head impatiently to cover that fact. "Man, you're some piece of work. Are you sure you can handle a job this big?"

"I can handle it!" Regis said fiercely, his manhood challenged and insulted by the implication that he couldn't.

"All I know is what I'm told; I don't care about the rest, and I've delivered my message," Casey recited impatiently. "Your girl's got the stuff. Wonder why *he* knows that and *you* don't." Jake smirked mockingly and left Regis standing there, enraged and offended, to try to scramble together what had been lost.

~ *Chapter Twenty-five* ~

"You know, Goldie," Michael said with terrifying quiet, "I can't tell you how irritating this whole thing is to me, and how much I don't want to be here right now. I've just about had it with this whole game. Now, we know you work for Regis Black. We know he's setting up a new drug that's supposed to make a lot of people rich, and fry the brains of the rest of the city. Someone pumped Detective Linden full of the drug the night they were supposed to make their first deal, and two *cops* beat him to death when they found out that he and Susan Ventry betrayed Black. Tell me where he is."

Sergeant Michael Camden was speaking to him, but Captain Philip Jackson stared Goldie down, and that's who held the young officer's attention. Philip Jackson, Precinct Captain, mad as a grizzly, with rejecting disappointment filling his entire face with disdain. "I don't know what you're talking about, sir."

"Oh, come on, Golden! Why else were you outside Kevin Larsen's home? Why did I hear you calling Regis, by name, and telling him that *they* were gone? Whose they?"

"I -" Golden was faltering, glancing between Jack and Michael in obvious panic. How did they know so much about everything? It was taking him completely off guard. He didn't know how to act or what to say when they were slinging truth after truth at him in this way. They seemed to have accurately recreated the entire night of Susan's betrayal, up to and including the drug deal that was supposed to have been made in the warehouse that night, who had been involved, and how Linden had been murdered. No doubt, Susan had already accomplished her tattling goal. They had been busted. No. *He* had been busted. There still seemed to be quite a few things Camden and his secret department didn't know.

"You know, Golden," Captain Jack finally interjected, "it isn't going to do you any good to lie. We already know everything. All we need to do is put a few names and faces together with our facts and - bingo," Jack snapped his fingers loudly to emphasize his point, "everyone involved is going to fry. Wouldn't you rather go down having provided a bit of the information so your sentence goes easier?"

Golden looked again at Jack's face as his words drilled into the silence Goldie had been hesitating in. The captain's eyes were still shards of ice, piercing into his soul. His face was still a mask of impenetrable, intimidating disdain, but conversely, his words offered the slightest ray of hope, although they weren't intended to do so. Perhaps... perhaps if he just spoke out at the right time...

"I - I - refuse to answer anymore questions on the grounds that it might incriminate me."

~ *Chapter Twenty-six* ~

A row of inspection booths interrupted the highway. There were, perhaps, ten of them in a line across the road as Kevin and Angela approached, but only two had the green signal light lit atop to indicate they were open. Kevin obediently fell in line to await inspection.

"Passport?" It seemed more like a demand as the Canadian Customs Inspector leveled a scrutinizing stare into Kevin's face from the seat within his booth. Kevin and Angela obediently handed over their documentation.

Both of them had crossed between the nations hundreds of times before. Both of them knew the system and what to do and say. It was normally a simple procedure, but today they had to concentrate hard to try to look relaxed, to act as if nothing was wrong, to pray to God they wouldn't be checked.

"What's your business in Canada this evening?" the young man asked, his face never wavering or even suggesting friendliness or a smile.

"We're just visiting The Falls."

Why did it look as though he didn't believe them? "How long will you be in Canada?"

"Just for dinner, maybe a show. Possibly overnight."

"Are you bringing anything in with you?" He meant anything taxable or illegal.

"Just a change of clothes."

The inspector seemed to consider that for the briefest of moments, which seemed endless to Angela. She tried not to look too much into the young man's face, and to smile without looking like she was trying to do so. She wasn't at all sure she had managed to look guiltless, nor was she sure what this man was thinking.

"Okay, go ahead," he finally said, to Kevin and Angela's utmost relief. They were free to pass.

With a friendly smile and a nod of his head, Kevin thanked the man casually and pulled away. "Are you okay?" he asked Angela, the slightest teasing grin at the corners of his mouth.

She caught the look, supposing that she wasn't such a good James Bond agent after all. "I think so. How can you act so calm?"

"I'm not so calm, but I do know how these things work. When we stop at the booth, our license plate number is monitored. When the Customs officer scans the number into his computer, they know immediately if there's anything wrong with the car or the occupants that should be driving it. When we approach, they check out the validity of the drivers with our passports and a few simple questions. If those questions are answered honestly, there usually isn't a problem. Besides when my plate number comes up, my name also comes up with it. *Lieutenant Kevin Larsen.* They pretty much know the name."

"Why? Do they know all the police officers' names?"

"No, but..." Kevin looked at her, a bit exasperated that everyone in the city seemed to have heard of him except this one woman, who he wished had. Like her maintenance man earlier this morning: He'd taken one look at Kevin and had not only recognized him, but had rushed forward to shake his hand as if he were a celebrity. Then, he promptly gave Kevin access to Angela's building without any question or delay.

She, however, didn't seem to be making any of the usual connections. He didn't want to tell her of his own exploits like a bragging teenager, but damned if he wasn't tempted to do just that; sit there and talk about himself to try to impress her. Why did he *want* to announce things to her that he wanted to hide from everyone else? "I... well... some people have heard of me."

"Why?"

Kevin rolled his eyes slightly and grimaced. "Last year, before I retired, I was... involved in a major drug bust."

Angela's eyes narrowed. The major drug bust... of course, the one Michael had been involved in. The main detective's name was... "Oh, my - Kevin Larsen! You're the detective that... your house was blown up."

"Yes."

"And you busted that big drug dealer and half the city's other drug dealers!"

"Yes."

"You and your daughter were presumed dead."

"Yes."

"That's how Michael was connected to you. I remember it, I just paid more attention to Michael's name at the time because I knew him."

"They only gave *him* one line in the paper!" Kevin said with sarcastic humor, implying that his ego had been brutalized. She'd given his son-in-law's tiny mentioning more attention than she'd given his days and weeks of full-page articles.

She laughed at his boyish response and looked at him again. This time his chest swelled with a certain pride in the way she perused him as if they were meeting for the first time. Her eyes were filled with awed wonder, as if he were, in fact, a celebrity. He decided she was utterly beautiful when she laughed.

"Wow. I guess I'm honored to have someone like you look after me."

"Well, you know, bodyguard was my second choice for a profession."

"Oh, I see. Well, you do it very well." The comment filled the entire atmosphere around them. It wasn't the words, it was the potent, gentle way Angela said them. Kevin found himself staring again, and Angela found herself moving quickly into a different line of conversation. "That's why that Regis person knew you in my parking ramp, isn't it? Because of your connections with drug arrests?"

"Probably. Actually, I'd never even heard of Regis Black until Michael told me about him, which is pretty disconcerting. I hate when they know me and I don't know them."

"Could he have been involved with that other drug dealer, the one you busted last year?"

"It's possible. I honestly thought he was a badge when he was attacking you. That's why I was so confidant to talk like a hot shot." He sounded self-recriminating about it now, and Angela had to smile at his sarcasm.

"Well, I'm glad you did exactly what you did, because I think you scared him."

He looked over at her with a smile of his own. "Yeah, he did look scared, didn't he?"

"He sure did."

"The only problem is, now I have to live up to my threats, with no police backup and two women who are being chased and terrorized by said criminals," he said drolly.

214

Angela laughed again, even though the truth of the words weren't funny, and she knew that despite the comical way he'd said them, they were very true. "I have every confidence in you, Lieutenant Larsen."

That swell of pride was filling Kevin's chest again. What was it about this woman that made him feel as if he could win an entire war if she would just smile at him? What was it about the way she believed in him and trusted his ability to protect her that made him feel as if he could accomplish it exactly the way she believed? He was determined to see her protection carried out, even if it meant sacrificing himself in the process. "Thank you," he said. It was quiet and caressing. "I'll do my best."

She was momentarily spellbound, but luckily, they were stopping the car in front of a tall, dilapidated house. They pulled around back, and with the most casual, almost comical air, Kevin got out and released the latch on the trunk.

Susan squinted severely, holding her hand up against the brilliance of ordinary streetlights. Her eyes were round for a moment, wary, before she realized that it was Kevin peering down at her, with a laughing expression.

"Did we make it?"

"Yes, we did. How was the ride?" he smirked with a full smile now.

"I feel like I'm going to throw up."

"That's what I thought."

Angela, who had met him step for step as he'd gone to release Susan, shot him an exasperated look before she rushed to help her out of the trunk of the car. "Kevin!" she reprimanded, "how can you think this is funny?"

"I don't know," he said unrepentantly.

When Susan actually stumbled, however, and her face went pasty white, Kevin reached a strong hand to steady her. Driving in a prone position in a dark, claustrophobic trunk had made her nauseous and shaky. If the inspectors had dared check the vehicle, her freedom would be gone! With sincerity that made both women stare at him with transfixed appreciation, he asked, "Are you all right?"

She grabbed onto his strong hand when it came toward her, and as she felt his support under her elbow, she answered, "Yes, I am, I just need to feel the ground under my feet."

"You sure?"

"Yes."

"All right, come on, let's get this over with. We have to be quick and quiet, okay?"

Susan led the way to her apartment, situated in the rear of an old, three-story house that was badly in need of repairs and a good coat of paint. As if this were a perfectly natural occurrence, she walked up to the back door and threw her weight against it two or three times to open the jammed, warped wood. Angela flinched toward Kevin. Susan definitely didn't live in any sort of luxury, and Angela wondered if she was really safe at night.

They trudged up the endless steps that actually led into the attic, then faced a door that stood completely alone at the top. Susan found the key, stuffed into the bottom of the ever-present green gym bag. When she pushed the door open, she stopped in momentarily shocked paralysis. Then, she shrieked in horror, and turned to bolt away. She ran right into Kevin, of course, and his eyes widened with protective alarm as he caught her and threw her to his side in a shielding motion. He looked up with an intense glower at the inside of her apartment, and drew his gun as easily and as quickly as he drew his breath. Something had frightened Susan, had made her want to run. Someone was in there.

When he could finally focus, he relaxed with a dramatic, if slightly irritated, rush. Michael stood there, staring at them. Kevin looked down at Susan as she tried to pull away and said, "It's okay. He's a friend."

"He's a cop!"

Kevin leaned back slightly and peered into her face with astonished levity. "How do you know that?"

She actually smiled a bit, and relaxed because of the trust that shone from his eyes, and the slightly humorous, impressed look on his face. "It's written all over him."

Kevin turned to Michael with even more easy humor. "You better get yourself a new look, Michael. You're giving yourself completely away."

Michael, dressed in an ordinary suit and tie, and perhaps slightly affronted that he so obviously looked the part of the police officer in it, saw anything but humor in this situation. His jaw dropped in disbelief because Kevin, apparently, did. Not only was he joking lightly, but by the way he was holding Susan Ventry, and the adoring, trusting way she returned his gaze, every suspicion Michael had been hoping to be false was confirmed as truth before his eyes.

Angela seemed to correctly interpret his exasperation, and take it seriously, before anyone else did. She smiled a bit warily, a bit apologetically, as she stood to Kevin's other side in the tiny amount of space the dark stairwell provided. She truly did not know what to think, and was unsure how much trouble Michael would cause them. She got her answer almost immediately.

"Kevin, what the hell are you doing? First, you harbor a suspect wanted in a drug and murder case, then you refuse to bring her in, now you smuggle her, illegally, across international borders. Are there any other crimes you've committed that I should know about?"

"None that I can think of at the moment."

"Real funny. Get in here before someone hears you out there."

Kevin stepped aside to allow the ladies to enter the tiny, dark room that Susan called an apartment. For a moment, that familiar protective compassion assaulted him when he saw the way she lived, but the hard, narrow-eyed look on Michael's face quickly eclipsed every other thought.

He was standing in the middle of the room with his arms crossed and his legs slightly parted, supporting him like tree trunks. He watched Susan enter with a curious glare as she stared at him with wide, dreading eyes. She looked scared and off balance, but unremarkable. He wondered what her real story was.

Following closely behind Susan, when she finally stopped moving and stood staring at the detective in her kitchen, was Angela, awkward at her side. She connected for just a moment with Michael, an apology, once again, in her eyes. He tried to look at her severely, to even make her feel accused for all that had gone so completely awry, but he ended up shaking his head in an exasperated fashion and smiling a slight, forgiving smile at her anyway. She was a beautiful person, and carried a lot more influence than she had the slightest clue about. She couldn't move his father-in-law, though, unless he wanted to be moved. On that note, he leveled his gaze upon Kevin. There was nothing funny about this situation.

"So, did you find your package?" Kevin asked before Michael could articulate the many rebukes he wanted to convey.

Michael glanced at Susan, then back to Kevin. "Yes. We did."

"And was everything exactly the way she said it would be?"

"It was."

"Here's another package for you." Kevin tossed the gym bag to Michael casually and watched closely as his son-in-law looked inside. The drug money, originally intended to pay for all the PCP they had just confiscated, faced him in banded clumps.

Michael pursed his lips sardonically. "She is still wanted for a serious crime."

"She's not innocent, Michael, but she's not as guilty as it seems."

Michael sighed a deep, reorganizing breath, closed his eyes, and shook his head again. "I want to hear that from her."

Kevin nodded toward Susan, urging her to speak. "Susan, this is my son-in-law, Detective Sergeant Michael Camden of the Drug Enforcement Administration of Niagara Falls."

Michael grimaced sarcastically at the obvious use of his entire title. If Ventry felt apprehensive before, she would be shuddering with it now. He looked at her, and her eyes rounded in fright. "Oh, my God," she whispered in defeat. Surely, she was in deep trouble now.

Kevin read the look on her face, and couldn't keep the edges of a smile away again. The title did have a rather daunting ring to it, and Kevin was proud to be able to call this young man his son-in-law. In spite of the intimidating sound of his name, and the growling, unamused look on his face, Kevin knew Michael would be fair. His very presence here, alone, spoke of how much he wanted to give leeway in this situation. In fact, that's why Kevin had brought Susan here: to escape the incredible danger that was present in The States, with everyone from cop to criminal looking for her, and to meet Michael, whom Kevin knew would be waiting for them.

"Susan, this is no time to be tongue-tied," Kevin encouraged gently. "You have a once in a lifetime chance to talk to the investigator in charge of your case one-on-one, in a neutral zone. Take advantage of it."

Susan swallowed hard, looking in anguish from Kevin to Michael, and back again. "H-hello," she finally stuttered.

Michael looked at her hard for a few seconds, apparently debating whether or not to greet her on a friendly level. "Hello,

Susan," he replied civilly. "I've been looking for you for quite awhile now."

"Really? Well, I - I - actually, I know."

"Kevin's already told me your story. It checks out, but I need some answers from you."

"Okay."

"Let's start with Regis Black. I don't suppose you know where we can find him?"

"No, I don't. We always arranged to meet at different places. Sometimes he'd come here and pick me up, sometimes I met him wherever he said to meet him."

"Where can we find Max?"

She was a bit surprised at how he used the name so knowingly. "I used to meet with him in an alley about three blocks down. The meetings must have been arranged beforehand, but I don't know how. Regis always took care of it."

"All right, what happened to the envelope you supposedly gave to Linden?"

"He threw it across the room of that pizzeria. I don't know what happened to it after that. He - he started chasing me."

"Was he high?"

"He was wasted! On that *Racer* stuff."

"Who had access to *Racer* that night? I mean, if you were supposed to supply the chemicals for it, and it wasn't made yet, who would have been able to get it to shoot Detective Linden with it?"

Susan's brow furrowed for a moment. She obviously hadn't thought about this question before, and Michael watched her closely. "I think only Marty and Nick had it then. Regis never took any of it with him, at least not the night we were together in that warehouse... Yeah," she said speculatively, "only Marty and Nick knew anything about it, or had any of it."

"Do you know any way of finding them?"

"No, I don't. I only met them a couple of times, I don't know where they live."

"Do you know where Regis lives?"

"No." It was a dead, flat statement.

"Where did you - uh - spend time together then when you were in The States?"

Susan hesitated in acute humiliation. This detective had obviously been telling the truth when he'd said Kevin had told him everything. "River Motel," she said quietly, unable to meet his gaze.

Michael noted her reaction once again. He was striking a few chords and surprising her with his questions, but she was answering honestly every time. "What about The Judge?"

"What about him?"

"Do you know who he is?"

"No, I just know he helps Regis not to get caught at anything, and I think he gives him money."

"Did Regis ever mention anything about city housing, or city inspectors, anything like that?"

At this, Kevin glanced up sharply, and Michael looked at him briefly before he studied Susan once again. "No, all he talked about was the drugs."

"All right, Susan." It was simple and final. "I need to talk to my father-in-law for a few minutes alone."

Angela stepped in immediately, assuming she and Susan were to leave. "Would you like me to take her outside?"

"No, that's not really safe. We'll use the front porch."

Kevin looked around himself disbelievingly at the single cramped room that surrounded him, which Michael had already become thoroughly familiar with. "Front porch?" he asked skeptically.

"Yes, I have a small porch in front," Susan confirmed, gesturing toward the furthest wall of the room.

Michael and Kevin looked toward the spot she indicated. A door stood there, ominously closed and quiet, but when they opened it a tiny sitting area did indeed face them. A small row of windows overlooked the street, and filled the space with needed light in the daytime. A dangerously steep flight of stairs that seemed, somehow, frighteningly suspended in mid air, fell immediately to the right of the room. Two folding chairs sat in the hopeless space to the left, with a tray-table between them and a vase of flowers on top. Susan had obviously tried to make this tiny area livable.

Kevin glanced back as he began to follow Michael through the door. "Susan, gather whatever you'll need quickly and get ready to leave. I'll be out in a minute," he said, speaking right into her frightened thoughts. She obviously didn't yet realize that Michael wouldn't cause her harm.

"All right," she said, immediately beginning to move about, with Angela available for any assistance she might need.

Kevin closed the door. Michael didn't look pleased, but he didn't say anything more about Kevin's uncharacteristic actions. "I take it this visit is unofficial, then?" he said to his son-in-law.

"Unofficial," Michael affirmed with straight, hard features. "Sort of. Actually, I'm here on business. There's a team down in the basement and one outside watching the house. That's how I knew you were here, they radioed me - and you've got to get out of here quick because you're interrupting police procedure, which I'm sure doesn't bother you in the least. We're expecting a visit from Regis Black or some other equally disagreeable stooge."

"You are?" Kevin sounded surprised. Why?"

"Jake Brown planted a little message. He told Regis this is where the PCP is. We're hoping to ambush him."

"Casey..." Kevin said with an affectionate smile and an admiring wag of his head. "That crazy bastard, he always did risk too much."

Michael smiled a bit himself. "Yeah, gets the job done better than anyone else."

"Does he know I've got Susan?"

Michael's smile promptly faded, and his eyes narrowed. "He knows."

"But Captain Jack doesn't, right?"

Michael looked downward guiltily. "No."

Kevin smiled once again. "Thanks, son." Then teasingly, almost goading, he added, "You're learning fast."

Distinct irritation washed over Michael's face at this direct reference to his defection from proper procedure for Kevin's sake. As he looked at his father-in-law, though, he couldn't contain his own reluctant smile. When they had worked together, this was always the way it had been. Kevin joked about things that weren't funny, and Michael, somehow, laughed along. Then, all of a sudden, just when it became absolutely necessary, they would shift, and become as sober and formidable as any cop could be. It was happening again now as they stood across from one another and began to talk in the pitifully small entrance room of a drug runner and murder suspect.

"Do you have any idea what you're up against?" Michael finally asked.

"Probably not, but why don't you tell me what's going on."

Michael sighed and forged ahead. "Well, Casey's out on Lex full time. We went to Armondo's, there is no envelope, but there definitely are signs of a struggle similar to the one Susan described. The dust in there is about three inches thick, so every move that was made left a mark, including... a large rectangular indentation about ten feet from the struggle sight... which looks suspiciously like an envelope was thrown through the air and landed there.

Unfortunately, there's also a set of footprints, different from the one's we're assuming to be Linden's and Ventry's, leading to and away from it. So, someone else must have been there that night, and has the envelope.

"The PCP, however, was right where you said it would be, and has been brought into proper custody."

"Good."

"It doesn't make her innocent, Kevin."

"Yeah, it does. It proves that she never wanted to be a part of this, and when it all actually went down, she wouldn't go through with it. She called Linden to help her; meaning she tried to contact the police *before* any of this went down... that makes her innocent."

"She's not innocent of running drugs over the border for the last four months."

"But she didn't know what she was doing."

Michael looked at Kevin then, skeptical, but ultimately seeing what his father-in-law was trying to convey.

"Michael, I'm not asking you to lie, or even shift the facts a little. I'm just saying - catch these bastards. After you do, what would be so bad about leaving her out of it? You know what could happen to her if she got before the judge and jury. The public won't be nearly as understanding, and the kid just needs a break; deserves a break."

The word "judge" struck Michael. Kevin was right. If Susan were put into the public position of having involvement with drugs the magnitude of *Racer*, and killing a cop, she would be eaten alive by it, and dissected piece by piece because of her involvement. Whether she deserved it or not. It wasn't Michael's job to necessarily care about that, but, in fact, he did. Even more so, he cared about Kevin, and how it might affect him.

"Well, what am I supposed to do about her name and face already being known as the number one suspect?"

"Just find the real killer. That'll vindicate her like nothing else will."

"And her other transgressions?"

"We've overlooked transgressions before."

Michael smiled lopsidedly. Indeed, they had overlooked many transgressions in the past to balance the difference between the law and justice. "All right, I'll do what I can, with the agreement that, if it doesn't check out, you'll bring her in. If she's really an innocent kid, and just got caught in a trap, I'll overlook a few things, but if not..."

"It's a deal." A knowing relief flooded Kevin's face. He was certain that Susan's story would check out.

"All right, then. Say, speaking of judges, we have a suspect."

"Yeah? Who? Does it have anything to do with asking Susan about city inspectors?"

"Yes. We did a bit of background on Armondo's, you know, to see what Linden was doing there in the first place. It's actually even more confusing because the place has been shut down since 2010; pipes are busted, there's no heat, no water - it's a rattrap. It should have been condemned a long time ago. Turns out, there's all kinds of red tape between the city and the owner because the guy is in a nursing home and can't maintain, or sell, the property. So, we checked out who the judge in charge of the case was. It's Judge Carlton Souza."

"Hmm. Is that all you got?"

"Yeah, but it's a start. Supposedly, the good judge has left Armondo's owner alone about it for quite some time. Wonder if he had a reason for doing so... At any rate, maybe Linden knew something, and that's why he went there. There was no forced entry. Who knows...? In any case, we found Goldie."

"You did?"

"Yep. He's just as slimy as you might expect, but he's clamped his mouth shut tight as a drum until he can speak with his lawyer."

"Good going, man, how did you find him so fast?"

"Like a fool, I was worried about *you*, that's how. I wanted to be sure you were all right, so I did a little checking around your house earlier tonight. You were already gone, but there was Goldie, watching it, too, and talking to Regis on the phone."

"You caught him while he was on the phone with Black!" There was a light of shock in Kevin's eyes, and again, a playful sense of admiration. "Did you get the number he was connected to from Goldie's phone?"

"Yeah, it's just the same damn bar we've known about for months," Michael drawled sarcastically. "Same phone Marcus called from that last night."

"Damn, I'll bet Goldie almost pissed his pants."

Michael stifled the flippancy at once. "Kevin, I wish this was all as big a joke as you seem to think it is. These guys know all about you, and believe me, they won't think twice about killing you to get to Ventry. For her sake and yours, why don't you bring her in? Let us protect her - and Angela - and you."

Kevin's eyes hardened. "No."

Michael sighed again. "You know, I can force you."

Kevin looked into Michael's face. "But you won't."

"If I do, it's only for your own good. Amy is sick over all this. She keeps asking me if you're all right, and I don't know what to tell her!"

A light flickered in Kevin's eyes, and a true smile lit his face. Not an amused smile really, more of a peaceful assurance. As Michael was noticing it, and wondering about it, Kevin answered him. "You tell my girl that I'm all right. Tell her I'm better than I've been in a long, long time."

Michael finally recognized the peculiar light, and smiled too. "Angela, huh?"

"She's quite a friend. Why didn't you tell me about her before?"

"Must have slipped my mind. Remember your assignment, though, lover-boy, I asked you to protect her, not get yourself killed by drug dealers."

"Don't you worry. I'll take care of all of us."

At that moment Angela screamed, a terrified, blood-curdling scream. *"Kevin!"*

*   *   *

Marty Rhodes and Nick Kline were truly an unusual pair. One was all business, and one was all pleasure, but together they were one mind, and that, perhaps, made them more dangerous than anyone had ever guessed.

"We gotta get out of here, Marty, I can't stand being holed up like this," Nick whined. He was definitely the smarter of the two, but his highly nervous edge and lack of confidence made Marty the stronger, more capable leader.

"We can't leave yet. Not until we know what the hell is going on."

"Well, we can't stay in here forever! I can't stand it anymore, I can't stand it!" Nick was sitting on the cement floor of the dark, cold basement warehouse they had hidden in three nights ago. His arms were wrapped protectively, pitifully, around his knees, and he rocked back and forth. "I gotta have some rock, Marty, just a little, then we can come right back."

Marty crouched down and leaned forward, looking at Nick with surprising sensitivity. Marty understood, all too well. He hadn't been home or been able to circle the streets in three days. Since that bastard Linden confessed he was a cop on the phone. Who would have figured? He was the best enforcer they had ever had, got right into the games and kept everything in control. It was quite a loss... and quite a slap in the face to discover he was a cop. Of course, Marty had to silence him, and Linden had deserved to pay by tasting the stuff he was trying to get a lead on. It was justice.

Marty hadn't counted on the hell that had broken loose after he'd been injected, though. The freak had flipped out with the drug in him for the first time; pushing, screaming, fighting like a demon. He couldn't be contained, and had run like a mad dog before Marty and Nick could catch him. Who knew where the hell he was going or what he would say, so Marty and Nick had immediately known to hide.

Now Linden was dead, and Marty had to be sure no one would try to pin it on him and Nick. He'd pumped him full of *Racer*, and had hoped he'd killed him with it at the time, but he hadn't beaten him to death; and wouldn't have been so stupid as to kill him in a park, where the police were sure to find him. Still, his guilt was obvious, and someone might be trying to set him up to cover their own hide. He couldn't let that happen.

At any rate, his crack supply had dwindled away while they sat here worrying day after day with nothing else to do, and now both he and Nick were desperate for a fix. "I know, buddy, it's hard, but we can't leave until we know what's going on. If you think this is bad, imagine what prison will be like. We can't take any chances."

"Well, let's get a hold of Regis, man, he can tell us what's going on, and get us some rock, too. I'll stay as long as you want, but I gotta have some!" It was a frantic, keening cry, pleading and pitiful.

"We can't, Nicky, I told you; before we went into the warehouse the other night, him and his freak girlfriend tried to run me down. They acted like it was a mistake - like she was just scared, but what if they were lying? What if Regis was in tight with Linden on the side? What if that's why the cop was setting up a meeting alone with his girl? We can't talk to Regis until we know."

"Well, we gotta do something, *anything!*" Nick had grabbed onto the lapel of Marty's coat, and was looking at him with the desperate, dangerous features of a drug addict. He was going to do something drastic, stupid, if something didn't happen soon, Marty could see it in his eyes.

"We'll do something tonight, I promise, just hold on a little longer."

Before Nick ever got a chance to respond, Marty was shushing him and releasing his imploring arms with a nervous shake. He heard footsteps in the alley. Nick began to sob with hysteria as Marty got up and went to the small window, typically positioned high on the wall of the basement room. It was covered in a dark, heavy blanket the two had nailed up there three nights ago. Very carefully, he pulled a tiny edge of it to the side and peered out.

Someone stopped directly in front of him, and Marty flinched, trembling with the fear of being seen, even through the heavy material and dark shadows. Perhaps it was possible, because the person proceeded down the alley, and a minute later, the warehouse door was opening. Stark, solid footsteps began to descend ominously into the basement; slow, agonizing, and sure of themselves.

Marty grabbed a crowbar and readied himself in a nervous, menacing fashion; his legs shaking, the crowbar raised over his head, ready to strike. He had no control over himself and was so petrified, he would strike at anything to avoid being caught. The footsteps stopped, and it was silent for several seconds. The intruder was listening, trying to assess the situation. Suddenly, with a command that was somehow both a comforting drawl and a vicious bark, the visitor spoke. "Marty!"

It took a moment for Marty to respond to the voice. It was steeped in the shadows at the bottom of the steps, and the speaker wouldn't come any closer. The crowbar was still poised above

Marty's head, and Nick was hiding his face and sobbing into his hands in a drugged world of paranoia that immobilized him. "Regis?" Marty queried as if it couldn't possibly be him.

"Yes, Marty, it's me. Put the crowbar down."

"No way, man. No way. You tell me what the hell is going on! I didn't kill that cop!"

Regis' brow wrinkled in confusion. "No one ever said you did. Susan is being accused of the murder, not you."

"Why was she talking to the cop like that?"

"Like what?" Regis asked, ice in his veins.

"She was talking to the cop like they was good friends, setting up meetings and everything. I heard him on the phone with her. He told her, straight out, he was a cop. Don't jerk me around; I want to know what the hell is going on! You two trying to set me up?"

Regis sighed deeply, and his shoulders slumped decidedly at this newest proof of Susan's waywardness. "I don't know what she was doing, Marty," he said quietly. "I've been looking everywhere for her."

"Oh, God! The deal's dead, man, it's dead!" Marty whined with genuine distress. He and Nick had slaved after the dream of having the kind of money *Racer* would have supplied them with, and of having the power and prestige that came along with their important positions in its process. It had all been ripped out from beneath them so suddenly, so unexpectedly.

"Not if we can help it," Regis reassured, careful not to show any of the real emotions twisting him, like fear, and desperation. He couldn't be disgraced within the system, the hierarchy he'd become the prince of on the streets. He must succeed; he could *not* let this opportunity be snatched away from him!

"Now, come on, you know I didn't deceive you," he said sensibly. "You know I ain't trying to pin this on you, right? Come on, put the crowbar down and I'll tell you everything. You got nothing to worry about, The Judge is taking care of everything. He wants us back in business. Come on Marty. I brought you a present."

A slight jolt rocked through Marty at first. Then the crowbar slowly came down. For several moments Regis ceased to exist as he held out a small flask-like container with several rocks of crack inside. Marty reached for it tentatively at first, then grabbed it with a swipe, turning his back on Regis. Nick jumped up now, still shaking uncontrollably, but with a more capable, if recklessly excited, edge. Fifteen minutes later they were beginning to relax, and the buzz was beginning to fade.

"So, what's with your girl, man?" Marty asked Regis, who was watching them patiently.

"I don't know... word is she gave an envelope full of information to the cop before he died, and now it's gone."

"Oh, hell, we gotta get out of town. The Judge must be nuts wanting to get things moving again."

"No, no, no, he must have his connections, as usual. I don't believe any of it is true. Susan wouldn't turn on me. I think this envelope crap is just a trick to screw us up. I say we relocate, sure enough, but we've got to get it moving again. The way I figure it, we've got to eliminate Larsen to do that; that bastard is always in the way."

"We gotta get rid of your girlfriend, too, if she ratted on us."

The ice was back in Regis' eyes. "I'll handle Susan, understand? If anyone touches her I'll kill him where he stands, got it?"

Marty's eyes bugged wide, and he stared at the hard determination that had suddenly frosted Regis' face. Since the previous few minutes had been full of easy camaraderie, this sudden threat was unexpected and extremely disquieting. Apparently, Regis was still the same dangerous bastard who'd snap in a minute if things didn't suit him. Marty would take care.

*   *   *

There was a beep on Michael's radio. His outside officers were trying to reach him to warn him of the sudden intrusion, but it was too late. Men were unexpectedly bounding up the steps of Susan Ventry's building with quick force.

That's when they heard Angela scream. "Kevin! Oh, my God! Kevin!"

Her cry was suddenly cut off and stifled as Kevin and Michael ripped through the entryway door, guns automatically pulled as they moved. "Police! Freeze!"

Standing before them were two of the darkest, dirtiest drug addicts they had ever seen up close. One had Angela by the throat, a long, lethal looking knife poised there to ensure her complete cooperation. The other was dragging Susan down the steps and out of her apartment.

"Stay where you are or the lady dies. I'll bet she bleeds a pretty shade of red, don't you, cop?" The man holding Angela spoke with evil confidence while his accomplice escaped behind him with Susan struggling in his hold.

Kevin and Michael stopped as ordered. In the instant they had to decipher this situation, something intangible within both Michael and Kevin knew these two men were Marty Rhodes and Nick Kline, the other pieces to this infuriating puzzle. Nick must be the one holding Angela, because Marty was reportedly the leader of this tag team and would have the more important task of getting Susan. This was obviously one of the reasons they were here. Regis, then, must be close by.

Kevin stared at the scene before him as Nick Kline held Angela with erratic ferocity. A whole world of pain flashed before him as he saw her like that, being pushed up against the filthy body of a drug dealer, with a knife at her throat. Only this addict's hyper, unpredictable whim would keep her alive, or see her dead. Once, long ago, Kevin had wished he could have been there when a man held a knife to the throat of the woman he loved. Now, blind fear almost paralyzed him as this woman was helplessly attacked. This one, very special woman.

Michael could sense Kevin's silence rather than see it, for he wasn't looking at his former partner right now, but at the episode before him. Susan Ventry, who he'd searched endlessly for over the last four days, was being kidnapped. Marty Rhodes was forcing her down the stairs, and Michael was trying to leap through the chaos to keep her safely within his grasp. Before him, however, stood Nick Kline, blocking the way with a knife at Angela's throat.

Michael began a slow, easy walk toward Nick. Angela's eyes were huge with confusion and terror that she suppressed in forced, shocked silence. She stood rigid and obedient against the man with the knife, but she watched Michael approach slowly, almost ethereally, as if he was floating.

At least that's the way he looked to Nick, who, in his completely inebriated state, was momentarily spellbound by the illusion. He stared in sidetracked fascination at the figure coming toward him. "Nick..." The voice was gentle and easy. How did the figment know his name? "You don't want to do this, right? You don't want to hurt this pretty lady, do you? Come on now..."

Nick's grip slackened, and Kevin inched forward silently, almost imperceptibly, having reached a firm and enraged conclusion. He would never let this woman die, and especially not at the hands of scum like this. Again, Michael sensed Kevin, rather than heard or saw him, and the trust and dependence upon his ability fell into place.

Just then, another shout broke free from the steps that Michael was trying desperately to get to. "Nick! Nick! Don't listen to him, Nick! Come on!"

Nick seemed to snap to attention. His eyes were suddenly not on Michael, the floating detective; they were on Kevin, the very real, tiger-eyed enforcer who was right at his side. With one jerky, terrified movement, the knife went up to Angela's throat to ward him off. He was just about to make the slit across it when Kevin raised one lightening quick arm and slapped the knife away with the barrel of his gun."

Nick was shocked, and felt truly threatened and endangered now. Weaponless, and losing ground fast, he scrambled backward, frantic to be free, dragging Angela back with him toward the door. "Get away from me, cop! Get away! I'll kill her!"

Kevin followed him step for step with the most intimidating, almost amused look on his face. Angela stared into his eyes almost unseeingly, yet, in a way, able to discern his every thought. He was winning, she could feel it.

Apparently, Nick felt it, too, and to defend himself against it, he attacked. With one sharp, angular movement, he brought his knee up hard against Angela's back. It was completely unexpected, and she cringed with a guttural, agonized cry, doubling over in pain. When she did, Nick flung her forward, turned around, and ran.

Kevin was outraged. When he saw the look of pain on Angela's face as she crashed into him, fury spiraled through him, and he reached for Nick with a vicious snatch. He missed him at first because Angela was stumbling into him, but he held her quickly to his side, and snatched again toward the steps just as Nick turned to fling himself down. Kevin caught the back of his pants and yanked so hard Nick crashed backward. His feet slipped out from under him, thumping down the first few steps uncontrollably while his upper body remained in place. His head slammed into the edge of the top step, stunning him into immobility for several seconds.

The sound of Kevin's gun being cocked was the next sound Nick heard, and then, "Don't move Kline, or I'll have to blow what little is left of your brain right off your head." Without even looking, Nick's hands went up, and he began to shake and cry in that familiar paranoia that so easily beset him.

In the meantime, Michael had raced down the steps after Marty Rhodes as soon as he'd seen that Kevin had control of things inside the apartment. Never had he been so glad to have his teams on hand for backup. They may be able to keep Marty from making his escape. Nick had delayed Michael and Kevin long enough to allow Marty to drag the kicking, screaming Susan down the steps, gnashing and scraping her body along as her unwilling frame bumped against each edge.

Marty looked back, though. He never had any intention of leaving Nick behind. When he didn't hear him follow, and heard, instead, Kevin Larsen's angry voice order him not to move, Marty had known Nick was caught. The next thing he knew, the rumble of what seemed like a whole platoon of officers was pounding up the basement steps. Others were rushing out from somewhere across the long, busy street in front.

Then came the other cop, crashing down the stairwell Marty had just struggled down himself. It was confusing, officers seemed to be coming from everywhere, running, shouting and aiming their pistols. Where had they come from? What were they doing here?

Marty had just made it to the car with Susan when the first of them emerged from the house, and the only thing Susan saw at that moment of terror was Regis' face.

"Give her to me, Marty, and get in the car!" Regis ordered as he grabbed for Susan's bruised body.

"No!" she screeched, as he lunged for her from behind the wheel. "Lieutenant Larsen, help me!"

That one plea coming from Susan's lips sliced into Regis' soul like nothing else could have. She was calling his enemy to save her from himself. How could that be?

He stifled her entire body in the enraged, determined strength of his arms. Strength that Susan knew only too well. The smell of him, the feel of him, engulfed her as he held her against him with easy familiarity.

Someone yelled, "Freeze!" in a terrible voice, but it was too late, and Regis was too determined. He shoved Susan's body down and into the car in a matter of seconds, using her as a shield as he started the car. The officers, three of them including Michael, stood aiming their guns and trying to get a good shot at Regis in the night's blackness, with the outline of Susan's head the only clearly visible target. Another two officers were now within sight as they ran from the other side of the street toward the house. Regis didn't wait for anyone else when he saw Michael come charging out of the house with his men close behind.

Michael flung his arm forward toward Marty, who was still hesitating over Nick. It only took one swipe, and Marty's frail, bony frame was face down on the ground and Michael was cuffing him.

Susan, however, had been captured, and before Michael really accepted that reality, Regis was pealing out of the parking area. With a direct glare that challenged Michael and sent rage exploding through him at the impudence, Regis stared at him through the distortion of the night, and drove away with Susan inside the car. The two other officers who had followed Michael out of the house chased on foot, and the team who had been surveying from across the street tried valiantly to block Regis' path as the car came crashing toward them. All to no avail. Regis was gone.

Marty screamed as he fought against the restraining hold Michael was pinioning him with. "Regis! Regis, help me, where are you going? Regis!"

"Shut up, fool!" Michael ordered. "He's not coming back for you! In fact, you're coming with us. Right down to the police station.

Because you got a whole hell of a lot of answers, and I got a whole hell of a lot of questions."

*   *   *

Kevin had trained his gun on Nick Kline, and dropped to the floor beside Angela. She could barely straighten herself from the brutal blow Nick had jammed into the small of her back. "You bastard!" Kevin screamed at him, as he lay there in a terrified, prone position.

Angela curled onto the floor at Kevin's feet like a baby in a fetal position, struggling for air. For a few horrifying seconds she couldn't breathe, couldn't move, and she thought the attacker had injured her seriously. She didn't even know what he'd done. All she knew was that one instant he'd been pulling her toward the steps, and the next instant riveting pain was slicing through her back.

She knew Kevin's deep rage as if it were her own. He glared at Nick between sweeping, agonized glances at her. Only his concern for Angela kept him from marching over to the steps and smashing the man's skull in. His hands upon, her, though, were gentle as she lay there, and he asked over and over again if she was all right. "I'm - okay," she choked. "I just got the wind knocked out of me, that's all."

"Are you sure?" He was peering into her face with rigid concern, as if he were afraid she would die.

"Yes, really," she moved stiffly, painfully, into a sitting position, "I'm fine."

It was then that they heard Susan scream for Kevin, and if the plea had sliced through Regis Black's soul, it tripled within Kevin as he stood three flights of stairs away from her, and she was taken away before he could stop it.

"Susan!" Angela shrieked, and hobbled in an attempted run toward the front window, hearing tires peal down the drive. The long black car blended completely into the night, and was streaking down the street with Susan locked inside.

Kevin, too, rushed to the window to watch helplessly as Susan was taken away, and his chest convulsed in fear and rage as he realized what had happened. Self-rejection flooded him. He'd failed. Not only had he taken Susan into his care, but he'd kept her away from Michael and the police who could have actually helped her. Surely, by his defiance and insistence on playing by his own rules, he had allowed her to be caught by the criminal she feared most.

It didn't occur to him at that moment that if he'd done things differently, he'd never have gone back to find her in Angela's shed; instead he'd have reported her. If he hadn't taken her in, she wouldn't have trusted him so completely, and never would have given him the information she did. Without that knowledge, they wouldn't have gotten even this far in the fight against *Racer*. As it stood, they now had Goldie, Marty and Nick. A pretty good start, specifically due to Kevin's intervention. Still, Kevin would have given anything to change it.

It was the look on Angela's face that Kevin wanted to change most, though. She was stricken, desperate, hysterical as she sagged into his arms and stared down the road again as if by straining somehow, she could figure out what had just happened, and tell where that madman had taken Susan. She turned to him and his heart clenched painfully. She was looking for answers, for reassurances. He could give her none.

"He took her away! He took her away! Oh, my God, he's got her!" Full, shaking sobs wracked Angela as she crumpled in delayed jerks against Kevin. "Do you think he'll kill her?" She looked desperately into Kevin's eyes to seek his answer. They were filled with compassion and as much uncertainty as her own.

"No! She's not going to die, everything is all right."

"It's not all right! He took her away! Oh, my God, he'll kill her!"

"I said it's all right!" Kevin insisted sharply, as if because he said so, it simply was. Amazingly, in her hysteria, that simple logic seemed reasonable. She calmed considerably, but still kept peering down the street into the darkness. Just this morning she had begun leaving for work like any other day. Now her whole world was starkly and irrefutably collapsing around her. She was in trouble bigger than she'd ever dreamed possible, and with people she had only glimpsed in her deepest, most dreaded nightmares.

~ *Chapter Twenty-seven* ~

Susan was stiff and immobile as she watched the wild-eyed glare in Regis' face. He held one heavy hand restrictively across her lap, actually gripping her hip in his attempt to hold her securely, looking back and around himself frantically as he drove. The bright street lamps whipped by like flashes of lightening, and the wind swished past in rhythmic, beating gusts. Headlights from cars traveling in the opposite direction beamed in front of them as they sped down the road, but no one followed. She was alone with Regis, and afraid to move, afraid even to look too closely at him. He was angry and full of resentment as he jerked the wheel of the car to and fro determinedly.

"Why the hell are you sitting there like there's an icicle up your back, Susan?" It was a biting question, hostile and goading, pelting into the thick tension mercilessly.

She looked at him with enormous, incredulous eyes. Was he really asking her why she was afraid? Wasn't it obvious? Surely, he was going to kill her for her betrayal, for her deceptions, for leaving him. "I - I - "

"Yeah... you turned on me, didn't you? You know you did," he said quietly, and looked at her with deep, inquiring pain.

Whereas a moment ago Susan had been afraid to look at him, now all she could do was stare. The picture before her was shocking and mesmerizing, because even though Regis was snapping his head around and inspecting their surroundings with a jerking anxiety, behind his eyes was a sincere anguish, a hurt tenderness that she knew all too well. She'd experienced that tenderness, and trusted it, so many times before. He wasn't going to kill her; he'd never intended to harm her at all. He *forgave* her! She realized with an unexpected rush that he must truly love her, as he'd always said he did.

He was so close to her. His hand still gripped her hip, his strong arm crossing over her entire chest at a shoulder to lap angle, but it didn't hurt anymore. He looked much less in control today than he usually did; younger, anxious and wild in a way, yet older and stressed at the same time. He smelled so good... he'd come to get her, and would not harm her.

"Regis... I..." That's all that could escape her throat. It was quiet and gentle, the familiar look of love shining through her eyes, but mixed now with a grown up decisiveness rather than a starry eyed, blind adoration.

She'd matured in the last few days, had made decisions on her own that she'd never thought she could make. She'd faced realities she didn't want to endure, and had come to find that the man she always thought she loved was real after all. He was beside her, loving her, even through the most difficult, costly betrayals she could ever have heaped upon him. Regis truly loved her.

His eyes darted down at her between glimpses of the road. When he saw the shocked adoration in her eyes, and her mouth hanging open in awe, his whole face seemed to relax. His arm suddenly swung upward and around her, pulling her into the warmth of his chest. He kissed the top of her head over and over again, as if he couldn't get enough of her simple presence.

She felt the hardness of his chest against her cheek first, then the all encompassing feeling of being safe in his arms. She began to cry, to finally spill out the anguish she'd experienced over the past few days: The hurt, the fear, the pressure, the huge irreversible decisions that she'd made. She cried for all of it, and clutched him to her as he continued to kiss her hair, the side of her face, her forehead, any part of her that he could reach without running off the road.

"It's all right, baby, it's all right. Everything will be better now, I promise. I'll take care of everything." He finally forced her face up and kissed her mouth hungrily for a split second. Staring into her eyes, he repeated his promise, "I'll take care of everything."

He seemed to phase into another realm then, a realm that dealt specifically with the trouble at hand. He still kept Susan possessively under his arm, but he stared straight at the road now, and concentrated on what was before him. He had just barely escaped being captured by the police. Cops were in the area right now, in fact, even aware of the moves he was making. They had known he would look for the PCP in Susan's apartment. What else did they know, and how the hell did they know it?

One of the most alarming parts of this debacle was that he was stuck in Canada now. He felt out of place, insecure, vulnerable here, but he couldn't cross back into the U.S. now. The authorities would spot him in a minute if he tried. It didn't matter much anyway. The project was dead. Everything was falling completely apart. Goldie, Marty and Nick had all been busted. The best thing he could do was stay in Canada with Susan, and try to regroup his life. Eventually he could try to build the empire he'd just begun in The States. Right now, he had to get away.

He turned the wheel of the car with a whipping jerk, and scooted his way into the traffic of "The Strip", one single street, officially named Clifton Hill, that stood between the calm, everyday city of Niagara Falls, Ontario, and the gushing wonder of the world Niagara Falls was. An entire avenue of activity was immediately at hand with everything from freakish attractions to movie theaters to fine restaurants, jammed together into this amazing quarter of a mile strip.

Neon lights flashed above various establishments, luring in the throng of couples, families and loners who walked the street in droves. Teenagers hung about in groups, assessing other such groups with the wonder, and danger, of youth. Where the U.S. side of The Falls was a long stretch of quiet, scenic parkland, this was the hottest tourist spot in the entire Niagara Falls vicinity, and was an easy walk from the incredible view the Canadian side of The Falls provided as well.

It was everyday life to Susan. She worked in a pizza joint on this very strip, and lived less than a mile away from it. To Regis, it was a sure means of escape as he pushed into the chaotic mix and blended easily. It was endless traffic sheathed in blessed darkness and it would be almost impossible to be seen in it. He inched his way along, watching behind him nervously and thoroughly until he neared the end of the street.

When they finally got there, he made an abrupt turn, and they were suddenly sailing down a dark, amazingly quiet, residential street. The further they drove, the quieter it got, and after at least a mile they made another turn, and another, bringing them to a very dark side of the city. A side that few tourists even knew existed, and wouldn't really care about if they did. Carefully, Regis pulled over to the side of the road and parked the car. "Here's where we get out, sweetheart," he said to Susan who was only barely conscious of anything except the warmth of his embrace.

She looked up and around her quizzically. "Get out? Here?"

"Yep, come on, we'll have to hurry."

Regis kept a careful watch behind them, sometimes actually stopping and pushing Susan up against a telephone poll or grimy shop window to listen intently to the sounds of the night behind them. Silence. Everything was quiet and they obviously were not being followed. Still Regis was cautious.

At one particular point he waited an endlessly long time, then finally turned to Susan. "Okay, let's go," he said, and was suddenly stalking into a dark, alley-type opening that kept the big two story houses from scraping together. When he was between one of them, with Susan's arm stretching tautly behind him as she tried to keep up, he began to run, and finally came out into another alley. Here they stood quietly again, and did nothing more than wait.

A creeping wariness had laid hold of Susan long ago: A familiar, disturbing sensation that she used to feel with Regis all the time. She'd identified that feeling five days ago, and had wanted to forget it a few moments ago. She wanted to forget right now! She wanted to remember the feeling of his love and protection, of being in his arms, of his promises to take care of everything. As he dragged her through the streets, though, she knew that the way he might take care of things wasn't at all the way she wanted them to be taken care of. They were still worlds apart, and she didn't belong in his circle.

"Regis, where are we going?" she whispered instinctively.

"For help."

"Help for what?"

"To keep us alive, and away from those cops, that's what," he said as if it should be obvious.

She was incredibly wary, and suddenly longed for the safety of Lieutenant Larsen and Angela. Lieutenant Larsen and Angela... Oh, God, they would try to find her. A stab of guilt sliced through her.

She wasn't supposed to be here by choice. She had been kidnapped. "Can't we just go away and forget this? We'll get jobs, live like normal people and put all of this behind us."

"That might be nice, but we're being chased by the cops at the moment." He stopped then and turned directly in front of her, scrutinizing her features as if he wasn't sure what her face really looked like. With a curious, slightly disbelieving intensity, he added, "And no, I can't leave it all behind. We were screwed out of our chance for success. These bastard cops wrecked everything, and made you turn on me. I can't forget that, Susan, I'll never forget that they used you against me. Besides, I can't walk away from this business. With any luck, we can relocate, and rebuild. You do have the money and the PCP, right? You didn't give it to those cops, did you?"

He was talking to her as if the past few days' events hadn't occurred. As if she were a willing part of his world. A wide-eyed dawning crept over her. Apparently, Regis didn't believe she betrayed him, and, that with her surrender to his love, she'd come completely over to his way of thinking.

"Do you?" he demanded harshly.

"Uh - do I what?"

"Still have the money and PCP," he answered with a horrible dread, shaking his head very slightly in wide-eyed denial.

"Uh - yes," she lied, more out of fear than anything else.

A huge weighted sigh of relief escaped him. "Thank God." He grabbed her into his arms and kissed her head again. Then, holding her to him, he closed his eyes in painful apprehension and asked, "Did you give the police an... envelope... or some sort of information against me?" He didn't dare look at her for fear of what he would find in her eyes, but kept her against his chest, and spoke into the air above her head.

"An... an envelope?" she said, fear sounding convincingly like confusion. "Why would I give the police an envelope?"

That was all she said, but Regis seemed to jump at it. "Oh, thank God, thank God, I knew you wouldn't betray me."

She let him hold her, and didn't say anything. What a crazy predicament she was in, and how badly she wanted to deny it. Her entire soul was shredded, and after a moment she latched onto Regis as he held her, and buried herself in his arms.

What was she doing? What was she supposed to do? If only she could get him to run away, leave everything behind them and start new. The trouble was, she knew he would never start new the way she wanted to. He would always be the violent drug dealer that he was now; who held one part of himself for her. A tender part. A part that truly loved her, and refused to believe she had betrayed him.

What would be so terrible about letting him live his life? Would she have to be so directly involved? If he loved her, maybe he would allow her to stay away from his business dealings. Maybe she could just stay with the man she loved, because when he held her this way, and looked into her eyes, what he did mattered so little.

As soon as he felt her relax into his arms, he pulled her face up and kissed her again. Susan was lost in that kiss. Her entire body was electrified, and nothing else mattered but this man. Everything and everyone else faded completely away... until she heard that voice.

"My, my, my, isn't this a touching picture."

Their heads shot up, and Regis' grip tightened on Susan, drawing her back just slightly, as if he were preparing to throw her behind him, if necessary. When he saw who had spoken, he relaxed, but didn't remove his arm from Susan, not even for a second.

Susan wished he would have thrown her back when she saw the face. Especially when the man took a long, lewd look up and down her body. She burrowed into Regis then, and he actually did take a step forward to shield her from the rude gaze. She wished for Lieutenant Larsen again. She wanted to scream for him to come and arrest them all, because the fear, the unrest, the utter filthiness of the drug world was all around her. It possessed no decency, and ran by its own set of lawless rules.

The man standing before her was Max.

~ *Chapter Twenty-eight* ~

"Something's come up," Regis said to Max in a hard voice.

"Really?" Max replied, dry sarcasm dripping from his voice in a way that made him seem aristocratic.

"Yeah, really!"

Max seemed uninterested in the trouble, as he looked at Susan. "So, you brought along your little girlfriend." A simple enough statement, but his greasy tone made Susan back up a few steps.

Regis lurched forward, and grabbed Max by the lapel. "Shut up, Max, and if I catch you so much as *looking* at her again, I'll kick your ass all over the street!"

Susan was amazed at how sharply Regis spoke. Max stood well over six feet tall, and had a thin, wiry frame that somehow made his strength repulsive. He carried himself with sure confidence and hooded eyes that always seemed to be lusting and offensive. When he spoke, the voice was quiet and condescending, like black, dripping oil. Wire rimmed glasses covered his eyes in the current style, but the thin hairline, combed carefully to the side of his head, still made him seem out of date, and freakish.

It was the aura around him that was most domineering and frightening, though. He carried an aggressive power behind the quiet exterior. A power that was marked by evil. This man would take pleasure in using, or abusing, anyone he must to satisfy his appetites. That very evilness, that willingness to cause harm without regret, made his less-than-impressive figure seem truly powerful.

Susan had always been careful when she'd had to speak to Max, much less ask for favors, but Regis wasn't careful at all. There was no form of respect or catering to him; just hard, cold demands that Susan was simultaneously grateful for and fearful of.

For his part, Max seemed completely unfazed by Regis' threats, but he didn't look at Susan anymore. Instead, he looked dead into Regis' eyes. "I know all about the trouble. What I want to know is what the hell are we going to do? I've got PCP all over the place, when is the next payment coming in?"

"Max!" Regis said with incredulous wonder, unable to believe he was still pursuing this, "we got *busted!*" The statement was simple, but the exchange was intense.

"And...?"

"Didn't you hear about the detective that got beaten to death a couple of days ago?"

"I heard. Little Suzy's in big trouble, huh? I saw her face all over the news, although I couldn't believe it. Who would of thought she had it in her to kill a cop?" A sort of perverse admiration laced Max's tone that was somehow lewd. It made Susan's skin crawl. "Anyway," he continued, "we can still move, just keep her hidden."

"Max! That cop was our runner!"

"Your *runner?*"

"Yes! He was an undercover investigator who's been living on Lex Street for over a year. You'd never have known he was a detective! Never! The night they were supposed to make the deal, Marty and Nick heard him trying to set up a private meeting with

Susan at our lab site, so Marty and Nick shot the bastard up with *Racer* to try to kill him, but he got away.

"In the meantime, Goldie and Hewitt cruise by the lab and there's this cop running through the streets; one thing led to another and *they* ended up killing him, *not Susan...* Whatever information he had, though, was enough, because cops have been all over us for days now! We can't even piss without them knowing. It's been crazy!

"Somehow this ex-cop, Kevin Larsen, got involved, and he almost busted me the other day; then Goldie gets caught trying to watch the guy; and just now we tried to get the dust from Susan's place, and they ambushed us! Now, Marty and Nick are busted too... We're fried!"

Max and Regis, hostile and belligerent one moment ago, seemed to connect into a world of interest and camaraderie now. Susan looked on incredulously, listening in silence. Max didn't even blink at the violence Regis summarized, but seemed intense with interest and concern nonetheless. "God, Regis... everyone's busted?"

"Everyone," Regis confirmed with hard eyes and deep anxiety he was trying to hide.

"Well, what the hell are they going to say to the cops?"

"I don't know!" Regis growled. "Hopefully nothing! They'll pin their own asses if they talk..." A shaking desperation was suddenly in Regis' voice. "I've got to get a hold of Dad."

"All right, all right, don't worry about a thing. I'll let him know. Nothing is going to happen to you, so don't worry." It was more of a demand than a consolation, but it was sincere and comforting, nonetheless.

Max switched his discerning gaze to Susan. She stood behind Regis with wide, guilt-ridden eyes, and sudden understanding of the intricacies of this relationship. Her long blond hair fell in front of her shoulders evenly. Max could see her mind blinking with realization, making the connections, learning more and more and more... Such an innocent piece, she was... uncertain, and so tempting in her vulnerability. "Why was the stuff at Susan's place?" he asked smartly, trying obviously to make sense out of the mess set before him. "She was supposed to bring it over almost a week ago."

Regis hesitated, and looked back over his shoulder just slightly. Susan stared at him, pleading with him, wondering herself, actually, how Regis had reasoned this through in his own mind. If he wasn't sure himself, how would he ever explain it to Max? God, this evil man was Regis' *brother*. "She kept it there when she heard about the bust."

"Oh, yeah...? And how did the cops know where to find it?"

"Look, Max, I don't owe you any explanations!" Regis was suddenly defensive, and an edgy lack of control was coming upon him. Max noted every difference.

"I told you I never trusted her, Regis. She's way too nervous for this line of work, and *way* too 'Miss Goodie Two Shoes'."

"She's fine!" Regis insisted simply.

"You're blind where she's concerned, and you better smarten up! *How did the cops find out where the PCP was?*" he asked in slow, distinct tones, as if he were trying to drill the question, and its relevance, into Regis' head.

"I told you! The detective that was hanging around busted us!"

"Busted what?" Max shot out sarcastically. "You killed him before he could say anything - so what did he bust? And that wasn't my question. My question was: how did the cops know where to get the PCP *after* the cop was dead?"

"How do *you* think, smart ass?"

"I think Little Miss Muffet, here, told them, that's how."

Susan was shaking so badly, and was so filled with unmasked guilt that she thought she was going to vomit. She took a few more steps backward and stared at Regis' back in desperation. She couldn't see his face, and didn't dare speak, she just pleaded with him in some deep recess of her mind not to give her away to Max. Surely, he would have no mercy on her, or Regis, if he were to know the truth.

"That's crazy! Susan would never tell the police anything about me!"

"She wouldn't, huh?" Max leaned completely around Regis so he could get a good, intimidating look at Susan. "What do you think, Susan?" he asked her loudly.

"What?" Susan jumped at the booming sound of Max's voice being directed solely at her. Regis shot around protectively, to watch her face as she answered.

"I said, what do you think? Would you ever talk to the cops about us?"

She looked back and forth between them, longing to rush into the protection that Regis' arms could offer, but he was looking at her with ice in his eyes again. Dead, frightening ice. Like the night he had taken her to the crack house, and she had seen that dark, violent side of him. In that particular frame of mind, he was her worst enemy, because surely the same emotion that committed him to her so intensely would enable him to shoot her through the heart if she wasn't with him completely. "No... I love Regis."

Regis' whole body relaxed, and a light entered his eyes, along with the hard dominance that he'd acted with when they first met Max.

"Then how did they know? And why didn't you meet with Marty and Nick that night like you were supposed to?" Max asked. Regis continued looking directly at Susan, waiting to hear her explanation for himself.

Susan wasn't thinking past her own immediate predicament and danger when she answered. If she had been, she never would have answered the way that she did. "I got lost on the way to the meeting, and I... stopped at a store to get directions."

"You got lost?" Max asked with sarcastic skepticism. "How many times have you been downtown, Susan? A few thousand?"

"No! Actually no, I was only there once. Regis and I never went there." It was the truth, in a way, but it also effectively skirted the question. For she had, in fact, only been on Lex Street once, but she knew exactly how to get there.

Dawning realization washed over Regis, and a rush of relief bolted through him. He hadn't had a chance to ask Susan how or why this had all come about, and deep within he hadn't wanted to know. Now he understood... the lady at the garden store... yes... It all finally made sense. With renewed power, and absolute conviction in his voice, he confirmed Susan's words as if he'd known this was the truth all along. "It's true, I only took her there once. It's this lady she asked directions from that caused all of this."

Susan instantly realized her mistake, and everything within her wished she could take her explanation back.

"What lady?" Max asked.

Regis answered, making his explanations, and Susan's excuses, as much to himself as to Max. "She asked directions at some garden store, and this busy-body lady got herself all hooked in. She gave the cops a description of Susan, and they traced her. That's how they found out who she was. They put her face on the news, raided her apartment, then they wouldn't let her go. I just had to kidnap her from them!"

"Why would this lady give a description of Susan? Some kid comes asking for directions and she just assumes there's some connection to a cop killing?"

"No!" Susan said desperately, trying to recover this, for she knew where it was leading. "She tried to help me. The detective told me the meeting had changed to Armondo's -"

253

"The *detective* told you? When did you talk to him?"

Susan hesitated for only a second. "He called me."

"He called you? Is that why you were on the phone with him?" Regis asked, enlightened and hopeful at the same time.

"Yes..." she answered slowly, wondering how Regis knew about the phone call. What else did he know? Enough to know she was lying?

"How did he know your number?"

"I thought you gave it to him. I guess - being a cop - he had ways of finding it out."

That made sense.

"Anyway, he told me you said the meeting had changed to Armondo's. I'd heard you talking about a lab, so I figured that's where it was," she lied. "When I got there the cop... he... attacked me."

"He what?" Regis demanded.

"It's true; he attacked me."

"What did he do to you?" Regis asked, rage in his voice.

"Nothing. Really. The lady helped me, I swear, but that's how she knew the cop was connected to me. She saw us together. She was just trying to help."

"Yeah, that's why she reported you," Regis said sarcastically.

Susan stood there biting her lip in guilt and terror. If she told Regis and Max that Linden had known Susan's name and what she did for their business because she had confessed it to him, they would surely slice her throat right there. As it was, they assumed, erroneously, that Angela had reported her to the police after she learned of Linden's demise. Susan couldn't tell them the truth now! Not here, alone as she was with them.

"The project is dead," Regis declared furiously, resentment boiling within him. "I've just got to get the hell away from here now. Maybe I'll drive into Montreal and get lost there for a while. After some time goes by, we can regroup and start over again."

"Do you realize the loss we've taken?" Max asked with deadly quiet, his eyes closing in anger, as if he needed to settle himself before he could go on.

"I realize every bit of it. If things die down, though, and I'm tucked safely away in Canada where the American cops can't reach me, we'll only need a couple of months to put it back together. We'll make it happen, and we'll be rich, too, I promise."

"Don't be stupid, Regis, do you think the U.S. cops haven't told the Canadian cops about you? As far as they're concerned, you just kidnapped their witness, in *this* country. There's probably a hundred units looking for you right now."

The thought of cops chasing him made Regis' insides churn in fright. It was all too true; detectives had seen him kidnap Susan. God, if they found out who he really was, an entire hell would break loose. With Goldie, Marty and Nick all in the hands of the police, any number of pieces of his life could be exposed. In fact, it was all too possible that someone would blow him in intentionally, to get their own selves off the hook. *He had to get away! Right now!* "I've got to get out of here!" he said desperately. I've got to get away from here before I get caught. I'm way too close here."

"All right, all right," Max said with pained capitulation. "You can take the money... don't worry about paying me back for now, just... go and keep yourself safe. I don't think you should travel through Canada as you are, though - with this little chit at your side, you'll be busted for sure. I think the best thing you can do is grab hold of yourself and we'll get you back into The States. From there, you can very easily, and very casually, get a flight out of the country tonight. That's the safest way.

It was a good idea. An excellent idea that seemed to bring a calming order to the chaos within Regis. He must move quickly, that was for sure, but if he just relaxed and depended upon the front that had been established for him long ago, he would be all right. There was only one problem... The money.

Regis' eyes narrowed in a mix of confusion and hesitancy to speak. Turning toward Susan he looked at her questioningly, but stilled himself from asking the inevitable question in front of Max. It didn't matter, though, Max was painstakingly aware of every nuance about the pair, and of every inconsistency about his brother. On the night the deal was supposed to be made, Susan had one hundred thousand dollars in cash, to be delivered to Max for the PCP he had fronted to Regis. Max never got the money. So, where was it?

Unable to hide his confusion and hesitancy any longer, and seeing that Max was reading him anyway, Regis looked intently at Susan and asked quietly, as if to keep Max from hearing, "Where is the money, Susan?"

Susan's head reeled, and her nerves stood completely on edge. Every second that passed brought about more tension within her; more need to escape. Regis was planning to take her away. At least she assumed that he was taking her with him. They would go to a far off country, and after a time he intended to start producing *Racer* again, with the PCP that he assumed was still at her apartment, the formula she had stashed in the envelope and given to Linden, and with the money she had given to Lieutenant Larsen. She couldn't keep this facade up any longer. Sooner or later, they would figure out the truths, the inconstancies would become evident. She had told everything, and given proof of it all, to the police.

She longed for the protection of Lieutenant Larsen again. His strong smile, his sure way, and the righteousness he represented; which caused every other strength he possessed to escalate into true power. And Angela... to be in the safety of her motherly embrace again... to know the love and acceptance she offered. Susan craved it. She *must* get back to them.

Both men stared at her again, their gazes unnerving her to a point of trembling. She wanted to run, to scream, to collapse in utter panic, but if she dared do any of that, she would not live through this night. She could see now the fine line of brotherly blood that ran between Regis and Max. They fought like they hated each other, but depended upon one another with a bond. Nothing, including her, would be allowed to harm the other, or interfere with that bond.

She had barely escaped the accusation of her betrayal and lied her way out of it in time. She couldn't tell them that she'd given the money to the police. She must do anything to make them believe that she was ultimately still with them. She was thinking fast. Too fast. "I left it in the shed."

"The shed?"

"Yes, I - stayed in that lady's shed after the attack. She was nice to me, and I didn't know where else to go. I hid the money there."

"Again we return to the garden store lady," Max said icily, as if he were suspicious of something. "She must be one hell of a lady."

A sinister vengeance entered his voice, a hatred that Susan could sense. He wouldn't let this woman's interference go unpunished, no matter how many times Susan tried to convince him that her reasons had been helpful. "What's her name?"

Susan clamped her mouth shut and refused to reply, but Regis had no qualms at all about blurting out the answer to that question. In fact, he did so with a relishing, biting contempt; ready to place blame, to hate the woman for causing the harm to Susan and himself that he perceived she had caused.

"Her name, is Angela Cahn..."

~ *Chapter Twenty-nine* ~

The ride back into the U.S. wasn't nearly as quick as the ride into Canada had been. Furthermore, as nerve-wracking and risky as that first journey was, Angela thought, it had been easy by comparison. Now, an armed escort rode before and behind the row of official police vehicles carrying her and Kevin, Michael and his men, and the two criminals they had apprehended in the country.

A whole line of questions had to be answered, and Customs inspectors checked everything from names and identities to the contents of each unmarked vehicle. They were completely cooperative in helping the U.S. police with their task, but every offense had to be properly noted.

None of that really affected Angela. She was part of the undercover team that had gone in, although she and Kevin hadn't presented any such identification for that task when they entered the country. It didn't matter. A point so trivial could be easily overlooked, and, of course, no one told the Canadian authorities that they had actually been smuggling in a wanted criminal at the time.

Angela was more concerned about Susan. She stared out the window of Kevin's car, watching through the large windows of the

Canadian Customs office as Michael and his men dealt with all the details Customs required. She'd calmed considerably since seeing the kidnapping occur before her eyes, but she was still frantic. Susan had been captured by Regis Black. God, she could be dead right now! A team of officers had gone out combing the area for her and Regis, naturally, but nothing had come up. Black had a good head start, and the proper restraining of Marty and Nick had caused enough confusion to give him even more time to get away.

He was gone; with Susan.

Angela closed her eyes despondently and tried not to panic, or cry. She felt like doing both, and yet could do neither. All she could do was sit and stare, and contemplate distantly the incredible things that had happened to her in the past four days.

A simple occurrence had taken place; a young woman asking for directions. Nothing highly irregular, nothing monumental, and yet the complexity of that incident was likely to affect Angela for the rest of her life. In fact, she knew that her life would never be the same again. Especially if Susan died.

She felt her lip quiver, and the burning sting of tears behind her eyelids. It was impossible to be so emotionally attached to someone she didn't even know. She was, though. She had wanted so very badly for Susan to be all right. All she could imagine now, as she took deep shaking breaths, was her sweet, frail frame being tortured and beaten at the hands of a dangerous drug dealer. So, the panic returned.

The door to the driver's side of the car clicked softly, and Angela spun her head around. She hadn't even noticed that Michael and his teams were coming out of the Customs office. Finally. Now a whole sea of disturbance was entering the cool, peaceful night air that had given Angela a few moments to sit and ponder.

Marty Rhodes was screaming uncontrollably as one of Michael's men hauled him out, forcing him into a waiting squad car. Nick

CHRISTY LAUGHING

Kline was whimpering pathetically as he followed, trying to scoot after Marty unsuccessfully. When the tough looking police officer behind him directed him toward another squad car, Nick got hysterical and started screaming for Marty. He was forced into the car anyway and Angela knew a moment of troubled pity for the man as he plastered his face against the window, screaming desperately, looking for the security of his partner.

Michael followed it all without expression, and nonchalantly got into his own vehicle. Just as he was about to shut the door, though, Angela caught him with his own troubled look. He seemed unfazed in front of the mob, but all of this, especially Nick's sensitive panic, bothered him a great deal.

Kevin slid into the car gently, as if any sudden movement would cause Angela to shatter. He didn't take his eyes off her face when he saw the tears, and the edge of bewilderment behind them. He sat perfectly still for a moment and regarded her. The rest of the groups were starting their cars and pulling slowly away from the Customs offices and into the lanes directly across from them that would take them back into the U.S. One Canadian official stood waving a bright orange flag to guide them through a specific, designated booth so they wouldn't be detained any longer.

"How's your back?" Kevin said in that quiet way.

"Sore, but it's all right." Angela looked at him then, and didn't say another word, but her eyes were filled with the many issues plaguing her. He wanted to reach for her so badly his hands flexed convulsively. He wanted to erase the blatant anguish that was in her eyes, ease the worry, feel her relax against him. He wasn't sure if she would let him, though, or where she wanted this relationship to lead. He didn't know, either.

She had come upon him so unexpectedly, and had wound her way around his heart without the slightest bit of effort. All he knew was the way he had felt when Nick Kline had a knife to her throat:

260

total, fearful despair, and direct, consuming rage. He would have done anything to save her at that point, anything. In fact, it had taken everything within him to remember to act rationally. Especially when he'd seen that vicious knee connect with her back.

"Everything is going to be all right, Angela. Really."

She just looked at him and shook her head. "You don't have to say that. I know how bad this is. If that drug dealer came after her, he did it for a reason. You know how afraid she was of him. She believed he would kill her if he caught her. She's got too much information against him."

Hell, she'd pegged the issue precisely. He threw his head back and leaned it against the headrest of his seat, closing his eyes and trying to deny the situation. "I wish I could have been there. God, I wish I could have been there so bad."

"Kevin, you couldn't have done anything differently."

"I just keep hearing her voice, calling me for help. I can't get it out of my mind."

She reached over and touched his arm. "There was nothing you could have done," she said firmly. "And I, for one, am glad you were there with me."

He looked down at her hand on his arm first, gentle even though she was trying to be tough, then looked at her. "I'm glad I was with you, too. I would never have let him hurt you, Angela. I would have shot him where he stood to keep you safe, I swear it."

She stared into his eyes, and her heart skipped several beats as he made this declaration. Slowly, self consciously, she pulled her hand away, making the gesture even more obvious. She was suddenly very afraid of the passion in his eyes, of the commitment that seemed to jump out of him toward her; of her own commitment that she appeared to have already given without proper consent or consideration.

When he saw her recoil, he looked away with a closed-off silence. "It all just got away from us so quickly," he said dismissively, as if all the incidents combined, including any personal feelings between them, were simply part of the procedure.

Angela blinked at the shift in mood and topic. She sensed his withdrawal, and wanted to pull him back to her, but she didn't know how, and was genuinely afraid to do so. "Yes, but you did a wonderful job." It sounded lame and manufactured even to her own ears, and she cringed when he turned the car on without even bothering to respond.

As they pulled away, the official with the orange flag stood impatiently, waiting for them to proceed through the special gate. Everyone else was far ahead of them now, and Kevin stepped hard on the gas pedal, trying to catch up, while he and Angela drove along in silence.

~ *Chapter Thirty* ~

Nick was still shaking the next day, still on the verge of utter panic, and still desperate for some reassurance. In fact, now that he was way past due for another fix, he was even worse. He would be the easiest target, the one who would break first, Michael was sure of it.

His footsteps crashed against the tile floor in resounding thuds as Michael approached the elevator. It would take him to the deserted halls of the third floor of the precinct. Special Team interrogation rooms were kept as private as the teams themselves, remote, and off in a completely isolated section of the DEA wing. They would be observed by Captain Jack and one trusted D.A. member only. Technically Marty and Nick weren't under arrest. Michael had purposely held off on an official arrest until the two could be sober enough to answer questions accurately, but without the interference of lawyers.

Interrogation was never easy, or fun, and Michael's day today would be full of it. First Nick, then Marty, then back to Goldie. Goldie's partner, Bob Hewitt, would be questioned, too. The evidence they had discovered would nail him. One of them *must* talk about Regis.

Nick's face was pasty white, and his nerves were obviously jumping. Michael smiled at him congenially as he stepped into the interrogation room, seeing his distress, and well prepared to use it ruthlessly to his own advantage.

John Casey followed Michael in, but he didn't smile. He looked positively livid, and determined to cut directly through any of the usual conniving criminals liked to dish out in these types of situations. When Michael sat across from Nick and casually sipped his coffee, Casey stood stubbornly off to the side of the room, resting an elbow high upon the wall as if he didn't have the time or the patience to deal with this.

It briefly crossed Michael's mind how well he and Casey worked together, and how good they'd become at this game. Casey swung right into the role of the hardened investigator, and Michael easily assumed the part of the considerate, reasonable officer of the law. It was all one big game, originated purposely to obtain results. Looking steadily at Nick, they began to play.

"Nick," Michael greeted calmly, quietly. Nick looked between the two officers as if he were watching a tennis match. They seemed so complex. One looked like he wanted to kill him, the other looked like he wanted to bring him home and reform his errant ways. Nick wished desperately for Marty. "Can I get you a cup of coffee?" Michael offered.

"No. Can I see Marty? I need to talk to him."

"Of course," Michael answered with level-voiced understanding, and a carefully non-condescending tone. "You can see him when we're through. But first we need to talk."

"I ain't got anything to say."

"No?" Casey shot out with biting intimidation. "You knowingly shot a police officer up with enough crack and PCP to kill him; used, manufactured and planned to distribute an illegal, mind-altering drug; broke into a police witness's apartment and assisted in her

264

kidnapping, possibly her murder. That's not to mention the fact that you held a woman at knifepoint while you threatened detectives, then assaulted her. And you've got nothing to say?"

Casey stepped toward the table angrily, and leaned his strong arms on it so he could peer right into Nick's face. "I think you've got a *lot* to say, and you better start now, or you won't ever see your friend *Marty* again."

Nick's eyes were huge, and his entire body was shaking. He fixed his eyes on Michael quickly and desperately, as if he were a lifeline. Michael leaned in and looked back calmly. Very gently he said, "Nick we already know that you and Marty are manufacturing *Racer*, and that Regis Black is your boss. You can't get out of here with that information over your head. We have proof from Detective Linden. He knew because he lived right out there with you, didn't he? Who the hell would have ever thought he was a cop, right?"

Nick didn't answer, but his expression betrayed him as Michael quietly drew him further and further into his persuasion. He even smirked a little, mirthlessly, and his eyes darkened with agreement when Michael referred to Linden.

"Why don't you tell me about Linden?"

"There's nothing to tell."

"Why'd you shoot him up with *Racer*?"

Nick pursed his lips tightly together and looked stubbornly toward the far wall.

"The man asked you *why!*" Casey roared.

Nick jumped as if he'd been shot at, and looked again at Michael, and away from Casey. "Who is this guy?" he asked, referring to Casey.

"This is Sergeant John Casey. He's the homicide investigator in charge of Detective Linden's murder."

"Yeah, and I asked you *why!*" Casey actually started toward Nick, threat in every movement.

"John, *John!*" Michael stood up and held him back. "Settle it down, huh?" Michael looked directly into Casey's face as he spoke, the words more of a warning than a suggestion. Casey backed away, and repositioned himself against the far wall, elbow resting high against it as he fixed an unblinking, raging gaze upon Nick. Nick flinched, and began shaking uncontrollably. Exactly the response Michael and Casey were looking for.

"I'm sorry about that, Nick," Michael said with calm consideration. "Sergeant Casey gets a bit excited at times. "Now... you were telling me about Linden."

Nick stared at Michael again, obviously taking a great deal of comfort in his reassuring presence. "I... Linden?"

"Yes, you were telling me why you shot him up."

Had he been telling these cops that? He couldn't remember, what with the crazy one flipping out on him like that.

Michael saw the confusion and hesitation, and spoke quickly. "Linden was your runner," he said, as if Nick had provided that information. "You found out he was an investigator, and you shot him up, right?"

"...Uh, right."

"Okay, how did you find out he was a cop?"

"Me and Marty was going into the bar and we seen him on the phone, looking real nervous-like. It was loud so he didn't hear us come up behind him, but we heard him talking to Susan. They was setting up private meetings alone. Then he hung up and called someone else, and starts telling them he had talked to 'his contact', and she knew he was a cop, and was going to meet with him to give him information. We knew he was talking to other cops."

Michael remembered that incident with a pang. The cop Linden had been calling was him. His voice was smooth and placid as he asked, "So, you shot him up?"

Nick nodded.

"Why did you do that?"

"To get rid of him."

Michael nodded as if this were a logical and reasonable response. "I see... was *Racer* supposed to kill him?"

"Yes."

"Too much of it, right? Too much will kill someone?"

"Yes, it can. Not him, though. He was a freaking monster. It made him ten times stronger, and he went ballistic."

"Yeah, I can imagine, he was a big guy to begin with, huh?"

"Damn big."

"He would have made a great runner... That's some stuff you got there, too, *Racer* is. How'd you create it without blowing people's heads up like Spacebase does?"

A new admiration entered Nick's eyes. This detective seemed to be very wise. "Well, that's our little secret."

"Is it complicated?" Michael asked with seemingly genuine interest.

"Not really," Nick laughed.

Michael laughed, too. "Does anyone else know how to make it?"

"Regis made me write the formula down once and give it to his girlfriend."

"Susan Ventry?"

"Yeah, we were supposed to go through her for everything."

"She was Regis' contact person?"

"Yeah, up until the time she ratted on us."

"So, did you go to her home to kill her for that?"

"No, we went to *get* her - and the goods."

"The PCP?"

Silence.

"Will Regis kill Susan?"

"No, he won't ever kill her. She's his girl."

"Hmm. He'll probably just set her straight then, huh? Beat her up, that kind of thing?"

"No, he won't ever hurt her. They work together."

Interesting, very interesting, Michael thought. "Did Susan give the *Racer* formula to Regis?" he tried to ask innocently.

"I guess... she was supposed to." Alarm registered across Nick's face very suddenly, as if he'd been startled into consciousness. Something in him closed up, and Michael knew from experience that the opportunity to get anything pertinent from this suspect was over. He didn't bother trying. What he'd already said was enough for now... They would talk again later.

*   *   *

Marty Rhodes was a different story altogether. It was the same interrogation room, with the same two police officers, except Casey, still belligerent, was pacing the room like a pent-up lion, and was the one asking the questions now. Michael sat quietly, offering calm stability as he watched the questioning take place. The difference here was Marty would respond to an authoritative battering before he would ever be swayed by soft talking camaraderie. So, Michael and Casey, obligingly, gave each man exactly what he needed.

"Come on, Rhodes - really - they're making a fool out of you. They're walking away free men, while you sit here, being blamed for all their crimes. According to my sources, not only did you manufacture a drug that you knew had death potential, but now they're saying you pumped a cop full of the drug, then beat him to death, too!" Casey badgered.

Bingo! They finally hit a nerve in this sullen bastard. He looked up with incredulous rage in his eyes. "Who said that?"

Michael answered calmly, as if he were breaking some very difficult news to a good friend. "To be very honest, Marty, we've already spoken to Nick and Goldie."

"*Goldie!*" Marty almost shot out of his chair, angry betrayal lashed across his features.

"Yes, we brought Goldie in yesterday."

"And he told you *I* killed the cop?"

"That's pretty much the way we were led to believe."

Marty made an obscure sound of utterly disbelieving shock. "Well, he's a lying S.O.B., and he knows it. I did *not* kill that cop!"

"Then who did?" Casey asked, as if this were an argument he couldn't believe at all.

"Goldie killed him, that's who! Him and his partner, they hang together and do all of Regis' dirty work. I ain't taking no murder rap, I ain't," he said with conviction.

"But you did shoot Linden up, right?"

Silence.

"Did Black go to get Susan Ventry so he could kill her?"

Marty let out a sarcastic rush of breath. "No. He *should* kill her for turning on him, but the poor sucker is in *love*," he mocked.

"Where would he have taken her then?"

Silence.

"To Max's?"

Marty's eyes rounded in surprise when Casey spoke Max's name, but he still didn't say anything more.

"Where can we find Max?"

More silence.

They knew they had gotten everything out of Marty that they could, for now.

*   *   *

269

Officer Dwight Golden entered the room looking pale and slightly jumpier than he had last evening. Jail, even a local jail, was not the friendliest place, especially for a police officer. Not only did the other prisoners torment him continuously, but his fellow workers came down on a regular basis to add their votes of hatred to the pile.

Goldie was wearing down considerably, and the mouthy arrogance that had always been his cover-up was being replaced by the sniveling weakness of his true nature. On top of that, Regis had done nothing to help him, or even contact him to offer assistance. He had the power to do so, too. Perhaps Goldie was the only one who really knew the extent of power Regis Black had.

Michael and Casey watched Golden as he was led into the interrogation room, his lawyer following behind dispassionately. They didn't move, they didn't react, they simply watched as Goldie and his attorney were directed inside. Michael sat in one of the seats opposite them at the table, and Casey assumed his place by the wall, but they weren't playing any games with Goldie. With him, they would talk brutally straight.

They'd been doing this all morning long. It was now early afternoon and they hadn't stopped for even a small break. They hadn't wanted to. The momentum of finding out pertinent answers was charging the air around them, and they were laying hold of it greedily. This case must conclude immediately if it was to conclude at all.

"Well, Golden... you're looking like hell," Michael greeted the man spitefully.

Goldie wearily lifted his wrists for the guarding officer to unlatch the cuffs before leaving Goldie with Michael and Casey. He didn't say anything to the two men as their gazes shot into him, but his eyes were unsure and afraid. His lawyer whispered something into his ear.

Without further comment or preamble, Michael lifted a file up from the table and threw it down in front of Goldie. It landed with a slap on his side of the table, and Goldie looked down at it. Normal curiosity might have caused any other person to pick the folder up and look at it. The whole precinct, as well as the city at large, would have liked to know what was in that folder. Not Goldie. His eyes rounded slightly before he tried to look cool, and he refused to touch it. It was labeled "Forensics".

His lawyer had no such hesitation as he reached for the folder. Michael smiled an unamused, intimidating smile. "Don't you want to know what's inside, Goldie? Or maybe you already know. It will convict you, you can be sure of that. Perhaps you'd like to talk first, and confess your crimes."

Goldie didn't say anything, but a distinct line of sweat began to bead on his forehead, and he swallowed convulsively several times, as if he couldn't get enough moisture into his mouth. His lawyer set the folder down, looking grim, and again, whispered into his ear.

Michael reached over and picked up the folder, staring at his prisoner the entire time. This fellow officer had beaten Linden to death with his own hands. He was a criminal that had chosen and accepted the call into police duty; the call to uphold the law, and protect the innocent. Then he'd used his authority strategically, and promoted the very crimes he was supposed to fight against. He'd murdered one of Michael's own officers; a man assigned from his department. Michael had no mercy for him.

"It says here that Linden died of repeated blows to the head which cracked his cranium. Do you know how hard, and how many times, a man's head has to be hit for it to cave in like that? But of course you do, don't you? It also says that his heart failed only minutes before he actually died, due to trauma and a lethal mixture of crack and PCP in his bloodstream."

Michael looked up spitefully and stared right into Goldie's face. "To sum it up, he was shot full of *Racer*, which caused him to literally go crazy, and his heart failed from the combined trauma of having the drug in his system, and the beating you and Hewitt gave him."

Goldie looked down, and Michael thought the man might cry, but he still didn't say anything.

"No denial? Well, I'll be damned. He isn't even going to deny it, Casey."

Casey smirked with complete derision. The lawyer continued to watch. These police officers had the legal right to question his client.

"Can you prove any of this?" Goldie finally asked in a choking whisper.

"Yes, Goldie, in fact, I can." Michael looked down again at the report, and began to read off of it. "Fibers were found on the victim that match the fibers of a police uniform. The victim was handcuffed with regulation police cuffs, which he fought so hard against he bled at the wrists and ankles. Yours and Hewitt's cuffs were then checked, and traces of that blood, and Linden's skin tissue, were found all over them. Stupid on your part - you both should have known to disinfect them thoroughly.

"Your fingerprint was also found on the victim's lapel button, indicating that you grabbed him - like this..." Michael suddenly reached across the table in a simmering rage and grabbed Goldie by the lapel, literally lifting him off of his chair, and leaving him dangling from his arm like a terrorized rag-doll.

Casey charged forward in shock, and grabbed for his friend, darting glances at Goldie's lawyer out of the corner of his eye. The attorney had stood completely to his feet and regarded Michael with wide, stunned eyes. "Michael! Let him go!"

"Yes, Sergeant, I suggest you let my client go if you don't want an assault charge slapped against you," the lawyer said.

Michael refused. Instead, he continued to speak right into Goldie's frightened face, and finished his list. "...And, the angle of the wounds indicate that he was beaten repeatedly, and specifically, from two different sides at the same time with regulation billy clubs. The force executed suggests the strength of two adult males. During that beating the wood on one of the clubs splintered and lodged into Detective Linden's skull, and the splintered wood came from *your* club."

Michael dropped him like a sack of wheat, and he collapsed into the chair with complete resignation.

"Now... do you have anything to say?"

Goldie breathed in and out raggedly, shaking so badly he almost fell off the chair. "I... killed him."

"Dwight!" his lawyer warned sharply. Goldie held up his hand to silence the man.

"I want a deal."

"Let's hear what you've got to say, then you can talk deals with the D.A.," Michael said, indicating the viewing room, where everyone knew an official would be watching.

His lawyer looked disgusted, but nodded to Golden, who in turn, nodded to Michael.

"You and Hewitt killed him?

"Yes."

"Because he could incriminate Regis Black?"

"Because he could incriminate *me*," Goldie said angrily.

"How?"

"He knew everything, that's how."

"Like what?"

"About *Racer* - who made it - who was selling it - who was funding it. He could have nailed us."

"And just think, fool, you got nailed anyway. Now, exactly who did he know about and what parts do they play?"

Goldie looked horrified that he would have to answer such a question, but after a short, cornered pause, he did so anyway. "He knew Hewitt and me patrolled, and kept things in hand. That we were involved in helping it move once it was manufactured."

"And? Who manufactured it?"

"Marty and Nick."

"Marty Rhodes and Nick Kline?"

"Yes."

"How is Susan Ventry involved?"

"She gets the stuff back and forth across the border."

"Why across the border? Why don't they just keep it local?"

Goldie hesitated. "The..." He took a deep, disgusted breath before he forged ahead. "We have a supplier over there. He gets us the dust for a good price, and he's sort of in business with Regis."

"Max?" Casey asked sarcastically, making it clear that there was no point in trying to hide names now.

"Yes."

"Is Susan Ventry aware of her part in this game?"

"Oh, yes! She's aware of everything she's supposed to do."

"Uh, huh. Do Marty and Nick maintain a lab for manufacturing?"

Goldie looked up incredulously, and for the first time since he'd begun to talk, he hesitated. These detectives knew a lot, but they didn't know everything, did they? It occurred to him to try to withhold this last crucial piece of the puzzle, to try to salvage what little he actually could at this point. Michael leaned in closely, however, and read the wide-eyed, sudden dawning that came over Goldie.

"You screw with me now, Goldie, and you will be eternally sorry you did so. Not only will you land in a cell at Attica with all the home boys that would *love* to get their hands on a real live *policeman*, but before you go, I'll let you loose in this station, where all your friends can show you just what they think about a cop-killer. Now, where is their lab?"

Goldie was shaking again, and his face was pasty white. Michael sincerely hoped that he wouldn't faint before he gave them the information they needed. Something crucial, something they hadn't known up until this point.

"Armondo's." Goldie squealed in a whisper that was barely audible.

"What?" Michael asked, legitimately shocked. Had he heard Goldie correctly?

Casey, who had resumed his place by the wall after Michael had stopped his attack upon their prisoner, stood straight up and looked at Goldie.

"Armondo's," Goldie said again, stronger this time, "on Cane Street."

Michael turned his back on Goldie then, to keep him from seeing anymore of the shock he was experiencing at this revelation. Marty's lab had been at Armondo's? How could that be? He'd checked the place out himself. Nothing was there but footprints. They would have needed, at the very least, a stove to heat the cocaine needed to process the crack. That would require gas or electricity. The place had been shut down for years now. There hadn't been any gas, electricity, or water running there since it closed down. Or had there been? Casey was looking directly at him with the same incredulous expression on his face, wondering... just like Michael.

With great effort, Michael recomposed himself, and pushed this discovery aside, trying to act as if it hadn't shocked him as much as it really had. When he turned around, his face was cool, his expression straight. "And Black?" he asked casually. What about him?"

"Nothing."

"Come on, Goldie, don't screw with me now!"

But Goldie's mouth was shut tight, and Michael could sense it. "Come on, Goldie! You've told us this much, we know the rest; it's only a matter of time before Black is brought in, too. He can't hide with this much evidence already against him!"

Goldie sat staunchly, the slightest mocking smirk and a supreme, unexplained confidence coloring his face. He looked directly at Michael and refused to speak.

"Racer is dead, Goldie, why are you protecting him? He isn't protecting you."

Goldie's expression shifted suddenly, and Michael knew he'd hit a nerve.

"You are going to rot in a cell for what you've done, and Regis will walk free. Doesn't that bother you? He's the one who started this whole thing, the reason you've put yourself on the line, and now he'll be free to get rich again, while you're being sodomized by your cellmates. We can make it a lot easier for you if you tell us where to find him."

"I don't know where to find him."

"Come on Goldie! You know how this goes! Do you want the maximum sentence? Either way we know his name, we know he's out there, he's already been incriminated!"

Something in Goldie finally snapped. "No one can incriminate Black, because no one knows what the hell he's really all about!"

Michael's brow furrowed. What was there to know about Regis Black that they had missed so far? He was just a common drug dealer. Wasn't he?

~ *Chapter Thirty-one* ~

Michael and Casey were exhausted when they finally emerged from the interrogation room. Most of their day was gone, and they were bleary-eyed from the intensity, the mind games, and the deluge of information that now had to be properly assessed and applied to the situation. In the meantime, the criminals were still at large, making plans that could devastate the city. They had to be stopped. That couldn't be done inside an interrogation room, and couldn't be done without the information found there, either. Michael wished he could be in two places at once.

Overall, the interrogations had been very productive, but they'd also confounded things all the more. Had they been blind where Regis Black was concerned? Could he be bigger and more obscure than they had thought before? It certainly was possible. The biggest influences in drug funding usually had immaculate businesses and identities. Hadn't Michael learned that before, first hand?

They walked along the corridor of the third floor in fatigued silence, planning to return to their office, have lunch, and dissect everything they had learned. This process would be equally long and exhausting, but a certain charged anticipation was, nevertheless, present. Michael and Casey wanted to eradicate this case, and would work non-stop until it was either under their control, or totally lost to them. The key to this whole situation was that *Racer* hadn't officially begun yet. How many times was a DEA office given an opportunity to stop a killer drug before it started? Almost never. They just *couldn't* lose it!

As they rounded the corner and approached the elevator corridor that led to their offices, Michael drew back slightly, and almost stopped in his tracks. Kevin stood there, leaning against the wall, waiting for him. The security glass walls on either side of this small elevator room prevented him from going any further on this floor without a pass, but apparently his influence could still get him into this section of the building.

"Hello, Michael; Casey."

John Casey stepped forward to shake Kevin's hand with a gleam of admiration in his eyes. Obviously, Casey was aware of everything, as usual, and appreciated the older man's unorthodox, if not outright rebellious ways. Kevin in turn, gripped Casey's hand firmly, and held on to it for an extra second. "How have you been, Casey?" he asked him with warm regard.

"Good, Kev, real good."

"Glad to hear it."

"What are you doing here?" Michael asked, as if he didn't already know.

"I just thought I'd come around to see what's up."

"Well... it's really not a good day, Kev."

"It's the perfect day," Kevin insisted

Michael sighed, and looked downward with pursed lips before he regarded his father-in-law over his lashes. "Kevin, I can't let you in on this. I just can't."

Kevin looked straight and tall, and conspicuously as though he'd never been denied anything in his entire life. "Michael, I'm already in on this - by *your* invitation. Now I have a very personal and extreme interest in it. Susan could be dead. I have to know what's going on."

"We have reason to believe she's all right."

"Reason to believe?" Kevin asked incredulously. "What am I, a common civilian? What have you got?"

"Look, I already pushed the limits by having you watch Angela. Jack was fuming when he found out I went behind his back. Your own highly illegal antics afterward certainly didn't help the situation. If you want access to anything else, you'll have to talk to him about it."

"All right," Kevin said with a certain haughty confidence, "where is he?"

Michael shook his head in profound exasperation. "He should be passing through here any minute."

Silence followed as they both stood there with Casey looking on. Apparently Kevin had decided to wait right there for Jack to actually arrive. The silence was thick and uncomfortable. Kevin and Michael, for the first time in their relationship, found themselves working on opposite sides. Neither of them liked it.

Michael looked at Casey, his partner, and Casey looked back with a huge, smiling gleam. He obviously wasn't going to be any help.

"Say listen, Kev, I really hope Ventry is all right," Michael said on a capitulating rush of breath.

It didn't help, Kevin still wanted answers, but he softened notably. "So do I. Angela would hardly even look at me when I dropped her off last night."

"Well, none of this is *your* fault," Michael said defensively. "She can't blame *you* for it."

"No, no, I don't think she does. But *I* do. She's just so heartsick... I can't stand it."

Michael and Casey stared as Kevin's eyes took on a pained, faraway look. "Awh, dammit! Come on!" Michael mumbled incoherently, stomping forward to lead Kevin through the locked corridors to his office. Something about how Kevin could always do this to him, could always make him talk, could always draw him onto his side.

John Casey followed the two with the same gleaming, amused smile.

* * *

"Nice office," Kevin commented as he entered the room, "maybe I should have kept this job."

"Yeah, maybe you should have, then all of this would be legal."

"Come on, Michael, I was a Special Team Lieutenant less than a year ago; retired with honors and keys to the damn city. It's not like I don't know about all of this," he waved his hand around at the tightly secured suite of DEA rooms. "Or like you're spilling your guts to a novice. I can help you, and this case."

Michael sighed. "I know, that's why you're here. Have a seat."

"I, for one, am glad to have you aboard, Lieutenant," Casey said as he took his seat behind his desk.

Kevin smiled and winked at Casey. "I hear you've been a pain in Black's ass, as usual," he said. "Fine job, Casey, as always."

"Thanks, Kev," Casey replied humbly. Kevin's words meant a lot to him, especially since he and everyone in the room knew that Casey hadn't *always* done such exemplary work.

"Now, what did you find out about Susan?"

"Well," Michael answered, "both Marty and Nick said Regis wouldn't kill her. Actually, they both say he was in love with her; maybe a bit obsessive in it, but love just the same. They either didn't know, or wouldn't tell what he intends to do with her, though."

"Yeah, that's the question, what the hell is he going to do with her? He has to know she betrayed him. In fact, I know he knows that. So, why does he want her back?"

"I don't know."

"Did you learn anything else?"

"Yeah, it went pretty well, actually. The biggest thing is that Armondo's was Marty and Nick's lab site."

"What?"

"Yeah. That's what Goldie says. Seemed like he thought we should have already known that, didn't it, Casey?" Michael looked to Casey questioningly.

"Definitely," he replied. "By the way, that means they must have cleared everything out of there right away, because I went in two days later, and there was no sign of a lab. In fact, the dust was already settled, and all the gas and electric records say utilities have been turned off for over a year. How do they manufacture any crack related drug without a stove?"

"Unless they hadn't used the lab yet. They were just now planning to make it big. Maybe they didn't need a lab until now," Michael observed.

"Well, who knew that Linden was going to make the bust that night? Could there have been anyone who might have warned Regis to clear out?" Kevin asked.

"I don't think so," Michael said with a rejecting shake of his head. "Only the teams knew, Linden, Captain Jack; that's it. Anyway, they were supposed to be meeting downtown. Instead, Susan calls Linden for help, and they meet *at the lab site*. How did Linden come to make his meeting place with Susan at that specific spot?"

"He obviously knew about it."

"Or she did."

"Why would they make a lab that far away anyway? I mean they're all from the Lex Street area, that's where the biggest drug sales take place, why move from there?"

"It's not *that* far away. Maybe it was for safety," Kevin rationalized.

"Oh, come on, you know as well as I do that the safest place for the dealers to be is right in the middle of it. They could have used any one of a hundred places on Lex and Powell for a lab."

"Not if the crowds were pressing in, as I hear they were, and beating and shooting the hell out of everyone once they were on the stuff. Maybe they wanted to get away from the addicts so they wouldn't get mauled, or robbed."

"That's possible."

"Maybe we're thinking too much into it," Casey stepped in. "Maybe they just needed a secure place, and found one."

"All right, but why that particular building, that particular location?"

"Now, there's a good question," Casey responded, reaching into his desk drawer to pull out a file. "And probably the best place to pick up from here. The Honorable Judge Carlton Souza, who, by surprising chance, happens to be in charge of the Armondo's case."

"He's our man. He's got to be our man," Kevin said.

"Problem is, he's clean as a whistle."

"Problem is, one of the properties he's got jurisdiction over should have been condemned a long time ago, and sits unattended so that drug manufacturers can use it as a lab," Kevin said with scornful realism.

"I agree, this guy should be thoroughly checked," Michael said solemnly.

"I agree, too," Casey replied, a bit of defensive insistence in his tone, "but I already did a background on the guy, I'm telling you, he squeaks." Casey looked down at the file in front of him and began to read off one of the pages. "He's been married to the same woman, Katrina, for thirty-five years. She, naturally, is a regular volunteer at her church, and also works with the local hospital's Aid's Babies.

"He's worked in urban development for twenty years now, supposedly trying to better the city streets. He's got two sons, Matthew Alexander, thirty-one, a science professor in Ontario who graduated from Princeton, and Raymond Gregory, twenty-seven, who attends Niagara Community; the judge likes to stay out of the limelight, and does his job fairly, and with excellence. Not even a scratch on him.

"Now, I'm not saying he's innocent, I'm saying we're going to have to dig a hell of a lot deeper to get anything, if it's there. I don't know if we've got the necessary time, either. We've got to be so careful investigating a judge. We can't just go asking questions around town. The press would grab hold of something like that before you could blink back your shock, and they'd be on us like glue. God forbid at that point if we're wrong about our theories; it could cause a chaos. Not to mention, more press coverage would make our targets crawl even further under their rocks, and we might never be able to dig them out."

"Well, we'll have to do what we can on this without letting that happen," Michael said. "We need to keep looking. Somewhere out there is a written formula for *Racer*, and Regis Black didn't want it for safekeeping. He can manufacture it without Marty and Nick, and I'll bet that's exactly what he intends to do. He won't let this die, I can feel it."

Something within Kevin was clicking, and he was far away from the conversation. He was remembering Susan's words as she had confessed to him about her dealings with Regis Black. Something she had said... about meeting him at Niagara Community College, and he was... yes... twenty-seven years old.

"Kev?"

"Huh?"

"What's wrong?"

"The judge. One of his kids is thirty-one, *graduated* from *Princeton,* and lives in *Canada.* The other one is twenty-seven, and is just now attending the local community college? Isn't that a little odd? Susan met Regis Black at Niagara Community, and says he's twenty-seven years old."

All three men stood still and silent for several seconds, looking at each other before Kevin spoke again. "I say we check out *Raymond Souza* and see what his story is."

*   *   *

Casey dialed Michael's number with a satisfied smile from the Student Center of Niagara Community College.

"DEA."

"I saw him!"

Michael, completely engrossed in files and glances at his computer, looked up. "What?"

"I saw Raymond Souza's student ID card, and it's him: the same face as the Regis Black I talked to at the bar. He's registered as a part time student, but he rarely attends any classes at all. In the past month he hasn't attended any - must be busy with other things, huh? His mailing address is listed as 19 Meadowlark Terrace, his father's home, but his friends say he didn't live with his father. One girl in particular used to date him, and said he has a hellhole of an apartment downtown on Polk Street."

"Great! Polk is right in the Lex and Powell area. Any specific address?"

"No, but I'll bet if you look up all the unoccupied buildings in that area, you'll find Judge Daddy is in charge of a few. If so, all we need to do is check them, and I'll bet we find Regis Black's home sweet home. Also... I spoke to a few fellow students, it seems that, among other things, he likes to make a joke out of calling himself Raymond Gregory Souza - *Black*, because he's the black sheep of his family. Put the initials together and you've got R.G.S. Black - Regis Black."

Michael smiled triumphantly. "*Yes!* Casey, we're going to have to start paying you double. In the meantime, I have something on him, too. Says here that Raymond Souza was arrested nine years ago for possession of cocaine. Thank God he made it to his eighteenth birthday or there wouldn't even be this record of it. Of course, he never served any time for the offense, and there is no record of any other arrests after that, but it does prove that at least once in his life he had illegal interactions with drugs. And... I did a check on Officer Dwight Golden. Ventry claims he was a relative of Black's. Took a little searching, but I found out that Judge Souza happens to be his great-uncle, which makes him Raymond Souza's second-cousin."

"We got him. We definitely got him. Now all we have to do is find him, and stop him. I'll bet everything I own that Matthew Alexander Souza plays the same name games as his little brother, too - Matthew Alexander - Max."

"I'll bet everything I own that you're right."

"What does Kevin think about all of this?"

"I don't know, I made him leave. I have a meeting with Jack at four, and I didn't want him to walk in and see Kevin sitting here."

"Are you going to tell Jack that Kevin is in on this?"

"Yep; straight out. I don't think he'll mind as long as he's told."

"You're probably right. So, where is Kevin now? Tearing up the courthouse?"

"No, no. He had more important things on his mind," Michael smirked, "he went to check on Angela."

~ *Chapter Thirty-two* ~

Angela slipped the phone into its cradle with utter defeat and stared listlessly at the work order that had just come in. Topsoil. Five bags of topsoil, the easiest and most ordinary order that could possibly come into a garden shop and Angela had completely botched the call. Did she even carry topsoil? Of course, she must have some somewhere. How many pounds came in a bag? She wasn't quite sure. And the clincher; did they have any in stock? Angela didn't have a clue.

The customer on the other end of the line must have thought she was a total nitwit! She just couldn't concentrate. She felt like lead was in her bloodstream. A draining fatigue invaded her every movement. On top of that, it felt like she hadn't been in her store in months, and she truly wasn't sure anymore of even the most uncomplicated particulars. In reality, she had only missed *one day*. Just yesterday, she had tried to leave for work and had gotten accosted. Then... Kevin had been there.

Lieutenant Kevin Larsen. She couldn't get him out of her mind. The way he had helped her, the way that masked attacker had backed away from him in fear, the way he had taken Susan into his heart. What an incredible man; ruggedly dominating and frightful, yet filled with understanding and compassion.

She had let him leave last night as if she couldn't care less about him. What a fool! The look in his eyes, though... it had frightened her. It had been so long since she'd allowed a man to look at her, much less get that close to her. This man, however, moved straight through any pre-set boundaries, and broke down even the most staunchly constructed barriers. He'd seeped into her blood. Now he seemed far away from her, as if when he'd left her safely in her condo last night, he'd left her for good. What a *fool* she was!

Then, of course, there was Susan. Always lately, there was Susan. She could be dead right now, in some Canadian gutter, possibly filled with the drug she had tried to stop. Angela couldn't face that! She couldn't face it! She stood up abruptly and began to pace, to straighten her desk, to try to think plain, solid thoughts to curb the panic. She couldn't think that Susan was dead. She could *not* let herself believe that!

She picked up the phone with shaking hands, her stomach turning over in compulsive, insistent fear, and dialed the number Kevin had left her last night. She must talk to him. She needed to hear his voice, to feel the security of his presence. The phone rang, and rang, and rang. Kevin wasn't there.

*   *   *

Regis held Susan against his side as they drove across the bridge into Niagara Falls, New York. What a ridiculously simple procedure the Customs inspection had been. Of course, Matthew Souza, University Science Professor and upstanding son of a U.S. judge, could pass through at any time. Naturally, he was going to visit his father. Regis and Susan had gone completely unnoticed by simply crouching down in the back of Max's respectable custom van.

When they had made it safely through, Regis led Susan attentively back up to the front of the vehicle.

"I won't leave Susan." Regis said with steel in his voice for at least the third time.

"Awh, for the love of God, you don't have to leave her!" Max said in profound disgust, having reached the limit of his patience with the two long ago. As it was, their insistent, revolting 'love' had caused more problems than would ever have been normally allowed, and now had probably erased Regis' chances of getting away safely. He should have been on a plane last night. Because of *her,* more and more delays would be necessary.

Max was fuming, and would have loved nothing more than for his brother to leave his sweet little Suzy in his care. "She'd probably end up getting lost on the way back from the airport, if you did leave her anyway, and *just happen* to run into the police commissioner," Max continued derisively. "It may take a few days to get her a change of identity and legal passport, though. A lot of time will be wasted. You should have left last night. If you were smart, you'd let me drive you to the airport right now. You might stand a chance that way."

"No way! Susan and I stay together!"

"Well, you're stupid then, as usual. The police are questioning Goldie, Marty and Nick. You don't think anyone will talk? The cops are probably talking to them right *now*. Even a few more hours could mean your ass."

Regis looked torn. Maybe Max was right. It would be easier and less obvious if he and Susan traveled separately. Together they were sitting ducks. Especially since her picture had been all over the news. People thought she was a cop killer, and the airlines were already, most assuredly, on the lookout for her... if not for him. How could he leave her, though? Could he trust Max to take care of her, and send her to him when the time came?

"No!" he said aloud. "We'll have to figure out another way. We can drive all the way into Texas if we have to, and cross into Mexico from there. No one would be expecting that, and I'm sure they don't have our pictures up in Texas. Me and Susan stay together."

Yes. That was a great idea. That's exactly what he would do. Feeling a sudden rush of relief and confidence that infuriated Max, he continued in a solid, certain voice. "In a few months we *will* regroup, and pick up where we left off."

"No, we won't. Everything is lost. Even if we *can* regroup, how are we going to make Racer without Marty and Nick?"

At this, Regis smiled smugly, and Max's fury escalated. He hated it when Regis was able to function without his direction, and with this project he was far, far too independent.

"Do you honestly think I would leave something of this size in the hands of *Marty* and *Nick*? I'm not that stupid, and I would never depend on those two dopers. They were valuable to me for just the reasons they are proving now. In case of any type of bust - it's their asses, not mine." He smirked haughtily, as if everything, all the upset and panic that had been igniting the air over the last eighteen hours, had only been a part of the plan. "*I* own *Racer*, and I have the formula," he said dominantly.

"You? How did you get it?" Max asked with genuine surprise.

"I *asked* for it," Regis answered sarcastically.

"What the hell are you going to do with it?"

"Use it. I'll get the PCP and coke, and I'll find another street junkie to mix it - which isn't hard to do - or I'll make it myself."

Thankfully, Max sat quietly for the moment, staring at the road before him in thwarted bewilderment, never asking where the formula was. Why would he? His brother had simply said he'd had it. There was no reason to question where it was.

Only Susan knew where it really was. In an envelope, that she'd let Regis believe didn't exist. During the long night they had spent waiting for daylight so they could cross safely and inconspicuously back into the U.S., they had talked and talked. The twisting tales of half-truths and outright lies had spun so tightly she felt they would choke her.

He'd looked fiercely into her eyes, as usual, searching; unable to comprehend that she might possess strength of her own. Then he said, "Goldie said when he found Linden running down Cane Street he was screaming about some envelope that you gave him - with information in it that'll incriminate our operations. Why would he say that?"

"Oh..." she had replied, a light of fear entering her eyes that wasn't lost on him. "I just said that to the cop to make him leave me alone. I didn't mean to get you into any trouble," she covered, letting him think her anxiety came from having implicated him somehow. "After he attacked me, I said I would - give him proof - if he let me go."

He looked at her for a long time after that, and had turned away with his own light of fear, a shadow of doubt, a longing to believe her - and an incapacity to actually achieve it.

She could barely keep track anymore of all the lies she was being forced to instantaneously concoct whenever a new question was addressed. Each deception had both assaulted her sense of guilt, and successfully kept her alive. She was beginning to tire, though, and she was getting confused. She couldn't remember anymore where the real facts began, and her invented version ended. The pressure of trying to walk that tightrope, on very little sleep, and anxiety that literally made her stomach cramp with nausea, was choking her.

As they drove along the interstate toward Angela's shed, to retrieve the precious money they would need to get away - money that wouldn't be there because Susan had actually given it to Lieutenant Larsen - she listened to, and really heard Regis talk now;

about Marty and Nick's "purpose" for him. Her blood ran cold, and her resolve was strengthened. Regis had set her up the very same way he'd set up Marty and Nick. She realized it now, no matter how much he looked into her eyes and held her close. When it all came right down to it, he used her like everyone else. To shield his own self from danger.

She was the contact. The runner. Regis' eyes, ears, and voice. He had set her up as the connection between his crimes and his criminals; so that if anything went wrong - it would be her life on the line - not his.

The formula for *Racer* had been given to her in the very same way, and for the same purpose. She was to get it from Nick, and keep it safe in her own care. She'd done that. Certainly, he hadn't expected her betrayal; and never at any time in the past four days had she been so glad she'd done it. Her own sense of smug satisfaction filled her, and a large degree of the guilt she'd harbored for her lies and offenses vanished. She would have the last laugh - the very last laugh... and cry.

*   *   *

Randy stopped completely dead in the middle of the stockroom aisle as he looked at Angela. The bag of topsoil he'd been heaving stilled effortlessly in mid air, and was left forgotten as it sagged to the ground by his feet. Angela hadn't taken even one day off in the past ten years, except for the occasional flu, and her yearly visits to her parents' home in Florida, which she'd always planned for meticulously months ahead of time. All of a sudden, a few days ago, she started going nuts; closing up unexpectedly early, never showing up at all yesterday, and now she wanted to know if he wouldn't mind her leaving in the middle of the day today!

Deep-set worry lines creased her face, and she wrung her hands and stared into space absently when she thought she was alone - or was so preoccupied that she simply forgot other people were present in a room with her. No one was going to tell Randy that everything was all right.

A police officer had come looking for her yesterday morning, for crying out loud, then she disappeared for the remainder of the day without a word, while strangely inconspicuous vehicles parked themselves conspicuously around the building. This morning she pops in trying to act like nothing was unusual about her actions, gives him some ridiculous story about the police just wanting to ask her to donate to the New York State Policemen's Fund, and can't function well enough to take a simple order! Something was definitely wrong.

"Please don't ask, Randy," Angela said in a hoarse whisper when she saw the look on his face. She held her hand up as if to ward him off, and there was a mixture of distress and total honesty in her eyes. She couldn't tell him anything, but she was at least admitting that something was up. Something far worse than raising money for the police fund.

He rested his hands on the corners of the topsoil bag, more or less holding it up around his knees. "Angela, just tell me... are you in trouble?"

"No," she was close to tears, "I promise, I am not in any trouble. Something has happened that I can't talk about, that's all."

"Something illegal? To do with that officer?"

"That officer is helping me. I..." She looked up and took a deep, cleansing breath, her eyes tormented, confused about what she should say, yet longing to share it with someone. "I witnessed a crime the other night. A terrible crime that I can't talk about, so please don't ask, but now I just... I just... can't get over it. I'm so afraid."

"Oh, Angela." It was the stricken look on her face, and the thought of her alone in her fear that caused the compassion within

Randy to charge into overwhelming proportions. He reached for her, and she cried full, wracking tears against the comfort of his shoulder. "Why didn't you tell me?"

"I couldn't. I shouldn't have even told you the little bit I just did. It's a criminal case, and... I'm a witness."

"Well, what was it that you saw?" He stopped himself and looked downward. "I'm sorry, I didn't mean to ask, but if you're in some sort of trouble - can I help?"

"There's nothing you can do. I'm not really in any danger, and I have some pretty awesome bodyguards looking out for me."

"Those cars that have been sitting across the parking lot?"

"Yes. They're there to watch out for me, but Kevin... Lieutenant Larsen... he's been wonderful. Do you remember Michael Camden?"

"The kid who used to work here?"

"Yes..." she smirked in slight dismay, "but he's not a kid anymore. He's a force to be reckoned with at the police station. He's helping me, too."

"Oh, God, Angela. Is it as bad as all that?" Randy asked, knowing, too, as Angela had known, that Michael was a prominent narcotics investigator now.

She didn't tell him anything more, and certainly nothing about Susan. Everyone in town had seen her picture and heard her name as Detective Linden's suspected murderer. He would be skeptical at best, and she didn't want him to make the connections, and know what she was talking about. She simply nodded and said, "Yes. So, that's why I've been so crazy lately." Recovering herself slightly, she reached into her pocket for a tissue. "I just... need to go home for a while. Please?"

"Of course. Hey *I* work for *you*, remember?" he smiled trying to inject a note of levity with his warmth. "Take all the time you need."

"Thanks, Randy. You're the best."

He nodded, feeling something churn deep within. He was afraid for her safety and her state of mind as she turned to leave, looking so alone, and so distraught. He felt stunned and powerless, as if he should reach for her and protect her somehow. Something about her, though, about the whole situation, had silently divided them, and he could sense that there was no place for him in this crisis. So, he just stared frozenly as she walked away, the showroom door closing slowly behind her. She was gone.

*   *   *

"Here's the shed," Max said with dangerous sarcasm, "where's the money?" He looked at Susan who was standing behind Regis infuriatingly. He was sick of her always hiding behind Regis. He was far beyond believing her anymore. In fact, he was rapidly becoming suspicious of everything she said, sensing her lies, and ready to do her some severe physical harm for them.

"I don't know. This is where I left it." Susan's stomach flipped over in fear. Her time had run out. She had successfully gotten them all back into The States, near to Kevin and the officers who could help her, but now she stood face to face with all of her lies, and no one was here.

The shed stood ominously quiet and void of any of the security she had depended upon when she'd huddled there a few days ago. Worse, she realized with edging panic that she had to stifle violently, she had led Max and Regis to Angela.

Max stared ice into her soul, and stood unyieldingly before her, but it was Regis who Susan was most afraid of at that moment. A peculiar silence settled over him when he looked into the empty shed and saw that the money wasn't there. It was a dangerous silence, and he turned slowly around to peer into her face and wait for her response. She was totally alone now. "This is where I left it," she insisted. "Right there." She pointed to a small space beneath the window. "Someone must have found it."

"Yeah... someone," Regis said softly, danger still in his voice, and menace in his eyes.

"Regis, you've got to believe me, I left the bag right there!" She pointed again, but no one looked.

"Did your *friend* by any chance know about the money?" Regis asked sarcastically with Max looking on in perverse satisfaction. Regis finally seemed to oppose her.

Warning bells sounded in Susan's brain, but she had to think too fast to heed them. "Angela? Angela wouldn't have taken it."

"Did she know about it?"

"Uh - umm..." Torment mangled her features, and it was easy to see that she didn't want to admit that Angela knew about the money.

"The garden lady knows," Max said to Regis, and Regis turned to face him.

"Yeah, she obviously does." He turned his head and shot Susan a derisive look, then turned back to Max to completely ignore her. "What should we do? We can't stand around here, and what if she turned the money over to the cops?"

"She wouldn't do that!" Susan spoke up, "I'm telling you, you've got it all wrong. Angela isn't involved in this!"

"Shut up, Susan! Okay? Just shut up. And until I see that everything you're saying isn't a total lie, don't speak again."

"But I'm telling you -"

"Shut up!" Regis lunged for her, gripping one of her arms with one of his hands and her upper neck with the other. For a brief second, she stared full into his face and a thread of restraint entered his eyes as he saw her. He held her in that position without moving for several seconds, obviously debating whether or not to strike her. Then he relaxed and said in a deadly whisper that worked far better than his loud order, "Just - shut - up."

She did, and from that point on, she simply followed along, was forced along, really, with one man convinced of her lies, and the other so unsure, he could just as soon kill her as wait to find out.

*   *   *

Angela drove with a panicked edge embracing her, almost pulling off the road a few times because she couldn't stand the tension within any longer. Forcing herself to continue, she finally reached her destination. One of them anyway. She walked up the steps of Kevin's home and rang the doorbell, her face twisted in anxiety. She had to see him, and when she did, she wouldn't leave him again until this whole nightmare had passed. Possibly not then, either.

Silence greeted her. She rang the bell again, then knocked insistently. No answer. With a disheartened resolve, she turned away from the door. What now? She could go to the police station, but what reason would she give for showing up there? Because she was having a panic attack over Susan's fate? That wouldn't be any good. They wouldn't tell her anything significant anyway. She could call Michael and get some answers from him.

Yes... She'd continue to try to get a hold of Kevin, too, for she needed him for much more than just answers. She needed him for peace of mind. It was a good idea, one that would at least afford her a bit of sanity, a bit of relief...

She reached immediately for the cell phone in her purse, then stopped. She'd heard about cell calls being easily intercepted by scanners and other listeners. Looking around herself in mild paranoia, as if she were suddenly on hidden camera, she decided not to make the call from that phone. She definitely *would* call Michael just as soon as she got home, though. So she turned in a rush, with renewed purpose, to do just that: go home.

~ *Chapter Thirty-three* ~

Kevin got to LCPU just a few minutes after Angela rushed out. So much had happened that he wanted to tell her about. So much had passed between them, too, that he didn't want to let go of. He couldn't, *couldn't* let this woman walk away from him.

He was increasingly fearful for her safety. Regis Black had escaped last night, with Susan, and had known enough about Angela's involvement in this whole mess that he'd tried to kidnap her for it. Why did that point seem to escape everyone? Why was Kevin the only one who seemed to understand the degree of danger that might put her in? *Regis Black was still out there.*

Kevin knew, too, that she would be frantic over Susan, and needing to be reassured. She was just that way; so very special in the way she cared, and so powerfully connected to that little lady. He would, most definitely, like to reassure her if he could.

He entered the door of LCPU, and as before when he'd entered, was impressed by the store. It had a quiet air of both professionalism and friendliness. It invited a person in to use its services, then paid careful attention once they were inside. A unique atmosphere. One that Kevin was certain had been created by Angela. Not for the first time, though, he wondered about her husband.

"Can I help you?" Randy began automatically. Then he looked closely and actually saw the person who had just entered the store. He left the display of lawn fertilizer he was working on immediately, and rushed up to Kevin. "Hello; Officer Larsen, right?"

"Just Kevin, please."

Randy took the hand being offered to him congenially, but his eyes looked sternly into Kevin's face; a hard look that tried to find fault, and assure himself of Angela's safety. Kevin noticed the glare and returned it, suddenly wondering if Angela might be involved with this man. If so, Kevin decided, he didn't like him.

"Is Angela here?" Kevin asked civilly.

"No, I'm afraid you just missed her. She - uh - wasn't feeling well, and went home for the day."

"Wasn't feeling well, huh...?" Kevin said knowingly. "Damn..." He looked upwards and spoke more into the air than to Randy. He wondered if the bodyguards Michael had assigned her were still being employed, and if so, how seriously were they taking their charge when everyone else seemed to be disregarding it? When Kevin looked back at Angela's manager, the man's eyes were scrutinizing and Kevin was taken aback by the hard discernment in his glare. "What time did she leave?"

"Just about ten minutes ago. Officer - Kevin - she told me that she's in some trouble and that you're helping her. Is that true?"

"That she's in trouble, or that I'm helping her?"

"Both - I mean, I know she's in trouble, but - are you helping her - and are you capable of helping her?"

Kevin glared back now and asked with smart, male suspicion, "What's your interest in it?"

Randy held Kevin's gaze. "She's very special to me - and my wife," he said pointedly. "She's family, and I'm concerned for her well-being."

Kevin relaxed and, seeing the genuine concern that came from nothing more than friendship, decided he liked Randy Tripp a lot. He had a smart sense about him - and he *wasn't* involved with Angela. Smiling slightly, with a sudden disarming gleam of admiration, he answered, "Yes, I think I can help her. I'll certainly do my best to try."

It was a reassurance, and Randy knew it. He also heard the deep meaning behind the words, and noticed the quality of man Kevin was. Relenting with a nod, and gentling noticeably, he returned the gleam. "Good. Is she in very much trouble? She really wouldn't tell me much."

"She's more worried than anything else right now, and that won't cause her any real harm. She's probably in very little actual *danger*. I would like to make sure of that, though, so if you don't mind, I'll try and catch up with her at home."

"Yes, please, go right ahead. Do you know where she lives?"

"Yes, sir, I do."

Randy paused at that for a split second, slightly amazed that there might be a side to Angela's life that he knew nothing of. This officer was obviously possessive of Angela in more than a professional way. "Okay, then," he finally replied, "take care, Officer."

"You, too, Mr. Tripp."

When Kevin got to Angela's condo, she wasn't there, either. He stood in the building's plush entranceway, with its soft carpet and matching chairs. It was grand in style and elegance, but a wall of thick glass closed the area off and isolated a caller from actually contacting a member of this condo. Kevin felt like ripping the exquisite chairs to shreds and throwing them against the wall. He buzzed her unit five times, laying his finger on the button insistently, but there was no answer.

"Officer Larsen?" The sound of the voice was unexpected and oddly familiar, the question hopeful, and full of unmasked enthusiasm. Kevin turned and looked toward it, and was overjoyed when he saw the maintenance man, Howard, in the doorway.

"Mr. Beck! Hello there!" Kevin reached to shake Howard's hand so enthusiastically, the man's chest puffed out with pride. Obviously, he'd found a new friend, and a famous one at that.

"Please, call me Howard."

"Howard, yes, it's good to see you again."

"Are you looking after Mrs. Cahn again?" Howard asked.

"Yes, I am. She was supposed to be home early today, have you seen her?"

"No, no, I haven't. Do you want me to let you into the ramp again, and you can see if her car is there," Howard suggested hopefully.

"I'd appreciate that, thank you."

Howard unlocked the security entrance, and for a second Kevin considered barreling the older man over and making a dash for Angela's condo. That would get him nowhere, though, he corrected himself guiltily, watching the man stand aside with a sweeping flourish to allow Kevin into the elevator. He considerately pressed the correct button on the wall, then stepped out importantly as if his talents were an invaluable assistance to police business.

Kevin smiled genuinely at the man. He was doing what he could to be helpful, and his trust in Kevin had just given him access to Angela's building. When he reached the garage, he could stop the elevator door before it closed, then he'd be able to move through the building without further hindrance. First, though, he would indeed go down to the basement level and see if Angela's car was there or not. Randy Tripp had said she left less than ten minutes before Kevin had gotten to her store. She should be arriving soon.

*   *   *

They waited. And waited. And waited. They thought they'd have to wait even longer than they actually did, though, for Angela to arrive. She surprised them all by showing up unusually early.

Regis had discovered yesterday how ridiculously easy it was to gain entrance through the underground parking ramp below Angela's building. The front garage doors leading down into the ramp had to be opened with a security card, which each member was given when they bought a unit in the building. For such a sanctioned dwelling, though, it was incredible how easily the member's cars could be accessed through the small door in the rear. Once inside, the large garage doors in back could be opened via a button on the wall, so Regis had opened it, and Max had quietly pulled his van inside, leaving the door open for a speedy escape once the deed was done.

A maintenance man milled about here and there, but he was occupied far up into one of the units right now, blissfully unaware of trouble, and never really considering that anyone other than authorized members or guests would be entering or leaving the building anyway. Unbelievable.

They sat in Max's van, watching. The tension within the silence was unbearable. Susan sat stiffly in the back seat. Every time she moved Regis' head would shoot completely around to look at her, to study her face with unmasked confusion; trying to discern which, if any, of the things she had spoken over the past day and a half were lies. He was still unable, or unwilling, to believe she had betrayed him, but they would all find out for sure very soon. As soon as they finally got Mrs. Angela Cahn in their clutches so they might ask her about the money.

What then?

"What are we going to do with her once we find out if she's got the money?" Regis voiced the question out loud, and Max, who had been measuring the tension in the air with satisfying notation, looked over at him.

"I guess once we find out where it is, we'll have to kill her for her knowledge, won't we?" Max said, looking in his rearview mirror to stare dead into Susan's eyes while he spoke.

A flash of rejecting anxiety crossed her face before she could hide it, and before she knew he was watching.

"Yeah... if she would have just cooperated in the beginning, none of this would have happened," Regis replied nonchalantly. Then, thinking the situation through, he spoke out with an irritated edge. "God, how long do we have to sit here? Every second that passes is more detrimental to us. We've got to get the hell away from here!"

"You're right, but you should have listened to me last night and already been gone! It's probably just as well anyway because it might take both of us to muscle the garden lady around and make her talk. Of course, we can threaten her with *Susan* if she refuses. Just hang on, it's going to be a long wait."

As if Angela heard those words and wanted to prove them wrong, the door to the front garage opened and she entered into the dark quiet of the ramp. She was completely preoccupied with her thoughts, and itching to get up to her home and make the call to Michael. She never saw the van, parked only two spaces away from her own marked spot, and wouldn't have thought anything of it if she had. It was stylish and smart, and fit in perfectly with all the other stylish and smart vehicles in the ramp. Until a door opened.

Sudden realization of danger assaulted her. For no apparent reason, she remembered, for the first time since yesterday morning, that Regis had been after her. Somehow, in Kevin's presence, and having seen Regis in Canada, kidnapping Susan, she

302

had figured he'd forgotten about *her*. Now something in her screamed that she was still very much in danger, and very much alone.

She looked toward the van apprehensively, trying not to seem overly dramatic, or to accuse where it wasn't warranted. Perhaps a visitor would emerge, or another member of the condo - with a new van - was getting home at the same time she was. There were any number of possibilities. Her mind was simply over imaginative right now because of all the stress.

A man emerged with a loose black sack over his head. She instantly turned to run, but he lunged forward the few steps it took to reach her Grabbing her arm, he spoke in a dangerous whisper that sent paralyzing chills down her spine as his words hissed in her ear. "Hello, Mrs. Cahn. As always, it's so very good to see you."

It was Regis Black. She recognized the voice and size of him from yesterday. A strange sensation crept over her as she looked into his eyes through the holes in the sack. For a suspended moment, he seemed to do the same, look at her, trying to find something in her eyes; the answers to her connection with Susan.

Susan!

"What have you done with Susan?" she asked angrily.

The question seemed to snap him out of his own haze, and an ugly rage entered his eyes. "What have *you* done to her is the better question."

He dragged her over to the van and held her before the opened driver's door, his fingers digging painfully into her flesh. As if to punish her, he shot an indicating hand out toward the scene inside it. "All this is your fault, lady."

Angela's eyes widened. Susan was held restrictively across the lap of a thin man who wore a sack similar to Regis Black's over his face. His hand was clamped across her mouth so tightly her skin stretched taut and white. There was something repulsive about the man, which Angela could sense rather than see. He seemed to take an obvious lewd pleasure at Susan's squirming body across his lap. She stopped when Angela's face came into view, and stared with a pleading desperation at the older woman.

"Susan..."

That's all that was said between them.

A loud cry sounded from behind. "Police! Freeze!"

It was Angela's bodyguards. She recognized them instantly as the pair that had been in the parking lot of LCPU this morning, except they looked very much like police now. Their badges were flipped open and attached to their coat pockets like flashing beacons. Guns stood out, larger than life, at the ends of their taut arms, stretched straight in front of them, and aimed directly at the group.

Angela was overjoyed to see them, but the two men assaulting her didn't seem to take them very seriously. Instead, Regis was in instantaneous rebellion against them. He threw Angela toward the van and with one mind his slimy assistant discarded Susan and reached to catch her, trying to pull her roughly through the door. Regis raced for entrance on the other side. They would bowl these two intruding officers over and get away with Angela and the information she had about their money.

Only one thing would stop them.

*   *   *

Kevin would have surely been spotted the minute the elevator door opened if Angela's bright red car hadn't monopolized the attention of those waiting in the van. She pulled in easily, and his heart gave a flipping kind of jerk within his chest. She was home. He could get her in sight and not leave her again, whether she liked it or not, until this was over.

He'd casually begun blocking the elevator door with the trashcan that stood conveniently off to the side when he'd seen the van door open. It had the exact same effect on him that it had on Angela. Something tangible entered the air with the movement.

A tall, masked man emerged from the van. Kevin's heart flipped again, this time in fear, as he saw the man stalk toward Angela, then lunge for her. Kevin set out immediately to lunge back. Years of investigating made him silent and agile as he slithered through the garage, behind the sparse supply of cars and guardrails, until he'd come close enough to reach for Black when the right time came. He was behind them now, and he could sense the sickening within Angela's gut when he, too, got a glimpse into the van. Susan was being held there, fighting against the unwanted hold of a lusty bastard. Max. Kevin knew it was Max.

The booming sound of the officers shouting their presence into the garage startled him, just as it had startled Regis Black and Max. They tossed Angela forward, but it was Kevin, coming up behind with striking speed, that got a firm grip on her. His arm pushed at Max's offending hands as he tried to stabilize Angela's sudden rushing weight and pull her into the van. He didn't stand a chance. Kevin's arms were around her, pulling back before Max could adjust to the change. Kevin and Angela flew backward from the sudden release and landed in a rolling pile beside a black BMW.

In the meantime, Susan had been released from Max's hold, and when she heard the commotion around her, knew this was the only opportunity she would have to free herself. She lunged for the big side door of the van, just as Regis occupied himself getting into the passenger door, and the mix-up allowed her the time she needed for escape. For some time to come she would regret the decision, but she couldn't have known what lay ahead.

"Susan! Get in the van!" Regis screamed clearly into the reverberating air of the garage. "Get in the van!" He held his hand out the door she had left open and she cringed away from him as Max laid on the gas and sped out the back garage door they had purposely left open. They passed Angela's guards, who chased them uselessly on foot as the charging van careened around and flew away from the building.

Kevin reached for Angela instantly and squeezed her to him. The concern he felt for her was evident in his eyes. Could it be just yesterday he had saved her in this same parking facility, from the same man? It didn't seem possible that so little time had passed, and that so much had transpired between them. Yesterday she had collapsed in his arms. Today he collapsed in hers, with relief, as she clung to him once again. It felt so right to have her there, safe, within his hold.

One of her guards was approaching now, as the van skidded away, Regis Black lost to them once again. It was incredible that he could escape twice this easily, when the best officers in Niagara Falls sought him. When the guard saw Kevin's face, and recognized both the rank he carried and the possessive way he held his charge, he slowed.

It was the other officer who shook their attention from one another. Kevin and Angela shot their heads up and looked around at a terrified young woman trying to run to them, who was stopped mid-step by the startling, guttural demand screamed at her. "Freeze!"

She froze, her hands flying above her head in the typical fashion without being told to do so.

"Susan Ventry! You're under arrest!"

~ *Chapter Thirty-four* ~

Max peeled away from Angela's building with uncharacteristic fear bulging from his eyes. He jerked the wheel of the van in and out, from side to side, as if the very hounds of hell were on his heels. He felt he would be caught. So rigid was the feeling, that it tingled his spine. He'd come in contact with police. That had never happened before. In fact, they'd completely surprised him, which made him wonder how long they'd been watching him survey Angela Cahn's building. Oh, God! The thought of being watched when he hadn't been aware of it intensified the tingling in his spine to painful, stabbing pricks of fear. He could *feel* himself getting caught!

Regis seemed not to comprehend the severity of what had just occurred. He just stared out the open van door in stunned silence as the scene disappeared behind him. His mouth literally hung open, and his eyes were rounded in pained disbelief. Susan had escaped him. Had *wanted* to escape him. So, she must, then, have betrayed him, too.

"Ray! *Ray!* Shut the damn door, will you? We're already in enough trouble without you drawing more attention our way!"

Ray Souza looked at his brother in a disoriented haze. With a jerk of realization, he slammed the door shut, then sat back on his heels for another moment. He was lifeless, numb, but Max wasn't. Max was running over with fear and anger. He had always been the family angel, smart to a fault, and full of all the right promises. He knew how to hide his true nature, where Ray did not. Max had always lived his life in pretense. Ray had insisted on being what he was.

All Matthew Souza really wanted was money and power, and he found both could be easily manipulated in the drug business. Especially when you already had money to invest, and you had a little brother who had paved all the dangers out of the way. Never, *ever*, had Matthew Souza thought he'd get caught, nor had he even dreamed of risking anything that would put him in this position.

Conversely, Ray Souza had lived with the pressure of street life since he was sixteen and strayed from the well-secured comfort of a stifling upper middle-class home. A home where he could never compete. Where he had always known he didn't measure up. Where he had always needed, *desperately needed,* to break free.

He'd never been this close to getting caught before, but he wasn't in an outright panic like Matt was. He knew from experience what would happen now. Like always, his father would cover his hide. He'd stretch those big, engulfing, utterly suffocating arms out to him, and promptly cover his hide. In fact, he saw the direction Matt had automatically pointed the van. The direction of his father's home.

So, as Matt prattled on in his undignified panic, Ray fazed out, still sitting completely motionless on the floor of the van. His body was large and solid, but his shoulders were hunched forward. The only relief he had ever gotten in life was when one certain little woman had gazed into his eyes and believed in him for what he was. Susan.

She had loved him unselfishly, had placed no demands upon him, and had looked up to him as her hero. Like all others, now, she was lost to him. He didn't care about anything else at the moment. It didn't matter that he had used her, had tried to force her into a life of crime that she detested, had set her up intentionally to receive blame if a situation like this ever occurred. All that mattered was the shock and pain of knowing that Susan had truly and completely betrayed him.

She was about to pay, too. He *might* go down, but she *definitely* would. She would find out soon, and she wouldn't have any idea of how this had happened. She had no knowledge of how completely she had been set up. From the very first day she had said "I love you," her name had been spread throughout the drug community as Regis Black's possession. The drug runner... known among the streets as 'Regis' girl, where the good stuff came from'. She never even knew it.

It had to be that way, because he loved her so much. If she'd stayed with him, she'd have been under complete protection, but as she did not, she was left stripped and alone to take the blame.

"Ray!" Max shouted in an agitated singsong.

"What!" his brother replied crossly, finally looking up and noticing Max's endless, annoying prattle. Regis' face was hard and accusing, a distinct loss of respect displayed there at his brother's lack of guts in such a crisis.

For a second Max looked at Regis, some sort of dawning shame colliding with his panic as he saw that expression. Much calmer, although it was an obviously forced calm, he said, "We just almost got caught by the cops. Do you think they were watching us?"

"I don't know."

"What if Goldie spilled, and told them who we are? We're busted if he did! How did they know we'd go back to Cahn's place for the money?"

"There's only one way," Regis said quietly, and finally pulled himself off the floor to squeeze into the passenger's seat next to Max. "Susan."

A renewed panic started in Max. "Oh, God. God, God... I knew she was no good, Regis," he shot out between his teeth.

"She won't go unpunished... so don't worry about it - and *don't* start with me! Just get to Dad's place - he'll take care of everything."

~ *Chapter Thirty-five* ~

In a college dorm, they ran through the halls, screaming in defiance, pounding walls and doors, throwing bodies out of their way. They were raging, frightening, and the other students backed themselves against the walls, or stayed securely in their rooms as the rampage ripped through the dorm. Security had been called, but they were no match for this level of volcanic anger. The two young students knocked the guards to the ground, and continued through the place with demon screams.

They reached the roof level of the building just as several police units arrived. The two young men looked downward in a muted haze. The red flashing lights from the police cars swam and mixed together as they spun about in circles atop the vehicles. The men watched the circles for a moment as they illuminated different objects and went around and around. The sight, the distraction, actually produced a strange sort of calm within them.

Then the torment began again. Both men screamed, almost at the same time, or perhaps one began first and disrupted the other. No one would ever know. As the student body watched from their windows and from below on the ground, both young men grabbed their heads, twisting and turning as if trying to get away from something inside. With a united purpose, they stepped forward, leaned in low, and jumped.

*   *   *

Broken glass covered Lex Street by midnight that night, and the hospitals were full of patients. A surge of extreme violence had routed the area, causing fights unlike any they had ever known, all at one time. Barrooms were in shambles all over the district, tables and chairs broken, walls caved in by pounding fists, their front windows shattered by flying objects and people alike. It was mayhem in the city.

~ *Chapter Thirty-six* ~

Susan was, indeed, under arrest. Michael sat across from her in much the same way he had interrogated Goldie, Nick and Marty. Except he was asking the questions alone this time, and was much gentler with her. Knowing what he did from Kevin, he wanted to understand her side of the story.

Even still, he was setting her up, and he knew she didn't know it. She'd waived her rights to representation during this questioning. A decision Michael knew was unwise, and knew sprang from her trust in him. As the interrogating officer, however, he was prohibited from cautioning her about it. Kevin would have cautioned her, had they let him get near her, but she had been separated from him and Angela immediately after the two officers had cuffed her in Angela's parking ramp. Now it was too late, and Michael was supposed to be feeling somewhat triumphant for this break. He wasn't.

Captain Jack stood rigidly in the middle of the viewing room, his legs spread apart like tree stumps and his arms folded across his chest. Susan couldn't see him through the dark wall of glass, but he most definitely could see her. One D.A. official stood next to him as he watched, and Kevin, having maneuvered his way through after

Susan had been taken from him, stood behind both, letting them listen to it all, hoping, praying to God, that they would hear what he had heard when she told him her story: Innocence.

"So, you're certain that Max is Regis' brother?" Michael asked her.

"Yes. They told me last night. Max told Regis to calm down, that he would tell 'Dad' everything."

"Do you have any idea where Max lives?"

"No, I really don't, but I assume it's somewhere in Canada, because that's where I always met him."

"Where? Where did you meet him?"

"In an alley off the strip. By the theaters. He was always there waiting when I had a delivery for him."

"Is that where you and Regis met him after Regis kidnapped you?"

"No," she answered evenly, as if to organize the conversation. She was in trouble, she knew, but these investigators were kind to her, and she felt that her best recourse was to be honest and helpful with them. "I don't know where we were then. Regis took me down the strip, I know that, then he kept turning in and out, and I wasn't looking at where he was going.

"Where were you looking?"

"I... I sort of... He was holding me under his arm."

"Forcefully?"

"Not really. He... kind of thought he had found me. He didn't realize I didn't want to be found. Anyway, after awhile he stopped the car and we walked through the alleys, but I'd never been down that way before. I didn't know where we were. Max just appeared out of nowhere behind this motel, and that's where we stayed that night."

"What was the name of the motel?"

"I don't know... Pine Court, or something. I didn't really pay that much attention. I was very nervous."

"Did you spend the night with Regis?"

Susan's face drained of color, then flamed. "Yes. I had to, or he would have known I'd betrayed him."

"So, you *acted* like you were still with him? On his side?"

"Yes. For my own safety."

"How did you come to be at Angela's home?"

The first light of fear, and regret, entered Susan's eyes. "Regis wanted to run away. So, he asked me where I'd put the money that I was supposed to deliver to Max the night of Linden's murder. Max said Regis could have it to get away. I didn't want to tell them that I had given the money to Lieutenant Larsen, so I told them that I'd left it in Angela's shed."

"Why would you even bring Angela into the conversation? Didn't you realize that Regis had attacked her just the day before, and drawing her into this would only cause her harm?"

"I - I didn't realize it until after I'd said it. I didn't want to hurt Angela, I was just - getting confused. The last place I had the money before I gave it to Lieutenant Larsen was in Angela's shed. So, I just said it was still there."

"All right." Michael leaned back in his chair and regarded her. What a tough spot he was in, what with Jack listening to everything. Michael tended to believe she was telling the truth about her involvement with Regis Black as she relayed the whole story over again, officially. He'd believed her the other day when he'd spoken to her at her apartment, just as Kevin had believed her. He wanted to give her a break, but this was out of his control.

Jack wasn't happy with anyone right now, and didn't know what to think. Michael knew he was observing all of this with a critical mind. He clearly felt that the two finest officers he had ever worked with, Kevin and Michael, had gone completely over the edge, and their judgments weren't to be trusted. Kevin had committed a serious crime by hiding this young criminal, then transporting her across the border. All of that had to come out in the open when Michael came clean about his father-in-law's involvement. Jack was astonished by the indiscretion.

Luckily his anger had been curbed just enough to keep Kevin out of a prison cell, based upon the exemplary work he'd achieved through his interference. He hadn't been appeased enough to listen and believe what Kevin said about Susan Ventry, though. Too much evidence was stacked against her, and while Kevin could handle Jack, like no other person Michael was aware of, even he couldn't stop the tide of motion that had already begun.

Michael took a deep breath. "So... you claim that in all the months you ran drugs across the border, you never knew what you were doing?"

"That's right."

"And you were never involved in the drug deals or Regis Black's operations?"

"No. Not until the end."

"And the first time you ever saw what was really going on was the night you saw that young man beaten to death? Is that right?"

"Yes." She was getting wary.

Michael considered her for a moment, then forged ahead. "I'm afraid I have evidence of a different version."

Susan's eyes crinkled in sudden fear and confusion, and a distinct lack of trust radiated from them as she looked at Michael. He had led her to believe he was on her side, and now he was springing something entirely new upon her. "What?"

"We have testimony from at least twenty different users that say you've been dealing drugs in the Lex and Powell area for over four months. Word is *you are* Regis Black's girl, but you're a willing part of his deals. *So* willing, that the neighborhood knew you were one of the connections to go to if they needed a fix."

"*What?* Who said *that*?" Her face was stricken and her eyes astounded at this summation.

"Every drug addict we questioned. Not to mention Marty, Nick and Goldie."

"*Marty, Nick and Goldie?*" she shouted, almost standing to her feet. "Goldie's nothing but a dirty cop who uses his position to bully people... and Marty and Nick *created Racer*. I never even knew who they were until a week ago."

"Unfortunately," Michael said with genuine compassion, "that's not what about twenty people told us on the street. Marty was *a* dealer, and you were another."

"*I never dealt drugs!* As soon as I found out about what I was really doing, I called Detective Linden! Why would I do that? Why would I give you all that PCP, and all the money?"

"Maybe because once you knew you were caught, you tried to make yourself look innocent."

"I *am* innocent! I was never a part of them, and I tried to get away! This is insane!"

Michael took another deep breath. "I'm afraid there's a particular group of people willing to swear that *you* sold *Racer* at the crack houses.

"*What? Me? It's a lie! A total lie!*" She was absolutely incredulous, and frightened, and she stood completely to her feet as she tried to convey her innocence. She couldn't believe what she was hearing.

"Susan, the problem is, none of this is adding up. Every person we've talked to says the same thing. You have been dealing drugs downtown for months. I can't battle against sound testimony, just because you say so. You claim to know everything, but you don't tell us anything we need to know. Things you should know, like who Regis Black is, where we can find him; who Max is, where we can find him."

"I don't know those things!" she tried to interrupt.

"Also, we can't find anything to support your story about that kid getting beaten to death. There's no body, no killer, no witness. Nothing in any of Linden's reports. A thing like that can't be so easily hidden, and we're beginning to wonder if the whole story wasn't just a fabricated lie you told to make your story sound plausible."

"No! It happened exactly the way I said it did! How could I make up a story like that?" she asked sarcastically. "That was the first, the very first, time I had even been on Lex Street, and I wanted to run away so far that I would never see anything I saw that night again! It was the first time I ever met Marty, and he was making a deal with Regis. That's why we were there. Marty wanted to show Regis the new drug. So, *he* went in and waved it around like it was candy, and *he* sold all of those people the *Racer*. I sure didn't. Then he came back in and told us that he had overdosed the five guys at the poker table."

Anger, at last, raised her head and caused a certain defiance that should have been there long ago. Except she should have stood up to Regis, not to Michael.

He leaned his arms on the table and looked across it into her face. Very calmly, too calmly, and with deadly quiet, he continued. "You tell us a story that we can't confirm - about a murder in a crack house. You claim to have given Linden an envelope that we can't find anywhere. Regis Black threatened Angela Cahn *looking* for it, which means that *if* an envelope existed, he didn't know about it until someone told him."

"That's because *I* made the envelope. He didn't *know* about it because I didn't *want* him to know! He would have killed me for what I was doing!"

"Or, it might mean that you'd already decided to strike out on your own, and were trying to meet with his runner to set up your own deals."

"That's crazy!"

Michael held his hand up angrily to shush her. "We're beginning to wonder, Susan, if you ever really had an envelope, if you ever really intended to come clean. You were the last one known to have had the formula for *Racer*. Even you admit that Black gave it to you. Now, *if* the *Racer* formula was in that envelope, and the envelope has disappeared, why have we had a resurgence of *Racer* related violence? Perhaps because you've had the formula all along, and have begun using it."

"That's *crazy! I* don't know how to make *Racer!* How would I even get a hold of the drugs necessary to -" She stopped, feeling cornered as Michael stared at her as if he could see into her soul. But he couldn't see. He couldn't see anything! She finally realized that she was being incriminated.

"I'd say you have quite a bit of access to the necessary drugs. Wouldn't you?"

"I gave you all the drugs, and all the money."

"Perhaps. Perhaps not. Perhaps you gave them over just a bit *too* easily, huh?" When she just stared at him incredulously, he softened slightly. "Susan, I'd like to believe everything you're telling me, I really would, but it all looks way too suspicious. Without any evidence to the contrary, you are still considered a drug dealer, who carried illegal drugs over international borders continually over a four-month period.

"Now, we know you didn't beat Linden to death, but did you know that he didn't necessarily die from the beatings? He died from heart-trauma. Trauma caused by the combination of finding himself full of a foreign drug, and being beaten to death at the same time. Your involvement with his death is still questionable.

Especially if you sold the crack/PCP mixture that caused him to die. Or maybe you contacted Detective Linden that night to lead him to Cane Street, away from Lex, so that Goldie and Hewitt could do their thing. If so, you're an accomplice. Unless you can prove, somehow, that what these folks are saying isn't true."

At this, she started to cry. A collapsing, defeated anguish of tears. "How can I prove that? Regis and his men have this whole damn city under their thumb, and I'm the scapegoat now, I see. Why don't you find *him,* and find the *judge* he works for, then you'll have the real criminals. *I am not one of them!"* She put her face in her hands in utter despair. Weeping into them, she tried to hide her entire soul away from the travesty that she had feared would come upon her from the beginning. A fear that she had surrendered, in order to trust one police officer who had promised to help her. Desperately she asked, "Where is Lieutenant Larsen?"

Looking sympathetically at the broken figure before him, Michael answered, "Lieutenant Larsen can't help you anymore."

*　　　　　*　　　　　*

Kevin watched through the viewing glass in horror as he saw where Michael was going with his questions. It all looked so very convincing, didn't it? When Susan collapsed in tears, and asked for him, Kevin almost collapsed, too.

"...Lieutenant Larsen can't help you anymore."

Kevin turned with a stalking anger and ripped the door to the hallway open, deciding with a force, that, yes, Lieutenant Larsen *could!*

~ *Chapter Thirty-seven* ~

John Casey approached the house at 19 Meadowlark Terrace with a quelling dread in his midsection. He'd checked this case out thoroughly in the past couple of days, and his theory about Judge Souza and his sons was almost surety. Almost.

Of course, he was sure inside himself, and the testimonies of Marty, Nick and Goldie were pretty conclusive. Regis Black funded *Racer*, they could pretty much prove that, and Raymond Souza's student ID card had the same face on it as the Regis Black at the Lex Street Bar. The man had specifically identified himself as Regis Black when Casey had asked, so they knew that Regis was Raymond Souza.

While the crimes against Raymond Souza could understandably be substantiated, though, they didn't know nearly enough about some other crucial aspects of the case. Like Matthew Souza's involvement. Was he Max? If so, they must bust him, for he was a serious threat to society, and an international link. If not, they must find the real Max. It was the question of the judge's own involvement that made what Casey was doing now so tricky. He and Michael hadn't had nearly enough time to investigate the man thoroughly, and they had no idea just how connected the judge was to any part of his sons' crimes. As far as they could tell, the judge was on the level.

Susan Ventry had claimed there was 'a judge' involved. Involved in what, though? Could her account even be believed as they once thought it could? Raymond Souza was in well-documented estrangement with his father. He could have told Susan anything to make the judge look condemned. He could even have told her exactly what to spread among the ranks of police officers should she be caught. Who really knew?

If the judge was involved, approaching him without the proper information was second only to formally kissing his crimes goodbye. Without concrete facts and supporting evidence of exact crimes, he would be absolved of everything before the case even glanced at a courtroom. Probably with a well-secured lawsuit against the Police Department to boot. The judge couldn't be arrested on what little they knew, and Casey had a feeling just as much of a fiasco could be made out of trying to condemn Raymond and Matthew Souza.

Casey was, nonetheless, about to walk this fine line. This case was way too volatile to let go for one more minute, and this afternoon Regis Black had tried to assault Angela - again. Who would have thought Black would dare come back into town so fast, and have the nerve to further attack his victim?

Why would he have done that? What was he still seeking from Angela? Did he honestly think himself so far above the law that he could enter a protected witness's home without consequence? He obviously thought the police had no idea whatsoever who he was, and didn't deem it especially important if they did. Either that, or he was just plain stupid. He had to have known that the van could be traced. Even the most naive idiot would have guessed that. Although the plate number hadn't been seen, the sharp black and gray custom design of the van was easily distinguishable. Lo and behold, Canadian records showed that Matthew Souza owned just such a vehicle. So, why sit in it, inside a witness's garage, and wait? How utterly foolish.

Or could it be that Black didn't know Angela *was* a witness?

Casey almost faltered as that thought struck him, and a nagging hint of realization sounded within his brain. They had heard so much conflicting evidence about Susan Ventry. First she was guilty, then she was innocent, then she was innocent of some things, but still guilty of others. As it stood now, she was a criminal, but as Casey thought about it, the only reason they knew anything about Ray Souza, or his father and brother, was because of Susan. If the man still felt big enough, and unconquerable enough, to proceed with his plans... then maybe Susan had led him to feel that way. To help the police.

There was no time to contemplate that further. Casey had arrived at his destination. Judge Souza's house. He didn't feel ready to approach the man, but ready or not, the time had come. Oh, well, they had wanted the case to move quickly...

The bell rang in a prolonged chime, just like a rich, sophisticated bell, in such an expensive area, was supposed to ring. A lovely older woman answered, and the first thing Casey noticed was the warmth of her smile.

"Hello," Katrina Souza said sweetly.

"Hello... are you Mrs. Souza?"

"Yes...?"

Casey flipped open his badge in the traditional way, and watched Judge Souza's wife look at it in confusion. She still didn't comprehend a threat. "I'm Sergeant John Casey - Narcotics division of the N.F.P.D - I'm... looking for Raymond Souza."

Her hand flew to her throat and she gazed at Casey, unmoving, unsure of what to do.

"Mrs. Souza, can I come in, please?"

He thought for an instant that she was going to say no, and deny him entrance into her home. Then she looked past him, around the lovely neighborhood, and suddenly thought better of letting a police officer stand outside her door and question the family. This would obviously be better accomplished inside. With her husband present. She stepped aside wordlessly and allowed him to pass.

The very second the door clicked shut, though, she was no longer silent, but left Casey standing in the entranceway to shout through the hall as she ran down it, "Carl! Carl, come quick!"

Judge Carlton Souza rushed up the stairs from his basement, his face strained and his eyes filled with worry at his wife's tone. Casey could see down the hallway where they reached each other. For a moment, they spoke so quietly Casey could only hear the distress in the air, but not a single word was discernible. The judge's face, however, spoke volumes when he turned his head toward John Casey.

This was a situation no police officer alive ever wanted to be in. The absolute audacity of a cop to enter a judge's home on an illegal matter seemed like something akin to insubordination. Except that Casey was fully justified in his reasons for doing so, and the law stood behind him.

Judge Souza thundered down the hall with the complete confidence and conviction of a judge, then stood before Casey with hard eyes. "Can I help you, officer?"

"Yes, sir, I have a warrant for the arrest of Raymond Souza."

Judge Souza's eyes flickered for a fraction of a second, so brief that Casey wondered if he'd really seen it. "Raymond?" he resounded, sounding confused. "What has he done?"

Casey looked passed Judge Souza for a second to consider his wife, standing in the background, frozen, with her hand covering her mouth, and her eyes filled with fear. "Well, sir, I'm afraid he's under arrest for dealing drugs, for supplying funds to manufacture drugs, overseeing the manufacture and distribution of said drug, and for kidnapping. As a result of an investigation into his involvement, an officer is now dead."

"What? That's ridiculous."

"I'm afraid it isn't, sir."

"What is your name?" Judge Souza demanded, as if it was a highly relevant question, and he was prepared to slay Casey with it.

"Sergeant John Casey."

"Sergeant, my son has had some problems, but he is not a drug dealer. He's in college now, he's beginning to make a life for himself."

"Well, I'm sorry this comes as such a shock, but we have some pretty substantial proof to the contrary."

The judge's face grew ashen. "Like what?" he asked with ill concealed fear radiating from him.

"Like testimony from convicted dealers."

"They named *my* son?" Judge Souza seemed to mock the idea, and an abrupt confidence came over him that Casey found peculiar. "That's impossible," he said matter-of-factly.

Casey's eyes narrowed, and in his mind, the judge's first conviction was made. He seemed to know that Raymond Souza's name was not one among the list of drug dealers in the area... and not one that the criminals recently questioned had specified. Slowly, knowingly, Casey replied. "Yes, I suppose it does seem impossible, doesn't it? Except that they don't name Raymond Souza, they name a man called Regis Black."

Casey watched closely and noted the colorless white that transformed Judge Souza's features. He'd expected just such a reaction. None of them had any idea that concrete connections had been made.

"The fact is, sir, your son has been an active part of drug distribution for quite some time now, disguising himself as Regis

Black." For measure, Casey added, "Do you know where he gets the name from? His initials. R.G.S. - Black - for black sheep... because he says he's the black sheep of the family."

At these words, Katrina Souza began to weep. She stood quietly behind them and held her face in her hands. Her husband looked back slightly, as if he wanted to slap the tears off her face, for they seemed revealing, but he looked at Casey instead. Shards of icy hatred shot from his eyes. Hatred that was rooted in fear. With a controlled quiet that was highly intimidating, he spoke as if Casey were a child who had stepped way over the line of pre-set rules.

"Sergeant Casey, when did the crimes my son was supposedly involved in take place?"

Casey's face wrinkled in confusion. We've been aware of the name for over four months, the specific crimes can be placed back as far as three weeks ago."

"Well, then, your Regis Black cannot be my Raymond. Because one month ago I personally put him on a plane to Dallas Texas. He's been visiting with my wife's mother, and is there even now. So, whatever crimes have been committed, whatever blame you're trying to place, and whatever facts you think you've come up with, are utterly, and completely, erroneous."

*   *   *

Katrina Souza looked up from her tears and stared at her husband's back. It looked like shock in her eyes, but Casey was too stunned himself to see it. With her head held suddenly high and her tears ruthlessly aborted, she looked at Casey, and with the utmost serenity and decorum, kindly asked him to leave.

~ *Chapter Thirty-eight* ~

Of course, Judge Souza's story checked out completely. Not only did Raymond Souza board a plane last month, but his brother met him there a week and a half ago to help take care of their aging grandmother. Katrina's mother confirmed it, the airlines confirmed it, the whole damn city confirmed it. They'd even had police officers in Dallas check on it, and sure enough, Ray and Matt Souza were at their grandmother's house, visiting amiably.

The only one who didn't confirm it was Susan Ventry, who swore after seeing Ray and Matt Souza's pictures that these were the criminals she knew as Regis and Max. A whole scandal was likely to erupt about the matter at any moment. The only reasons it didn't were because the DEA was so desperate to keep the case quiet, and Judge Souza was adamant about keeping his family name unsullied.

Thank God, Michael thought to himself as he read over the reports once again. Thank God the man didn't want to raise a hell because he certainly wasn't working with the system willingly. By the few conversations Michael had with him, his lawyers in full, intimidating tow, he knew the man would love nothing better than to divest the entire Special Team Department.

Judge Souza's lawyers had a disclaimer for every charge in the case, based on the fact that they could prove Ray Souza's whereabouts for the past month, in which time the most main crimes had taken place. He couldn't have walked into a crack house nine days ago and funded drugs to a dealer, who then purposely overdosed several young men. He couldn't have watched callously as one of those young men was beaten to death. He couldn't be responsible for the epidemic of deaths and violence that had been reported in the city over the last month, much less connected to the death of Detective Linden. Lastly, he couldn't have attempted to threaten and abduct Angela three days ago, and successfully abduct Susan Ventry later that night, if he wasn't even in the city to do it!

"Damn!" Michael said aloud as he whipped the file onto his desk. "Damn!" he said again, louder this time, and slapped the whole thing to the ground in frustration. Papers scattered everywhere, and he felt like ripping them into tiny pieces and grinding them into the linoleum. He just barely stopped himself from doing it.

How did they get Ray Souza out of town like that? It had to be a trick of some sort. If so, they must break through it and find proof of the truth. If not, then that left open the question, who the hell was Regis Black? There wasn't the time to waste sitting here figuring out which way to begin searching. Yet, damned if that wasn't what Michael was doing right this minute: Sitting here in a stupefied haze, trying to figure out what had gone wrong, and where to go next. If they wasted too much time on the one, the other would be lost.

What about Susan Ventry, who loomed over him like a phantom? She was either totally innocent, and the only one who could prove their theory right, or totally guilty, and the biggest liar in The Falls. She'd sworn when she'd seen Ray Souza's picture that he was Regis Black, and that he'd been in Niagara Falls throughout the past month, committing every crime they had wanted to nail him with. Again, Judge Souza's lawyers dispelled any theories that couldn't be factually proven with a simple waving of the law before the eyes of Michael's department.

Susan Ventry had been proven, by Michael's own office, to be a conscious liar regarding this case. Her crimes had not been acquitted, she was still considered guilty. What made the DEA think that now, when they wanted to prove their theory, she suddenly wasn't a liar anymore? They couldn't say that, and they couldn't give her testimony credence. Michael wondered continually about her.

The only thing that could prove Susan Ventry true was the envelope she claimed to have given Linden. Inside was a tape of Regis Black's voice, discussing specific *Racer* related issues with Goldie. *That* would be indisputable proof that Regis Black *was* Raymond Souza, regardless of where the hell he'd been over the last month.

As it stood now, it was common knowledge that *Regis Black* was known to have committed all of these crimes. No one even bothered denying that, but there was no proof that *Ray Souza* was *Regis Black*. That's where the judge's lawyers kept confounding the situation.

When Michael brought up the issues, they never denied them, or debated Regis Black's involvement. They simply maintained that Regis Black, by irrefutable proof, could not be Raymond Souza because Raymond hadn't been present in the area to commit any of the crimes.

Even Goldie, Marty and Nick's testimonies were void in this area. The three men had spoken of Regis Black, there was no denying that, but as if they were one mind, all three had denied that the picture of Ray Souza was the real Regis Black. Therefore, once again, the lawyers maintained that Regis Black was *not* their client, Ray Souza.

Casey was willing to swear before a court that he had seen Ray Souza in the Lex Street Bar just three nights ago, and had led him to Susan's apartment. He knew it was the same man. He'd seen Souza's student ID, then had asked him specifically if he was Regis Black. The lawyers still held their ground with an almost mocking intimidation.

"The room was dark and probably rather smoky, Detective, was it not?"

Casey had looked dead into their eyes and refused to answer in the affirmative. He would refuse until his dying day to give any of these manipulators a bigger platform. His silence spoke louder than any affirming words would have anyway.

"Yes, of course it was," the lawyer had answered himself with manufactured consideration. "And in that dark, smoky room, it's understandable that you might have been just *a bit* mistaken. Because my client was not in town at the time, he was fourteen hundred miles away.

"Also, as far as the van that you all claim belonged to Matthew Souza..." The attorney had fished through a notebook melodramatically, searching for his facts. "Exactly two hundred and nine custom vans bearing the highly common colors of gray and black exist in Western New York and Ontario, Canada alone. That number is conservatively rounded off to newer vehicles *less than* two years old. So, gentlemen, I'm afraid that without a plate number, you have no proof that *any* of my client's family were involved in such atrocities."

Their last hope was in trying to pull Regis' voice off of Angela's answering machine. Although the caller hadn't identified himself as Regis Black when he'd threatened Angela, if they could trace the voiceprint to Ray Souza that would at least be *something*. That became hopeless, too, however. Angela couldn't erase that voice fast enough from her machine at the time. Consequently the machine had reused the space repeatedly by the time they realized its pertinence. Regis Black's voice could barely be made out, let alone accurately identified through it.

Casey and Michael, both, were numb. They had come so close, and now their prime target was slipping away. Not only that, but they had exposed the case. Now it was known, probably to Regis Black himself, that the DEA was involved. While they had the *Racer* inventors, and they had Linden's killer, they did not have the roots of the crime. They did not have Max, the cocaine and PCP supplier. Therefore, the crime could spring up again at any time, in any place. In fact, it already had. Some polluted form of *Racer* had already leaked out, and people were killing themselves as they took it.

Was Susan Ventry responsible for that? Or could Regis Black still be out there, perhaps trying to produce Racer without Marty and Nick's guidance? Or, perhaps trying to pin his existence on the innocent son of a judge. Could the real Regis Black have concocted a plan like that? Could this department have been running in circles all along?

Who knew?

Who *really* knew?

~ Chapter Thirty-nine ~

Judge Carlton Souza sat silently before his fireplace with a full glass of whiskey swirling around in his hand. Except for the light of the fire, the entire house was steeped in darkness and radiated silence, as if the structure itself sensed the mood of its master.

Judge Souza stared at the flames in somewhat of a haze, then took another gulp from his glass. The Honorable Judge Carlton Souza. What a joke. He smirked without humor, and reached to set the glass next to the shoebox-sized chest he'd removed from his safe. He'd tried for so long to do everything right, to bring his sons up properly. How had everything gotten so completely out of hand?

He was tired, His Honor was. So very, very tired, and perhaps for the first time, he was seeing his sons for what they were. Dirty drug dealers. He supposed, when it came right down to it, he was a dirty accomplice to their crimes. He'd hidden them away for so long, had covered all of their erring tracks so strategically. It had been exhausting, he realized now, to be under so much constant pressure. He'd done it all, though, and now he stood to pay for it.

His sons would be freed. He, himself, would walk away unharmed. Eventually it would all fade away, but he would still pay; inside himself. He wondered if it would ever really pass away.

After all this time, would his sons really change? How had such evil entered into them?

Raymond didn't really surprise him, although at first his dealings had come as a shock. When Judge Souza had learned his son's true nature, he'd gone numb. That's when he'd promptly made reservations for his departure to Dallas. He'd known then that Raymond would need an alibi, if not at that immediate time, then in the future.

It had been simple to arrange for Ray, or a man that looked very similar to him, to be seen on the flight out of the area. Everything had been simple, and Raymond, by default, made things even simpler. He was never in class, so he couldn't have been seen too often on campus, and when the entirety of it all erupted, he hadn't shown up in school at all. This, of course, only confirmed their alibi.

Finding out about *Matt's* illicit behavior was what had devastated the judge. Why had he never seen that Matthew was as wrongfully involved as Raymond? Why had it never occurred to him? It had killed something deep and precious inside of him to find out. Matthew was an international drug supplier to his brother. That realization had caused the first wave of ice to cover Carl. When Judge Souza had found out just how much they'd been using *him* was when his heart froze. How, after all the times he had shielded the boys, had they the face to *use* him?

Armondo's Pizzeria, a derelict building in his files, had a sudden resurgence of life. Luckily, a friend at the gas company had notified him that utilities had been requested for the property, to be turned on the following day. Fortunately, his friend had arranged to 'lose' that information and delete the order. Carl had gone himself to check out what was going on. He'd seen far too much.

He knew Susan Ventry was telling the truth in her account of the crimes. He'd been the one upstairs at Armondo's that night. He'd been trying to stop what was happening. Instead he'd become further embroiled. Regis Black was Raymond, and Susan herself was innocent; of everything except loving Raymond.

He'd heard her confession to Linden when they'd been downstairs at Armondo's. He'd heard everything. Her knowledge, her relief to have finally reached Linden, her admissions when she'd handed over the envelope. Then her confusion when she'd seen his condition, and her fear when she'd seen the violence.

The judge knew from experience what loving Raymond brought a person, and when Raymond and Matt had come racing to his house a couple of days ago to tell him of their newest predicament, it came as no surprise that Ray had set Susan up. She would take the blame, and Carl would continue to insist on his sons' innocence; would continue to cover for them, protect them, lie for them. He was neck deep in it anyway now.

He'd cleared Armondo's completely out when he'd seen the various paraphernalia that could identify it as a lab. When Ray had exploded about the interference, Carl had to tell him about Angela Cahn, and that she'd helped Susan. He'd even assisted Ray, when he'd desperately needed to get to Angela so he could find Susan. Not only had he driven the black Buick that day to help his son, he'd almost helped him succeed in abducting the woman. When Ray had continued to follow her, and she'd gone to the police, Carl had finally put his foot down and refused to help him further. In truth, he was still doing just that: helping him.

He hadn't told his son everything he knew, though. He never told him of Susan's outright betrayal. Ray had learned that on his own. He also never told him what he'd heard that night at Armondo's. He'd felt so sorry for Susan, had even sympathized with her plight. She, apparently, could do what he, an honorable judge, could not. She could do what was right.

Now his son had the nerve to further plead for Susan Ventry's life. The judge was incredulous, and this latest proof of his son's selfishness had snapped the final shard in place. Ray had come begging, after all Carl had done to keep his name clean, that he rescue Susan as well. It was an impossible request.

Judge Souza was justified in defending his own family, but he had no business helping Susan Ventry. Especially when Ray had created the mess in the first place by setting her up for blame, and she so easily skirted suspicion away from the Souza family. Interfering with her would not only draw attention to himself, but everyone involved would undergo a rekindling of suspicion.

The request, perhaps irrationally, had set Carl completely off, and had closed his soul once and for all. Raymond appreciated nothing, and was never satisfied with the endless sacrifices that were made for him. Further, he never considered the danger to others that his schemes put them in. All that mattered to him was what he felt at that moment. Which, in this instance, was desperation for Susan.

Strange how she had touched Ray in a way none of them ever could. She was very special, Judge Souza knew. He'd seen her honesty and loyalty - and victimization. In his mind, she was much more worthy than his son. She'd been smarter and stronger than Regis had ever given her credit for, too, hadn't she? Too bad she didn't have a judge for a parent. Too bad she didn't have a parent at all who could help her...

He gazed into the fire in a mesmerized state. Full of pain, yet somehow numb, he lifted the lid off the box that stood to his side. Wearily, he reached into it and removed the envelope he'd picked up off the floor of Armondo's the night Susan had tried giving it to Detective Linden.

The fire loomed before him, ready to dissolve everything that would hinder his family further. Could it really burn the difficulties away...?

~ *Chapter Forty* ~

Kevin studied the back of a familiar old gas station, and for a moment, an overwhelming sense of recollection claimed him. In this dark, dangerous hellhole was where everything that had transformed his life in the past two years had begun. With him watching the back of this building. He'd seen crimes go on here that he'd never have imagined possible, not so much because they were too much for his sensibilities, but because of the source he'd discovered they came from. He'd busted it, but it still hurt. Damned if it didn't still hurt.

That was over now, and this is where the pain would end. Life had come back into his veins in the form of Angela Cahn, and, to a lesser degree, in the form of Susan Ventry. He knew she was innocent, but he couldn't figure out how to prove it. So, he would find the answers himself, right here where the problems began. On Lex Street.

Not much had changed since he'd been here last, but the atmosphere had toned down some. The residents here knew now that cops might be present among them, and they feared busts to a greater degree. That didn't mean the debauchery ended, though.

It had slowed for a while, but it hadn't ended, and Kevin wondered if it was even worth trying to fight against.

Now the residents just moved their affairs indoors, where they couldn't be so easily seen, and they had sharper control over who participated. It was still a loud, dangerous area, though, where you could as easily be robbed and killed as looked at, if you weren't careful.

The gas station had always stood apart from it, even though it stood right in the middle. Apparently, that hadn't changed, either. It was still quiet and seldom-touched in back, while debauchery reigned across the street. Kevin leaned against a tree, hidden by shadows, and looked at it. Just a building. It was up for sale now, without any interested buyers. Property of the State, since the owner was in prison for life.

People had openly stated that Susan was a dealer around here. A certain group had even named her as one of the dealers who had sold drugs at the crack houses. If that were true, then *someone*, somewhere around here, must know if a boy was beaten to death in one of those houses. It seemed a little far-fetched, even to Kevin, that not one among those questioned by the police who had invaded the area in the past few days, knew anything about a death. Not that they were about to say much to the cops anyway. Strange that they would so readily mention Susan's name, though, wasn't it? That's why Kevin was here. Officially unofficial, to find out about that death. Casey had finally gotten a lead on it. Finally, some progress just might be made.

Angela was a basket-case about the whole situation. She cried continually, both from the tragedy that had befallen Susan, and the unbearable amount of stress that seemed to have snapped the last vestiges of her control. Kevin and Randy both tried to convince her to take a break, to go visit her parents for a while and relax, but she adamantly refused.

Kevin was secretly glad. He cared about her state of mind, and would have willingly supported her decision to go, but the thought of her being so far away from him twisted his insides. She had elected to stay and see that Susan got a fair trial. Along those lines, she had secured one of the best criminal attorneys in the area to hear her case. Not a small gesture, and not an inexpensive one, but Kevin wholeheartedly agreed it was best and would share the costs. There was hope; not an extremely vibrant hope, but there was hope just the same.

"Kevin?" The voice intruded into his quietude and shocked him dangerously. He whipped around with his pistol drawn, and found himself aiming it right at John Casey. If Kevin hadn't known Casey was coming, he probably would have shot the man through the heart. As it was, he jumped and cocked the trigger before his eyes adjusted in the darkness and he focused and relaxed.

"God! Casey!" Kevin almost threw the gun on the ground to get it away from him. "What are you doing sneaking up on me like that?"

Casey smiled and moved closer, never even blinking when Kevin jumped at him with the gun. Apparently, he trusted this man's instincts and self-control better than the man himself. "I wasn't sneaking, I'm meeting you here just like we agreed," he said dryly.

"Well, you could rustle a few leaves or something, you know?" Kevin replied sarcastically.

"That wouldn't be too smart, would it? It's not good to draw attention to yourself in a place like this," Casey informed him with joking sarcasm.

Kevin scowled at him. "Casey, I was scouting this area before you had hair on your chest... You do have hair on your chest, don't you? Never mind... What's the lead you've found on this phantom teen murderer? Does he really exist, and did he kill that kid the way Susan claims?"

338

"I seriously think so. In fact, I'm willing to bet that the kid I've found is the kid we're after. And yes, I do have hair on my chest."

"Good," Kevin replied with a gleam. "How'd you find him?"

"Well, as it happens, I was checking on Susan's story about the kid getting beaten to death in that crack house long before you asked me to dig deep. To be honest, Michael and I wondered if it was true, or if she was just inventing stories to make it sound real."

Kevin's eyes narrowed. "Her story is true," he said ironly.

Casey looked straight at him. "You may be right... because, as I've asked around town and kept my ears open, I heard that there is a new kid doing Regis Black's business, and supposedly he's in hiding. I started to really track him over the last two days because of this Souza thing. *If* the kid committed murder, maybe I can convince him to deal a little. If he'll tell me what he really knows... maybe we can keep him out of jail for the crime."

"Possible - very possible. But will he turn against Black?"

"I don't know, I'm hoping he's running scared and the sight of a badge will make him sing. All I need is another person to identify Souza. That's what's killing me about this. All we need is someone who can confirm that Ray Souza is Regis Black. It's so simple, yet we can't find anyone that the lawyers won't twist to a pulp on a witness stand. Anyway, if the kid does exist, and this is him, he'll also know if Susan really sold *Racer* around town."

Kevin smiled. "Casey, you are a constant wonder. If ever I knew a man who cared about everyone else's loose ends while he tied up his own, that man is you."

Casey looked away. "I just want justice - for all. I hope Susan is innocent, I really do, but I really want that kid to tell me something about Souza. I know that bastard is Regis Black, and it makes my blood boil to see his daddy and his high priced lawyers getting him off. If I have to, I'll fly into Dallas myself and question everyone in the city to make sure he's *really* been there over the past month. Ten to one he hasn't been."

Kevin knew that passion. "Well, I hope you get him, Casey, I really do." Kevin said soberly.

"But you want Susan Ventry cleared even more, don't you?" Casey smiled.

"Only because she's innocent."

Casey nodded with a knowing smile.

"So, why are we meeting here?" Kevin asked.

Casey looked toward the gas station they stood behind. The place where memories could blind-side them both. Neither one of them wanted to go in there, and both knew why. "I think he's hiding in there," Casey said, and nodded at the building.

"In the gas station?"

"Yep."

"How do you know?"

"I've been watching, and I saw someone go in a couple times over the past few days. The new *Racer* manufacturer is supposedly hiding out, and this is an abandoned building..."

Kevin looked at the structure. Definitely abandoned. "So, we should go in there and check," he stated, trying to cover the anxiety he felt with blandness. He didn't quite achieve it.

"Yep."

Kevin looked at Casey. "Well, let's go then," he said edgily, "it's just a damn building."

"All right. Let's go."

So they went; beginning a cautious walk, then a quick trot toward the building, while they kept their senses keen toward their surroundings. Their guns were drawn, and they checked each other often as they approached.

Kevin couldn't have described the feelings that rushed him as they took the first few steps. It was utter exhilaration to be sleuthing again, outright revulsion to be entering this hellish place again, and an intangible surge of instinct that sensed they were onto something. They must be careful not to blow it.

They approached a heavy door that they knew existed to the side of the building. It was unlocked. This was their first clue that something was amiss. This entire structure should be securely locked and shut tight. It wasn't. However, the weight of a heavily jammed chair against the knob kept them from entering freely. Their second clue. Someone, without a proper key, had barricaded themselves inside.

They looked at each other triumphantly and walked completely around the building as if the place belonged to them. They knew just where to go, what to do, and were ready when they finally gained entrance by breaking a front window and unlocking the door from the inside. It was a tactic they had not wanted to use because from the front they could be easily seen by the multitudes that gathered across the street. There hadn't really been a choice, though, and there was truly no more time to stand back and be cautious.

With blood pumping and eyes sharply alert, they stalked through the building. Everything was shut down and deserted, but that didn't surprise or deter them. They knew exactly where they were going, and made their way hastily through the dark. Past the garage was a small hallway, and down that hallway stood the door they had tried to gain entrance through just a few moments before. There stood the chair rammed tightly underneath the doorknob just as they had suspected.

A few steps further down was another door, and they both knew it led into the basement level of the building. Kevin glanced at Casey before he reached for the doorknob. A line of sweat beaded his forehead and his knuckles turned white as he held his gun straight down at his side. Casey had nearly been shot to death last year, in the basement room they were entering. His eyes were expectant, and intense. When he saw Kevin glance back at him, he smiled very slightly and said, "Ready or not..."

The descent into the dark gloom of the basement was like something out of a horror movie. Anxiety rang in the air so starkly it was almost audible. Cobwebs hung in huge sprays that covered entire corners of the walls. The musty smell was thick enough to hinder free breathing as they entered into it, and the squealing sound of frightened rats chattered through the place as their territory was invaded.

Kevin could feel the perspiration beading along his brow line as he continued down and finally reached the bottom. There was no light except that which came from the flashlights Casey had the foresight to bring. They were powerful tools, but did little to combat the sensation that something was about to spring at them.

Kevin, in the lead, flashed his light around the room. It, too, like everything else around here, looked very similar to the last time they had seen it. Except it should have been completely emptied now, as the DEA had confiscated every last item for evidence. Instead, a very rudimentary setup of what had been here before stood in its place.

Kevin walked over to it and looked around at the small wooden table that replaced the rows of lab tables the DEA had removed. On top of it was a simple propane burner, a kerosene lantern, and a few scattered items, like pans, baking soda, and plastic bags. A far cry from the industrial size drug lab that once was here, but it was a drug lab just the same.

Kevin looked at Casey knowingly. "Looks like someone's been busy."

"Sure does. Are there any drugs around?"

As one, they flashed their beams around the table, under it, over the walls, behind it. Everything was barren. "None that I can see, but let's have a look around."

Sidling along like jewel thieves, they continued through the tiny cell-like box of a room. A simple flashing of the light in each direction gave them a fairly all-encompassing grasp on the scene. There was nothing but empty concrete facing them.

The room was empty.

"Damn," Casey said harshly when the light hit the last corner, and the room was found barren. "If the kid isn't in here, we lost him. After breaking in the way we did, he'll never come back."

Kevin grimaced and lowered the light slightly. "Damn," he repeated in agreement, feeling hollow and stunned.

As the flashlight moved downward from Kevin's movement, a tiny flash caught Casey's eye. He strained to see what it was, then said with an anticipatory edge, "Look, there's a door over there."

Kevin flashed his light deliberately into the direction Casey was pointing. Sure enough, a small half-door blended into the wall, with a latch hook barely closing it. "Let's check it out," Kevin said.

They started for the door, intention in every step. When they reached it, Kevin took a deep breath and moved to the side of it with his back placed firmly against the dusty wall. Casey, too, positioned himself automatically against the wall on the other side of the door. With guns stretched out, Casey gave a nodding signal when he was ready, and Kevin jerked the latch open. The movement was sudden and seemed to electrify the air for a split second. Kevin shined his light into the closet and Casey pointed his gun. The combination effectively paralyzed the boy inside.

Kevin and Casey, both, had waited for this moment with deep vehemence. They'd searched for this boy for days now, and had their own personal and professional reasons for wanting to catch him so badly. Gazing down at the boy's terrified features, however, as he tried to shield his face from the blinding light, neither could remember their vengeance. All they knew was pity. He was crumpled into a ball in the corner of the closet, obviously trying to hide from them. His face was drawn, the skin yellowed, and he looked little more than sixteen. A teenager that had once been big and strong, a leader among the crowds, now cowered before a simple flashlight, and the police officers behind it.

Kevin lowered the beam instantly so that it just lit the small space he was in. "Hey there," he said gently, "everything is all right. We don't want to hurt you, we just want to talk."

The young man didn't look capable of putting up a fight about it, and didn't seem to want to. He looked tired and resigned, almost relieved, especially when he heard the soothing timbre of Kevin's voice.

Reaching in very cautiously, while Casey's gun aimed directly at the boy, Kevin grasped a hold of his arm. With a gentle lift that took more strength and effort on Kevin's part than it should have, he pulled the boy up and slowly drew him from the closet. He was shaking so badly that Kevin had to secure him under one arm and walk him to the table where the lab was set up.

The boy collapsed in the chair that stood there, and Kevin lit the lantern. In the illuminating light, the boy looked even worse. His clothes were filthy, and raw body stench reeked off them. His blond hair looked like it was streaked with black oil and plastered against his head in an unwashed mess. His eyes were tired and afraid, bulging out, in fact, with fear and sleeplessness. His convulsive shakes worsened as the two strangers studied him.

Kevin removed his coat and draped it over the young man. "Are you all right?" he asked, genuinely concerned.

The boy nodded.

Kevin regarded him for a minute, and Casey finally lowered the gun. "What's your name, son?"

After an initial hesitation, the boy croaked, "Jimmy."

"Jimmy what?" Kevin asked.

"Jimmy Brandt."

"Do you have parents, Jimmy?"

"I live on my own."

"How old are you?"

"Nineteen."

Kevin nodded. "What are you doing down here?"

"I live here."

"Oh, I see. Are you aware that it's against the law to live in a building you don't own or pay rent for?"

Jimmy nodded.

"Well, did you always live here?"

"No."

"When did you move in?"

"Last week."

"Why?"

"Because I needed a place to live."

"A place to live? Or a place to hide?"

Jimmy looked up, guilt plaguing his features.

"This isn't going to be easy, Jimmy, but we have to talk," Kevin said. "This is Sergeant John Casey, and I'm Kevin Larsen."

"*Lieutenant* Kevin Larsen," Casey corrected pointedly.

"Right... Jimmy, I'll tell you what; Sergeant Casey and I have a theory about you, and I'm going to tell you what it is, and you tell me if I'm wrong, and what parts I leave out, okay?"

Jimmy nodded wearily, looking down into his lap, knowing these cops had pegged his situation accurately.

"Okay. We think you're hiding in here. The reason we think you're hiding is because you killed someone. Is that true?"

Jimmy began to shake again, and an agony of torment covered his features as he continued to look down; but he didn't answer.

Kevin continued, speaking very gently into the shattered soul before him. "We think that last week you bought a drug at one of the crack houses. A drug called *Racer*. When you were high, you got into a fight with one of your friends, and you beat him to death. Is that right?"

Tears fell in huge drops that landed in Jimmy's lap. "He was my best friend..." That's all Jimmy said, then he collapsed in sobs. "I didn't mean to... I didn't mean to... I was just... stoned."

Kevin looked at Casey. They had their link, but there was no triumph in it. Nevertheless, they would milk every morsel of information they needed out of him.

Casey pressed a button on a tiny tape recorder he kept forever ready at his belt loop, as Kevin consoled Jimmy. "It's all right, son, it's all over now, and you can help us. You can help yourself, and your friend, you can help everyone."

Jimmy nodded, understanding that he would be asked official questions about an official case, and he was about to become an official snitch. He didn't care. The relief of confessing to the authorities, of coming clean with the story and the torment, meant more to him at the moment than life itself. He repositioned himself and dried his eyes with the grime of his shirtsleeve. "What do you want to know?"

"First of all, I want *you* to know, for your own sanity, that you were *purposely* overdosed that night. The dealer, Marty Rhodes, was trying to prove a point to his boss - Regis Black - and he wanted to show the bastard what *Racer* could do." Kevin paused a moment to let that sink in. As he knew it would, a light of anger entered Jimmy's eyes. "Can you tell us what happened that night?"

Jimmy told them the exact same story Susan had, but from a different perspective. He seemed relieved to tell it, eager to tell it, even eager for the punishment that would come with it. There was no questioning its truth. When he was finished, Kevin asked, "Was your friend, Rich, dead when you left that night?"

"No, he was alive then, but later in the night he kept spitting up blood. Then he just collapsed and..."

"All right, all right. I want you to stay with me now and focus," Kevin commanded when Jimmy started to panic at the memory. At least now they knew why Linden never reported this death. When Rich left that night, he was still alive.

"Jimmy?" Kevin persisted until the boy looked up at him with clear eyes. "Let's continue. Now, are you certain of the man who sold you the *Racer*?"

"Yes."

"It was...?"

"Marty." It was a flat out reply, with no hesitation.

"Marty Rhodes?"

"Yeah."

"Did he always sell the drugs around here?"

"Yeah."

"Have you ever heard the name Susan Ventry?"

An unexpected fear crossed Jimmy's eyes. Peering into Kevin's face as if to latch onto some sort of stronghold, he replied, "I've heard of her."

"How?"

"She's Regis Black's girl."

"Have you ever gotten drugs from her?"

"No. I've never even seen her. But I've heard of her. She deals for him."

Kevin's face fell. "For Regis Black?"

"Yeah."

"Have you ever seen Regis Black?" Casey stepped in to ask.

Jimmy's lip began to tremble again. "Yeah. He hangs out at the bar sometimes."

"How come when we ask around no one seems to know him?"

"No one knows anyone that the cops are looking for around here. It's common rules. Especially Regis Black, you don't know nothing about Black, cause he'll either kill you himself or land you in jail."

"Really? Why are you talking then?"

"Cause I'm already going to jail, ain't I? And I can't stand it no more, I just can't stand it!"

"Can't stand what, Jimmy?" Casey asked when his reaction seemed more intense than it should.

"Hiding. I can't stand hiding anymore, trying to act like I didn't kill Rich. He makes me hide, and he tells me that if I talk he'll send me to jail. He said he'd take care of Rich's body and make sure no one can ever find it if I do what he says. But I *did* kill Rich, okay? I *did*. So, send me to jail, that's where I belong anyway!" Jimmy stated with hysterical passion.

"What doesn't he want you to say, Jimmy?"

"He doesn't want me to tell anyone about Regis, and since Marty and Nick got busted he wants *me* to make the stuff. I don't know how to make *Racer*. *I don't know how!*"

"Wait a minute. *Black* wants *you* to make *Racer*?"

"Yeah, he says he still wants it out there so they can't blame Regis for it."

"What?" Kevin and Casey looked at each other in utter confusion. The boy was talking in circles.

"He wants it to look like Regis is innocent!" Jimmy insisted impatiently, as if his words were clear and shouldn't need clarifying. "So, he's pinning me with it, but I don't know how to make *Racer*, and I don't want to do it!"

"So, you've been making the new *Racer* that's driving everyone over the edge?" Kevin asked, still bewildered, but beginning to see.

Jimmy nodded.

"Wait a minute, wait a minute!" Casey said fervently, trying to get a grip on this conversation. Regis was threatening him, but Regis didn't want Regis to get caught? It didn't make any sense. The kid must be hysterical. He pulled out the snapshot of Ray Souza that he'd brought along for just such a situation. "Jimmy, is this Regis Black?"

Jimmy looked at the picture, but Casey wondered if he really saw anything. "Yeah!" he said with boiling frustration, as if this were a secondary point.

"And he's the one who's threatening you; right?"

"*No!*" Jimmy yelled in provoked annoyance. "Not *him*, his father... The judge!"

~ *Chapter Forty-one* ~

Kevin stared at Judge Souza's house in a daze. It was three-thirty in the morning, and sleep was impossible. Instead, he pondered what was about to go down so unexpectedly. On everyone's part, this was indeed unexpected, but on the part of Judge Souza, it would be devastatingly abrupt. He'd thought he'd crossed all his T's and dotted all his I's, hadn't he? The police officers had thought so, too.

Jimmy was in jail right now, and probably considered it a haven compared to what he'd lived in over the past week and a half. The story had been relayed to Michael before Jack and the D.A. It was concrete and convicting. Judge Souza and sons had been involved in dealing drugs, and in the manufacture and distribution of a lethal drug.

Racer could effectively be stopped via their busts, especially with the fear that had radiated through the city about the drug. Even the street addicts were afraid of it now. The original formula, which gave them the high they were looking for, had been replaced by the devastating form Jimmy had produced. Because it was so early in the drug's history, *Racer* had developed an adverse reputation.

Michael was ecstatic. So was Kevin. Except Susan was still a part of the overall crime. Nothing had been eradicated from her list of guilt. At this point Kevin just wanted to know the truth. He believed in her, he really did. He'd seen the truth in her eyes from the moment she had looked into his face through the rearview mirror in his car and said, "I'm not innocent, but I swear to you I didn't know what I was doing."

She could be just a good little actress, but Kevin didn't think so. The facts, however, were confounding, and he found himself looking more closely at them. She had been in all the wrong places at all the right times, hadn't she? She'd known a hell of a lot without knowing anything truly significant, too. There were witnesses everywhere who could name her as a dealer. Even Jimmy, who would become the main witness in the case against the Souza's, had named her as a dealer. None of them had ever seen her, that was true, but they knew of her just the same. Could it be? Could it possibly be that she was a part of the whole world she claimed to despise, and had set them all up with one lie after another from the beginning?

Angela said no, that couldn't be, but she wasn't exactly an expert on such matters, and her emotions were clouding her thinking lately anyway. Kevin was supposed to be the expert. Years of detective work should have seasoned him to be able to discern this situation - but he didn't know, either.

Now, he looked at Judge Souza's house and war waged within him. He had only one final recourse, and once again he found himself battling against the law to take hold of it. It could seriously jeopardize the arrest that was imminent as soon as dawn broke later this morning. If he didn't do it, though, Susan's life could be lost forever.

He opened the car door with a quiet click that seemed prolonged in the stillness of the night. Stepping out of the car with purpose, his decision was made. He approached the house, and very quietly rapped on the door. Amazingly, after only a few seconds, he heard footsteps approaching, and the judge himself peered out the narrow, rectangular window at the side of the door. When he saw Kevin standing there, he stopped as if every breath and muscle in his body were paralyzed.

For a moment, the air was tense. Kevin looked steadily back through the window into the darkened face of the judge, almost with a knowing compassion. Their paths hadn't crossed too many times in the course of their professional lives, but they still knew each other by sight. Indeed, they had even worked different ends of the same case at times. That wasn't why Judge Carlton Souza stood there staring, though, almost not even surprised by the call, even if it had immobilized him.

Like everyone else in the city, Kevin's involvement in narcotics investigations was well known to the judge. He himself had seen Kevin helping Angela Cahn the day Ray had tried to accost her. Kevin Larsen, somehow, had maneuvered himself onto this case.

Resignedly, Judge Souza moved toward the door and opened it. He was dressed in a tailored shirt and suit slacks that looked as though he'd put them on three days ago. The shirt hung out and was unbuttoned several inches down his chest. His belt was unhooked and gaped open at the front of the pants, which were wrinkled, and hung down as if they didn't fit anymore. Kevin looked at him as he stood there silently, just gazing back at the man on his doorstep at three-thirty in the morning.

"Your Honor," Kevin greeted respectfully, with a nod.

"Don't call me that," Judge Souza said, and stepped aside to allow Kevin into the house. Everything was dark and quiet except for the light of a fireplace coming from a sitting room toward the back of the house. The judge turned without a word, his countenance resigned and fatigued, and began walking toward that room. Kevin followed, attentive and quiet as the judge set the pace perceptively.

He sat down in a leather chair that faced the fire, and began looking into it as if Kevin weren't there. In fact, he was aware of every nuance of him, and Kevin knew it. He didn't sit, instead he walked in front of Judge Souza and asked, "Do you know why I'm here?" It was a genuine question. Kevin hadn't exactly been prepared for this easy admission into Judge Souza's home, and certainly not for this knowing resignation that seemed the fill the judge's entire soul.

"No. Not exactly. But I'm sure I can make a fairly accurate guess as to what it's about."

Kevin rocked slightly on his feet and continued to stare. "I came to tell you that you'll be under arrest in about four hours."

Judge Souza blinked and nodded so slightly it was almost imperceptible.

"Your sons, too," Kevin added.

The judge still didn't move, but closed his eyes against the fact. "So, why are you telling me about it?"

Kevin breathed in quietly and hesitated. "Because I guess, even after all that's been said and done, you deserve to be prepared."

"Wrong, Lieutenant. I deserve very little."

Kevin finally deciphered the mood the judge was emitting. Self-recrimination. He knew what he'd done, what his son's had done, and there was a distinct shame present for it. "What proof did you find?" he asked quietly, needing to know.

"Jimmy. We found him and he... confessed."

Judge Souza nodded again. "Good, I hope you can do something to help him."

"They'll try, I'm sure." It became quiet again before Kevin continued. "I came here for something else, too," he said levelly, unwillingly connecting with the man. Judge Souza finally looked up at him. "I came to ask if you know anything about Susan Ventry."

A wry sarcasm filled the judge's eyes. "Susan. Of course. Everyone wants to know about Susan." Derision filled the man's voice and it scared Kevin a bit, because he couldn't trust it, and wondered if the judge would refuse to speak the truth.

"Judge, please... She's become very special to me; like a daughter. I can't just let her waste away in a prison cell if she's not guilty. She says she's not, but there's an awful lot of evidence against her. All I want to know is the truth."

Kevin's eyes were filled with emotion, and intense with his searching. Judge Souza stared at him, touched and sympathetic. Then his expression stopped, changed into sudden anger, as if he was remembering something, and he laughed humorlessly.

"She's like a daughter to you? *Like* a daughter? Should that matter to me? I've done everything for my sons, Lieutenant. Everything. I've coddled them, I've protected them, I've cleaned up every pile of crap they've lain down. I've even broken the law to help them. All I've ever wanted was for them to be okay. For them to grow into productive adults. I loved them with everything I had within me, and when that was expended, I loved them with more. It gets you nowhere. So, do you think I should care at this point what happens to *your* special child? A young lady who is *like* a daughter to you? I'm afraid not."

Kevin bent his entire body at the knee to level himself before Judge Souza. He stared with genuine compassion as Carl spoke his tirade. The judge looked so torn up, so convicted for his crimes, and so genuinely ashamed, he didn't even try to hide it.

"Yes. You should care. For everything that you've done wrong, and everything that's been done wrong to you, you should care if this girl is innocent. Should she be blamed just because she loved

Regis? Or is it because she betrayed him and caused all of this that you won't help her?"

"No!" Judge Souza shot out with strength so surprising Kevin blinked. "That's not what it is..." He stopped himself quickly, and Kevin leaned in, desperate to know what he knew.

"Please, Judge," Kevin implored, "I have to know."

He calmed considerably, then said quietly, "She did what I should have done a long time ago. She's not guilty, Lieutenant. Everything she's told you is true."

Kevin leaned back on his heels and expelled a great, relieved breath. She was innocent. He'd felt so sure that she was; now it was confirmed. He would pursue that innocence with great confidence now. "Will you testify for her?" Kevin asked tentatively.

"Lieutenant..." the judge began as if he hadn't heard the question, "will you escort me down to the police station? I'd... rather turn myself in quietly than go through the humiliation of being arrested at my home, or worse, at my job." He almost laughed at the notion. A judge being arrested and taken away from his own courtroom. It would cause a press-frenzy!

Kevin stood up and watched the judge curiously. Had he heard Kevin's question? Kevin was sure he did. He was purposely ignoring it. "Yes, sir, I'll escort you, but -"

"I heard you." With gentle purpose, Judge Souza reached to his side and maneuvered a small box into his lap. Kevin flinched and reached instinctively for his pistol. The judge looked up dryly and opened the box. "I'm not going to pull out a gun and shoot you, Lieutenant." He stood up. "I want to give you this."

Kevin's eyes rounded and shot back and forth between the object Judge Souza held out and the eyes of the man giving it. "The envelope..." he said, almost reverently. This was the envelope Susan had insisted she'd given Linden. He knew it instantly. It was large and gold, unremarkable and plain, but contained more crushing proof than any other single item. "How did you get it?"

"The night Susan met with Detective Linden, I was at Armondo's. I have a friend at the gas company who informed me that utilities had been requested for the property. I knew what was happening immediately so I went to stop it. While I was there, I heard all the commotion of Detective Linden entering the building, and everything else that followed.

"All of it is exactly as Susan claims. She tried to give Linden the envelope and confess the crimes to him, he attacked her, and Angela Cahn rescued her. The hammer Linden used in his assault is in here, too." The judge tipped the box to reveal its bottom. Kevin's eyes lit with comprehension.

"Undoubtedly, Lieutenant, Susan is quite a girl - and definitely innocent."

Kevin nodded appreciatively with a proud smile as Judge Souza gathered his coat to be escorted to the police station. As they were leaving the sitting room, where the fire still burned brightly, Judge Souza stopped and looked at Kevin intently. "I want you to know, I wasn't going to allow it." He smiled, defeated. "For the first time in Ray's life I was going to say no. I wish I would have gotten the chance before everything got out of hand."

Kevin held Judge Souza's gaze. Suddenly all of Carl Souza's additional crimes, like forcing a young boy to produce *Racer*, seemed unrelated to the actual person standing before him. The sorrow Kevin felt was evident. "I wish you would have, too, sir," he said. "I really do."

~ *Chapter Forty-two* ~

Perhaps the hardest part of Susan's entire ordeal with *Racer* occurred after she was released from jail. It was a relief to be freed, unbelievably so, and she was glad it was over, but another, somehow worse, trauma awaited her - Detective Linden's funeral.

It was her first obligation, and had been scheduled shortly after all the convicting evidence came in. She'd felt rather like a celebrity in a way, and decided she hated the role. Especially since every part of her involvement was cast in a semi-negative light.

Sure, it was common knowledge, that she'd been released, and that she had turned the tables on the drug dealer and had stopped an epidemic of crime; but the public didn't really know the issues. They couldn't know, and a dark shadow still surrounded her. She'd live through it, no doubt, but this day... would she ever truly outlive this day?

A mass of people were present at the funeral, and as she paid her respects she couldn't help but feel that, somehow, she was responsible. She was one of the last people to see Linden alive; and hadn't he died trying to help her? Hadn't she, in fact, caused him to blow his cover by calling him? He died with honors in the line of duty, and was highly regarded throughout the city as the public mourned the loss.

Something within Susan died that day, too, and perhaps then, at the moment the casket was lowered into the earth, she saw everything clearly. She saw the stark differences between the world she had known and the world she'd been swept into because of Angela and Kevin. Silently, she promised the detective that his life was not in vain, and that she would be a living testimony to his death. "Good came from your life, Detective," she whispered to him, "and I'll make good come from your death, too. Through me. I promise." With that, she, and the hundreds gathered together, bade him his final, honorable, farewell.

She wasn't sure at this point which had been harder, that funeral or meeting Judge Souza. 'The Judge', as Goldie and Regis – Ray - had called him. Ray... she couldn't get used to his name being Ray, although he'd told her once that Black stood for 'black sheep'.

The Judge had requested a meeting with her, specifically, and had brought the evidence to free her. She couldn't stop thinking about him, he was so different from what she had pictured him to be. She'd imagined an evil, lofty man who manipulated the law and his position to get what he wanted. Someone like Goldie. That wasn't the case. Everything this judge did, he seemed to have done out of love. Totally misguided love, but love just the same. He was Regis' *father*. Somehow, she had never pictured Regis with real parents, and she despised him for the torment he had put them through. God, if she had one half the father that Regis had...

Then there was Katrina... what a pitiful, heartbroken wreck she was over all of this. Her husband and her two sons faced long-term prison sentences. Of all of the Souzas, Katrina would have the hardest time recovering from this, and it was she who least deserved what had come upon her.

When Susan had been brought up from her cell and placed in the DEA interrogation room, Judge Souza had been sitting there, lawyers and police alike surrounding him. He was ready to divulge everything, add all the answers to the questions, and wanted her there to hear it all. She'd gotten the immediate, uneasy feeling that he knew her, while she'd never even seen him. He'd looked right at her with gentle compassion and true regret, and said, "Hello, Susan. I'm so sorry for what you've been put through... I guess we're both sorry we loved him."

Those words replayed in her mind over and over again, not so much because of the statement itself, but because of the deep, instantaneous connection that had transferred between the two when he spoke them. She'd been seated after that, and had listened to his every confession, which had answered all of the *Racer* questions for Michael and his men, and all of the involvement questions for her. Charges against her had been dropped immediately.

Regis and Max had been flown in from their grandmother's house. To say they were shocked by the prospect of being turned in by their father was an understatement. They had been convicted on all counts for their involvement. Years of prison were their reward.

Susan, however, would receive a second chance at life. Disconcerting at best. She wasn't sure how to go about living anymore, or how to assimilate the changes she'd gone through into her lifestyle. Luckily, there was Angela. Angela seemed to always be there now, and she'd led Susan out of the jail, with Kevin surrounding them both. She'd been staying with Angela since that day. There were all kinds of legal issues about her actually residing permanently in the U.S., but while she was in college, at least, she could stay with Angela for a while. They'd have to see where it all went from here, but for now it felt like family.

When she'd seen the anger Angela displayed about where she was going today, she knew it really *was* like family. Susan had smiled warmly, but insisted, "Angela, I have to see him."

"Why? It's not good for you, Susan, he's not good for you!"

"Do you think I don't know that? I still need to see him." Her face took on a forlorn look. "I loved him; and while I could get over that, I can't seem to get over the fact that *he* loved *me*. He really did."

Angela looked at her deeply. "Susan, he set you up to get caught. That's not love."

"I know," she said matter-of-factly, "but he loved me in his own way, the best that he could. Don't worry, I wouldn't go back to him, even if he *wasn't* spending the better part of his life in prison. I just need to tie up those loose ends - give the matter closure."

Angela still hadn't agreed, but here she was at Allenwood Federal Penitentiary, with Kevin standing protectively off in the distance, watching her as she sat at a round table and Regis was brought in to receive his visitor. She felt like she should cry when she saw him in his muted green prison uniform, and noted his haggard appearance, but she couldn't. The first step of closure had begun. She didn't feel sorry for him, or for herself, at all.

"Hello, Susan."

"Regis..."

"I'm glad you came."

She could hear the attraction in his voice, and see the desire to connect within his eyes. She didn't return it. Truly, she didn't return it. "I wanted to see you, Regis... one last time. I wanted to say goodbye. I felt you... deserved that much."

He saw the lack of warmth in her gaze. She looked strong, independent, sure. He didn't like it.

She didn't care. He held nothing over her any longer. It didn't matter what he liked or disliked. She was free from the bonds he'd placed upon her. A second sense of closure washed over her.

"You look good, Susan. It's hell in here."

"I'm sorry." Neither one of them was exactly sure what she was sorry for. The fact that things were hell, or that he was there in the first place, or that she had ultimately put him there.

"I'm sorry, too."

She nodded slightly.

"You know, I really loved you," he said raggedly.

"And I really loved you..." she replied shakily.

"Then what happened to our love, Susan? What happened?"

"I don't think we interpreted love the same way. We definitely didn't interpret life the same way."

"But to go this far... to send me to prison... didn't our love mean anything to you?"

"It meant everything to me! Too much! I couldn't even see that you'd set me up from the beginning. That's not love, either, is it?" she shot out pointedly.

He had the grace to look profoundly ashamed and full of regret. "I'd like to make sure you're taken care of, Susan. It doesn't have to end between us... my mother could help you."

"I don't need any help," she cut in coldly.

He hesitated. "How will I know you're all right?"

"I'm fine," she said, and looked at him searchingly for one last moment. Plenty of heartbreak, but no regret. He didn't even understand what had gone wrong. She knew by the look in his eyes. He was still besotted by the unreality he invented.

"I... am fine," she repeated with peaceful conviction that spoke volumes. Then she got up from the table, and walked away. She never looked back as she closed the door behind her.

~ *Epilogue* ~

"I'm getting a little sick and tired of attending awards ceremonies on your behalf," Michael said playfully, proudly, as he walked into Kevin's bathroom to find him. "I mean, you're not even a detective anymore for crying out loud." His smile deepened and the admiration and respect he had for his father-in-law radiated from his eyes.

Kevin returned the smile with equal affection as his son-in-law barged into his bathroom unannounced. "Yeah, well, I'm getting a little sick of it myself. Does this tie look straight?"

"Yeah, it looks okay to me."

"Good. What do you say? Are we ready to go?"

"Just waiting for you, *Dad*."

The two men walked out of the bathroom and into the living room where Angela, Amy and Susan sat jabbering away as if there was nothing else to do tonight but sit and talk. They stopped in unison when the men appeared, and Amy got up immediately from her perch upon one of the dining room stools and came over to them.

"You men... look *so* handsome." She smiled lovingly at them both, then wrinkled her eyes at Kevin. "But, hold on, Dad, your tie isn't straight." Kevin glanced over her head as she went to work on the tie, and shot a withering, sarcastic look at his son-in-law.

Michael guiltily feigned a more detailed inspection. "I thought it looked okay."

"Yeah... right *son...* thanks a lot."

All three ladies were surrounding them now, looking beautiful in their formal best. Kevin had eyes for only one as she moved toward him. She was breathtaking, and he had to remind himself that there were others in the room as she caught his gaze and returned it. Angela...

"There," Amy said with finality as she patted down the ends of the bow tie. That looks right, doesn't it, Angela?"

"Yes. It looks perfect."

"Would you two like to be alone?" Michael asked sarcastically when they continued to stare at each other.

"Honey, leave them alone," Amy admonished, "I think they're sweet."

That did more to alleviate the passion in the air than anything else. Kevin looked around at them all sarcastically, but as he spoke, he secured Angela under one strong arm. She fit perfectly against him. "I'll have all of you know, that I am *not* sweet. In fact, I'm a real bastard, and I refuse to have my daughter calling me that. Especially tonight."

They all laughed at the expressive, comical way he spoke, as if he'd been called a foul name. Angela spoke up above the noise, though, and defeated his words by saying, "Oh, yes, he is sweet," in a knowing singsong that caused the laughter to intensify, and Kevin to redden.

Maybe when he stands up to receive his award I'll tell everyone that," Michael said in mock threat. "And presenting," he continued in the voice of a circus announcer, "this year's Citizen of Valor Award, going to, Lieutenant *Sweetie Pie* Larsen."

The laughter escalated into sarcastic oohs and ahhs. "You say anything like that - and you're not my son-in-law anymore," Kevin retorted.

"Michael feigned horror. "You can't disown your son-in-law."

"Oh, yes I can."

"Come on, girls," Angela said, trying to relieve Kevin a bit, "let's get our coats."

The ladies walked back into the living room where their coats were lying carefully across a chair. Kevin was glad Angela had connected so well with his daughter. He'd worried about Amy meeting a woman he had grown so close to, but the admiration had been almost instant.

Susan was still shy around all the healthy banter and solid relationships, but she was, more and more, becoming a welcomed addition to the family. She was fascinated by the love she saw, and cleaved to it hungrily. She was learning, he observed, as she allowed Amy to unhook her necklace from her coat, which had gotten tangled when she'd put it on. She was definitely learning.

"Come on, everyone, we better get going. Casey is meeting us there with this new girl he's been wanting to date. If we're late and he's stuck in an uncomfortable lapse of conversation, he'll kill us," Michael said to the crowd.

Amy and Angela were instantly at attention. "Oh, who is she?"

"A new nurse at the hospital. He has a group of hard guys he takes there for counseling, and she's the shrink's assistant."

"Oh, I hope it works out for him," Angela said almost dreamily.

"Me, too," said Amy. "He's such a nice guy."

"I know..." Angela, Amy and Susan walked out without another thought, all chattering meaningfully about the wonderful, inherent qualities of John Casey.

Kevin and Michael watched, openmouthed. "We better hurry, before we lose our dates," Michael said sarcastically.

"I say we leave Casey sitting there, and purposely come in an hour late," Kevin countered.

"By the way, Amy and I will take Susan with us since you and Angela seem preoccupied with each other," Michael said on the way out. "We wouldn't want the poor kid getting a complex from being ignored."

"Thanks, buddy," Kevin gleamed with an overly large smile.

Michael rolled his eyes, and followed him out.

*   *   *

"Whatever happened to all the other guys involved with Regis Black?" Angela asked Kevin while they drove to the banquet.

Kevin shot his eyes around at her. "What made you think of that *now?*"

"Why? What did you want me to think about?" she asked playfully.

"Kevin had no defense against that smile, and returned it seductively. "Not that," he sing-songed.

"Well, I was just thinking about the award you're getting - I'm so proud of you - and then I thought of why you're getting it - and then I thought of everything else."

"Well... they were all convicted, and they're in prison."

"I knew *that*," she said saucily. "I mean, what *happened* to them?"

Completely not comprehending the depth of her question, he answered in the typically factual male way. "Nothing. Marty and Nick got ten to twenty each for manufacturing. Goldie and Hewitt got life for murder. That's all there is to it."

Angela shook her head, not bothering to seek any more profound information. "The whole thing is such a shame. I still find it hard to believe things like that go on."

"They go on. Not only that, but this big bust doesn't really solve anything. Tomorrow there'll be a new crime, a new drug, a new dealer to take over where these left off."

"Is that why you got out of it?"

Kevin thought that through for a fraction of a second, then said quietly, "No... not really. I mean, I guess that was *part* of it, but I never really noticed that I wasn't accomplishing anything until..." He broke off.

"That case last year?"

"Yeah. After that, I just sort of lost my will to fight."

"Why?"

Kevin pursed his lips. "There were things about that case the public didn't know about."

She looked at him for a long while, sensing a depth of pain that he simultaneously wanted to shield himself away from, and spill out to her in great torrents. "Anyway... that's all over with now. You make me want to fight again, and live, and be alive." He reached for her hand and squeezed it lovingly.

"I'm not so sure I want to make you fight!" she said with a laughing smile, "but I like it that you want to live."

"Did you and your husband fight?"

She looked at him in surprise. "Not very much."

"You loved him a lot, huh?"

"Yes... He was my whole world."

"Is that why you stayed single for all those years?"

"Yes. He was a wonderful man, and I was very young when we met - and when he died. I never thought I'd find another man to fill that void, I truly didn't. Until you."

He smiled, and a certain tension drained from his face. "Hey, speaking of living, the lake is open for sailing this weekend. I promised myself that as soon as it opened I'd be there on the boat. Can you get Randy to cover for you Saturday?"

"Oh, Kevin... I don't know... this is the busiest time of year... I can't leave him alone."

"Well, get Susan to help him."

"I don't know if she's ready. If we get any type of rush they'll go crazy."

"How about if we all work until three, and then go?"

She laughed softly, her eyes sparkling with the desire to say yes.

"Please?" he asked in a little boy tone.

She laughed louder this time. "Definitely sweet."

"Oh, don't start that again!"

"Are you actually willing to come into the store and help out?"

"Sure; why not?"

She gaped at him for a minute. "You'll lug fertilizer and bags of stone all morning long? Just so I'll go on the boat with you?"

"You bet. I'd do anything for you."

"Okay, then, I'll go."

"Good! And don't be inviting the kids along, this is just for us."

Her heart flipped over. Very quietly, and with a small blush, she said, "Deal." After a few seconds she looked at him, and with a hesitating gentleness said, "Can I ask you something completely off the subject?"

"Sure."

She reached up to his face and traced a long scar that flitted into his cheek and went straight down until his shirt collar hid it. "Where did you get this scar?"

He winced, whether at the topic or the gentleness of her touch, he wasn't even sure himself. "I got *that* from last year's bust, too."

"When your house exploded?"

"Yes. I was hit by the flame."

"Is it bad?" she asked sensitively.

"A mess. My whole back is a mess. I hope it doesn't make you sick."

"Kevin, you could never make me sick. I think you're beautiful. Inside and out."

"And I think the same about you."

It was quiet for a few minutes, both of them contemplating.

"Tell me about it, Kevin," Angela blurted out suddenly. He looked at her with wide, startled eyes. "I know it hurts you. Please tell me what happened with that case. What could have been so terrible that it made you leave police work? Was it just the hopelessness of the job?"

He snorted a humorless laugh. "No, it wasn't the job at all. I loved my job – in some twisted part of myself. But that case... well..." Kevin thought of the brother that had been lost to him... "That case was another story..."

*   *   *

The table of eight where Kevin reposed was one of the rowdiest at the banquet. Not that anyone there was behaving rudely, or even inappropriately, but the laughter coming from it made other tables turn to stare. Susan sat with Michael's parents at the next table, engrossed in deep discussion with Reverend and Mrs. Camden. They possessed fascinating words about the love of God that Susan was starved to hear. She never even looked at the table next to her where all the commotion was coming from.

That left Kevin and Angela to sit with Michael and Amy, Randy and Joanne, and Casey and his date Becky, who Amy and Angela eyed curiously. They'd been having a fabulous time, and creating quite a din by the time Captain Jack stood at the platform and they were forced to stifle themselves. Kevin was only one in a long line of honorees tonight. He would receive precinct award for Citizen of Valor, for his assistance in the *Racer* case. It was a long stretch to call him 'an average citizen' for he was surely more than that, but he was well deserved in receiving the award.

It was an exhausting exercise in boredom to hear each honoree's name called and their attributes declared as if they were the only one present. Kevin had been here before, many times in fact, and would have much rather been alone with Angela at her condo. Later, he thought, as Jack finally called his name.

"For the award of Citizen of Valor, we name Lieutenant Kevin Larsen."

The crowd applauded with smiles as he stood, but the two tables of close friends that were there with him went a little crazy. They stood completely to their feet and cheered raucously, much to Kevin's embarrassment. He reached the platform and stood across from Jack, a potent expression between them. Jack simultaneously addressed the crowd at large, and spoke to him personally.

"I've known Kevin Larsen for many years now, and it's always been a privilege to be associated with him. He's been a crucial part of many police investigations throughout the years, so it comes as no shock that he's still an excellent investigator. Except that he's a retired police officer now, and has, as in the past, gone above and beyond the call of duty to assist in a case that could have devastated this city. In the process, he has spared precious innocent lives. The Citizen of Valor award is well bestowed on Lieutenant Kevin Larsen."

The crowd applauded again as Kevin reached for the award, and his two tables of friends, again, went a bit overboard. There were only two faces in the crowd that he saw as he turned modestly to nod his acceptance. They, too, had risked much, had fought hard, had gone far beyond their call of duty. He searched for their faces very briefly and when he connected with their gazes, he bowed slightly and saluted Susan, then locked eyes with Angela. How could he stand here and be honored while she was present? She should be up here receiving this award, not him. Everything that had happened had happened because of her. She was responsible for Susan's freedom, the arrest of Regis Black and his men, and the containing of *Racer*, which would have crippled the city.

Most important to Kevin, she was the one responsible for the life that flowed through him once again. Blessed life. She brought the best out in him, caused him to fight for what was right again. Angela was the one who went furthest in her sacrifice, goodness and duty. Causing Kevin to go furthest in his.

~ The End ~

Take a look at the continuing challenges Kevin, Michael and Casey face in their next adventure...

United We Fall

Coming to Amazon and Kindle in January of 2013
Also Available at: www.laughingalltheway.net

United We Fall

by

Christy Laughing

…Caleb snatched the wallet away, and calmly drew a pistol from the inner pocket of his jacket. Detective Sergeant John Casey stopped short and recoiled in surprise. He'd been caught. "This *isn't* the identification I was looking for," Caleb said menacingly as he opened the wallet and displayed the obvious picture ID. "Identify yourself as a Sovereign."

Casey stood stock still, his mind racing to know how he could do that. Nothing whatsoever came to him, and for the first time in his undercover career, he felt defeat. He'd been in difficult spots before, had had situations fall completely through his fingers before, but never had he known entrapment like he knew it now. His instincts had been right when he'd first cleared the mountain. His doubts should have made him turn around and retreat. These brothers were smarter than he'd given them credit for, knew each other more accurately than he had ever guessed, and were involved in something way deeper and more dangerous than he was prepared to handle.

"Just as I thought," Caleb said as he watched Casey stand there in numb silence. "Who are you?"

"I'm a friend of Arthur's."

"Don't lie to me!" Caleb seemed livid for all of his quietly controlled words. "I don't like to be deceived, and I most definitely don't like to be mocked by the likes of *you!*" He looked disgustedly up and down Casey's physique, and dug the gun into the flesh of his throat.

Casey glared at him, not a hint of fear reaching his eyes.

"You're a cop," Caleb stated, panic forming like a pit in his stomach. He'd worked so hard, for so long. How could police have found out about him?

Casey continued to glare, unmoving, a slight, mocking lift to his brow.

"How did you find out about the brethren? Did Arthur tell you?" Caleb asked, needing to know, desperate to find out how much the authorities knew, how completely he'd been discovered.

Casey still stood and stared without saying a word.

The gun pressed tighter underneath his chin.

That's when they heard the sounds of men in the camp. At least two of the others had arrived together, and Casey's heart began to rip through his chest painfully. Caleb he could easily maneuver, if he didn't shoot the hell out of him first, but a group of them? With this level of insanity their binding tie? He didn't think so. Nevertheless, when Caleb turned toward the bawdy voices, which collided into the quietude of the trees, Casey struck.

His hands were like lightening as they raised and crashed downward on the back of Caleb's neck. Caleb screeched and crumpled, but he held the gun and kept enough presence of mind to scream through the thin walls of the cabin, "Brothers, help me!"

Casey successfully cut the words off as he grabbed for Caleb's face and yanked backwards. The little runt of a man collapsed like a fallen tree and lay straight on the cabin floor, looking up into Casey's determined face, his hand digging into the thin hair on top of Caleb's head. He had to get out of here. Right now, before Caleb's men found him beating their leader. It would only take one good hit to this tiny man's chin, and Casey knew Caleb would be out like a light. Then he would run through the trees and escape to his truck. He would notify Michael immediately and they could have a team from the Weapon's Ordinance there within minutes.

This in mind, he simply drew his fist back to make short work of it. That's when he, and Caleb, noticed the gun. To Caleb it was almost a reactionary movement. It was doubtful by the terrorized look on his face that he realized the gun was still in his hand. He just lifted his arms up to protect himself from the lashing Casey was obviously going to bestow. When he felt the weight of the gun, he fumbled with it and tried to fire.

For Casey, it was much the same. He suddenly saw the gun come into his line of vision as his fist came down. He aborted his movement ruthlessly, and swiped at the flailing hands instead, trying to gain possession of the gun they held. Caleb had managed to cock it, and the real battle began.

It was a fight for their lives, they both knew, and so they fought desperately. Nevertheless, it was over quickly, and as the two other brethren burst into the cabin, the gun was fired. Blood spattered instantly, and everywhere at once. Stunned silence stood suddenly thick in the air, the movements of the two men in the doorway stilled in mid-motion.

"Caleb...?" one of them questioned, his eyes unsure and wide with panic. "Caleb?"

At first, it was just the similarity in the names that caught Casey's attention. He didn't comprehend that the two young men in the doorway were dazedly speaking to him. He was numb and in shock, and just looked up toward the sound of someone speaking his name, or a name very similar, he realized, as the men stared in dismay. His gaze was hard, deadly, and not because of any acting ability he possessed. This was born of survival, the need and determination to fight every last Sovereign to the ground and escape. Surely it was either that or be slain where he stood because of what he'd just done. He'd killed their leader.

"Caleb?" the young man repeated. Casey finally realized that the man was looking at *him*. He glanced down at the bloodied form of the real Caleb, lying dead on the floor of the cabin with Arthur Penn's ID fallen across his chest. ID with Casey's own muddled features staring back at him. He grabbed the wallet as if he were trying to get a closer look at the damage he'd done to the dead body, and held it tightly closed. There would be no way of identifying this body on sight. The face was blown completely off. Casey shoved the wallet deep inside the breast pocket of Caleb's jacket, more to get it immediately out of sight than anything else. He blinked for a few horrific moments, comprehension coming slow, in convulsive waves. Caleb was dead, and the men of his congregation thought *he* was their leader.

Slowly rising, Casey glanced down only one more time at the unimpressive form laying dead at his feet. The sight was gruesome. Brain tissue and bone fragments had scattered in a swatting spray, leaving a trail of blood that was already spreading into a wide, pooling river. Casey's mind was screaming for clarity and direction when he finally looked up, stared dead into the eyes of the two terrorists, and finally answered, "Yes, brothers, it is Caleb."

United We Fall

Coming to Amazon.com & Kindle January 2013
Also Available at: www.laughingalltheway.net

ABOUT THE AUTHOR

Christy Laughing was born and raised in Buffalo New York. She and her husband are happily married and have three grown sons between them. Her very first award for writing came in the 6th grade. "I was asked to write a poem using the letter "O". I wrote about 'Ollie the Octopus.' My teacher immediately pulled me aside and began the encouragements.
Mrs. M., if you're out there, thank you!"

During the past ten years, Christy has focused mostly on writing for business, but creating a story is her favorite kind of writing. *She really wants her readers to be on the edge of their seats!*

CLOSER THAN A BROTHER, released in August of 2012, was the first novel in the **CLOSER THAN A BROTHER BOOK SERIES**.

BEYOND THE CALL OF DUTY, was released in *December of 2012*

In *January of 2013,* **UNITED WE FALL,** the third book in this series, is scheduled for release.

Christy maintains a website, **www.laughingalltheway.net**, in hopes of helping others cope with life's day-to-day tough spots. **Her books can also be purchased at this site.**
Her goal is to keep writing!